. . . from Novel 5: . . . the Indian Nation

Black Horse broke in, "You're stalling, Marshal. I want you to say right now that we get the reward and the money Boyle stole."

Longarm had made up his mind. Casually, as though impelled by habit, he brought up a hand and began fingering his watch chain. He said, "Black Horse, the stolen money's not mine to give away. I'd be stealing it myself if I let you have it. I'll try to see that you get the reward, though."

Black Horse stood up. He shifted his revolver to his left hand and slid a long knife from his belt sheath with his right. "Then you'll have to die, too. The reward money's not enough."

Late Morning Star gasped loudly and Black Horse glanced at her involuntarily. Longarm tugged his watch chain and the derringer leaped into his hand. He fired. Black Horse crumpled to the floor while the flat report of the derringer was still echoing in the little hut.

. . . from Novel 6: . . . the Loggers

Longarm stepped past the door and flattened himself against the wall. With the barrel of his Colt, he gently pushed open the door. As it began to swing into the room, he gave it a final shove. When he heard it slam into the wall, he sprang into the room, crouching low, his six-gun in front of him, waist-high, his elbow bent. Nothing. No flash of gunpowder lancing through the dark.

He heard the bedsprings creak—and a girl's voice, low and seductive, laughing softly. Waiting a moment for his eyes to adjust to the sudden darkness of the room, he saw something long and pale stir on the bed.

"My, my," the girl said. "You must be awful nervous to enter like that . . ."

Jove Double Editions by Tabor Evans

Longarm Double #1: Deputy U.S. Marshal

Longarm Double #2: Longarm of the Law

Longarm Double #3: Frontier Justice

◆•TABOR EVANS•◆

DOUBLE #3

FRONTIER JUSTICE

JOVE BOOKS, NEW YORK

THE BERKLEY PUBLISHING GROUP
Published by the Penguin Group
Penguin Group (USA) Inc.
375 Hudson Street, New York, New York 10014, USA

Penguin Group (Canada), 90 Eglinton Avenue East, Suite 700, Toronto, Ontario M4P 2Y3, Canada
(a division of Pearson Penguin Canada Inc.)
Penguin Books Ltd., 80 Strand, London WC2R 0RL, England
Penguin Group Ireland, 25 St. Stephen's Green, Dublin 2, Ireland (a division of Penguin Books Ltd.)
Penguin Group (Australia), 250 Camberwell Road, Camberwell, Victoria 3124, Australia
(a division of Pearson Australia Group Pty. Ltd.)
Penguin Books India Pvt. Ltd., 11 Community Centre, Panchsheel Park, New Delhi—110 017, India
Penguin Group (NZ), 67 Apollo Drive, Rosedale, Auckland 0632, New Zealand
(a division of Pearson New Zealand Ltd.)
Penguin Books (South Africa) (Pty.) Ltd., 24 Sturdee Avenue, Rosebank, Johannesburg 2196,
South Africa

Penguin Books Ltd., Registered Offices: 80 Strand, London WC2R 0RL, England

This is a work of fiction. Names, characters, places, and incidents either are the product of the author's imagination or are used fictitiously, and any resemblance to actual persons, living or dead, business establishments, events, or locales is entirely coincidental.

LONGARM DOUBLE #3: FRONTIER JUSTICE

A Jove Book / published by arrangement with the author

PRINTING HISTORY
Jove edition / May 2011

Copyright © 2011 by Penguin Group (USA) Inc.
Cover illustration by Milo Sinovcic.
Longarm in the Indian Nation copyright 1979 by Jove Publications, Inc.
Longarm and the Loggers copyright 1979 by Jove Publications, Inc.

ISBN: 978-0-515-14939-5

JOVE®
Jove Books are published by The Berkley Publishing Group,
a division of Penguin Group (USA) Inc.,
375 Hudson Street, New York, New York 10014.
JOVE® is a registered trademark of Penguin Group (USA) Inc.
The "J" design is a trademark of Penguin Group (USA) Inc.

PRINTED IN THE UNITED STATES OF AMERICA

10 9 8 7 6 5 4 3 2 1

NOVEL 5

—————•◆•—————

Longarm
in the
Indian Nation

Chapter 1

Snapping awake with all senses alert wasn't anything new to Custis Long. He'd done that every morning for almost as many years as he could remember. What was new was snapping awake in a bed far softer than his own, in his rooming house, and as different as his own bed was from the rough shakedowns on the ground that he'd gotten used to in the field. For a moment he was startled by the unaccustomed luxury of satin sheets and pillowcases brushing his bare skin, the scent of patchouli and musk heavy in his nostrils, and a soft, warm feminine form cuddled up to him.

For a moment, Longarm resisted two temptations. The first was to lever himself out of bed the way he usually did the instant he was awake. The second was to nestle down again with the woman, who was still asleep, and enjoy the pleasure of rousing her.

He didn't resist the temptation to recall the night from which he'd just awakened, and memory brought a smile of pleasure to his face. The evening had started badly. He'd swung off the train at Julesburg to find the station agent waiting for him with the yellow flimsy of a telegram. The wire had been from his chief, Marshal Billy Vail, ordering him to get back to Denver as fast as possible while Vail dispatched another deputy to take on the Julesburg case. Longarm had gotten enough messages from his boss to distinguish between the ones that meant what they said and those that gave him a choice of obeying them or ignoring them. The telegram, together with his badge, enabled Longarm to persuade the stationmaster to flag the Limited, which would get him into Denver that night.

* * *

While the westbound Limited puffed impatiently, Longarm swung aboard the baggage car, where he dropped off his saddle and gear. Then he made his way through the train, looking for a seat. There were only two chair cars, both full, and the Pullmans were just as crowded. He didn't find a seat until he'd walked all the way back to the observation car, which was also the club car, and where he'd probably have wound up in any event for a drink while he waited for the first call to dinner.

Years of riding trains to and from his case assignments had given Longarm a good eye for the recurring types of passengers he encountered. He figured the man standing next to him at the tiny corner bar while they were both waiting for service for a traveling salesman, a drummer; the back-tilted gray derby hat and the flashy stickpin in an overly ornate cravat were both earmarks of the type. It was easy to see, from the drummer's red face and unsteady hands, that he'd been spending too much time with the bottle. The man hadn't gone in to the dining car when the chime-tapping steward came through making the call to dinner. In fact, he'd ignored all three announcements. Longarm went in on the second call, and in the diner he noticed the woman. She was sitting with another woman and a man, and it would have been impossible not to notice her. She was the most attractive feature of the otherwise drab dining car.

Longarm shared a table with three other men—stockbrokers, judging from their conversation in which he took small part. Their talk of stock issues, debentures, convertibles, and options held small interest for him, and they were too engrossed in business talk to spend much time chatting idly with a stranger they'd never see again. After the meal, he returned to the observation car and took his after-dinner dram of Maryland rye out onto the platform to enjoy the crisp night air, which grew progressively crisper as the Limited huffed and swayed gently in its climb up the foothills of the Rockies. The first hint he had of trouble came when the door to the observation platform opened and the woman he'd seen at dinner came flying out.

Longarm grabbed her just as she was about to hit the brass rail that ran across the end of the platform, "Hey, now!" he said. "You ought to be more careful. You could've fallen right off the train!"

Whatever she'd been about to say in reply was lost in a bull-roar from the drunken traveling man who rushed after her onto the observation platform.

"Don't play hard to get with me!" he shouted. His face, Longarm could see in the light from the open door, was even redder than it had been before supper. "You fancy dames are all alike! Lead a man on, then run away!"

"Please! Let me alone!" the woman pleaded. "I don't know you, and I don't want to!"

"You weren't acting this way inside!" he charged.

"I came out here to get away from you!" she snapped.

"You came out here so I'd follow you and we could be by ourselves," he retorted, with drunken lack of logic. "That's just fine, girlie. Now we can play!"

Longarm stepped between the drummer and the woman. Obviously, the drunk hadn't noticed him before, for the man's eyes bugged out when he saw him. Longarm said, "I heard the lady tell you she wants you to leave her alone."

"Who in hell are you to butt in?" the man demanded. "Try-ing to cut me out with the dame, are you?"

He swung. Longarm had no trouble grabbing the slow-moving wrist. His calloused hands cut into the soft skin of the drummer's arm as he pushed the man to the side of the obser-vation platform. Before the startled drummer knew what was happening, Longarm had grabbed his other arm and was hold-ing him out over the edge of the platform, his legs swinging in rhythm with the swaying of the speeding train, nothing but the thin mountain air below his feet.

Looking down at the ground rushing past below him had a very sobering effect on the drunk, especially when the wind took off his derby and sent it sailing into the dusk. He gasped, "Jesus, mister! Don't let go of me! If you drop me, I'll be killed for sure!"

"Let me hear how nicely you can apologize to that lady for troubling her," Longarm ordered.

"Now, I didn't mean anything! I was just—"

"Please!" the woman said. "Don't hurt him on my account!"

Longarm didn't answer her. He gave the drummer a shake. "Find your tongue fast, mister! If I let you go now, it'll be a long walk to Denver!"

"Lady, I'm sorry I stepped out of line," the man gasped. "If you'll overlook it—"

"Yes, yes! I'll accept your apology," she said quickly.

Longarm pulled the man back onto the platform and released his arms. The drummer wiped the sweat off his red face with trembling hands and fled into the coach.

"My goodness!" the woman said. "You certainly have a way of dealing with people who upset you. I hope I never get in your bad graces! But I'm very grateful that you stepped in to stop that man from annoying me."

Longarm took off his Stetson and made a little half-bow. "I'm glad I was on hand, ma'am, to save you trouble."

"You must be very strong," she smiled. "That man weighed at least two hundred pounds, but you handled him like a sack of peanuts."

"Well, even if he was three sheets to the wind, he ought to've been able to tell you're the kind of lady who wouldn't appreciate somebody like him trying to get fresh with you."

The woman looked abashed. "I suppose it was partly my fault. I made the mistake of coming back here to the observation car for an after-dinner glass of port, instead of having it served in my compartment."

"Your friends I saw you with at dinner didn't come back with you, then?" the lawman asked.

"Why, they weren't friends. Just people I was sharing a table with, as one does on a train."

"I guess it wouldn't have mattered to a gentleman, even if you were sitting down drinking by yourself, on a train. In a saloon, now, it might've been different."

The woman's hand flew up to her breast. "Goodness! I wouldn't go into a common saloon, even with an escort! I'm Julia Burnside, by the way."

She extended her hand, palm down. Longarm didn't know whether she expected him to kiss it or shake it, but thought it wasn't quite his style to be kissing a lady's hand, so he grasped the hand and shook it, while with his other hand, he touched the brim of his hat.

"My name's Long, Miz Burnside. Custis Long, deputy U.S. marshal from the Denver office." He hesitated, then asked, "Would I be presuming if I asked if you are related to the late general?"

"No." She smiled. "We are not related, though I do hope I have better luck than he did. But my father's family lives in Georgia, and I think the general came from New England. And it's *Miss* Burnside, by the way."

He smiled. "I wasn't aiming to be nosy, ma'am. Just wondering." Again Longarm hesitated. Then he suggested, "If you'd like to go back in the car and finish your glass of wine, I'd be honored to sit with you. It might keep somebody else from bothering you."

"Why, thank you, Mr. Long. Or should I call you Marshal Long? I'd enjoy your company."

"It doesn't matter a bit what you call me, ma'am. I don't set a lot of store in titles, but I've gotten sort of used to being called Longarm. Here, let me open that door for you."

They sat chatting in the observation car, Miss Burnside with her glass of port, Longarm with a fresh glass of Maryland rye, while the Limited steamed up the long slope to Denver. Without being obvious about it, Julia Burnside encouraged Longarm to talk of his experiences, and he enjoyed their conversation thoroughly, as would any man who finds an attractive young woman interested in what he had to say.

When the conductor called the first warning for the Denver stop, they joined the flurry set off by other passengers who were getting off at the Colorado capital. Longarm decided to write off the incident as a pleasant but inconsequential evening. Even so, he hated to see it end. He'd found Julia Burnside's dark beauty and her slow, sensuous way of smiling exceedingly attractive. She was past the age of kittenish youth, but not yet overly mature. Longarm didn't expect to see her again after they parted in the excursion car, but when he'd picked up his gear from the baggage master and was carrying it out of the depot, he saw her standing on the top step. A porter with a loaded luggage cart waited behind her. She was surveying the long line of hacks and carriages with impatient bewilderment.

"Something wrong, Miss Burnside?" Longarm asked.

She turned toward him, obviously pleased to see him, but puzzled. "My carriage isn't here. I sent our housekeeper a wire from Omaha, telling her to have Duffey meet me." She shook her head. "The staff wasn't expecting me back so soon. I suppose they're treating themselves to a few days away from their jobs."

"Your family had to travel somewhere else, then?"

"There's only my father and me. Mother died several years ago. We'd planned to spend another week in Atlanta, but he got a telegram that called him to New York, and I decided to come home alone."

"Well, now, you ought not go to an empty house by yourself, at night. Suppose I just escort you home?"

"Really, Marshal Long—Longarm—there's no need for that. I'm not a baby. I can go home without worrying or being afraid."

"Just the same," he said, "I bet you'd feel better if somebody was with you."

"Well, if you're sure I wouldn't be imposing. The house is in quite a lonely part of town, some distance out on Sherman Avenue."

"All the more reason I should see you home. And you ain't imposing one bit," Longarm assured her. "I don't have a wife or anybody waiting for me. I'll just see that you get home safe and sound."

He whistled up a hack and saw that her bags were properly stowed away, then tossed his own gear onto the rack on top of the vehicle. He was wondering if he'd been too forward in making his offer. Julia Burnside's dress and manners had marked her as being prosperous, but a home on Sherman Avenue meant more than mere prosperity; it meant wealth. His conversation during the drive was somewhat inhibited, but his companion more than made up for it with a stream of light, somewhat nervous chatter as the hack passed beyond the zone of lighted streets and into the city's outlying residential section.

When he saw the Burnside house in the veiled moonlight of the autumn night, looming huge and dark in the center of an acre or so of newly planted lawn and shrubbery, Longarm whistled softly to himself. *It must look bigger than it really is,* he thought. Then the hack turned onto a semicircular driveway that led to the front door of the imposing structure, and Julia said, "I'll go on ahead and light a lamp in the hall, if you don't mind seeing that the driver gets all my bags."

Longarm jumped out of the carriage, helped her down, and then helped the cabman assemble the luggage. When they got to the house, the door was open, and a lamp was glowing in the hallway. Involuntarily, Longarm took a step inside. While the hackman was arranging the luggage on the floor just inside the doorway, Julia Burnside appeared at Longarm's elbow.

Turning back from his quick glance down the long, dim corridor, Longarm volunteered, "You've got a pretty good-sized house here, Miss Burnside. If it's been left by itself very long, it might be a good idea for me just to walk through it and make sure there's nobody lurking in any of the rooms."

"I was hoping you'd offer to do that, Marshal. It'd make me feel a good deal safer."

"I'll just tell the hackman to wait." Longarm started after the driver, who was already halfway back to the hack.

"There's no need," she said. "I've already paid him and told him to come back for you at six. And I warned him to be sure nothing happens to your saddle and other equipment."

Longarm said the first thing that popped into his mind. "I didn't expect you'd invite me to stay."

"I didn't plan to, until we were halfway out here." Julia pulled the jewelled pin from her hat and tossed the hat down the dim hall. Before his eyes, Longarm saw a prim-and-proper young lady suddenly transformed into a flashing-eyed temptress. She went on, "Then I asked myself, 'Why not?' And, do you know, I couldn't think of a single reason why I shouldn't, so I did!" And she threw back her head, laughing huskily.

As pleasant as he found the memory of what had followed, Longarm couldn't lie still while he exhausted the recollections of the night. Habit was too strong to overcome; he simply wasn't comfortable lying abed of a morning, with the day and his duty waiting. The soft satin sheets slithered luxuriously over his skin as he slipped out of bed. There was enough of a glow coming from the coal fire he'd lighted in the bedroom's small fireplace to enable him to locate a window. He opened the heavy velvet drapes wide enough to see the graying sky. It wasn't quite six o'clock yet, by his reckoning.

Moving as quietly as he knew how, he dressed by the grate's soft glow, adjusting his gunbelt and holster by feel, and forgoing the routine which he usually followed each morning in his own room, of inspecting his weapons closely. He didn't know when Julia would wake up, but when he turned toward the bed after slipping his arms into the sleeves of his Prince Albert coat, she was sitting up, propped on the pillows, watching him dress. Her hair was tousled into dark curls around her face, her full lips were slightly swollen, and her shoulders gleamed in the fireglow that turned her creamy skin a rosy pink and accented the dark, pebbled rosettes of her upthrust nipples.

"How did it get so late so soon?" she asked, stretching languidly.

Longarm smiled. "Time's got a habit of hurrying, when you're enjoying yourself."

"I'd enjoy having you come back to bed, even for a little while."

"Now, Julia, you know I can't. It's getting on toward six, and that's when you said the hack would be back."

"Tonight, then?" she asked hopefully. "If the servants show up, I'll send them away, and we'll have the house to ourselves again."

"You know I'd like to. The only problem is, by tonight I might be headed out for God knows where. I told you my chief wired me to hurry back here, that he's got a case waiting for me."

"Yes, I remember," she pouted. "When you come back, then?"

"Sure. I don't know when that'll be, but I'll find a way to let you know."

"Let me find you, Longarm. My father resents any man with whom I make friends. He seems to want to choose all my companions himself. Of course, he always has his own 'companions' in a cozy little nest that he keeps in town, near his office. And I've decided that if he can choose his, I have a right to choose mine."

"Just have somebody ask at Marshal Vail's office in the

Federal Building." Longarm stepped to the bed and bent to kiss her. "When I get back, then."

He let himself out the big front door just as the hack rolled into the driveway.

A few minutes after eight, fortified by a hot breakfast and freshly shaved, Longarm walked into Billy Vail's office in the Federal Building.

Vail looked up from his paper-strewn desk and grunted, "Time you were getting here."

"If I'd known you were in that big a hurry, I'd've come right here from the depot last night," Longarm said mildly. "Only I didn't expect I'd find you here, then."

"I might've surprised you," Vail replied. He made a face, clasped his hands over a stomach that was beginning to bulge, and belched. "Damn soggy fried potatoes I had for breakfast. Nobody cooks spuds the right way anymore. Well, now that you're here, sit down and listen."

As Longarm settled into the red morocco armchair across from his chief's desk, he said, "The way that wire you sent me read, I didn't think you'd give me a chance to sit down before I had to leave on whatever job it is you pulled me back for. What's come up that's so all-fired important?"

Vail answered with a question. "Was Cady Martin in the outer office when you passed through it?"

"Cady? The sheriff from Teller County? If he was, I didn't see him. The only one out there was your pretty little sissified pen-pusher."

Pressing a button on his desk, Vail waited impatiently for the door of his office to open. When the young, pink-cheeked stenographer-clerk stuck his head inside, Vail asked, "Has Sheriff Martin showed up yet?"

"He just this minute came in," the young man replied.

"Well, tell him to trot on in here." Turning to Longarm, the chief marshal went on, "It's really Cady's case, so I asked him to wait over in town to tell you about it."

"We're handling county cases now?" Longarm asked incredulously.

"We're handling this one, because Frank and Harry Warde have a connection with it. And if we don't take it on at Cady's request, we'll be getting one from the senator as soon as Cady gets back to Cripple Creek and the Wardes have time to telegraph Washington."

Longarm nodded. "All right. I get what you're driving at."

Cady Martin came in. A Colt swung from his hip, a leather vest with a star pinned on it hung loosely from his shoulders. Cady was a lanky, sandy-haired man with an untrimmed tobacco-stained mustache that drooped wearily down on either side of a long, protruding chin. His eyes were red-rimmed and he needed a shave.

"'Morning, Billy," he said. "Longarm. Sorry I'm late, but I saw the elephant and heard the owl last night. Seemed to me I was entitled to cut loose after all the riding I've done the past week."

"No harm," Vail told him. "Sit down, Cady, and go over what you told me yesterday. I want Longarm to get it firsthand."

Martin pulled up a chair from the row ranged along the wall and let himself down into it carefully. "Not a hell of a lot to tell. These three gophers, Scud Petersen and Dob something-or-other and Eddie Boyle, they got tired of scratching hardrock, so they figured they'd change their luck by robbing the Miner's Bank, there in Cripple Creek. That'd be three, close to four weeks back. Well, I don't know how much experience them yahoos had robbing banks before, but they fucked this one up real good." He paused to squirt a stream of amber tobacco juice into the spittoon beside Vail's desk.

Longarm took the opportunity to ask, "You mean they didn't pull it off?"

"Oh, they pulled it off, all right. Got something like thirty thousand dollars, mostly in gold and silver, but a few greenbacks. Only Jimmy Clark, the teller at the bank, ran to the door and cut loose on 'em with a shotgun after they got outside. Tim Andrews heard the ruckus, and he come running down from his office, and when the smoke cleared away they'd shot both Tim and Clark."

"Sorry to hear that," Longarm interrupted. "Tim was as good a town marshal as I ever ran into."

"Yep, he was all right, Tim was," Martin agreed. "Only good thing about it was that Tim shot Scud first, dropped him cold, and the one called Dob took so much lead from the shotgun that he died a little ways out of town. I was up to Gillel when it all took place. By the time I'd got word and made it back to Cripple Creek, Eddie Boyle was long on his way, with all the loot. I took Sid, and we dogged after him on a cold trail. For all we knew, he might've been shot up, too, and had to hole up someplace close by."

Martin stopped to spit again and Longarm observed, "Only I get the idea it didn't happen that way."

"Sure as hell not," the sheriff agreed. "To cut it short and sweet, if Boyle was hurt at all, which I don't guess he was, he wasn't hurt enough to slow him down. He left a trail a mile wide, buying fresh horses every town he came to that had a livery stable. We didn't have no trouble following him."

Vail said, "You don't need to go through all that, Cady. Just tell Longarm what you wound up with."

"Like I told you yesterday, Billy, we wound up with what the little boy shot at," Martin snorted. "Boyle cut east to La Junta and then made tracks straight on south to the Indian Nation. Sid and me got as far as Fort Supply before we ran into a couple of Pawnee Indian policemen. They spotted our badges and told us to hightail the hell back to where we had jurisdiction."

"Well, they were right, in a way," Vail said. "It's federal territory, down in the Nation. I don't say they should've turned you and Sid back, but the Indian police never did take kindly to anybody from outside butting in on their home grounds."

Martin slammed a palm down on Vail's desk. "Damn it, Billy, it wasn't like Eddie Boyle's an Indian! He might be a breed, come to think of it, but he robbed a bank in my territory! You'd think them redskin bastards would give me and Sid a hand, instead of chasing us off!"

"It doesn't work out that way," Longarm put in. "They don't make us welcome in the Nation even if we wear federal badges the same as they do."

"Sure. I know that," Martin said disgustedly. "But that didn't leave us much legroom. Thing is, while I was coming back to Cripple Creek from Gillel, Sid found out a little bit about Boyle. Seems he used to talk a lot about a woman he was sweet on down in the Nation. Hottest piece of ass he ever had, he used to say. He was always getting ready to go back to her."

"Now that's interesting." Longarm frowned. "Whereabouts does she live?"

The sheriff shook his head irritably. "Damn it, I don't know! We never could find that out. But we were on a good trail, when we got pulled off it. Anyhow, we didn't come off so good when we tried to argue with them Pawnees, so we just turned around and headed home. Then, on the way back, I got to thinking. That Miner's Bank belongs to the Warde brothers, and I know neither one of 'em is going to be satisfied till they see Boyle on the business end of a hanging rope. So I figured I better stop on up here and get Billy to pick up where me and Sid left off."

All three of the men sat silently for a moment. They knew what the sheriff had been thinking. The big mining and financial syndicates that had dominated Colorado's commercial life since the days when it had still been a territory had grown even stronger with statehood. The syndicates were almost a government unto themselves; they'd taken the Cattlemen's Association as a model and had assembled a band of enforcers, a loosely knit, small private army, that worked in parallel but not always in cooperation with the authorities. There was one big difference. The enforcers weren't bound by laws and rules of evidence, and often recovery of the loot from a mine or gold train or bank robbery was secondary to punishing the perpetrators as examples. Usually, the punishment was a lead slug.

"Well?" Vail asked Longarm. "How do you see it?"

The deputy pulled absently at a corner of his mustache for a moment, then replied, "About like you do, I guess, Billy. The Warde brothers are going to be pulling strings as soon as Cady reports back to Cripple Creek. You called the turn a while ago."

Vail said, "If their men go into the Nation looking for Boyle, they're sure to rub the Indian police raw. I want a man down there to keep trouble from exploding—to get Boyle first. You've had more cases down in the Nation than anybody else in the office. Your warrant's ready whenever you are."

Longarm nodded slowly. "All right. Give me time to sit down a minute with Cady and find out what else I can about this Boyle fellow. Fort Reno's as likely a place as any for me to work out of, so I'll take the early train and connect up with the Rock Island spur that runs down to the Nation. Expect me back when you see me, I guess."

"And try to take things as easy as you can," Vail said. "The last time I heard, things were nice and quiet down there. Don't get me blamed for starting another Indian war, whatever else you do!"

Chapter 2

For the first two or three miles of his ride from the end of the Rock Island spur track to Fort Reno, Longarm couldn't make up his mind whether the seat of the jolting army supply wagon was more or less uncomfortable than the bench in the caboose where he'd spent the previous night and half the morning. Finally, he decided there wasn't much to choose between the two, and devoted his attention to the landscape.

There was as little to choose between the country he was seeing now and that which he'd watched while the freight train rolled south from Wichita into the Indian Nation. Both landscapes were virtually featureless, and both bore the same kind of vegetation. The land between the Indian agency at the Darlington railhead and Fort Reno, ten miles farther south, was perhaps a bit more rolling, but on it grew the same blackjack oaks, gum trees, and mesquite patches.

Although the primary reason for Darlington's existence was the Indian agency that served the Arapahoe-Cheyenne reservation, the agency had attracted a few other enterprises. There were a blacksmith shop, a notions store, a tintype gallery, and a pharmacy. There was also a big authorized trading post, which was also a general store, and housed in the same building with it were a hotel, a dining room, and a saloon. There was no livery stable.

Not that it would make any difference, Longarm thought as he shifted position trying to find a soft spot on the wooden seat. *I'd pick an army-trained nag any day over what I might draw from a liveryman's outfit in a place like this.*

"Something I've always wondered about," he remarked to the teamster on the seat beside him. "Why in hell does every fort in the Indian Nation have a railroad line running close to it, but not ever any spur tracks built right *to* the fort?"

"Beats me, Marshal," the man said around his chaw of cut plug. "But did you ever see the army do anything the easy way?" The teamster joined in Longarm's chuckle, then added, "Besides, if they built the railroads right up to the forts, us teamsters wouldn't have no jobs. And I'd a damn sight rather skin mules than get saddlesores on my ass chasing Indians all over hell and Texas."

"Still having to go out after runaways, are they?" Longarm asked.

"Maybe not as much now as we used to. The boys at Fort Sill do, though. Them Comanches and Kiowas down there jump the reservation a lot worse than the Araps and Cheyennes around Fort Reno."

"Comanches and Kiowas are a sight wilder than most, I'd say," Longarm remarked.

"Damn right," the driver agreed, "and a sight meaner, too. Not that the ones up here are much better. I tell you, Marshal, I'm just as glad that agency's where it is, instead of jammed up to the fort. We don't get a lot of 'em wandering around, maybe slipping a rifle or pistol up under their blankets if they get a chance. And them Indians damn sure ain't going to be collecting their beef allotments and butchering the critters in smelling distance of our barracks."

Longarm nodded abstractedly. He was already plotting a course of action in his mind, to be refined after he'd studied the maps he'd pick up at the fort. Chiefly, he was wondering how far he was going to have to backtrack to pick up the trail of the missing Eddie Boyle. He'd forgotten a lot of the distances that he'd learned from his previous cases in the Nation, but seemed to recall that Fort Supply, where Cady Martin had been forced to leave the fugitive's trail, was a good hundred miles northwest of Fort Reno.

"How's the lay of the land between here and Fort Supply?" he asked the teamster.

"About what you'd expect. Dry and cold at this time of year; will be until the snow starts next month. Then it'll be just plain *cold*. Why? You heading up that way?"

"Soon as I can pick up a horse at your remount depot and draw some rations from the quartermaster's stores."

"Well, I wish you good luck." The teamster spat around the end of the wagon. "You're going to need it, if you're going into the open territory."

Mounted on a roan gelding, the best of the horses he'd seen at the remount corral, with jerky, hardtack, bacon, pintos, and a bag of coffee beans bulging his saddlebags, Longarm started back to Darlington in the waning afternoon. He didn't intend to hit the real trail until morning. After a night and a day rattling around on the hard seat of the Rock Island caboose, he felt he was entitled to sit down to a dinner he hadn't cooked himself, and to sleep at least one night in a real bed before he set out. Once he'd left Darlington, there wasn't any way of knowing how long he'd have to get by on rations of bacon, beans, hardtack, and jerky, with perhaps a rabbit now and then, or how long he'd sleep in his bedroll on the ground. The maps he'd gotten at the fort showed only one settlement between Darlington and Fort Supply.

His second look at the settlement that had grown up around the Darlington Indian agency didn't change the opinion Longarm had formed of the place when he'd first stepped off the freight. He'd thought then that there wasn't much to it, but it was better than nothing at all. Looking at it again in the low-angled sunlight of the dying day confirmed his first impression.

About fifteen buildings formed the agency itself; isolated by the river from the settlement, they stood in a neat, open square in the middle of plowed area that had obviously been used in growing farm crops of some kind. Longarm could almost discern the purpose of each building just by looking at it from the outside: dwellings, an office, workshops, a church, a school, warehouses, barns; a corral stood off one corner of the square. The agency buildings were all neatly painted, white with dark gray trim, and they shone fresh and clean in the early evening sunshine.

In contrast, the trader's settlement that had seemed imposing from a distance was shabby and scruffy-looking when seen up close. The main structure was the all-purpose, three-story building that dominated everything. From the placement of the signs that hung on it, Longarm saw that the Murray Hotel occupied the two upper floors, and Baker's Store and Trading Post the main floor, with one end given over to the dining room. The saloon was housed in an ell that had been added on to one end of the structure as an afterthought.

When new, the big building had been painted with a single coat of drab gray paint. It seemed to be the only shade available in the Nation, except white. Now, the paint was scabrous and splotched, and beginning to peel, showing the raw boards in places. The white trim that had outlined the eaves, doors, and windows had weathered, until it almost matched the gray walls. Behind the store stood a large new warehouse, built of bricks.

To the northwest, the rolling plain fell in a gentle slope to form a saucer within a sweeping curve of the Canadian River's north fork. A narrow trace of beaten earth, neither wide enough nor distinct enough to be called a road, wandered at random across the plain. Longarm counted eleven houses spaced irregularly along the trace within a distance of perhaps three miles. All the dwellings stood in stubbled fields checkerboarded by irrigation ditches. The fields hadn't been plowed after the summer harvest; they were covered with sheared stalks of corn and maize.

All the houses were uniform in size and shape—small cubes with roofs shaped like pyramids. Chimneys stuck up from the roof peaks. They were all painted with the same sodbuster-gray that covered the trader's building. Beyond the houses, the conical shapes of tipis marked the location of an Indian camp. Past the camp, the river formed a broken silver line that curved between low hillocks, its course bringing it toward the agency's edge. The stream was shallow now, little more than a series of small pools connected by thread-thin trickles, waiting to be replenished by the rains that had not yet set in.

Longarm reined in at the long hitch rail that stretched from one end of the trading post building to the other. His stomach told him it was nearly time to eat, but curiosity was more commanding than hunger. He went into the store, where he found the interior cavernous, dim, and empty of customers. At the back, at a desk behind a long, scarred counter, a man sat checking over ledger sheets.

"Help you with something?" he called when Longarm entered.

"Some information, maybe." Longarm picked his way through the maze of bales, boxes, and barrels that were scattered on the floor. "My name's Long, deputy U.S. marshal from Denver."

"Asa Baker," the man said. "I'm the trader here."

"Figured that out from your sign," Longarm said, as he looked around the store's deserted interior, at the same time taking stock of Baker from a corner of his eye. The trader wore a fringe of beard, his upper lip clean-shaven. His beard was gray, but his hair was still dark brown. His eyes were closely set and his eyelids were slitted under brows that appeared to be drawn together in a perpetual frown. Longarm went on, "Trade don't seem real lively, right now."

"Too close to suppertime. Well, Marshal, who're you after?" Baker's voice reflected long-suffering impatience. "You're bound to be looking for somebody. Every damned outlaw that finds things too hot for him outside heads for the Nation, and the law follows him."

"I guess that's about right," Longarm agreed. "The one I'm after is a bank-robbing killer named Eddie Boyle."

"What's he look like?" Baker asked. "Names don't mean much here; a man on the dodge, first thing he does is give himself a new one. But I guess you'd know that, if you're who you say you are."

"Just to set your mind easy—" Longarm took out his wallet and flipped it open to show his badge. "That satisfy you?"

"Looks real enough, all right. Well, what about this Boyle you're after, Marshal? Colorado badman, is he?"

The deputy nodded. "Cripple Creek. Last one of a gang that robbed a bank and killed two men getting away. About all I've got is his description. Early twenties, just under six feet, sort of slim, dark-complected. He's got a nose that's been busted twice, high and low."

"There's plenty of men with busted noses around here, but none of 'em are strangers to me. How long's this fellow been on the prod?"

"A month, give or take a few days. He'd've showed up here

not more than a week ago, I'd guess, if he kept moving after he got across the Colorado line."

Baker shook his head. "Afraid I can't help you. There's only been two or three strangers pass through here in the last two weeks, and none of them had busted noses. You sure your man headed this way?"

"Not too sure. All I know is he was headed south."

"Guess you'll have to backtrack, then. There's not too many places up in the Cherokee Outlet where a man can get provisions. Outside of a few whiskey ranches just above the reservation border, there's only New Cantonment, Fort Supply, and Beaver City." Looking thoughtful, Baker added, "Unless he just cut though No-Man's-Land and hit into Texas. There's enough cattle ranches in the Panhandle now so a man could go from one to the other and keep eating pretty regular without ever showing his face in a town."

"I've thought about Texas, sure. The thing is, I've been told that Boyle has a lady friend someplace here in the Nation."

The trader scratched his fringe of chin whiskers pensively. "That covers lots of ground. Whereabouts in the Nation?"

"Now, if I knew that, I'd be making tracks for the place instead of standing here jawing with you, wouldn't I? Tell me something, Baker. You been the trader here very long?"

"Going on four years. Moved over from the Creek lands a little while after the army begun herding the Cheyennes and Araps southward, and needed a trader on this reservation. Why? What's that got to do with anything?"

Longarm wondered why the trader's voice suddenly took on a note of hostility, but ignored it. He said casually, "I just wondered how well acquainted you might be with the Indian police on these stations here. If you were me, which one of 'em would be best to ask if he'd keep an eye out for this Boyle?"

Baker snorted. "None of 'em. Have you ever worked in the Nation before now, Marshal?"

"Some. Not lately, though. It used to be that the Indian police wouldn't go an inch out of their way to help a white lawman, even if he wore a federal badge the same as they do. I hoped things might've changed."

"They haven't. But if you feel like you've got to ask one of 'em to help, I'd say an Osage named Short Bear is your best bet."

"Thanks, Baker. Where do I find him? At the agency?"

"Tomorrow, maybe. If you want to talk to him sooner, he'll more than likely be in the dining room next door at supper-time. Unless you plan to push on tonight?"

"I figure to stay here, if there's a room open in the hotel."

"There is. As far's I know, Mrs. Murray's only got one room rented out right now. They'll be starting to dish up supper in a few minutes. If you're thirsty, better stop at the bar first. No liquor in the dining room 'cause it's open to the redskins."

The lawman would have enjoyed a tot of Maryland rye, but decided to wait until after supper. He didn't want to miss the chance of talking to the Osage policeman in the dining room.

"Thanks, but I'll wait a while," he told Baker.

"Sure. You come to the bar after supper, I'll set up the drinks myself. You tell Short Bear I said for you to talk to him. Maybe he'll listen, but I don't guarantee anything."

"I'll do that." The deputy turned to leave, then turned back, "Oh, one more thing. Does the hotel have a barn or stall where I can put my horse tonight?"

"Nope. Hotel guests use my corral; it's out back of the warehouse. If you need feed, I've got oats and grain for sale."

Carrying a small bag of oats and another one of corn, Long-arm led his roan back to the corral, unsaddled the animal and fed it, then climbed the stairs to the hotel lobby, carrying his saddle gear, and signed the dog-eared register. Mrs. Murray—at least, he assumed she was the landlady—showed him to a room down a dark corridor, looking out at the warehouse's blank wall.

"No drinking or carousing in your room, now," she cautioned him. "I run a nice, respectable hotel, and I expect my guests to behave, not go wild and break up my furniture. Now then, you can eat supper in the dining room if you get there inside of the next hour. It's open for breakfast at five."

"Thank you for the information, ma'am." Longarm glanced at the mismatched furnishings: an iron bedstead with chipped paint and a sagging mattress; a pine straight-backed chair; a fumed-oak bureau spotted white with watermarks, its mirror mottled with age. "I'll be right careful of your furniture. Now, if you'll be so kind as to send up the porter with some hot water—"

"Porter!" she exploded. "Mister, in this hotel, I'm the porter and the maid and the desk clerk, too!" Mrs. Murray looked incredulously at Longarm. He'd kept his face straight and serious during her outburst, and this seemed to confuse her. After a moment, she relented. "Oh, all right. I'll get you a pitcherful from the dining room. They wouldn't give it to you if you was to ask. But you'll have to fetch it from the desk."

"I'll be glad to, ma'am. And I'm real grateful for your help."

"Don't worry, it'll be on your bill," she retorted. "Hot water comes extra with my rooms."

With the cinder dust from the freight train and the red trail dust from his trip to Fort Reno washed away, freshly shaved and wearing his clean shirt, Longarm entered the dining room a half hour later. The two long tables that stretched side by side down the length of the room weren't crowded, but as Longarm studied the table arrangement, he saw that he faced a problem.

Two Indians wearing tall, round-topped hats and blue uniform tunics sat side by side, facing in his direction. There were vacant chairs flanking them on both sides, but Longarm knew that if he made it obvious that he preferred to sit next to Short Bear, he ran the risk of offending the second Indian. Without asking, there was no way to determine which of the two was the Osage Baker had said was friendly. If he sat beside the wrong man and then had to change his position, that would be a serious loss of face to Short Bear's companion. Indian pride was touchy that way, he knew, and the last thing he needed was to offend either of the two policemen.

With this in mind, he decided to sit across the table from them. That way, he'd be talking to each of them on equal terms. More importantly, he'd be able to watch their faces for their reactions during the conversation. There were vacant chairs across from them, but the seat directly opposite was occupied by a woman. Her back was turned toward him, and he couldn't tell a thing about her, but it had been Longarm's experience that if a man ignored half a dozen empty chairs and deliberately sat down beside a lone woman, she was apt to take the act as an insulting advance and raise a ruckus. He didn't need that, either, because then he'd be forced to apologize, and apologizing to a woman in public would reduce his stature to the Indians.

Typically, he decided to solve the problem by meeting it head-on. Going down the side of the table on which the woman was seated, he took off his Stetson and stopped behind her. He said, "Beg your pardon, ma'am. I hope you don't think I'm being forward, but I'm a deputy U.S. marshal, and I need to talk to these two officers on official business."

Turning in her chair, the woman looked up at him, and for the first time he got a look at her face. He realized with surprise that she was young, very young indeed. His guess was that she couldn't be a day more than twenty, and might not even be that old.

She said coldly, "It just happens that I'm talking with these gentlemen on business, too, Marshal. And I might point out that I was here first."

Longarm bowed his head diffidently, then raised it again and looked her steadily in the eye. "I'm sorry, ma'am, but I'm going to have to insist. I've got to leave here before daylight tomorrow, and I need to get my business done tonight."

The color rose in her cheeks, and she said angrily, "Marshal, are you suggesting that I'm planning to spend the entire night with these two men? Do you mean to imply that I'm a lady of the evening? Is that what you thought I meant when I said I was talking business with them?"

"Now, ma'am, that wasn't in my mind at all—" Longarm began, but before he could continue, the girl had risen to her feet and slapped him sharply across the cheek.

Longarm knew he had to do something. To let the woman's act pass by would cause the Osage policemen to classify him as, at worst, weaker than a woman, or at the very least, as a man of no consequence, a man to whom they wouldn't listen. The feelings of the girl and the possible reaction of the other diners in the room were a lot less important at the moment than the impression he made on the Indians. Longarm promptly caught the girl around her waist, propped one foot on the rung of a chair, bent her over his knee, and spanked her three or four times on the buttocks.

Everyone in the dining room was watching, but nobody moved to interfere. It wasn't a habit among them to butt into another man's affairs. For all the diners knew, Longarm might have been a father paddling a disobedient daughter, or a husband punishing an errant wife. Only the Indian policemen knew the reason for the spanking, and they were too busy laughing and nudging one another to pay any attention to the rest of the onlookers.

As for the girl, she was too indignant to speak when Longarm released her. She stood staring at him for a moment, then stamped a foot angrily and hissed, "You'll hear more about this, Marshal!" Then, her face red with anger and embarrassment, she ran from the dining room.

Longarm took the chair she'd vacated and looked across the table at the Osage policemen. As though nothing unusual had happened, he asked in a quiet voice, "I suppose one of you is Short Bear? My name's Custis Long."

"I'm Short Bear," the bigger of the two said, then jerked a thumb in the other's direction. "This is my partner, Fat Beaver."

"I'm sorry I busted up your confab," Longarm told them. "Who was the lady, anyhow? A missionary, or something like that?"

"She told us she's a writer," Short Bear answered. His English was as good as Longarm's. "She said she wants to do some stories about what life is like here in the Nation."

"The hell you say!" Longarm frowned. "Maybe I ought not to've butted in. She sort of riled me, though, when she sassed me that way."

Short Bear nodded sagely. "A woman should speak softly to a man." He began eating his interrupted dinner. "If the girl wants to talk to us later, she knows where to find us."

Longarm studied the two Osages, who were now ignoring him. Fat Beaver had gone back to his meal while Short Bear and Longarm were talking. Longarm decided the best thing he could do was to follow their example. He pushed the girl's plate aside, took a clean one from the setting next to him, and helped himself to boiled beef, potatoes, squash, onions, and carrots. He started to eat, following the example of the Osages by ignoring them. He noticed that they were watching him covertly.

After a few moments, Short Bear asked, "What's your business with us, Marshal? Did some of our people break off the reservation and go kill a few Texas steers?"

"No. A little thing like that wouldn't bring me here from Denver. I'm after a killer—a bank robber who murdered two men up in Colorado. The sheriff's posse that was chasing him got run out of the Nation by some of your men up around Fort Supply, so I'm here with a federal warrant to find him and bring him back."

"You mean to *try* to find him," Fat Beaver put in. "Or that you want us to find him for you. No, Marshal Long. Our job's with our own people, not chasing fugitives who've broken laws outside the Nation."

"Now hold on!" Longarm protested. "So far, I haven't asked you men to do anything at all. You might let me tell you what I want before you start saying no."

"We'll listen to him," Short Bear told his partner. Then, turning to Longarm, he said, "Fat Beaver's right, though. Unless your outlaw's an Indian, or somebody who's going to cause trouble with our people, we're not very interested in guiding you around while you look for somebody who hasn't committed a crime in our territory."

"I'll give you credit for one thing," Longarm told them. His words caught their attention, and he made the most of it, chewing and swallowing a bite of beef before continuing. "You sure don't waste any words laying things right on the line."

"Our people don't say an antelope is a buffalo," Short Bear observed.

"So I've found out. Well, I'll lay it to you straight, too. I don't expect you to do my job for me. All I want is for you to keep an eye out for this man I'm after. As for him making trouble for your people, he just might, in one way. I'm pretty certain he's got a lady friend someplace in the Nation. My guess is that he's figuring to move in with her, maybe get himself a gang together from among her friends. What kind of trouble that might start is something you'd know better than I do."

For the first time, the Osages showed a flicker of real interest. Short Bear frowned and asked, "One of our women?"

Longarm nodded. "That's what I was told."

"What tribe does she come from?" Fat Beaver asked.

"You got me there. That's something I don't know."

Fat Beaver shook his head. "You might as well go back home, Marshal. It's not like it used to be, here in the Nation. In the old days we only had ten or twelve tribes living here. Now there are thirty tribes and ten times as many of us as there were then. If you don't know more than you've told us so far—things like the tribe this woman belongs to—we can't do anything to help you."

"Damn it, I just told you I'm not asking for help!" Longarm said. "All I want you to do is keep your eyes and ears open while you go about your job, and pass the word to the rest of your force that I'm after a fugitive. Now, don't tell me that's too much for one federal lawman to ask another one to do for him!"

"If you put it that way, I guess it isn't," Short Bear said. He looked questioningly at Fat Beaver. "You agree?"

Somewhat reluctantly, Fat Beaver nodded. "It's reasonable." Then he asked Longarm, "Suppose we run across this outlaw's trail. How will we get word to you? We won't know where you are."

"Well, I damn sure won't be hiding. Just pass the word to your stations or offices or whatever you call your headquarters. When I'm close to one of 'em, I'll drop in, and if there's a message for me, I'll get it, all right."

Short Bear nodded his agreement. Then he asked, "Marshal, tell me something. Do you share Indian blood with us?"

"Not that I know of. Why?"

"Because you ask us instead of ordering us. And you show more patience than most white lawmen I've run into." The Osage smiled. "What you ask is reasonable; we'll do it. Now tell us what your outlaw looks like, and if any of our people cross his trail, you'll hear about it."

While they finished their meal, Longarm gave the Osages the only description he had of Eddie Boyle, and outlined details of the Cripple Creek killings. The Indians left, and Longarm finished his own supper. Outside the dining room, he took a cheroot from an inside pocket, centered it between his lips, and looked along the dark street. There were lights in some of the buildings at the agency, and pale yellow squares of light in the farmhouses beyond. He took out a match, struck it with a thumbnail, and touched the flame to his cheroot. The only signs of life close at hand were trickles of voices coming from the store and the saloon. He shook out the match, and stuck his head in the door of the store; Baker, with two clerks helping him now, was busy. Half the people who'd left the dining room seemed to be doing their shopping.

Old son, Longarm told himself, *the best thing you can do tonight is to get a bottle and go up to your room. Tomorrow's likely to be a long, rough day, and you ain't exactly had a whole lot of shut-eye lately.*

Aside from the back bar, which was lined with small kegs instead of the more usual bottles, the saloon might have been in any one of a dozen towns he'd visited. The barkeep wore a stained apron hitched up under his armpits, a gaudy striped shirt, and a macassar-oiled mustache. He didn't put a bottle on the table in response to Longarm's call for Maryland rye, but filled an empty bottle from one of the kegs. He drove a cork in its neck with the heel of his hand and set the bottle on the bar.

"That's two dollars," he announced.

Longarm didn't argue. He was used to the inflated prices that saloons in isolated areas charged. He tossed a half-eagle on the bar, and while the barkeep turned to the till for change, he pulled the cork out of the bottle and took a sample swallow. The barkeep stacked three silver cartwheels in front of Longarm. Instead of picking them up, Longarm shoved the bottle back to him.

"I guess you didn't hear me, friend," he told the man. "I asked you for Maryland rye. This here's Monongahela whiskey, and it's watered down, to boot. Now suppose you just pour this slop back in the keg and fill my order the right way."

For a moment the barkeep seemed ready to argue, but when he took Longarm's measure with his eyes and saw the bulge made by his Colt under the frock coat, he said quickly, "Sorry, mister. I guess I just didn't hear you, like you said."

He brought out a bottle from beneath the bar. Longarm held out his hand. Wordlessly, the barkeep laid a corkscrew in it. Longarm drew the cork, sniffed, then tilted the bottle and tasted. He nodded. "That's better."

Picking up his change, he tucked the bottle under his arm

and climbed the stairs to the hotel lobby. A lamp burned on the desk, but no one was there; he decided Mrs. Murray must be finishing her day's work by helping to clean up the dining room, though she hadn't mentioned that job when she'd listed her duties earlier. The hotel register lay open on the desk. Longarm glanced at it and saw that the signature on the line above his was "E. Cochrane, Pittsburgh, Penna." It was written in a firm, bold, broad script. As he walked down the dim hallway, he chuckled at the recollection of Miss Cochrane's embarrassed indignation as she'd stalked out of the dining room after his token spanking.

Longarm checked the matchstick he'd wedged between door and jamb on leaving his room, and found it undisturbed. He supposed there was no reason it should have been bothered, because, aside from Miss Cochrane, there wasn't anybody in the Nation mad at him. At least nobody he knew about. In his room, he groped for the lamp in the darkness. He finally had to strike a match to find it, but managed to get the chimney off and touch the match to the wick before the flame died out.

He hadn't been very nice to Miss Cochrane, Longarm decided as he shed his coat and vest and hung his gunbelt on the head of the bedstead. He settled down in the room's only chair and propped his feet up on the edge of the bed. After taking a long swallow from the bottle, he lighted a cheroot and let its smoke caress his throat and smooth the pleasant bite of the whiskey. It tasted so good that he took a second swallow and another puff. Idly, he wondered what the "E" in Miss Cochrane's name stood for. Emma? Evangeline? Ellen? Eugenia?

An almost imperceptible scuffling sound in the hallway broke in to interrupt his thought. The noise was so faint that he wasn't really sure he'd heard anything, and then it occurred to him that if he had heard something, it was probably a rat going to or from the kitchen on the floor below. Then, distantly, a murmur of voices began, too low in volume and too far away for him to distinguish anything except that they were voices. His professional curiosity was aroused. Longarm brought his feet down from the bed and set them silently on the floor. He was still sitting down, straining to hear more than the soft shushing of sound filtered through the door when he heard the beginning of a woman's scream, quickly stifled.

Pausing only long enough to slide his Colt from its holster, Longarm threw open the door of his room and looked down the hallway. Light streamed from an open door on the opposite side of the corridor, between his room and the lobby. In black silhouette, he saw the Cochrane girl struggling in the grasp of a man whose hand was clamped around her mouth. The girl was between him and the man; Longarm couldn't shoot without the risk of hitting her.

"Get your hands in the air!" he commanded, He pressed against the wall and leveled his pistol at the struggling pair.

There was a gleam of bright steel in the dim light. Longarm, looking into the glare of lamplight streaming through the open door of the girl's room and from the lobby just beyond it, didn't see the knife whirling through the air until it hit him. The blade went through his shirtsleeve, creasing his arm with swift, sudden pain and pinning his gunhand to the wall by the cuff. At the same time, the intruder shoved the girl away and turned to run.

Before Longarm could shift his pistol to his free hand, the man had covered the few steps to the lobby and was out of sight down the stairway. Longarm stood immobilized, the blood from his slashed arm soaking into his cuff and beginning to drip off his fingertips.

Chapter 3

"You're hurt!" the girl cried, as Longarm wrenched the knife out of the wall and let it fall to the floor.

"Nothing to worry about," he told her. He flexed his gun hand and found that it still responded normally. "You stay here. I'm going after that knife-tossing buzzard."

His bootheels clattering on the uncarpeted stairway, Longarm took the steps two at a time, and ran into the street. Light spilled in yellow rectangles from the doors of the store, the hotel, and the saloon, breaking the darkness of the gravel roadway. He stopped in a dark patch between the lights, squeezing his eyes closed for a moment to speed their adjustment to the darkness, risking the chance that his quarry was still close by, watching. Except for a babble of voices coming through the saloon door, the street was silent.

There was no place a man could hide across from the hotel and store building. Longarm circled the yellow slit of light that came from the hotel door and hugged the side of the dining room to the corner of the building. The brick warehouse loomed, a solid black hulk in the starlight, as he peered around the corner. There was no movement, no noise of feet crunching on the hard earth. Still, he didn't give up. He moved cautiously through the dark passageway between the two structures, and scouted the area beyond them. By now, he'd gotten his night vision and could see a reasonable distance across the barren ground beyond the buildings. Nothing moved.

"Missed the son of a bitch," he muttered. "And not much use in trying to find him now. He knows the layout here a lot better than I do."

Tucking his Colt into the waistband of his trousers, Longarm went back up the stairway. The girl was still standing in the hall. There was a worried look on her face.

"Did you find him?" she asked.

"Not hide nor hair, ma'am. He must've just kept on running."

"You'd better let me look at your arm," she suggested. "It's still bleeding, and I don't suppose there's a doctor within a hundred miles of here."

"It'll be all right. All I got was a scratch." He picked up the knife and looked at it. The weapon was a homemade blade with a leather handle and a lead butt-cap. The blade was honed razor-keen, double-edged for two inches back from the point; it was a weapon designed to be equally effective for stabbing, slashing, or throwing. "Maybe somebody'll recognize this. I'll ask around tomorrow."

"You'll come into my room right now, and let me fix up your arm," she told him severely.

"I can look after it myself, Miss—"

"Cochrane. Elizabeth Cochrane. And I'm not going to take any excuses, Marshal. If you think I'm still angry about that little scene in the dining room, you're right. You had no business handling me like I was a naughty schoolgirl. But if you hadn't tried to help me a minute ago, when that man attacked me, you wouldn't be bleeding now. Please don't argue with me. Just step inside and let me put a bandage on your arm."

"Well, then, if you insist—"

Longarm followed the girl into the room and sat down in the lone chair it held. She watched him fumble with his cuff button, using his left hand, and then she brushed his fingers aside impatiently, unbuttoned the cuff, and pulled the sleeve up above his elbow. The wound was a short slash across Longarm's forearm, a couple of inches above his wrist. Blood still oozed from it slowly.

"You're lucky, Marshal—what's your name, anyhow? I never did hear you mention it, downstairs."

"Long, Miss Cochrane. Custis Long. From the Denver office."

"Well, you're lucky that knife didn't go any deeper than it did." Elizabeth Cochrane turned Longarm's wrist to show him the cut left by the blade. "Another fraction of an inch, and that big vein would've been slashed."

"No use worrying about ifs, Miss Cochrane, as long as it didn't hit the vein. I told you it wasn't bad—just a scratch. Won't do any damage to my gunhand, or slow me down a bit."

"That's important to you, isn't it?" She'd gone to the night-stand on the opposite side of the room, and was pouring water from the pitcher into the washbowl.

"Maybe a lot more than you'd understand, being from the East like you are," he replied shortly.

"Not all Easterners are ignorant of the West, Marshal," she retorted, bringing the basin to where Longarm sat and putting it on the floor beside his chair.

Longarm studied her while she made her preparations. He'd been too busy with the Osages at supper to pay much attention to her. He couldn't quite decide whether Elizabeth was a mature girl or an unusually young-looking woman. Her face was unlined, her skin smoothly youthful and without wrinkles, and she moved with the quickness of the very young. But there was something in her eyes that made him question what his own eyes saw.

Elizabeth's eyes were deep, a dark violet, and he'd seen them grow dark and snap with anger. He'd also seen them soften when she smiled, and shade down when she became serious. Her eyes didn't match the youthfulness of her face, the firmly rounded small chin and rosebud lips that were full but capable of being drawn tightly severe. He wondered what the rest of her was like, under the fluffed-out blouse and full skirt.

She'd tucked a towel under her arm. Now she soaked a corner of it in the tepid water and gently washed the blood-stained arm and hand. Her touch was sure and gentle as she worked. The rough cloth scraped Longarm's skin, but she never allowed it to touch the wound itself. Reversing the towel, she dried his wrist.

"You've done this kind of thing before, haven't you?" he asked.

"A little bit. I thought I wanted to be a nurse at one time. Now"—she rested Longarm's hand on his knee—"just hold your arm still, and I'll fix up some antiseptic solution for it before I put on a bandage."

"Aw, I don't need a bandage on that little henpeck scratch. It'll heal up in a day or so."

"Just let me take care of things, Marshal. If your shirtsleeve sticks to that cut, it'll be painful when you take it off. You'll probably start bleeding again."

There was an authority in the girl's voice that surprised Longarm, coming as it did from one so young. He found himself wondering about Elizabeth Cochrane—who she was, why she was there. He watched while she opened her portmanteau and took out a vial of pale pink crystals. She poured water into a tumbler from the pitcher on the nightstand and shook a pinch of the crystals into it. The water turned a deep reddish purple as the crystals dissolved.

"I'll paint the cut with this potassium permanganate," she told him. "Heaven only knows what that knife's been used for, or how dirty the blade is. It might be carrying some very infectious germs, for all we can tell." She swabbed the cut with a corner of the towel after dipping it into the tumbler. The antiseptic left a deep purple stain on Longarm's wrist. The swift assurance of her movements matched the authority he'd heard in her voice, and Longarm couldn't hold back his curiosity any longer.

"What're you doing out here in the Indian Nation, Miss Cochrane? Come to help out at one of the hospitals or something?" he asked.

She shook her head. "Nothing like that." She hesitated, then said, "I suppose it won't hurt anything to tell you. Since you're from Denver, you wouldn't be caught up in any of the sordid affairs that I've heard rumors of. I'm a newspaper reporter, Marshal."

"A—a newspaper reporter?" Longarm couldn't hide the incredulity that was in his tone as he echoed her.

"Don't be so surprised," she snapped, "Women can see things as clearly as men do, and write as well as men."

"But, you're sort of—well, I mean to say—" Longarm floundered.

"I'm young. Isn't that what you're trying to say?"

"I guess so. At least, you sure don't look very old to me."

"I suppose that's flattering. Well, I'm not going to tell you my age; that's a woman's privilege that I'll reserve for myself. But I'm old enough to know my own mind, and to take care of myself. In fact, I've been in much wilder country than the In-

dian Nation for the past three months, and as you can see, I'm
still doing quite well."

She looked around the room for a cloth with which to make
a bandage. The pillows on the bed caught her eye; she stripped
a case from one of them and used the attacker's knife to start a
rip along its hem so that she could tear a strip from it.

"This is about the cleanest piece of cloth we're likely to find,
I suppose, but with the permanganate on that cut, I don't think
you'll get any sort of infection from the cloth."

Neatly and efficiently, she bandaged the wound and tied off
the strip of cloth by ripping it into halves for a few inches from
the end. Longarm had seen messier bandages applied in hospitals and frontier doctors' offices.

"That'll do fine," he told her. "And I'm right grateful to you
for taking the trouble."

"Oh, I'm not through yet. I assume you're traveling light; I
know *I* can't carry any extras. Take off your shirt, and I'll wash
out that blood before it sets."

"You don't need to do that, Miss Cochrane. I can dip the
cuff into my own washbasin when I go back to my room."

"Please don't argue with me, Marshal, I feel responsible for
your having been wounded, and I intend to do whatever's necessary to save you trouble."

"Now that you mention it, how come that fellow set onto
you like that? You stepped on any toes since you been here?"

Elizabeth Cochrane shook her head. "I haven't been here
long enough to make any enemies, Marshal. Actually, I haven't
really begun to pry around at all. I just got here yesterday."

"You never saw him before, then?"

"Not that I can remember. But I really didn't get a good
look at him. His back was toward the light in the hall, and his
face was shadowed by the door of my room. Then, when he
grabbed me, he kept his hand over my mouth and was squeezing so hard it started my eyes to watering. I never did see his
face clearly."

Longarm frowned. "Neither did I. He had his hat pulled
down low, and I wasn't looking at much except to find an angle
I could wing him from without hitting you."

"I suppose I was lucky to be able to make enough noise for
you to've heard me. I remember asking him what he wanted,

and then when he didn't answer right away, I asked him again, louder. That was all I had time to say before he grabbed me."

The deputy looked thoughtful. "There's got to be some reason why he came looking for you."

"I can give you the only reason that comes to my mind," the young woman said. "He'd probably seen me earlier in the day, when I got off the stage, or when I was in the store or the dining room, and either decided I was a new whore come to town, or that I was somebody he could rape."

Longarm whistled. "For as nice-spoken a lady as you are, you sure use some rough words, Miss Cochrane."

"Don't pretend to be shocked, Marshal. I'm sure you've heard all the words before. Used them, for that matter."

"Well, I suppose I have. But I don't generally hear young ladies spit 'em out like they were just saying dog or cat."

"Marshal Long, I told you I'm a newspaper reporter. I've covered just about every kind of story during the three years I've been with the *Dispatch*, and I've gotten accustomed to hearing plain talk. And talking plainly myself, I suppose." She smiled.

Longarm nodded slowly. "I can see how that'd be. This newspaper you report for; is it in New York?"

"No. It's published in Pittsburgh, Pennsylvania. But it has a very wide circulation. Next to the New York *World* and James Gordon Bennett's *Herald,* the *Dispatch* is about the most widely read newspaper in the East. It's always concerned with things that are important to the ordinary citizen."

"I'm not much of a newspaper reader, myself," Longarm said. "I look at the Denver paper when I'm there, but you can't believe much of what Bonfils and Tammen say."

"So I've heard." Elizabeth smiled. "But my boss—George Madden—insists that we get all our facts straight and write them up truthfully."

"I'll have to look around for your paper, if it gets as far as Denver. I know some men reporters, of course, but you're the first woman one I've run into."

She smiled. "You won't recognize my stories unless you look for the name I sign them with."

"You don't use your own name, then?"

"No, Marshal. It's too long, for one thing. And too hard to remember."

"Now, I don't think I'd have any trouble remembering it."

"But you're not the average newspaper reader. They forget names that aren't short and easy to say."

"What name do you write under, then?"

"Nellie Bly. I took the name from one of my favorite Stephen Foster songs, except that I changed it a little, called myself Bly instead of Gray. It rings a little better, and I didn't want anybody to think of me as a gray-haired spinster." She reached out, took hold of the end of Longarm's black string necktie, and tugged until its knot was freed. "Now, don't think I can't see through what you're doing, Marshal. If you're bashful about taking off your shirt so I can wash the sleeve, you needn't be. There's very little I haven't seen—or experienced, for that matter. I won't be in the least embarrassed by seeing your bare chest."

"Well, then, if you're going to insist—"

"I am. I'm responsible for your shirt getting soiled, so I'll wash it and mend the place where the knife cut, so it won't ravel out and tear."

Longarm gave in. He unbuttoned his shirt and took it off, removing his Colt from his waistband before pulling his shirttail free. Nellie took the shirt and put the cuff and the bloodstained portion of the sleeve to soak in the washbasin.

Turning back to face him, she said, "It'll take a few minutes for the water to work on the bloodstain. If you feel embarrassed, I'll bring your shirt to you when I've finished mending it. Or if you want to wait, I'd like to ask you a few questions about the Indian Territory. I know you're a lot better acquainted with it than I am. In fact, I wasn't really aware of what the Indian Territory was until I heard some talk about it on the train coming back from Mexico."

Longarm frowned. "You mean you've been to Mexico? That's a pretty far piece from Pennsylvania."

"Distance doesn't matter to George Madden, Marshal. When he heard about what was happening in Mexico under Porfirio Diaz, he sent me down there at once to see if the stories were true."

"You found out they were, I bet. I had some brushes with Diaz's *rurales* myself, a while back, on a case that took me down thataway."

"What we'd heard wasn't only true," she told him. "It was a lot worse than anything I could imagine."

Longarm shook his head. "I guess you must be a pretty smart woman, Miss Bly—or Cochrane, if you'd rather."

"I'd be pleased if you'd just call me Nellie. That's what most of the men in the office do. Except George. He calls me Eliza, which I hate, even if I know he's just doing it to tease me."

"Miss Nellie, then."

"Nellie without the 'Miss,' Marshal."

"Whatever you say. My friends have got a nickname for me, too, if it'd be easy for you to use it. Mostly, they call me Longarm."

"Because you represent the long arm of the law? Well, with your last name being Long, and your job taking you almost anywhere, I can see how that'd come about." She smiled, a friendly smile this time. "Though I must say, I didn't appreciate the hand on the end of your long arm being applied to my bottom earlier. I can understand now why you lost patience with me, though. Can we forget that little scene in the dining room and start fresh, as friends?"

"I'd be proud to, Nellie."

"Good." She sat on the edge of the bed, gesturing toward the chair. The tall deputy turned it so that its back faced the bed, threw a leg over it as if it were a horse, and sat, folding his arms on the top of the chair's back and resting his chin on his forearms. "Now," she continued, "what're you doing here in the Indian Nation? I've already told you why I'm here."

"Shucks, my case here's not all that big. I'm chasing a bank robber that shot down a town marshal up in Cripple Creek. He got into the Nation before the sheriff caught up with him, and my boss in Denver sent me down after him, mainly because it's federal territory, and because I've been here on other cases."

"That's why you were looking for the Indian policemen, then? To have them help you locate the man you're after?"

"Mostly. Things here in the Nation ain't like what 'most anybody's used to, Nellie. The government gave the land to the

Indian tribes, but Washington keeps on trying to tell 'em how
to run things. They've got no marshals stationed here, and the
Indian police are supposed to keep things peaceful, so when
somebody comes in from outside, it sort of gets their backs up.
I can't *tell* 'em to help me, you see. All I can do is ask."

Nellie nodded thoughtfully. "I can see how that'd rub them
the wrong way. And what about the army? And the Indian
agents? And the traders? Where do they come in? What authority do they have?"

"I guess nobody rightly knows. The army's got a lot of Indian
scouts, mostly Blackfoot and Osage, and a few Delawares and
Pawnees. Other tribes don't much like the Pawnees. They used
to be cannibals way back years ago, like the Tonkawas still are."

This matter-of-fact statement seemed to ruffle her composure slightly. "Cannibals? I didn't know there were any cannibals among our own Indians!"

"There always were a few cannibal tribes, the way I heard
it. Up in the Northeast and along the border with Canada, way
back when us white men first came here. It lasted a lot longer
with the Tonks, is all."

"I didn't mean to interrupt you, Longarm. You were about
to tell me where the army fitted in."

"Well, I'd say the army fits in just about any place it feels
like it wants to. Most of the officers figure their Indian and
breed scouts have got as much authority as the Indian police,
so there ain't much love lost between the police and the army.
And if one of the tribes gets rambunctious, like the newest
ones settled in the Nation do—the Kiowas and Comanches,
say—it's always the army that goes out to tame 'em down."

Nellie sighed. "It sounds like nobody really knows who's
in charge of anything here. I can see where there'd be a lot of
conflict."

"Oh, I'm just getting started. The army doesn't get along
with the Bureau of Indian Affairs, I guess because both outfits
are headquartered direct in Washington. And the BIA men,
that's the traders and storekeepers and agents, are usually set
up in their jobs by some congressman or senator, maybe even
by the President himself. So they figure they don't really have
to answer to the Indian police or the army, either. And the army

sutlers don't like the traders cutting in on their business. Nobody in the Nation really gets along with anybody else, and the Indians are always on the bottom of the pile."

"I don't see how the Indians put up with so many bosses. From what I've heard, they don't even follow their own tribal chiefs, if they think the chiefs are in the wrong."

The lawman stroked his mustache with a long forefinger. "Well, you're like most folks from the East, I'd say. You've got the idea an Indian chief's picked out by a whole tribe, Which ain't exactly the case. You see, there's tribes inside of tribes— little tribes or clans or whatever you'd call 'em. The Sioux have got maybe ten or twelve different ones, and the Comanches have got four or five, and the Kiowas have got three I can recall, maybe more. And every little tribe's got its own chief, who won't follow any chief of one of the other tribes, even if they're both Sioux or Comanche or whatever."

"It sounds to me like a terrible mess," Nellie commented.

"It is. Except for the Five Civilized Tribes—that's the Cherokees, Choctaws, Seminoles, Creeks, and Chickasaws— nobody really knows who's their boss. And them five tribes don't cotton much to the other ones, because they were promised the whole Indian Nation back before the War Between the States, when they were moved here from the East."

"They look on the other tribes as intruders, then?"

He nodded. "Pretty much. They call 'em the wild tribes, even if some of 'em did come to the Nation not long after the so-called civilized bunch did."

"Do the Indians fight among themselves, then?"

"Some. It's mostly undercover fighting now, though. The army held onto the reins long enough for things to settle down between the different reservations."

The young woman looked slightly surprised. "How many reservations are there, for Heaven's sake? I thought this was all one big Indian territory."

"It's a long way from being that, Nellie." Longarm scratched the back of his neck. "I ain't been down here for a spell of years, but let's see if I can sort 'em all out and give 'em to you straight."

"It'd be a big help if you can. I'm planning to stay here for a month or so, trying to find out if the rumors I heard are true.

If they are, I'll be here longer, digging out the facts for my story."

"Well, I'll do my best. There're two big reservations over on the Arkansas side of the Nation—that's the Cherokees and Choctaws. Down to the south, next to the Choctaws, you've got the Chickasaws. The Osage reservation's up along the Kansas border to the north. There's a whole mess of little reservations— the Kaws, Quapahs, Tonkawas, Poncas, and Otoes—up in the north part. In the middle there's another little bunch of tiny ones, the Iowas, Kickapoos, Sacs, Foxes, Seminoles, and Potawatamies. On the west, next to Texas, is where the Comanches, Kiowas, Apaches, and Wichitas have got their reservations, and then up where we are now, it's the Arapahoes and Cheyennes." Longarm sighed and stopped. "I guess that's it, unless I forgot one of the little tribes."

Nellie smiled, obviously impressed. "I don't see how you could possibly remember all of them. And there's no central authority over all the reservations, like our states have the federal government?"

"Not unless you count the army and the BIA people."

"But from what you've said, they don't get along together at all."

He stretched his long legs out to either side of the chair, resting his heels on the floor. "Well, it looks to me like the federal government in Washington doesn't get along much better, most of the time, so I guess it's pretty much the same thing here."

Nellie shook her head. "I don't understand, though."

"Don't understand what?"

"Some of the things I heard on the train on the way back from Mexico. Things that made me decide to come here to the Indian Nation and do some investigating instead of going directly back to Pittsburgh."

Longarm arched an eyebrow, cocking his head to one side. "What kind of things?"

Nellie hesitated for a moment before she said, "I'm not quite sure I can explain them to you, Longarm."

"You might give it a shot. Like you said a minute ago, I know the Nation better'n you do. Maybe what doesn't make sense to you would make sense to me."

"I'll feel like a fool if it doesn't, though."

"If it turns out that way, you ain't lost much, except a little bit of time. But if it's something serious, maybe I'd like to know about it, too."

"I'll have to trust somebody," she said, more to herself than to Longarm. "And even if we did get off to a bad start, I think I know an honest lawman when I meet one. God knows, I've known both kinds in the East."

"Try me," he suggested.

"Oh, I intend to. Maybe you can understand why there's some sort of group, I think they're ranch owners or cattle raisers, who have their eye on a lot of land here in the Indian Nation. It doesn't make any sense to me, after hearing you explain how the Nation's divided up among—well, I couldn't keep track of the number of tribes you named a minute ago, but there must've been fifteen or twenty."

"More like thirty than twenty," Longarm put in.

"That many?" When he nodded, Nellie went on, "If all the land in the Indian Nation's divided up among those thirty tribes, it doesn't seem to me there'd be any left for white ranchers trying to get some for themselves."

He held up a hand, palm forward. "Now hold on. I didn't say all the land in the Nation's been used up. It ain't that way, Nellie. There's maybe a fourth or a third of it that doesn't belong to any tribe at all."

"But you said—"

"Never mind what I said," the deputy interrupted. "Or what you thought I said. There's a long, thin strip up on the northwest of the Nation, in between Texas and Kansas, that doesn't belong to any tribe. They call it 'No-Man's-Land,' because so many owlhoots use it to hide in when the law's hot on their trail."

She nodded. "I did hear somebody use that term, but I didn't connect it with the Indian Nation."

"Oh, it's part of the Nation, right enough," Longarm assured her. "And that ain't all. To the east of No-Man's-Land, there's a big chunk that was put aside for the Cherokees back when the Nation was first set up. But when Stan Watie and his bunch joined up with the South during the War, it made the government mad, so the land's never been passed on to the tribe, even if it's still called the Cherokee Outlet. And right below it, just east of where we are now, there's another big chunk that's called the unassigned land. It's supposed to go to the other tribes that might be put on the Nation some day, or else split up between the ones who're already here."

"Are there counties in the Nation?" she asked.

"Not that I know about. Why?"

"I heard Greer County mentioned," she replied.

"Greer County's down southwest of here," Longarm explained. "It's a Texas county that had its boundaries set before Texas joined the Union. There never was much reason to do anything about it before the Nation got set up, so Texas and Washington are still fighting over who it belongs to."

"Now things are starting to come together," Nellie said thoughtfully. "Tell me something, Longarm. Is there enough land in this part of the Nation that still hasn't been given to an Indian tribe to make it attractive to ranchers or cattlemen who want to expand?"

He nodded emphatically. "You're damn right—I'm sorry—"

"I've heard the word before, even use it myself now and then," Nellie assured him with a sudden smile.

Longarm rose from the chair and stretched languidly. "Well, there's plenty of land still open. I don't rightly know how much. Maybe about two thousand square miles, give or take five hundred."

Nellie frowned. "You mean acres, don't you?"

"No, ma'am! I mean just exactly what I said. Square miles. Nobody measures land in acres when they get west of the Missouri River. Everything's in sections out here, and a section's a square mile."

Nellie looked at the ceiling for a moment, as if she were calculating silently, then she blinked, and said in an astonished tone, "That's as much land as there is in the state of Pennsylvania!"

"Well, I wouldn't say that. But it's a big hunk of range land, any way you want to look at it."

Her lips tightened into a thin line. "And somebody's looking at it with the idea of grabbing it from the Indians, who were promised it would be theirs."

"That ain't so unusual either, Nellie." Suddenly Longarm's

tone grew very serious. "How certain are you that you heard what you think you did?"

"A few minutes ago I wasn't sure at all. Now, after what you've told me, I'm sure I'm right. Why do you ask?"

"Because if what you heard is true, it means there's got to be a whole bunch of people in cahoots," he explained. "There's got to be graft and bribery and a whole hell of a lot of corruption. And stopping a thing like that's part of my job."

"You mean you'd help me investigate?"

"If you can convince me you're right."

"Oh, Longarm! I could kiss you! In fact, I *am* going to kiss you!"

Nellie stood up, put her arms around Longarm's bare chest, and kissed him—not with passion, but where her skin touched his, electricity flowed between them. Longarm couldn't tell whether he was being kissed by a girl or a woman. Nellie wore no perfume, and he was aware of the faint aroma of her body— totally female. He started to embrace her, to return the kiss, but from somewhere deep in his mind a voice of caution made itself heard.

Old son, the inner voice told him, *just hang back here. This little girl ain't old enough for you to monkey with. She's just about as old as your own daughter'd be, if you had one. Now ease off. Don't start robbing cradles, getting something started that you'd be sorry for later.*

Firmly, he reached up and took Nellie's wrists in his calloused hands and broke the embrace.

Chapter 4

Nellie didn't seem to be offended, and Longarm told himself that she hadn't meant her embrace to be anything but friendly. He said, "You don't need to thank me for a thing, Nellie. Not yet, at least. Remember, I said I'd help you if I thought you were right about what you'd overheard. You've got to convince me I won't be going off half-cocked over some pipe dream you've had."

"It wasn't a dream," she replied firmly. "Even if I didn't understand everything those men said, I got enough of what they were talking about to know there was something wrong in the plans they were discussing."

"All right. Suppose you start out at the beginning and tell me all about it—how you heard what they said, and where, and who they were, if you know their names. After I've listened a few minutes, I'll know whether you had a pipe dream or not. I guess you do remember all those things, don't you?"

"Better than that. I took notes of what they were saying. Remember, I'm trained as a reporter. I've got to have my facts straight before I can write a story that George will publish."

"All right," he said. "I'm listening. Go ahead."

"You said for me to start at the beginning. That was in Laredo—I suppose you know where that is?"

"Sure. Down on the Texas-Mexican border. The only place the railroad crosses the river, or at least it used to be. I hear there's a line running south from El Paso now."

"There is, but I wanted to come through Texas. I've heard so much about how big it is, I wanted to see it myself."

"All right. You got on the train at Laredo."

"Actually, in Mexico City. I changed trains at the border, from the Mexican railroad to the Southern Pacific line. I was going across Texas, through San Antonio and Houston to New Orleans, because I had never been to any of those places before and thought this would be a good chance to see them."

"Wait a minute, now. When I said tell me everything, I meant to start at the time you first stumbled across this business."

"Well, it was on the train to San Antonio that I heard about it for the first time. There was a man named Scott sitting in the diner when I went in for dinner the evening I got on the train. He was—oh, I guess a few years older than you are, and I didn't take him to be anything but a businessman when I first saw him. The waiter took me to the table where he was sitting, and told me I'd be safe with Mr. Scott. We hadn't said more than a few words to each other—you know the kind of things you say when you first meet somebody, how do you do, and so on— before the train stopped and another man got on. He came into the dining car and sat down next to Mr. Scott. His name was Bob, or at least that's what Mr. Scott called him."

"This Scott fellow—he didn't introduce you?"

"He certainly didn't. He forgot all about me as soon as the one he called Bob sat down by him. First they started talking about Herefords, which I figured out after a while must be a breed of cattle, then they began comparing Herefords to longhorns, which I'd heard about ever since I was a little girl as being a kind of cattle that grows in Texas."

"I guess everybody knows about longhorns," the lawman observed. "Even you folks from back East, where mostly all you've got is dairy herds."

"Well, almost everything else they said went right over my head for a while. They were talking about ticks and how their herds were suffering, but what finally caught my attention was something Mr. Scott said about a deal he was working on for some land up north. He didn't come right out and explain things to his friend, but he did warn Bob—whatever his last name was—that there'd be a lot of money spent in bribes. After that, I really started to listen." She held up an index finger.

"I don't want to make any mistakes when I tell you," she said. "Wait just a minute. I'll get out the notes I made when I went back to my seat after I left the diner."

She walked around the bed and bent over her portmanteau. She rummaged in it and came up with a small notebook. Quickly, she leafed through the pages until she found the one she was looking for.

"Bob said, 'That's going to make the land too expensive, isn't it?' and then Mr. Scott told him, 'No. The land's not going to cost anybody one damned penny. But you'll pay what it's worth in the money that's going to have to be used in greasing palms.' Bob asked, 'Whose palms?' and Mr. Scott said, 'If you're really interested and want us to cut you in, I'll tell you, provided you give me your word that you won't say anything if you decide to stay out.'"

Nellie stopped, frowning at her notebook. She was silent for such a long time that Longarm became restless.

"Well?" he asked her.

"Please don't hurry me. My shorthand isn't really very good, and the train was going over a rough stretch of track or something when I was writing this part. At least, I guess that's why it's all squiggly and run together."

She studied the notes a few moments longer, then her face brightened. "Now I've got it. Bob promised he wouldn't say anything, and Mr. Scott dropped his voice to a whisper. That's why I had trouble; I could only catch a few words of what he said. They didn't make much sense to me, they're so disconnected."

"Go on," Longarm said. "Read 'em. Maybe I can figure out what he meant."

"Here's part of a sentence," Nellie said. She read, "'. . . officers who're placed high enough to pull their rank and stop questions from being asked . . .' Does that mean anything to you?"

Longarm nodded. "Sure. I'd say he's got next to somebody in the army who's pretty high up in command, who's got enough rank to sit on any junior officer that might try to raise a ruckus."

"Yes," she agreed. "That'd make sense. And these initials— I've got them jotted down two or three times—B, I, A. I didn't connect them up until now, when you said something about the Bureau of Indian Affairs."

"That'd cover the agents and the traders, sure. What else have you got in that book of yours, Nellie?"

"Not a great deal, I'm afraid. There are some names I didn't know how to spell; I suppose they're Indian."

"Likely they are," Longarm concurred. "I guess you couldn't be expected to spell them out. I can't pronounce half of 'em myself, even after I know how they're spelled."

"About the only other thing that might be important is what they said just before they left the table," Nellie continued, after she'd studied her notebook again. "Bob said he didn't much like the idea of going to jail for passing bribes, and Mr. Scott just laughed and told him not to worry. Then he said, 'Nobody in Washington gives two hoots in hell what happens to the redskins in the Indian Nation.'"

"That's what tipped you off that it's the Nation the two of them were talking about?"

"Yes. I didn't really know anything about the Nation. I still don't, for that matter, except for what you've told me this evening. But I did know it's on land the federal government gave to the Indians, and if there's some sort of plot being formed that's going to involve large-scale bribery, I thought it was important enough for me to travel out of my way and try to find out what's going on."

"I'd say you did a right good job of putting two and two together and coming up with a number real close to four."

"It does make sense to you, then?" Nellie asked hopefully.

"Yep. Let me see if I can fill in the gaps for you." Longarm reached automatically for a cheroot. His hand slid over his bare chest before he remembered that he was shirtless. He reminded himself that he had intended to cut down on the cigars anyhow, and went on, "You just didn't get all of it because you don't know much about Texas or cattle ranching."

"I never said I did."

"Well, I don't know all that much, either, but I guess I've been around it more than you have. You see, Texas was settled with land scrip, ten cents an acre it was worth, and you could even claim land just by promising to work it for a few years and then to pay the scrip price. So after a while, Texas just about ran out of cheap land. And in dry country like they have up in the Panhandle, it takes twenty or thirty acres a head to graze cattle."

"I don't think I understand that, either," Nellie told him.

"What I mean is, if you've got ten steers, you've got to have two or three hundred acres to feed 'em for a year."

"I see," she nodded. "There's enough grass to feed more for a short time, but you've got to have enough acreage to graze them for a year, if you're going to succeed."

"You catch on real quick, Nellie," he said. "Now, then. Pretty nearly all the land in the Panhandle's taken up, a lot of it by outfits that ain't in Texas. They belong to stock companies in England and places like that. A Texas rancher who wants to grow has got to look around, and when he looks, he sees all this land over here in the Indian Nation. Chances are, he's got some kind of grudge against the Indians anyhow, if he came to Texas before the Comanches were whipped, which wasn't such a long time ago. So if he can get ahold of Indian land, that fellow from Texas sort of feels like he's getting back what's his by rights."

She frowned thoughtfully. "You mean he's willing to bribe government officials to let him bring in his cattle, thinking that once he's gotten hold of the land, nobody's going to be able to put him off. I suppose I can see how that would work out."

"I'd say that hunch you followed up here was a pretty good one," Longarm told her. "If something like that's in the wind, and I can track it down and stop it, it's going to save somebody digging up the mess after it's happened and been buried."

"I'm going to track it down with you," she said. "After all, it's my story."

"Now, wait a minute! I've got another job to finish first, before I can dig into what you been telling me about."

"All right," Nellie said stubbornly, "I'll follow you on your first job, too, then I'll be right on hand when you start digging into the second one. The story of you tracking down a bank robber who's also a killer ought to get big play back in the East."

"Now, that's something I don't aim to let you do, Nellie," Longarm said.

"Why not? I can take care of myself," she replied indignantly.

"I don't doubt that. The thing is, I've seen too many men

ruined by the kind of stories newspapers printed about 'em back East. It was a bunch of blown-up newspaper yarns that got Bill Hickok shot in the back, and swole Bat Masterson's and Wyatt Earp's heads so big they couldn't find hats to fit 'em. No, sir—I mean, no, ma'am, I don't want my name in your paper."

"But you owe me something for giving you this lead."

"I grant you that, Nellie," the deputy said. "I owe you, and I'll see that you get your story about whatever kind of grab those Texas fellows are cooking up. But just leave me and Eddie Boyle out of it."

"Is that the name of the man you came here to find?" she asked.

"Yep. And that's all I aim to say about him, except that I'm going to find him and bring him in, if he's still walking around."

"All right, Longarm. If you feel that strongly about it, I'll promise not to write a story about you."

Nellie got up to put away her notebook. As she passed the nightstand, she noticed Longarm's shirt, with its sleeve still soaking in the washbowl. She lifted the shirt and looked at the cuff.

"It looks like the bloodstain's gone," she said. "I'll wring it dry and mend the knife cut."

Longarm went to the stand and took the shirt from her. "Now, I told you not to bother about doing any sewing for me, Nellie. That little bit of a cut won't hurt anything."

Instead of letting him slip the shirt on, Nellie grabbed it back. "No. If you try to wear this before it's mended, it's just going to rip out more and more. I've got needles and thread in my sewing kit, and it'll only take a minute to sew the place up."

She tucked the shirt under her arm and bent down again to rummage in her portmanteau.

Just as she stooped, the windowpane shattered with a musical tinkle. Splinters of glass showered both Nellie and Longarm as a bullet thudded with a flat slap into the ceiling.

Longarm dove for the floor, and pulled Nellie down beside him. He snapped, "Don't stand up! Lay right where you are, and don't get up off the floor, or even move, till I get back!"

He was already moving for the door as he spoke, scrabbling

on hands and knees. Habit had brought his hand sweeping up to draw the Colt from his waistband before the last shards of broken glass had hit the floor. Once in the protection of the windowless hallway, Longarm stood up and raced down the narrow stairs. This time, he took three of the steps, in each leap. Less than a minute had passed before he was again standing in the dark street, straining his eyes for any sign of movement.

He'd gotten there too late. There was no movement in the darkness that he could see, but the batwings of the saloon were swinging open as the few drinkers still inside came tumbling out to see what was going on. Longarm ignored their babbling voices. Before they could ask him any questions, he'd ducked back into the hotel doorway; most of the men from the saloon didn't even see him.

"Did you find him?" Nellie asked, as he entered the still-open door of her room.

"Not a chance. He must've begun running as soon as he let off that shot."

"Maybe if you'd looked out the window—" she began.

Longarm cut her short. "That's a fool's move, Nellie. All I'd've done if I'd looked out was give him a clear target. That's how greenhorns get themselves killed." He suddenly realized that Nellie was still lying on the floor in obedience to his command. He said, "Crawl over here past the window. When you get to where the light won't throw your shadow on the shade, you can stand up."

"You're sure it'll be safe?"

"Safe enough. Whoever that jasper was, he's long gone. There's still some gawkers down in the street, anyhow. He won't come back, even after they move on."

"Who do you think it was?" Nellie's eyes were wide, but Longarm couldn't decide whether her expression was one of curiosity or fear. He shook his head. "No way of telling. I'd guess it was the same fellow that tried to drag you out of your room, though."

"You're saying somebody's trying to kill me? Why?"

"Might not be for any reason at all. Might be that the men you heard talking on the train caught on that you were listening."

"Couldn't it have been somebody trying to shoot you, though? That outlaw you're after—Eddie Boyle?"

"I guess it could've been. Him or one of his friends. The thing is, outside of those two Osage policemen, the only one I've told what I'm here for is the trader in the store downstairs."

He saw that Nellie was turning pale. He said, "You need something to steady your nerves. Just a minute. I'll be right back."

Longarm went down the hall to his room and came back carrying the bottle of rye. He uncorked it and poured some into the glass from Nellie's nightstand. "Here," he said. "Drink this."

"What is it?" she asked suspiciously,

"Nothing but a swallow of good Maryland rye. It won't hurt you a bit, and it'll steady your nerves."

Obediently, she swallowed the whiskey. She coughed and gagged, grimacing. "I'm not used to taking whiskey. All I ever drink is a glass of wine now and then."

"Right this minute, you need something stronger. You'd better sit down, now, while we try to figure this thing out."

Longarm waited until Nellie settled herself down on the side of the bed. Her hands were shaking with the realization that she'd been the target of an unknown assassin's bullet, and Longarm looked around for something he could give her to keep them busy. He spotted his shirt, picked it up, and handed it to her, then dragged her portmanteau around to where she could reach it.

"Here. You might as well be doing that sewing you'd started on, while we talk."

Nellie responded automatically. She found her sewing kit in the bag and took out needle and thread. When she tried to thread the needle, her hands were shaking so badly that she failed on her first attempts. She persisted, and after several tries, managed to get the thread through the needle's eye. Longarm had seen this trick work before, of forcing a person unused to violence to concentrate on a familiar task in order to settle his nerves. After Nellie had taken the first few stitches in his shirtsleeve, her hands grew steadier and her face became calm once more.

Sitting down in the chair facing her, Longarm said, "Now, then. The two men on the train—did you notice where they got off?"

"One of them, Bob, got off at San Antonio. That's where I had to change my ticket to come up here instead of going on to New Orleans. The other man, Mr. Scott, was on the train all the way up to Amarillo. He got off there, and I didn't see him again."

"How'd you get to the Nation, then?"

"Oh, I found out from the conductor that I could take a stage from Amarillo to a little place called Mobeetie. That's right near Fort Elliott, and there's a stage that runs from Fort Elliott to Fort Supply and then down here to Darlington and Fort Reno. I think it goes on back to Fort Elliott from here. It was an expensive trip, too, a lot more than my train fare from Laredo to San Antonio. Why, it cost me thirty-five dollars just to travel from Fort Elliott to Darlington."

"Never mind all that, Nellie. Did this Mr. Scott show up at the stagecoach station?"

"No. I told you, I didn't see him after we both got off the train in Amarillo."

"Who else rode on the stage with you?"

"A preacher and his wife. They got off at Fort Supply to go on east to one of the reservations."

"Nobody else?"

"Two soldiers. One got off at Fort Supply, and the other one came on to Fort Reno, I guess. He stayed on when I got off here. And there were the driver and his helper, of course."

"How about the stage you took from Amarillo to Mobeetie?" Longarm knew Mobeetie's reputation as the toughest town in Texas, north of Fort Worth. A lot of the wanted circulars that came to the office in Denver contained the phrase, "believed to be in or near Mobeetie."

"There was the minister, his wife, and three men."

"What'd the men look like?"

"Why, just like cowboys, I guess. They had bottles and kept on drinking until they went to sleep."

"Nobody along the way paid any special attention to you?"

"Well, the cowboys tried to make up to me, until the preacher told them to behave. Then they just drank."

"Damn it!" Longarm caught himself. "Excuse me, Nellie. Think hard, now. Did you tell anybody along the way that you work for that newspaper back East?"

"Only the conductor on the train I took from Laredo. I mentioned it to him when I was asking about getting my ticket changed."

"He's the one that set you at the table in the diner with this Mr. Scott?"

"Yes. I told you how that happened." Nellie's violet eyes grew wide again. "You think it was him who sent somebody to follow me? To kill me just because I heard him talking to his friend on the train?"

"Well, Nellie, when you see a critter that waddles like a skunk, and has got black and white fur like a skunk, and stinks like a skunk, it's a pretty safe bet you're looking at a skunk. Yep, I—"

A peremptory knock sounded at the door, and almost immediately, it flew open. Mrs. Murray stood in the hall, her lips compressed angrily.

"You! You, Mr. Long, and you, Miss Cochrane! I told you both, I run a respectable hotel! I warned you, I won't stand for any loose conduct in my place!"

"Now, Miz Murray—" Longarm began.

"Don't 'Miz Murray' me!" she snapped. "Look at you! Sitting there in this woman's room, half naked, late at night! A whiskey bottle on the dresser! The two of you alone with the door closed! Now, I want both of you out of my place this minute!"

"Hold on, Miz Murray!" Longarm said angrily. "Don't go getting wrong ideas. There's just one reason I'm in here, and that's because this 'respectable hotel' of yours has turned out to be downright dangerous for decent folks. What do you say to that?"

"What—why, I don't know what you're talking about!" the landlady stuttered.

"What I'm talking about is that this young lady was set on by some drunk who must've wandered in off the street. When I tried to help her, he came at me with a knife." Longarm held up his bandaged arm. "Miss Cochrane fixed up the place where he cut me. Then, just a minute ago, somebody fired a bullet through that window, there. I tell you something, Miz Murray, if there was another place to stay in this town, we wouldn't be here now!"

Mrs. Murray's jaw dropped. She looked questioningly at Nellie, and made a woman-to-woman appeal. "Is that right, Miss Cochrane? Did all them things happen the way Mr. Long said?"

"He told you the exact truth," Nellie replied coldly. "And I'd like to know where you were when all this was going on."

"I had to go out to the agency farm and get garden truck for the dining room for tomorrow. I was just taking a final look around, and happened to hear you two talking."

"And jumped to the worst possible conclusion." Nellie's voice was tremulous with indignation.

"I—I guess I spoke too quick," Mrs. Murray admitted. Before either Longarm or Nellie could comment, she asked, "How about my broken window? Glass is expensive. Who's going to pay for it?"

"I'll tell you what, Miz Murray," Longarm suggested. "Let's the three of us make a deal, right here and now. Miss Cochrane's finished sewing up my shirt that got ripped by that fellow with the knife. The shot didn't hit either of us. So, suppose I just take my bottle of whiskey that I brought from my room to settle Miss Cochrane's nerves after the shooting, and take my shirt, and go back to my own room? We won't blame you for badmouthing us, and you don't blame us for the busted window. Does that sound fair? Don't forget, you've got to think about your hotel's reputation."

"Well." Mrs. Murray's expression showed that she comprehended the idea behind Longarm's words. "Well, I guess maybe that *is* the best way to settle it. Get your shirt and your bottle, Mr. Long, and let Miss Cochrane go to bed. But I'm going to be sitting out by the desk until I'm sure everything's settled down for the night."

Longarm and Nellie suppressed their smiles as they exchanged glances. He took his shirt and bottle and started down the hall. He could feel Mrs. Murray's eyes on his back until he closed the door to his own room.

Chapter 5

Habit snapped Longarm awake at six o'clock. He sat up, the creaking springs of the strange bed reminding him that he wasn't in his own room. The warm air, so different from the September chill of mile-high Denver, prompted him to throw back the light blanket he'd automatically pulled up around his chest the night before. He looked at his bandaged wrist and twisted it then felt it experimentally. Except for a slight soreness when he pressed directly on the cut, it seemed in good shape.

Across the room, the bottle of Maryland rye gleamed invitingly in the soft light that filtered through the tattered windowshade. Rolling out of bed, Longarm stretched hugely. He walked over to the window and reached for the shade, but thought better of raising it when he recalled the shot that had shattered Nellie Bly's window the night before.

Stepping to the dresser, he gripped the cork of the whiskey bottle in his strong white teeth to pull it, then let the cork drop into his free hand and tilted the bottle to his lips. The bite of the rye freshened his mouth and drove the night's stuffiness out of his nose. He snorted, put the bottle down, poured water from the pitcher into the basin, and splashed his face. His fingers encountered the stubble on his jaw, and he thought idly of shaving. Then he decided that he wouldn't be the only man in the Indian Nation with a day's growth of beard, and let the notion drop. There'd be time to shave later, after he'd made up his mind which way he'd be having to move after breakfast. If he decided to push along right away on Eddie Boyle's trail, shaving would be a useless gesture. It would only expose raw skin to the alkali dust carried by the Nation's gusting winds.

Longarm made short work of dressing. His flannel shirt, skintight britches, wool socks, and low-heeled stovepipe cavalry boots went on quickly. He broke his routine of dressing only once, for a second wake-up swallow of rye. As he lowered the bottle from his lips, the mend in his shirtsleeve caught his attention and he stopped to look at it closely. Nellie's stitches reminded him of the girl herself; they were neat, evenly spaced, workmanlike. He wondered how she'd slept, after an evening that must have been wilder than any she'd experienced before in her short life. Until now, she'd been a spectator, reporting the news. This time she'd been part of the event.

Although he'd fired neither his Colt nor the doubled-barreled derringer that dangled on the opposite end of his watch chain from his Ingersoll pocket watch, Longarm spent an extra minute checking the tools of his trade. Then he put a bit more time than usual into getting the set of his holster precisely correct, high on his left hip, with the short-barreled .44-40 Colt carried butt-forward under his black Prince Albert coat.

Satisfied that he'd done all a man could do to meet the unknown challenges of the day, Longarm closed the door of his room, locked it, and inserted his alarm signal, the broken stub of a matchstick, between the door's edge and the jamb. Then he strode confidently down the hall to the stairs and descended to the dining room.

He'd half expected Nellie Bly to be at one of the tables, but she wasn't. Mostly, the faces were the same ones Longarm remembered seeing at supper, although the pair of Osage Indian policemen were also missing. He selected a vacant chair near the end of one of the long tables, where he wouldn't have to make conversation with anybody. It was time, he'd decided, to do some serious thinking.

Food came before thought in Longarm's morning timetable, but even before he'd reached for the egg platter, the flimsy, cloth-screened door of the dining room swung open to admit a pair of newcomers—a man and a woman. The couple stood inside the entrance for a moment, which gave Longarm the opportunity to inspect them while they looked over the dining room.

They were as unlikely a pair as he'd ever seen. The man was too tall for the breadth of his chest and shoulders. He stood on thin giraffe's legs that rose from a pair of narrow, ornately stitched boots with feet longer than any Longarm could remember ever having seen before. His arms were disproportionately long, too. They ended in oversized hands that dangled midway between his knees and his hips. His face was mournful, naturally hangdog. It was a narrow rectangle that started out at a square, dimpled chin and ended a foot higher in an elongated forehead that gave him the appearance of being prematurely balding in spite of a generous bush of ginger-colored hair. He was clean-shaven; his lips were invisible, or nearly so, a thin line of pink in a sallow face marked by high, craggy cheekbones and a jutting triangle of a nose.

His clothing was standard for the time and place: a well-rubbed vest of suede leather over a shirt with small black and white checks; the customary Levi's denims of the prairie; and a black bandanna folded into a triangle for a neck scarf. The hat in his hand was as narrow and tall-crowned as the man; it had a rattlesnake-skin band. His gunbelt was a bit too wide and carried cartridge loops as well as a polished black leather holster. Longarm studied the holstered pistol without letting his interest show too obviously. The weapon had staghorn handles chased in silver, and, judging from the length of its barrel and the contour of its butt, it was a single-action Colt .41, the "long Colt" favored by some gunslingers because its extra-length shell gave the slug tremendous stopping power, although the weapon wasn't noted for long-range accuracy.

Old son, Longarm told himself, *that pistol's all you need to see. You're looking at a shooter standing there.*

Now he turned his attention to the woman. *Flashy* was the first word that came to his mind. She looked just a little bit too polished, though she was not a caricature of a woman as her companion was of a man. She wore her hair high, fluffed around her head and gathered on top into a low coil, held by a circle of heavy tortoiseshell hairpins studded with small brilliants; her hair itself was an impossible shade of pinkish orange. Eyebrows of the same hue were almost invisible from across the room against the tanned skin of her forehead; her complexion deepened to a rosy hue on her high cheekbones. Her eyes were a brilliant green that flashed between heavy lids with unusually thick, dark lashes. Her nose was prominent but not overpowering, and her lips were a bit overfull, moistly and brilliantly scarlet. Her chin was wide and firm.

Standing beside her overly tall companion, the woman looked shorter than she was, an illusion helped by her calf-length riding skirt. A blue linen blouse and denim jacket, both cinched in at her small waist, accentuated her full and jutting breasts. Her wide hips added to the illusion that she was a short woman, but her hands were large and she used them vigorously as she and the man held a whispered conversation that fell just short of being an argument.

That lady, Longarm told himself, *knows who kept the tally and how much it came to, and where whoever tallied made a mistake.*

Suddenly it dawned on Longarm that he was the subject of the newcomers' discussion. Their eyes turned his way again and again as they talked. Finally, the man shrugged and followed the woman when she came directly to the table where Longarm sat.

"Excuse me," she said. "Aren't you Marshal Custis Long?"

Longarm rose as he answered, "Yes, ma'am, I am. But I don't recall that we've ever met. I'm right sure I'd remember you if we had."

"No, we haven't met before, Marshal. I'm Zelda Morgan. This gentleman here is Brad Steele. It was Brad who recognized you, just in case you're wondering."

"I heard too much about the man everybody calls Longarm to be wrong in spotting you," Steele said. His voice was light, almost as high-pitched as that of a young boy. "You mind if we set by you and eat our breakfast?"

"There's plenty of room," Longarm replied. Since he hadn't invited them to join him, he didn't think it was necessary to make them welcome with a show of false cordiality. He'd planned on having a solitary meal, during which he could do some thinking.

Steele sat down on one side of Longarm, Zelda Morgan on the other. Neither of them made any effort at conversation while platters of ham and bacon, hard-fried eggs, biscuits, and corn pone were passed back and forth, and coffee was poured from the heavy ironstone pitcher that stood in the center of each table.

Longarm marveled at the voracity with which Steele ate. For a man so thin, he had a brawny appetite. He put away four

eggs, two slices of ham, several rashers of bacon, and a stack of
biscuits, while Longarm was eating his usual two eggs with a
single slice of ham and a pair of buttered biscuits. Zelda Morgan
picked at her food, eating only the egg yolk, a rasher of bacon,
and half a biscuit. Longarm was aware of the eyes of one or the
other of the couple fixed on him at intervals during the meal.

Finally, Steele pushed his plate away and said, "Guess you're
wondering why we butted in on your breakfast, Marshal."

"Not especially," the tall lawman replied. "I figured if you
got a reason, you'll get around to telling me, sooner or later."

Zelda said, "We've got a very good reason for wanting to
talk to you. Show him the flyer, Brad."

Steele fished a folded paper out of his vest pocket and
passed it over to Longarm. Opened out, the paper proclaimed
in large, heavy type that a reward of ten thousand dollars in
gold was being offered by the Rocky Mountain Investment
Corporation, owner of the Miner's Bank at Cripple Creek, for
the delivery of one Eddie Boyle, alive, or for proof that the
claimant was responsible for Boyle's death while trying to
avoid capture. Longarm had seen several dozen similar circulars advertising other wanted men. He wondered why it had
taken the Warde brothers so long to get theirs into circulation.

He shoved the circular back to Steele. "You're working for
the Wardes, then, I take it?"

"Not on your life!" Steele replied a bit too quickly and emphatically. "Zelda and I are operatives from the International
Investigations Agency, in St. Louis. We just didn't happen to
have a case in hand right now, so our boss turned us loose to
see if we could pick up a little reward money."

Privately, Longarm thought that if somebody were to look
behind enough doors at the International Investigations Agency,
they'd find a connection between it and the Rocky Mountain
Investment Corporation, but he didn't pass his suspicions on to
Steele and Zelda.

He said, "How'd you happen to wind up down here in the
Indian Nation?"

"Why, we did what any trained investigating team would,"
Zelda replied. "We talked to the sheriff in Teller County and
found out where Boyle was headed the last time anybody
saw him."

"And Cady told you I'd most likely be here, I guess?"

"He did mention your name," she confessed.

Longarm nodded. "Well, it's a free country, and this part of it's quite a bit freer than some others. You're welcome to hunt for Boyle, just like I am."

"That ain't exactly what we had in mind, Longarm," Steele said. "Three heads are better than two. We thought you might like to join forces with us. It'd make the job a lot easier, if we worked together."

Longarm didn't respond to Steele's suggestion, not wanting to accept it or to reject it summarily, without some thought. Before he could work out a suitably diplomatic reply, Nellie Bly came into the dining room. She glanced around, saw Longarm, and made a beeline for the table where he was sitting.

Longarm foresaw problems looming. The last thing he wanted was for Nellie to start talking about the land-grab plot she'd discovered, to tip off Steele and the Morgan woman that there was a potential for blackmail money in the offing. From bitter experience, he knew the breed they represented: unscrupulous opportunists eager to cash in on any chance of picking up quick cash without working for it. His memory flashed involuntarily to the Crooked Lance-Cotton Younger affair, in which his association with another such bizarre man-woman pair of detectives had nearly cost him his life. He was reluctant to initiate another such relationship. He jumped from his chair without excusing himself to his table companions and intercepted Nellie before she'd selected a seat across from him.

"You didn't have to escort me to the table," she protested when Longarm took her elbow. "I can select my own seat, and pull my own chair up after I'm in it."

"That's not the reason I came over, Nellie. Those two people I'm sitting with call themselves private detectives, they're after the same man I am, only their idea's to collect the reward that the bank he robbed is offering now. I've got to talk to them private-like."

"Well, I certainly wouldn't interrupt any conversation you might be having with them."

"I know that. But if it's all the same to you, I'll ask you to sit someplace else until after I get through talking to 'em."

"If you're afraid I'll overhear something that'll embarrass you, I certainly wouldn't want to join you," she said. Her smile faded and her voice was hung with icicles. "Now, if you'll just let go of my arm, I'll find a place to sit down and have my own quiet breakfast, by myself."

Pulling her arm from his hand, Nellie flounced away and seated herself at a table as far removed from the one occupied by Longarm as she could manage. He stood gazing helplessly after her for a moment, then returned unhappily to Steele and Zelda.

"Having trouble with a lady friend?" Zelda asked. Her voice had an edge of malice. "I must say, she's a bit young for you, or seems to be."

"She's just a little girl from the East I happened to run into by accident," Longarm explained.

Steele was staring at Nellie. "Well, Longarm, if there's nothing between you, maybe I'll try my hand with her. She's a right pretty young thing after you look at her twice."

"I'd advise you to stay away from her, Steele." Longarm's voice was cold. "I sort of feel responsible for seeing she gets home without anything happening to her."

"Brad won't try to cut in on you, Longarm," Zelda said with assurance. "Will you, Brad?"

"Oh, no, no. I was just making a joke."

"Suppose we get down to business again," Zelda suggested. "You never did say what you thought about our idea of working together." She leaned forward, her full breasts pressing as though by accident against Longarm's biceps. "It could be profitable for all of us."

"Now, Miz Morgan, you know the rules I've got to work by. I can't tie up with anybody when I'm on a case."

"Rules, pooh! Who cares about them? They're only made to be disregarded."

"We sure as hell wouldn't snitch on you," Steele put in. "If it got out that we'd tied up with another investigator, our boss might fire us. No need to worry about anything leaking out."

"I'd have to think about it real careful," Longarm said. "Maybe we can talk some more later on, and see how it looks after I chase the idea around a spell. Are you folks putting up at the hotel upstairs?"

"We ain't decided to stay here yet," Steele replied. "We just rode up in time to come in and set down to breakfast."

"We had the same thought that must've occurred to you, Longarm," Zelda said. "The sheriff in Teller County told us where he lost Boyle's track, so we came this far into the Nation with the idea of doubling back and possibly cutting him off, or at least running across his trail. If he's passed this way, we'll find out."

Slowly, Longarm nodded. Her explanation rang true. She and Steele had done what most trained investigators would: get ahead of a fugitive and try to intercept him after figuring out what trail he'd be most apt to take. His respect for this unlikely team rose a notch. As Zelda had just pointed out, they were using the same tactics he'd decided on himself.

Longarm made a quick decision. There'd be no harm in telling the newcomers that Boyle hadn't gotten to Darlington; they could find that out in a short time themselves. The rest of what he'd learned, even though it was next to nothing, he'd keep to himself.

He said, "I'll give you this much. Boyle's never shown up here. He's either stopped someplace, or slanted off east or west. Fact is, I don't plan to hang around here very long. As soon as I decide which way looks most likely, I'll be heading out, trying to pick up his trail up north. I reckon Teller's already told you that he lost the trail at Fort Supply."

"Does that mean you're heading north right away?" she asked.

"Maybe today, maybe tomorrow. No use barking up an empty tree after the coon's gone." He shoved himself away from the table. "But we'll talk before I go."

Zelda looked at her companion. "Brad, suppose you stay and finish up your breakfast. Here." She set the egg platter and then the meat platter in front of him. "While you finish eating, I'll walk along with Longarm." Brad opened his mouth to protest, but Zelda cut him off. "I said finish your breakfast, Brad!"

"Oh," Steele said. "Sure. I'm really hungry this morning."

Zelda faced Longarm. "You wouldn't object to a little walk, to settle our meal, would you?"

Longarm decided to satisfy his curiosity. "Not a bit. It'll be a real treat to walk with a pretty lady like you."

Longarm avoided Nellie's eyes as he followed Zelda out of the dining room, but he was sure he could feel her angry glare burning the back of his neck.

Outside, Zelda stopped and looked at the sun-baked street. "I suppose it doesn't make much difference which way we go."

"Not a bit. There's nobody likely to hear anything we talk about, whichever way we go."

As she tucked her arm into his and led him away from the buildings, she said, "I can understand why you didn't want to say much in front of Brad. If we decided to double-cross you, there'd be two of us who'd be witnesses. Or that little dolly-girl you acted so concerned about might take a notion to join us, or somebody else could butt in and overhear. This way, it's just your word against mine, and I agree with you, it's a lot safer."

"You act like you're getting set to talk business. If you are, oughtn't your partner to be along?"

"Not necessarily. Brad will go along with whatever you and I agree on."

"I told you inside, Miz Morgan—" Longarm began.

"Please, Longarm, call me Zelda. Or Zee. We're in the same trade. Let's don't be formal with one another."

"If that's what you want, sure. Now, what I was about to say was, I can't be right sure it'd be safe to strike up a deal with you and your friend."

"From everything I've heard about you, Longarm, you're not a stupid man. Don't try to act like you are. I know exactly how much you're paid as a federal marshal. You've got to have side deals, like the one we're talking about, if you're to make any money at all."

Being tagged as a venal lawman galled Longarm, but he did his best not to let his feelings show. For all he knew, Brad and Zelda might have more up-to-date information than had been given him before he'd left Denver. If they had, it was his job to dig it out of them.

He said, "You know the law about us marshals not taking reward money. Now, that's not just rules like we were talking about a while ago. That's a law that a man can be put in jail for breaking."

"Don't try to convince me you're afraid to take a chance, if the pay's good enough."

"It'd have to be almighty good, to tempt me. How good is what you've got in mind, Zee?"

"We split the reward three ways. Brad and I will pay the agency percentage out of our share."

"Doesn't seem like that'd be fair to you two. Are you sure Steele will go along on a deal like that?"

"We've already talked it over. He'll go along, all right."

"You must be pretty certain of me, then, if you've already talked about how to split the take."

"We're sure of one thing, Longarm—that you're a smart man. Look at it my way—that is, Brad's and mine," Zelda urged. "You've probably got a better chance to run Boyle down than we have. We're betting you've got more information right now, and we're sure you can get help from places we can't, just by showing your federal badge."

"Well—" Longarm sounded thoughtful. "I guess you could say that without me giving you much of an argument."

"But if you do take Boyle first," she pressed on, "what the hell do you get out of it? A pat on the back from your chief, and another star on your record in Washington. And you can't spend either one."

Longarm cast a sidelong glance at her as he adjusted the brim of his Stetson. "I've got to agree with you there."

"Think about what you can do with over three thousand dollars! Why, you can take that pretty little dolly you made so unhappy back there, and show her New York, or even Paris and Rome."

Longarm sighed. "You've still got the wrong idea about that young lady, Zee. All she is is a little girl I feel sort of responsible for."

"You'd better be sure she knows that's how you feel."

"Do you want to explain what you're getting at in plain words I can understand?"

"I mean, she's fallen for you. She might not know it yet, but I know women. No matter what their age is, I can tell."

"That's just something you're imagining. Anyhow, it's got nothing to do with our business."

"We are going to do business together, then?"

"Well, you put up some pretty convincing arguments. I'm still not ready to say yes, but I sure don't mean to say no, until I do some more studying about it."

The woman grasped his elbow, and turned him around so she was looking him in the eye. "Will you answer a straight question, Longarm?"

"I never was much of a hand at lying. What's your question?"

"Do you know where Eddie Boyle is right now? Or where he's most likely to be heading for, here in the Nation?"

"No. Right this minute, I don't know any more about him than you do. And I'm in just about the same boat as you and your partner. I haven't been here long enough to find anything out."

"We're on even terms, then?" she asked.

"Sure looks that way," Longarm agreed.

"That being the case, what have we got to lose by working together? The money's good, if we find him."

"You're pretty good at persuading, Zee."

"I can be even better, but don't let that give you any ideas. Brad's inclined to be a little bit jealous. Of course, I can handle him without any trouble. Do I make myself clear?"

"I've followed you without any trouble, so far. That doesn't change my answer, though. Give me a little time to study it over."

"How much time?" she asked. A hint of sharpness crept into her voice, which until now had been seductively promising.

"I'm not planning to go anywhere, not today, anyhow. I don't guess you and Steele are, either. Let me sleep on your scheme. Now, we'd better be turning around and walking back to the hotel, or your partner's apt to come looking for us. And I don't want any trouble between him and me. At least, not yet."

Chapter 6

Brad Steele was waiting outside the dining room when Zelda and Longarm returned.

"Well?" he asked. "Have we got a deal?"

Longarm didn't reply directly, but said, "Zelda'll tell you how things stack up. Right now I've got some chores to take care of. We'll talk about a deal later on."

"How much later? Me and Zelda want to get after this Boyle before somebody else nabs him and collects that reward money. If you ain't going to throw in with us—"

"I don't say I will and I don't say I won't," Longarm snapped impatiently. "You and her talk over what you want to do. If you feel like you're better off on your own, go ahead."

Zelda put her hand on Steele's arm. "Don't get impatient, Brad. Longarm's explained to me why he needs time to think about our offer. It won't hurt anything for us to wait a day."

"Well—" Steele gave in reluctantly. "If you say so, Zee."

"We'll talk after supper," Zelda said to Longarm, "if that suits you?"

"It's as good a time as any. Now, I'd better be moving."

Nellie was not in the dining room. Longarm went up the narrow hotel stairs and tapped at her door.

"Yes? Who is it?"

"Me. You feel like talking to me, now?"

She opened the door. Her eyes were snapping. "I don't know whether I do or not. You certainly didn't waste any attention on me at breakfast."

"I had good reasons. I was hoping you'd understand when I told you who they were and what they're after."

"But why didn't you want me to sit with you? I promised

you I wouldn't write anything for my paper about the case you're on. Don't you trust me?"

"Sure I do." Longarm looked at the doors that lined the hall. "Come on, Nellie. Let's go walk around a few minutes. I don't want anybody to interrupt us, or hear what we're talking about."

Nellie hesitated for a moment, then, joining Longarm in the hall, she shut her door and locked it. They walked downstairs and along the street. Brad Steele and Zelda Morgan were nowhere in sight. Longarm waited until they had reached the open area between the store buildings and the Darlington Agency before he said anything.

"Nellie," he began, "you know how big this land-grab scheme is that you've turned up. It's a lot more important than me catching up with a small-time crook."

"I wouldn't exactly call a murderer who stole thirty thousand dollars a small-time crook," she said dryly.

"Well, maybe not. But the other thing's a lot more important. And I didn't want those people sitting with me in the dining room to get wind of it through something you might let slip, not meaning to."

"You don't give me much credit, do you, Marshal? You think I'm just a little half-grown-up girl playing at being a newspaper reporter. Well, let me tell you something. I'm good enough to hold my job on one of the best newspapers in the country, and I'm going to be something big in the newspaper field one day. I've made up my mind to that."

"Oh, I give you credit for knowing what you're about. And I can see how smart you are. But the point is, I can't do anything about your land-grabbers until I catch Boyle, and those two are bounty hunters who're out to get to him before I do."

"You mean they're after the reward?" Nellie asked.

"Maybe more than just the reward."

Nellie frowned. "You'll have to explain that to me."

"That's what I want to do," he said patiently. "That's why we're walking out here by ourselves. The way of it is, I've got a real big hunch that they're on the Warde brothers' payroll."

"Who are the Warde brothers?"

"Bankers, stock dealers, money men. They're involved in a lot of different kinds of business, but mostly banking. And when one of their banks gets robbed, they don't want the robbers caught as much as they want 'em killed."

"You mean murdered? But that's a worse crime than robbing a bank!" she exclaimed indignantly.

"Sure it is. But a dead bank robber's a mighty persuasive lesson to somebody else who might be thinking about holding one up."

"How do they get away with ordering people killed? I know a little bit about the gangs in Pittsburgh, but you're talking about men who ought to be upholding the law."

Longarm nodded. "Now, that's the way I feel, myself."

"And you really think that man and woman will kill this Boyle, if they find him before you do?"

"I'm dead sure of it, even if I can't prove it. There's more to it than that, though."

"I don't see how there could be. What you've just told me is bad enough."

"Don't forget, Nellie, wherever Boyle is, he's got thirty thousand bucks worth of bank money, take away what few thousand he's spent getting down here to the Nation. If Steele and the Morgan woman get him first, there'll be damn little—excuse me—there won't be much of that loot left to go back to the bank."

"Why, that's terrible!" she said, shocked. "I thought criminals in the East were bad, but your Western criminals are worse!"

"Outlaws're outlaws wherever you run onto 'em, Nellie," he observed sagaciously, "But I've got to agree, there're some pretty sorry specimens out here, and a lot of 'em are in the Nation. That's why I've been fretting about you."

"Fretting? About me? Why, for Heaven's sake?"

"Because I've got to go after Eddie Boyle in a hurry, and that means I've got to leave you here, or put you on a stage or train for home."

"Now, wait just a damned minute, Mr. Marshal Custis Long! I'm on the trail of a story, and I'm not going to drop it!"

"You know Eddie Boyle's got nothing to do with your real story, Nellie. You already said that."

"It doesn't make any difference. If I let you go off without me, how are we going to get together again when it's time for you to help me uncover the land swindle scheme?"

"You asked me a minute ago did I trust you, and I said I did. Don't you trust me to come get you after I've got Boyle?"

"It's not the same thing!" Nellie protested.

Longarm held back the retort that came to his mind. Instead, he gave Nellie a minute to calm down, then asked her in a casual tone, "How good are you at riding horseback, Nellie?"

"Why—I've never been on a horse in my life. Why should I? I've always lived in a town or a city."

"If you don't ride horseback, how do you aim to go with me after Boyle? Because that's the only way I can travel. A buggy or a wagon's too slow. Besides, there're lots of places only a horse can get to."

"Now, that's not fair, and you know it!"

"You'll see it's the way things are, after you get through stewing," Longarm said soberly. "The plain fact is, I've got to travel fast. You can't. And it ain't because you're a woman or a newspaper reporter either one, so don't say I'm just using it as an excuse to get out of taking you with me."

They walked along in silence for a few steps. Finally, Nellie said, "You're right, I suppose. But what am I going to do while you're gone?"

"I've been thinking about that, too, and I've figured out something. I sure don't aim to leave you by yourself, without somebody to keep you safe in case that fellow who tried to get you last night's still lurking around."

"But there isn't anywhere to stay, except the hotel."

"Yes, there is," Longarm said.

"Where?"

"At the agency headquarters—if you don't mind being around preachers and Indians, that is."

"I've been around a lot worse than that, covering some of the stories I've done for the *Dispatch*. Neither the preachers nor the Indians will bother me a bit." She brightened and added, "In fact, I might be able to get some good background material by being around them."

"I'll bet you can. Is it settled then?"

"I suppose so. Yes, it's settled."

"Good enough. Let's get on back to the store and stop there for a minute, then I'll figure out a way to get you and your suitcase out to the agent's house."

"Why do we have to go to the store?"

"I'm going to buy you a present."

"What kind of present?"

"Never mind for now," he said mysteriously. "You'll find out soon enough."

For all Longarm knew, Asa Baker hadn't moved a muscle since the night before. The trader was still sitting at his desk, going over ledger sheets. He took his time in looking up when Longarm and Nellie came in. Finally, he put the sheets down and said, "'Morning, Miss Cochrane—Marshal Long."

Nellie replied to Longarm's surprised look, "Mr. Baker directed me to Mrs. Murray's hotel when I first got here."

"I hope you don't hold that against me, after the trouble I heard you had last night," Baker said. His expression and tone of voice didn't change.

"I figure it was some kind of mistake," Longarm said.

"Could've been, at that," Baker agreed. "Well, how can I help you folks this morning?"

"If you heard about last night, you ought to be able to figure out what we came in to buy," Longarm told him.

Baker nodded. "My stock of guns isn't very big, but I guess I can show you something that'll suit you." He led them to a locked cabinet in the back of the store, fumbled through the keys on a big ring that he hauled from his pocket, and unlocked the heavy doors. "Government regulation," he explained. "Can't keep weapons in the open where the Indians might see 'em and be tempted."

He swung the doors open and Longarm glanced at the firearms inside. There was a motley assortment of old and new rifles leaning higgledy-piggledy against the cabinet walls, and a scattering of pistols on the bottom. Longarm inspected the pistols. Most of them were large-caliber revolvers of recent manufacture, though there were a few percussion pistols that dated back to prewar days. He was about to turn away when he saw the butt of a derringer sticking out from behind a rifle stock in one corner. He took out the squat little pistol and examined it carefully.

"It's not new, but it's in good condition. And made by Henry Deringer himself, you'll notice," Baker said.

"So I see. I take it you've got .41 loads for it?"

"A few boxes, your choice of Remington or Winchester," Baker assured him.

"How much?"

"Well, for a genuine derringer like that one, I'll have to get six dollars."

Longarm shook his head. "It's not worth more'n four. Got some rust specks on the barrel. It ain't been looked after too carefully, I'd say."

"Take it for five, then," Baker compromised.

"We've got a deal, if you'll throw in a box of cartridges."

"I guess I can go that far." Baker hauled a tattered ledger book out of the drawer that held ammunition, laid it aside, and rummaged until he found a box of cartridges. He picked up the book and said, "I guess this is going to be Miss Cochrane's purse-pistol?"

Nellie looked questioningly at Longarm, who nodded. Baker went on, "Fine. I'll need your full name, Miss Cochrane, and proof that you're not an Indian and that you're over twenty-one years old."

"Why?" she asked.

"More government red tape. I can't sell guns to Indians, you see, so I've got to keep a register of anybody who buys one from me. A lot of foolishness, if you ask me. If an Indian wants a gun, he'll go out and steal one somewhere."

Nellie pulled at Longarm's sleeve. He leaned down and she whispered, "I can't show him my passport, Marshal."

"Why not?"

"Because it gives my age. I'm not over twenty-one."

"You—" When he'd recovered from his surprise, Longarm asked her in a whisper, "How old are you, Nellie?"

"Twenty. I won't be twenty-one for four more months."

"There's a way to get around that." He said to Baker, "I'll sign your book, seeing as I'm the one paying for the gun. What I do with it after I buy it ain't no business of the government or anybody else."

Baker neither agreed nor argued, but handed the registry book to Longarm, who signed it and returned it.

"You won't need it wrapped, I guess?" the trader asked. "It's sinful how expensive wrapping paper and sacks have gotten to be."

"I'll just slide it in my pocket," Longarm told him, and did so. Outside again, he asked Nellie, "Did you ever shoot a gun?"

"A shotgun, a few times. I'm an only child, you see, and my father started out to bring me up as a boy, until Mother stopped him."

"That would've been a plumb waste, I'd say. Well, now we've got to get you out to the agency. I guess you'll have to ride double with me, if you don't object."

"You seem to have taken charge of what I'm going to do. Would it do me any good if I did object?"

"Oh, we can always walk. It ain't more'n a mile or so."

"It's too hot to walk. I'll ride double."

With Nellie's portmanteau dangling by its handle from the McClellan's saddle strings, and with Nellie herself sitting sideways in the saddle and Longarm on the gelding's rump, stretching one arm around Nellie to hold the reins, holding her in place with his other arm around her waist, they rode out to the agency. Although the sun was not directly in their faces, its brilliance in the unclouded sky made them squint.

Longarm said, to make conversation and keep out of his mind the feeling of Nellie's soft waist and the natural, unperfumed aroma of her lithe young body, "If you're going to stay around here, you'd better find yourself a hat with a brim that'll keep the sun out of your eyes. You don't want that pretty face of yours all wrinkled up with squint marks."

"Do you really think my face is pretty?" Her question wasn't coquettish; she sounded genuinely curious.

"Sure it is. You're a real nice-looking girl."

She turned her head to look back at him, and smiled. "Thank you. A lot of people don't think so, I'm afraid. Especially when I'm trying to worm information out of them, or get them to talk about something they're not proud of. I'll bet you didn't think I was pretty a while ago, when I was trying to find out why you didn't want to take me with you."

"Wasn't that I didn't want to," Longarm corrected. "Couldn't."

"All right, then. Couldn't. But I do hope you'll be back real soon. I'm anxious to get started on my story."

"Best I can say is look for me when you see me. But you can figure I won't be wasting any time."

They were at the agency office now, and Longarm reined

in. He swung down and helped Nellie off the gelding. She followed him inside. A stocky, gray-haired man looked up and greeted them.

"Howdy," Longarm replied. "I need to talk to the agent, I guess, or whatever they call the man who's in charge of things."

"You're talking to him. My name's Seth Edmonds. I'm the agent."

"Custis Long, Mr. Edmonds. Deputy U.S. marshal out of Denver." He extended his hand, and the agent shook it. "This young lady's name is Miss Elizabeth Cochrane; she's a reporter for a newspaper back East, looking for some stories about the Indian Nation."

Edmonds smiled. "I'd say you've come to the right place. You couldn't get much closer to the middle of it. And if you've come to me to ask for help, I'll be glad to do anything I can."

"I'm right glad to hear that," Longarm said. "It's like this, Mr. Edmonds. I've been sort of keeping an eye on Nellie, because there're some pretty rough characters around. Now, I've got to ride up north for a few days on official business, and I just don't feel right about leaving her to stay at the hotel by herself. You think you might put her up for a few days?"

"I'm sure Mrs. Murray'd do her best to look after you, Miss," Edmonds told Nellie. "But I can see how the marshal feels, with the store and saloon and hotel all together, there. I'll be glad to put you up, though. We have a few rooms that we use for guests."

"I'll pay for my room and board," Nellie offered.

"Since I'm sure your paper's paying your expenses, I won't refuse. How long do you plan to be here?"

"Just until the marshal gets back—a week or less."

Edmonds said, "It won't be what you're used to back East, but it'll be clean. And if you're looking for stories about the Indians, you'll certainly find them here."

"You're all taken care of, then," Longarm told Nellie. "Now, I'll get back to town and get ready to travel. And, Mr. Edmonds, I do thank you for helping out."

Although Longarm considered himself a truthful man, he had no compunction about bending truth to serve his needs when he was dealing with those outside the law. He neither avoided Brad Steele and Zelda Morgan nor looked for them.

When he was ready to ride out, with his saddlebags packed, and his Winchester in its saddle scabbard, and he still hadn't run into the bounty-hunting couple, he left a brief note for them with Mrs. Murray, telling them he'd been called away on urgent business and adding that if they waited for him at Darlington, he'd talk with them on his return. Then, with the noon-day sun beating down on him, he started north, heading for the twenty-year-old "temporary" army camp known as New Cantonment, his first stop on the way to Fort Supply, a hundred miles distant.

The Indian Nation wasn't a new place to Longarm, but the earlier cases that had taken him there had all been in the eastern half—the area settled more than half a century earlier when the Creeks and Cherokees had trodden what they called the Trail of Tears. The western part of the Nation might have been on a different planet. In the east, rivers ran wide and deep all year round, and countless springs fed small creeks to keep the land green. Trees abounded on the gently rolling hills and in the wide, shallow valleys of the eastern part. Here in the west, the grass grew short, and dried out soon after the rains stopped in early summer. Vegetation was sparse, except along the sides of the few waterways. There were wide, raw canyons that cut through the flat prairie, and sudden bluffs that jutted in stark isolation above the level plain. Mottes of pin oak, an occasional bois d'arc or redbud tree, and a few clumps of sage, broke the monotony of the browned grass.

Longarm followed a well-defined road. It had been used by army supply wagons before rails penetrated the Nation, and its surface was deeply rutted by their wheels. He rode steadily through the afternoon, seeing no other riders. Two or three times, distant herds of antelope pranced over the prairie in the distance, and jackrabbits zigzagged ahead of the gelding frequently, often in groups of a half dozen or more. Once, a rattlesnake buzzed a warning from its sunning place on a flat rock beside the road, and several times he had to detour around prairie dog towns that had extended their colonies into the old roadway. He crossed three small creeks, tributaries of the Canadian River; they were running low, almost dry. Always, though, there were pools in their beds where he could let his horse drink.

When the sun slanted close to the edge of the flat horizon, Longarm began looking ahead for a place to spend the night. Distantly, a line of dark green showed through the shimmering haze, marking a creekbed. The line ran north on one side of the road, angling to cross it beyond the horizon's rim. On the prairie, a man on horseback can see ten or twelve miles through clear air, or somewhat less if the air is heat-hazed. Longarm chose the line of green as his campsite, and turned the gelding off the road to reach the trees and ride along the creek while he looked for a good spot to stop.

He'd covered a bit more than half of the distance when he saw the spurts of gunsmoke, and before the flat crack of the shots reached his ears, he'd kicked the gelding into a lope. The haze seemed to recede ahead of him as he rode toward the spot. Fresh shots were sounding there now, irregularly spaced.

As diminishing distance reduced the blurring effects of the haze, Longarm could see riders dashing back and forth in front of the line of trees. The riders were still too far away for even Longarm's keen eyes to determine whether they were whites or Indians. He could tell only one thing about the skirmish: the mounted men were besieging others who'd taken cover in the foliage bordering the creekbed. He couldn't guess at their numbers. The shooting wasn't as regular now, but it still continued.

Old son, he told himself, *don't be in too big a rush to get mixed up in whatever kind of fight's going on up ahead. You don't want to pick the wrong side to help.*

That decision was taken away from him when he was still beyond rifle-range of the trees. He could see some details now, and Longarm could tell that there were three attackers—Kiowas, judging from the way they sat their horses—besieging whoever had taken cover in the creekbed. Even though he was still out of range, he slid his Winchester from the saddle scabbard and, using a lot of Ozark elevation, sent a slug in the general direction of the fracas.

His shot fell short, as he had expected, but the rifle's report drew the Indians' attention to his approach. The three attackers drew back a score of yards from their objective and pulled their horses together while they talked over the situation. This drew a couple of fresh shots from the trees, and Longarm let off another round just for emphasis. The Kiowas got the message. They galloped off along the line of trees, not anxious to get caught in a crossfire, and Longarm rode on to the creekbed without difficulty.

There was a rustling among the short salt cedars that grew down the banks of the dry creekbed. Longarm dropped his rifle's muzzle to cover the area of moving limbs. The man or men who'd been besieged by the Indians might not be any friendlier than their attackers. The cedar limbs parted and a hat showed, waving back and forth.

From the thicket, a man's voice called, "Hold your fire, mister! I'm leaving my rifle back with my horse, and I'm coming out with my hands held out from my gun!"

"Come ahead," Longarm replied. "I've got no hankering to shoot anybody. All I wanted to do was stop the fighting."

A young man followed the outthrust hat from the brake. True to his promise, his hands were extended from his sides. He stopped and looked Longarm over. "Name's Frank Turner," he announced. "If you're a lawman, I ain't wanted for anything. If you're a gun-prod, I got no money, or much of anything else on me."

"You can settle down," Longarm told him. "Robbing stray cowhands ain't my style." He saw that Turner's left sleeve was bloodstained, and went on, "Looks like you caught a slug in that arm. Let's see how bad it is."

"Just a graze. Stings a little bit, but it's quit bleeding. I guess I owe you for spooking them redskins away. Don't know why they jumped me, anyhow. I never did a thing to them."

"Hell, you've got a horse and saddle, and a rifle and pistol. If things are the same as they used to be in the Nation, the Indians'd rather have them than money."

"Hadn't thought about that," Turner said. "Maybe I'm luckier than I realized. If they'd kept pushing me, I'd've run out of ammunition after a while, then they'd've had me cold."

Longarm dropped from his saddle. "Let's take a look at that arm. I'm not much on doctoring, but I can tie it up, which is something that ain't easy for a man to do by himself, with only one hand to work with."

Turner had described his wound accurately. The rifle slug that had hit him had traveled shallowly through the flesh of his upper arm, just above the elbow, missing both bone and muscle. Longarm dug a fresh bandanna out of his saddlebag and improvised a bandage after sponging off the dried blood with water from his canteen. He drank from the canteen after he'd completed the bandage, then offered it to Turner.

The cowboy shook his head. "No thanks, mister. I wouldn't want to run you short."

"Ain't there some water in the creek?" Longarm asked, surprised.

"Not here, there ain't. I followed the creekbed from where I hit it, about ten miles back, looking for a pool I can camp by tonight."

"There's bound to be one up ahead. Where are you headed for, by the way?"

"New Cantonment," Turner replied. "Didn't have grub enough to hold me to Fort Supply, which is where I set out for. I was just getting ready to settle for a dry camp tonight when them Indians jumped outta the brush, yelling and shooting."

Longarm looked at Turner more closely than he'd had a chance to until now. Except for sun-wrinkles, the young man's face was unlined. It was neither a handsome face nor an ugly one. Turner's nose was straight, not the nose of a barroom brawler. His lips were firm under a straight-cut mustache, and his eyes were a light brown. He had a three-day stubble of beard, but it was free of ingrained grime. His rolled-up sleeve showed a well-muscled arm, his hands were the hard-leather ones of a working cowhand, and his denim jeans and jacket were bleached from regular washing. Longarm decided that he'd make a safe traveling companion, at least for the short distance to New Cantonment.

He said to Turner, "We're on the same trail, looks like. If you're agreeable, we can ride on till we find a water hole in this dry gully, and camp together tonight."

"Suits me fine. Those Kiowas might not've jumped me if I'd had some company."

"Haven't had time to tell you my name. I'm Custis Long, from Denver."

"You're a ways from home, then." Turner smiled and added, "I guess you could say I am, too. I been riding up from the Palo Duro country. That's south from Amarillo."

"I've heard about it," Longarm nodded. "You looking for

work, or just passing through? Because if it's a job you're after, I'd say you won't find very much in the Nation. The Indians that run cattle keep the jobs in their own tribes, mostly."

Turner hesitated for a moment, then said, "I'm not after a job. What I come up here for is to find out more about something I heard my old boss talking about just before I quit him. I was about to ask you if you knew anything of it, but I recall you said you're from Denver."

"I hear things, though. Try me."

"Well. A little while ago, I hit a wide streak of luck in a poker game. First one I ever had, and it might be the last. Anyhow, to cut it to the bone, I quit my job to set up on a spread of my own."

Longarm frowned. "You can't mean here in the Nation. All the range belongs to the Indians, if you don't count Greer County; I hear there's still Texas cattle being run down there."

The young cowhand nodded. "I know about Greer County. The man I quit's got a little bit of range in it, but his main one's by Palo Duro Canyon. What brought me up here was something he said about things changing, that the Indian range was going to be opened up. I figured if that's so, I better get my bid in early."

It was Longarm's turn to hesitate. Turner's story matched what Nellie had heard, which might mean the news was getting around. He might find out more, if he stuck with Turner a while. He said, "Well, if we're going to camp tonight, we better start riding and looking for a water hole. It's early yet, so we don't have to push. Then, after supper, we can swap lies while we drink our coffee."

And I hope what you just said about the range land opening up in the Nation ain't among the lies we'll swap, he thought, as the two men mounted and rode off.

Chapter 7

Before they found a water hole, Longarm shot a young ante-lope for their supper. The yearling buck leaped from the brake along the creekbed and bounded directly in front of their horses. Longarm didn't bother reaching for the rifle in his sad-dle scabbard. He drew his Colt and killed the animal with a shot through the heart.

"That's supper and breakfast," he said. He reined in and dismounted to bleed and gut the antelope. "Not much more, though. These little things don't have much more meat on 'em than a jackrabbit."

"Fresh meat'll taste real good to me," Turner said as he got off his own horse to help. "I've been living on bacon and corn pone since the day after I set out."

"All I'm carrying is jerky and hardtack, and some beans and rice for when I feel like cooking," Longarm told him as they worked. "We'll cook both haunches and eat one tonight, hang the liver and have it for breakfast, and tote the other haunch to eat at noon tomorrow. We ought to hit New Cantonment about noon the day after that."

Two miles farther on, they came to a small spring that formed a pool in the creekbed. The water wasn't exactly sweet, but it wasn't too alkaline, either, and both the men and the horses made up for a thirsty day on the trail. After supper, Longarm lighted a cheroot while Turner rolled a Bull Durham cigarette and put an ember from the campfire to its tip. They leaned back against the warm earth wall of the dry creekbed. Their horses, hobbled for the night, stood resting at the edge of the pool.

Longarm set about testing his new companion's story. "I shy away from prying into a man's private business," he began. "But what you told me back a ways don't hang together, Frank. I'll admit I'm a mite curious. You mind if I ask you something?"

"Ask away," Turner invited. "I've got no secrets to hide."

"Didn't figure you had, or that you'd tell them to me even if I asked you. Before you came out of the brush, you told me you were broke. Later on, you said you had money enough to start a cattle spread. That doesn't make sense, and I'm sort of puzzled."

Turner chuckled. "If I remember, I didn't exactly say I was broke. I just told you I didn't have any money, which is true. I'm not enough of a damn fool to carry a load of cash across wild country like this. My money's safe in a bank in Amarillo. All I've got on me is traveling money, and most of that's sewed up in the edge of my saddle blanket."

"Which wouldn't have been much use to you if those Kiowas had gotten away with your horse," Longarm pointed out.

"Hell, Long, a man who loses his horse in this kind of country, he's almost as good as dead anyhow. You know that."

"I guess you're right," Longarm agreed. He puffed his cigar back to life before asking, "If it ain't too personal a question, what do you figure to pay for a section of land here, if you can get it?"

"That's one of the things I've come to find out, after I take a look at the range. For all I know, the few thousand I've got won't be enough even to get me started. But Forest—that's the fellow I was working for, Scott Forest—said the land he's getting here in the Nation's just about being given to him."

Longarm's memory clicked. Nellie's "Mr. Scott" had left the train in Amarillo, which wasn't more than a crippled crow's hop from the Palo Duro country. The chance that there'd be another rancher with Scott in his name in that part of the Texas Panhandle was a lot slimmer than the chance of finding balls on a heifer. The odds on it were a lot less than the odds on the coincidence that had brought him and Frank Turner together. There weren't that many places to go in the Nation, or that many people traveling to what few places there were, to set high odds on such an accidental encounter.

He said to Turner, "What I can't figure is how that boss of yours thinks he can get hold of land the government's already given to the Indian tribes."

Turner scratched his stubbly jaw, then sighed and said, "I don't know that, either. I've thought a lot about it, though, and my idea is that Scott and a bunch of his friends in Greer County have got an inside track on some move the government's about to make."

"Either that or they're going to pay off somebody who can let them in on the land in secret," Longarm prodded. "Which might not be exactly according to the rules, but I suppose if a man's land-hungry, he'll do just about anything to feed himself."

"Not me, I won't," Turner said emphatically. "I thought about that, too, and I wouldn't put a trick like that past Forest. But I've already made up my mind—if that's what he's cooking up, I'll go look somewhere else."

"I'm right glad to hear you say that, Frank." Longarm's opinion was that the young cowhand's story held up, and that it was time to try to enlist his help. "I didn't tell you this before, because I wasn't sure about you. What you just said eased my mind somewhat."

"Meaning just exactly what?" In the gathering twilight, Turner's open young face showed his curiosity.

"Meaning I can tell you what my job is. I'm a deputy U.S. marshal." Longarm fished out his badge and showed it.

"Well, now I'll tell you something, Marshal Long—"

"Those who deal straight with me, I let call me Longarm," the deputy interrupted.

Turner smiled. "Good enough—Longarm. I've been wondering which you were, a lawman or an outlaw, ever since you knocked over that antelope. I've seen men draw fast, and I've seen other men shoot straight, but I never saw one man draw so fast *and* shoot so straight before, and I figured you had to be one or the other."

"If you were worried, why'd you tell me where you had your spare cash hid away?"

"Because after I'd thought it over, I decided that if you were an outlaw, you wouldn't waste time on such small potatoes as the few dollars you'd get from me. I tagged you as a shooter, maybe chasing down rustlers for the Cattlemen's Association or something."

Longarm grinned. "You think pretty good, Frank. That makes it easier to go ahead."

"You're down here looking for somebody, is that what you're getting ready to say? I figured that out when you told me what you do, and all I can say is, I'm damned glad it's not me."

"Come to think of it, so am I," Longarm said. "But the man I'm after's a lot older than you, and he's got a nose that's been busted more than once."

"What'd he do?"

"Robbed a bank and killed a town marshal, up in Colorado. I'm backtrailing now; I figure to run across his track up around Fort Supply. That's close to where the posse that chased him from Colorado lost him." Longarm puffed on his cheroot for a moment. Its tip glowed in the dusk. Their supper fire, a scant one made from small, dry branches picked up along the creek-bed, was now a tiny spot of red, almost out.

Longarm went on, "It was the bank robber that got me down here, but now I've stumbled onto something new. It's got to do with that land you heard was going to be handed out for ranches."

Turner was suddenly sober. "It's a crooked scheme, ain't it, Longarm? There's going to be bribes and pay-offs made, am I right?"

"Looks that way from where I'm sitting. When I first ran across it, the whole thing seemed like it was too farfetched to be real. But what you've told me's changed my mind. As soon as I catch up with that bank robber, I'm going to start digging into it."

"Damn it to hell!" Turner cursed. "I ought to've known it was too good to be true!"

"You'd just better be thankful you found out in time," Longarm told him soberly, "Now, I'm going to ask you a favor."

"I think I know what it is, and my answer's yes. I don't owe Scott Forest and his friends one fucking thing." Anger flared in the young cowhand's voice. "He treats his hands like dogs, and that's the main reason I quit him. Even if I didn't have a dime in my jeans, I was going to leave, anyhow."

"You'll give me a hand in unraveling things, then?" Longarm asked. "I'd better tell you before you get in too deep, it's likely to be a mite dangerous."

"It couldn't be any worse than dropping a loop over a lo-coed steer that's coming at you. When do we start?"

"Whoa, now. You take on a job like this the way you eat an apple, one bite at a time."

Turner smiled. "I guess that's the best way to miss swallowing a worm. Well, you're dealing the hand, Longarm. I'm ready to play whatever cards you give me."

"Thanks, Frank. There's no way I can pay you for helping me, but I'll sure be grateful for it."

"Forget about it. Maybe I'm doing it because I don't like Scott, or maybe I just feel mean enough not to want him and his friends to have something I don't feel right about taking."

Longarm stood up and stretched. "We'll talk more about it while we're riding on to New Cantonment You might recall something you've overlooked. Right now, I feel like turning in. We've still got a lot of riding ahead of us, you know."

It was a warm night, and Longarm remembered that dew didn't form on the prairie. He didn't bother to do more than take off his boots and lay them under his blanket for a pillow. Five seconds after he lay down, he was asleep.

"Well, there it lays," Longarm said.

A full day of steady riding had brought the tall lawman and Frank Turner back to the looping course of the Canadian River's north fork, and they'd followed the old wagon road that ran roughly parallel to the stream. They'd started early on the second morning, and now, with the sun almost directly overhead, they'd just sighted the huddled buildings of the army outpost, New Cantonment, their first stop on the way to Fort Supply.

"You might be lucky and pick up the trail of that hombre you're after," Turner suggested.

"Not much chance. Oh, I'll have a stab at it, of course, but if I'd been on the run, with a posse right behind me, I'd've bought enough grub and stuff at Fort Supply so I wouldn't have to show my face again till I got where I was planning to stop. An outlaw who's smart enough to do that can break his trail for sure."

"Maybe this one wasn't that smart."

"I don't know yet. But we'll know pretty quick if he came this way after he left Fort Supply."

They rode on in silence as the buildings of New Cantonment grew larger and larger and the sun got hotter and hotter. *It's likely to be snowing in Denver*, Longarm thought, *or at least raining now and again*. As little as he liked snow, he half wished he was back in the Rockies, where a man didn't sweat his life away like he did on the prairie. He'd noticed that the heat didn't seem to bother Turner, and had wondered why, until it occurred to him that the young cowhand was used to the same kind of heat on the Texas prairie that they were encountering on the prairie of the Indian Nation. Longarm pulled out his bandanna and wiped his face again, and looked ahead to the army depot, where there were buildings to shade a man from the sun.

New Cantonment's promise of relief from the burning sun was more of an illusion than a reality, Longarm discovered when they arrived. The outpost was still considered a temporary camp, though it had been standing in the same spot for more than twenty years. Because of its classification, army regulations did not officially allow for the construction of any permanent buildings. There were some, of course, but these were of the most basic type, with bare board-and-batten walls and shake roofs. They were unpainted, and their interiors were unfinished. They did little more than trap the heat that beat down on their roofs.

Longarm and Turner headed for the sutler's in search of something cold to drink—a request that was greeted with a loud guffaw by the grizzle-jawed veteran who limped to greet them from the cane-bottomed chair he'd been sitting in behind the counter.

"You come at the wrong time of year," he told them. "Stop by next winter. Then, anything you get'll be half froze. Right now, the best you'll git is beer outta that tub of water over in the corner. It ain't what you'd call cold, but it ain't as hot as the wind, anyhow."

"I'll settle for that," Turner said. "At least it'll be wet. Anything to stop me from spitting cotton any longer."

"Guess I'll have to join you," Longarm said. Then he asked the sutler's whiskery helper, "You got a bottle of Maryland rye in your stock, old fellow? If you have, I'll take it. It'll help me wash down the beer."

They stood in the doorway, trying to catch any breeze that

might be moving, alternating swallows of the lukewarm beer with sips of the biting whiskey. The combination didn't cool them off much, but it cut the dust and made the heat seem less oppressive. Turner had just handed the rye bottle back to Longarm when he saw a soldier leading a big black stallion along the dusty street that ran in front of the sutler's establishment.

"Damn it, I know that horse," he said. "There can't be two like it. Longarm, it looks like you're going to get a chance to start finding out something about Scott Forest's land-grab scheme sooner than you'd figured, because that's his favorite horse going by, and where the nag is, you'll find Forest."

"You sure about the horse?" Longarm asked

"Dead sure. If you get up close to him, you'll see he's got a scar on his neck just ahead of the off-shoulder. The buster who broke him in scraped his hide with a spur when he got throwed."

"I guess you ought to know, Frank." Longarm took another swallow of beer and washed away its flatness with a sip of the rye, while he puzzled out which way to move. Then, dropping his voice, he said, "Now listen right careful, Frank. You remember what we talked about last night, and while we were riding yesterday?"

"Sure. I'm going to introduce you to—"

"Never mind going over it," Longarm interrupted. "Just be sure you've got it all straight, how we'll play things. I didn't aim to get into this deal so sudden—I wanted to round up Boyle first—but we've got a chance here that's too good to pass up."

"I'll follow whatever play you make, Longarm."

"Good enough. We'll just wait in here until your old boss shows up, then we'll saunter over and go ahead like we figured on doing."

They didn't have long to wait. A few minutes after the trooper had tied the stallion to the hitch rail, a tall, burly man came out of the building and loosened the animal's reins. Turner nodded in response to Longarm's questioning look. Side by side, they walked the short distance to where Scott Forest was getting ready to mount.

Longarm used the few moments that their walk required to

study the rancher. Forest was a craggy man, with a face that might have been chiseled from a boulder. It was all planes and angles, and his body was built the same way. The only visible signs that set him apart from a working cowhand were a big diamond ring on his left hand and a creamy, wide-brimmed Stetson that looked as though it had just come out of its factory box. His gray eyes were granite-hard under full, dark brows. His thick eyebrows lifted in surprise when he saw Longarm and Turner.

"Frank Turner? What in hell are you doing here? I thought you headed north when you left the Box S."

"Well, this *is* north, Mr. Forest," Frank said. "And it looks to me like pretty good country for a range herd, just like you said."

Forest frowned. "I don't follow you."

"Oh, sure you do. After all the talking you did about the cheap range up here, don't you think us hands got the idea you planned to come up to the Nation and stake out some for yourself? I figured if it was good enough for you, it'd be good for me, too."

Longarm noted that this man Forest was beginning to look distinctly uncomfortable.

"Look here, Frank," the rancher said. "If you've got some idea about starting that spread you've been daydreaming about, I'd advise you to look somewhere else. Not here."

"I don't see why," Turner persisted with wide-eyed innocence. "Let's see, how'd you put it? Plenty of land at the right price, if I remember. Well, that's what I'm looking for."

Forest's face began to grow red. "You haven't got what it takes to get in on the deal you heard me mention. I know you made a big killing in that poker game in Amarillo, but that's not enough to swing this kind of deal."

"Maybe I've got some help you don't know about."

"Your friend there?" Forest looked Longarm over. "From his looks, I'd say he hasn't, either. Who is he, by the way?"

"The name's Long, Mr. Forest," Longarm said. "Custis Long."

"Did Frank spin you a wild yarn of some kind about getting in on a land deal here in the Nation?"

"We might've talked some along those lines."

"Well, Long, I don't know who you are or where you came from, but I'll tell you this. Turner's using stolen information to rope you in with him. If you know what's good for both of you, you'll forget the Nation, and start looking somewhere else."

Longarm's voice was mild, but steely. "Oh, I don't know. We've been looking things over up here. We both like what we've seen."

Forest glowered at the young cowhand. "Damn you, Turner! You've got no right to use private information you picked up while you were working for me to try cutting yourself in on my deal!"

"You never made much of a secret about what you had in mind!" Turner shot back.

"I didn't think one of my own men would be ungrateful enough to pull a stunt like you're trying!"

"I don't owe you a damn thing, Mr. Forest. What you paid me, I worked hard for. I figure we're quits."

Forest was silent for a moment. He was obviously getting his temper under control, and when he spoke again, he was calmer. "Now look, Frank, you're just trying to get started for yourself. You don't understand how deals like this one of mine are set up. It's taken me a lot of time and cost me money, and it'll cost a lot more. Even if you could afford it, I couldn't bring an outsider in on a deal of this kind. There'd be too much danger of him fucking things up. It's not just you; I'd say the same to anybody."

"Make me an insider, then," Turner invited.

"I'll see you in hell first!" Turner snapped, losing control for the first time. "This pie's cut into enough pieces already. We don't need to take out another slice."

Longarm said, "Looks like we'll just have to cut our own slice, then. You think about that, Forest." He waited long enough to let his words percolate through the rancher's mind, then added, "I've seen enough deals like yours to know what can happen when outsiders begin poking into corners and asking questions. It makes people nervous, and they start to pull in their horns." He turned to the young cowhand. "Come on, Frank. We'll cook up our own deal."

"If you butt into this, it'll be at your own risk!" Forest hissed. He brought his hand up and rested it on his gun butt. "And I'm ready to back up what I'm telling you."

Turner matched Forest's gesture. "If you want to make a shooting affair out of it, I'm ready."

"Now, let's hold up," Longarm said sharply. He stepped between Turner and the boiling-mad Forest, and faced the rancher. "I ain't one to let my mouth run away with my good sense, Forest. You never saw me before, and I never saw you, so we've got no past arguments hanging over us. Why don't you and me step off to one side and talk quiet? Maybe we can figure something out."

Forest hesitated, but like most men who'd pulled themselves up by their own bootstraps, he recognized in Longarm's voice the authority earned by a man's own efforts. He stared at Longarm for a long moment, then nodded. "All right," he said, and tossed the stallion's reins back over the hitch rail. "You sound sensible enough. I'll listen to you."

Frank took the cue, and shook a finger at Longarm. "Don't sell me out, now!"

"Don't worry," Longarm said with great sincerity, "you know me better'n that."

Longarm established the initiative by stepping out first, forcing Forest to follow rather than leading. He emphasized his control by selecting the direction in which they walked, and by keeping a half-step ahead of the rancher until they were out of Turner's hearing. Then he slowed and let Forest walk beside him.

"If I see this scheme of yours clear, Forest," Longarm began, "you're depending an awful lot on people you can't control—government people."

"I'm not a fool, Long, They've all been taken care of."

"Maybe. Your scheme looks chancy as hell to me. If word gets back to Washington, you'll be in real trouble."

Forest smiled coldly. "It's not going to happen that way."

"Don't be too sure about that. I sure as hell ain't local."

"Are you telling me you're in the federal government?"

"Justice Department, Forest. That's the one that keeps an eye on what people in places like this get into."

"I don't like to be threatened, Long." Forest was getting angry again. Longarm made no reply, and they walked on for a few steps in silence. Forest asked, "Just what do you do in the Justice Department?"

"I'll let that pass for a minute. If we get along together, it won't make any difference. If we don't, you'll find out fast enough."

"Long, if you're not telling me the truth, you're the most convincing goddamned liar I've met in quite a while."

Longarm turned his gunmetal-blue gaze on the rancher. "Do I strike you as a liar, Forest?"

"No. And that's what bothers me; I don't see you as a bluffer, either. You don't act like a man who's trying to pull a fiddle."

"I'll tell you this much. I'm not a real high mucky-muck in Washington, but in my job, I can hurt you or help you. And that's about all I need to say, ain't it?"

"I suppose you can prove this?" Forest asked.

"When the right time comes. But I damn sure won't give you any handle on me now. I'm no more of a fool than you are."

Forest reached up and pushed back the brim of his hat. His diamond ring flashed in the hazy sunshine. "Did Frank Turner come to you and spill my plans? Was he trying to get you to make trouble for me?"

"No. He came to me for help, because he needed somebody like me to back up his play. It looked good enough for me to go in with him. If you think I've got my hand held out for a payoff, the answer's no. I came in as Frank's partner."

"In that case, I don't suppose there's anything I can offer you to get out and leave me alone," Forest said thoughtfully.

"Not one damn thing. I can offer you something, though, if me and Frank are in. There's enough land; all you and your friends have to do is cut a few sections apiece off your shares to take care of us. That looks like a pretty cheap price to me."

"Have you got the money to match what we've already put in? And what we'll still have to put in?"

"Up to about any reasonable figure you name," Longarm replied confidently.

"Up to twenty-five thousand dollars?"

"Up to double that, and more if it's needed. And enough on top of that so I can help Frank out if he's short. You're getting ahead of things, though, Forest. From what I hear, things ain't ripe yet."

"No, but they will be in a few weeks. It'll take me a little time to talk my own partners around to letting you two in. By the time I've done that, the deal will be ready to close."

"Except that there won't be a deal to close if me and Frank ain't in it. Can you make your friends see that?"

"I can deliver what I promise, Long. I'm not sure yet that you can, though. I want to see your money."

"You will. Look, Forest, you know how careful a man in my place has to be. I can't keep too much cash in one spot. My money's spread around. I don't keep enough in any one bank to start folks asking questions. It'll take a while to get it together."

Something akin to admiration crept into Forest's voice as he said, "By God, Long, I'm changing my opinion of you. I'm beginning to think you're really shrewd enough to make it worthwhile to take you in, even if I do have to take Turner to get you with us."

Longarm saw that he was winning. It was time to push his streak. He said, "I take it I've satisfied you, then. Now, it's up to you to satisfy me about something."

Forest arched a bushy eyebrow.

"What's that?"

"I figure you've come here to talk to one of the men who's pushing your scheme, somebody in the army or the Indian bureau. I want to hear him say things are working out all right."

Forest stiffened. "Not on your damned life! The army and BIA people who're in on this are gun-shy enough as it is. They're caught between a shit and a sweat until this thing's closed up. I can't take a chance on upsetting them by bringing in somebody new."

"I'll remind you of something before you make your mind up firm, Forest. If this deal falls through, all you'll be out is a wad of cash. You'll go right on and work up something else. If I get in it and it falls through, I'm finished with the government."

Forest thought this over with a frown. Then he said, "I can't say I blame you, Long; I respect a man who covers himself. All right. I guess it won't do any harm to introduce you to Captain Rogers. But you'll have to be careful of what you say."

"I'll guard my mouth," Longarm promised. "If it makes you

feel better, me and Frank won't be hanging around here once we're sure things are all set. I imagine we'll be pulling out in the morning."

"I've got to get on up to Fort Supply, myself. That's where we'll close things up, by the way. You and Turner will have to be there in about three weeks. Is that going to be enough time for you to get your money together?"

"Plenty," the deputy said with assurance. "We'll be there. And we'll wait for you if you're late, just like we'll expect you to wait a day or so for us."

"That's understood. I know how hard it is to keep to a time-table in a thing of this kind. If it's settled, then, let's go see Rogers. I've got to get on the road to Supply without wasting any more time."

Chapter 8

Turner, waiting at the hitch rail, looked questioningly at Longarm as he and Forest approached. Longarm nodded, and when they got closer, he said in a low voice, "It's all set, partner. I'll tell you the ins and outs, later on. Right now, we're going in to meet Captain Rogers, and Forest's going to let him know about us."

"Just be careful of what you say," Forest told Turner, repeating the warning he'd already given Longarm. "I've already explained to Long how edgy these army people are."

"Maybe you'd better let me and Forest do the talking," Longarm suggested. "It'll be safer that way."

Frank nodded. "Whatever you say."

Forest led the way inside. The New Cantonment headquarters was as barren within as it was stark without. A pair of field desks stood on opposite sides of the big central room, and there were maps tacked on the walls, and papers stacked in corners. The captain was seated at one of the desks. He looked up with surprise.

"I thought you'd left, Forest."

"I ran into these associates of mine outside," Forest explained. "It seemed like a good idea to introduce them to you, so you won't be worrying about what they're doing if they stay around a day or so. Mr. Long and Mr. Turner, Captain Rogers."

Rogers didn't offer to shake hands, but bobbed his head to acknowledge the introductions. He said to Forest, "I thought we'd agreed to confine any personal contacts to you and me."

"Suppose something happens to me?" Forest asked. "It'd make things easier if you know at least one or two of the men I'm working with."

"If you put it that way, I suppose it would," Rogers agreed.

Longarm had been studying the captain from the time they'd entered the office. Rogers was a type he'd seen many times before: an aging veteran of the War, one who'd probably carried a brevet rank of colonel until the swollen wartime military force had been forced to tighten its rosters. Reduced to his regular grade, put in command of a small outpost in an isolated spot, he was waiting for retirement with nothing more to look forward to than a captain's pension of forty dollars a month. The commandant had the florid face and venous nose of a man who enjoyed the bottle too much for his own good. Longarm guessed that his involvement in Forest's scheme was a way to put away a nest egg against the lean retirement years that lay ahead.

He asked Longarm, "You're just looking over the terrain, I suppose?"

The lawman nodded "Something like that. There's a lot of things maps don't show."

"A sensible idea. Will you be here long?"

"Not very. We've got some more looking to do, then we'll be going on up north," Longarm said.

"Too bad. I know Mr. Forest's leaving right away, or I'd invite you to dine with me at the mess this evening."

"Another time," Forest said quickly. "I should be on the road right now, in fact." He stood up. "We'll be leaving you to your work. If anything should come up, you know how to reach me."

"Yes, of course." This time, Rogers made the gesture of standing and bowing. "Good day, gentlemen."

When they were outside again, Forest turned to Longarm. "Well? Are you satisfied now?"

"It looks right good."

"Just do me one favor," Forest went on. "Stay away from Rogers until things are wound up. You saw how edgy he is."

"Don't worry," Longarm assured him. "We'll be on our way, too, pretty soon. Now that we've got a deal, I'm going to have to get on the move, so I'll have the money all gathered up by the time we meet at Fort Supply."

"Good." Forest swung into his saddle. "I'll see you there in two or three weeks, then."

Longarm and Turner watched the rancher until he was

well on his way out of New Cantonment. Longarm expelled the deep sigh of relief he'd been holding back.

"It was pretty close there, a time or two," he told Turner. "But I've got to give you credit, Frank, you put on a mighty good show for your old boss."

"I'd rather have punched his nose a few times," Turner said. "Do you really think he swallowed that yarn you spun him?"

"I'll tell you three things about crooks," Longarm replied. "First thing is, they've got to believe everybody else is as crooked as they are, so you don't need much of a story to convince 'em. Next thing is, they're always looking for an edge, something that'll guarantee that their scheme's going to work, or that'll keep 'em out of trouble if it doesn't. You hold that out to 'em, and they'll grab without looking to see if it's bait with a hook in it or not. And the last thing is, they're always bluffing that they ain't worried, but all the time they are. If you show a tough face, you can generally count on 'em to fall in with most anything you want 'em to."

Turner whistled. "That's quite a sermon."

"And preaching it's made my mouth go dry. Let's get on back to the sutler's. That warm beer he's got don't beat horse piss by very much, but it's the only beer in a hundred miles."

As they walked toward the sutler's, Turner asked, "What do we do while we're waiting to meet Forest in Fort Supply?"

"I don't know what you'll be doing, but I've got to find that Eddie Boyle and tuck him away. Once I've got my hands on him, I can keep him in one of the Indian police jails while we go on to bust up Forest's plan. The trouble is, if I try handling both jobs at the same time, I'll have to move so fast I'll meet myself coming back. I ought to be asking around here to find out if Boyle's showed his face in New Cantonment."

"I don't see any reason why you can't do that."

"There're handbills out on Boyle. If I start being nosy in a little place like this, it's going to get talked about, and that Captain Rogers might hear what I was doing. That could start him to wondering and asking questions. You saw how nervous he is."

"I could ask," Turner said thoughtfully. "Say he's some kind of relative, a cousin or uncle, who's supposed to be traveling in the Nation."

Longarm smiled, impressed with the young man's ingenuity. "You know, you could, at that. As long as you don't call his name, just describe what he looks like."

"That's easy. You described him for me. We might as well start at the sutler's, while we're having a beer and buying our supplies."

"That's a prime idea. Then we can go over to the army stable and you can ask there, too. There can't be so many strangers passing through that he'd've missed being noticed, if he was here at all."

Nosing around the camp trying to uncover a trace of the fugitive took up most of the afternoon. Longarm and Frank made an early supper on cheese and hard sausage at the sutler's counter, and set out for Barrel Springs, the campground that had been used by the army before New Cantonment's relocation on the riverbank. The campground was still a stopping-place for Indians and other travelers for whom the military wasn't obliged to furnish accommodations. From the instant he'd met Captain Rogers, Longarm had realized that he couldn't afford to disclose his identity to receive the courtesies given by the army to federal employees. They'd covered less than a mile of the distance to the springs when Longarm's horse began to falter and miss steps.

"Hold up," he called to Frank as he reined in. "This damn nag's either picked up a rock in his frog, or he's got a stone-bruise."

Examining the gelding's hoof was easy; the moon was full, the night almost daylight-bright. Longarm found the hoof free of rocks, but when he ran his hands up the horse's leg, applying pressure, the animal flinched.

"Stone-bruise," he announced. "And there ain't any way for me to get another one from the remounts at New Cantonment without tipping Rogers off to who I am."

"Where does that leave us, then?" Frank asked.

"It leaves us stuck, damn it!" Longarm replied. "I ain't fool enough to set out tomorrow with a crippled horse. I've got some liniment in my saddlebag, but that ain't going to cure him up short of a day and a night."

"We'll lose a day, then."

"Looks like it. If we give the critter's leg tonight and all day tomorrow to get better, maybe we can start by sundown tomorrow. The moon's full and it'll be a little easier on the horses, traveling when it's cooler."

"It'll be a lot easier on us, too," Frank observed. "Seems like a shame to lose the time, though."

"I'll make it up," Longarm promised. "I ain't figured out how yet, but I'll work it out."

With the limping horse slowing them down, the ride to Barrel Springs seemed endless. When they got there, they spread their bedrolls on a knoll a short distance from the water and dropped off to sleep in the bright light of the round moon; to the accompaniment provided by a wakeful mockingbird that lived in the brush around the water hole.

Morning brought a bright sun in a cloudless sky. While they waited for coffee to boil, Longarm said, "We're just going to have to lose a day, there's no way out of it. We'll rest the horses till an hour or so before sundown, Frank. If the gelding makes a mile or two without going lame again, he ought to get to Fort Supply without trouble. I can get another horse there from the remount station, then I'll be all right."

Dozing and swapping stories, they rested through the day in anticipation of the long night ahead. Longarm kept the gelding's leg wet with the strong, smelly liniment, and when the sun dipped to within two hours or so of setting, he pronounced the animal fit for travel.

"We'll have to take it easy, though," he said. "He really ought to rest another day. But I guess it won't be as bad as it looked at first. If we'd started this morning, we couldn't've done anything at Fort Supply until tomorrow, anyway."

Saddled and mounted, they took to the road. Longarm kept their pace easy, alert to any indication that the gelding's sore leg might be getting worse. The animal seemed to have recovered, though, and he said to Turner, "Looks like we'll make it to Fort Supply without any trouble. If I'm lucky, I'll pick up Boyle's tracks there and start running him down, while you wait for me."

"I thought I was going along," Turner said.

Longarm shook his head. "Better not. It ain't that I don't enjoy your company, Frank, but when I get on a trail, I've got to keep moving. You ain't used to it. Besides, if I'm late getting back, you ought to be there to make sure Forest and his bunch don't start making their deal without waiting for us."

"That makes sense," Frank agreed. "I won't argue against your plan."

"Tell you what, though," Longarm said. "First place where the road swings close to the river, we'll stop and cook a bite before it gets too dark. It'll give the horses an extra rest, and maybe save trouble later. Then we won't have to make any more long stops till we decide to sleep."

They left the road where a pool twenty yards or so distant from its ruts offered a good place to stop. Frank cooked while Longarm put more liniment on the gelding's leg. They ate without haste, and had stowed their gear into their saddlebags, ready to mount and ride, when the rapid thudding of hoofbeats sounded from the road. Longarm looked up just in time to see a buggy sailing by. He blinked and shook his head, not believing what he'd seen. The buggy was being driven by Nellie Bly.

"Godamighty!" he gasped, swinging into his saddle. "Frank, kick up that horse of yours! Catch up with that buggy and stop it!"

Frank didn't pause to question the odd command. He forked his mustang and rode. By the time Longarm caught up with the buggy, the young cowhand had brought it to a halt and was holding the horse while Nellie stood on the seat, swinging her portmanteau at him, unable to reach out far enough to land a blow.

"Hold on, Nellie!" Longarm called. "He ain't trying to hurt you!"

She turned at the sound of his voice. "Longarm! Thank God! This man's after me!"

"No he's not," Longarm assured her as he reined in beside the buggy. "He's helping me. I had him stop you because I had to favor my horse. It's lame."

Turner doffed his Stetson. "I'm right sorry I scared you, Miss. If the marshal hadn't told me to, I sure wouldn't've come after you like I did."

"This is Frank Turner, Nellie," Longarm said, "Frank, meet Miss Cochrane. Only I guess you might as well get used to calling her Nellie, like I do. That's the name she writes under for a newspaper back East."

Nellie had recovered from her fright and anger. "I was sure you had something terrible in mind. I'm glad to find out you're a friend of Longarm's."

Longarm rubbed his chin. "Well, what in tarnation are you doing here, Nellie? I thought you were safe back at Darlington."

"I had to come after you. You hadn't been gone very long when that Indian policeman, Short Bear, came looking for you. He'd found out somehow about the woman you asked him to look for, Eddie Boyle's half-breed Pawnee."

"How'd you find out about her?" Longarm asked Nellie. "I don't recall mentioning anything to you."

"You didn't. I had to pry the information out of Short Bear. Honestly, a ward-heeling political grafter could take lessons from an Indian in saying a lot without telling a reporter anything."

"But you got Short Bear to loosen up?"

"After I convinced him you'd left me to take whatever messages might come for you while you were away. It took an hour to persuade him. By then, it was getting late, but I knew I had to get word to you where the woman is. So I took the buggy and hitched it up and started after you."

Longarm stared at her in disbelief. "You took the buggy? Didn't you ask the agent if you could?"

"I was afraid he'd refuse. Besides, it was just standing out there by the stable. Thank goodness, I used to help Father hitch our mare, so I knew what to do."

"Damn it, don't you know they hang people for stealing horses and buggies in this part of the country?"

She dismissed the question with an impatient wave of her hand. "Oh, I've heard about that. Wild West stories. Besides, I left Mr. Edmondson a note telling him I'd take good care of his horse and I'd bring the buggy back."

Longarm chewed at the edge of his mustache. He couldn't see how such a smart young girl could manage to be so pushy and get herself into so much trouble in such a short time. He said at last, "And you came all the way up here by yourself?"

"Of course. There's only one road, I found that out before I left. And I had my gun, in case anybody bothered me."

"If they had, I guess you'd've tried to beat 'em off with your suitcase, the way you were whaling away at Frank?"

Nellie gasped. "I forgot all about it, I was so excited!"

"I'm just as glad you did, ma'am," Frank said. He'd been listening to their conversation with his mouth hanging open.

Longarm asked Nellie, "What'd Short Bear tell you about Boyle's woman?"

"Her name is Late Morning Star, and she's at a Pawnee hunting camp on Buffalo Creek. He said that's a creek that runs into the Cimarron River northeast of Fort Supply."

Longarm frowned thoughtfully. "Did he say how long she'd be there?"

"No. That's why I was in such a hurry to catch up with you. If you don't find her now—"

"Yeah, I know. Well, I'd say you did right, Nellie, even if I don't think you ought to've risked it. Now I've got to figure how to pull everything together. One sure thing, we can't stand here in the road palaverin' all night. Frank, you lead my horse a spell while I ride in the buggy with Nellie. As soon as I get things all worked out, we'll stop and talk some more."

After they'd ridden silently for a short distance, Longarm told Nellie, "I didn't want to seem to be scolding you in front of Frank, and I'm grateful for what you did. But you took a real risk, coming up here the way you did. That young fellow up ahead there'd be laying dead and scalped someplace along the Canadian if I hadn't happened along in time to spook a bunch of Kiowas that had jumped their reservation and set on him while he was on the way to New Cantonment from Texas."

Nellie's eyes widened. "That really happened?"

"You can ask him to show you the fresh bullet wound he's got, if you don't believe me."

"I didn't think things like that still happened out here, Longarm. I thought the West had been tamed. I saw a lot of fighting and shooting in Mexico, but they're having a revolution there. I just thought it'd be different in the United States."

"This ain't the United States," he reminded her. "It's the Indian Nation. And the old bad feelings last a long time."

Nellie had already recovered her composure. She said, "Nothing happened to me, so there's no use worrying, now. I want to find out what happened after you left me."

"Find out about what? You just told me what I've been waiting to hear about Boyle's woman."

She wouldn't be put off so easily. "Don't beat around the bush, Longarm. You've run across something else. I can tell by the way you've been acting."

Longarm hadn't been conscious that he was acting any differently than he always did, but apparently Nellie's training in news-gathering had alerted her to something of which he wasn't aware. He said, "I don't see how you figure that. Frank and me stopped at New Cantonment to buy grub and ask about Boyle, if that's what you mean."

"I think you've found out something new about the land-grab scheme. You've been so careful to avoid mentioning it that I'm suspicious."

Longarm chuckled. "All right. I wasn't aiming to keep it from you, though. I just wanted to save it until we could all three sit down and Frank could fill in places I might've missed."

"Frank Turner, the young cowboy riding up there ahead of us?"

"He's the only Frank hereabouts."

"Don't be like Short Bear, Longarm. Tell me, don't make me dig it all out of you."

"I guess it's time." Quickly, he filled her in on Frank's connection with Scott Forest, and Forest's relationship with the land-stealing plan. When he'd finished, she leaned forward and Longarm could see her violet eyes gleaming with anticipation in the bright moonlight.

She said, "Everything's working out perfectly, isn't it? Now I can go on with you to look for Late Morning Star, and Frank can go ahead to keep an eye on Scott Forest in Fort Supply."

"Now, just a damn minute!" Longarm began.

Nellie cut him short. "No, Longarm. You put me on the shelf at Darlington, but I'm not going to let you do it again. These are my stories, and I'm going to follow them both."

"You said you weren't going to write me up!" he protested.

"I can write the story without making you the central character," she reminded him. "And that's what I'll do. But I intend to stay with you and be in on everything that happens."

"You're a real determined young lady, ain't you?"

"If you'll overlook my language, I sure as hell am!" she retorted. "It's the only way a woman can be, if she's going to get along in a world that's run by men!"

"Be reasonable, Nellie," he pleaded. "A Pawnee hunting camp's not any place for a white girl. It's smelly and dirty and rough."

She gazed evenly at him, and said in a voice that bespoke a maturity far beyond her years, "Longarm, I've seen men who've been murdered and women and children who've been beaten to death or burned to death in fires. I've got a strong stomach, and I don't think my mind's weak. I'm going with you, and that's my last word!"

Longarm realized that there wasn't really any way he could keep Nellie from following him. She knew where he was going, and she'd find a way to get on his trail if he left her behind; what had happened at Darlington proved that. At least, if she was with him, he'd be able to keep her out of trouble. What was more important, he'd be able to keep her from kiting off in all directions and causing trouble for him.

He sighed and nodded. "All right, Nellie, if that's what you're set on doing. First thing, though, we better pull up and get ourselves all pulling the same way."

He whistled shrilly, pulling on the buggy reins. Frank looked back at the whistle's sound and saw the buggy stopping. He turned back to join them.

"What's wrong?" he asked.

"Nothing. I just finished my plan. I need to look at my map to make sure of a thing or two." Longarm got out of the buggy and took the map from his saddlebag. The moonlight, nearly day-bright, made it easy for him to follow the lines on it. He located Buffalo Creek. It flowed almost due east into the Cimarron, joining the river about ten miles north and twenty miles east of Fort Supply. He studied the map for a few moments, setting landmarks and distances in his mind, then folded it and put it away.

Longarm told Frank, "The best thing for you to do is to go on in to Fort Supply. I'll go in the buggy with Nellie to the Pawnee camp and see if I can find Boyle's woman. As long as she stole the damn buggy, we might as well get some use out of it. Anyway, that gelding needs a good long rest. You lead him on in to Fort Supply. I'll just get my saddle and gear off him, and carry it in the buggy."

"If you haven't got a horse, what do you need the saddle for?" Frank asked.

"I'll find some use for it, even if it's just as a pillow," Longarm replied in a casual voice. "All right, you might as well go on. We'll tag along till we come to the place up ahead where the road cuts pretty sharp to the west. Then we'll get off the road, go straight north, and follow the creek till we come to the Pawnee camp."

"And you want me to stay in Fort Supply until you get there?" Frank asked. "How long do you figure it'll be?"

"A week, more or less. If I've got to take a long trail after Boyle, we'll swing past Fort Supply, and Nellie can stay there where you'll be around to make sure she's safe."

"No!" Nellie exclaimed. "I told you, I'm going to stay with you, no matter what kind of trail you have to take."

"Now you listen to me," Longarm told her severely. "I'll take you along to the Pawnee camp, like I said I would. If I find Boyle there, that's an end to it, but if he's gone and I've got to chase after him, I'll be moving too fast for you to keep up, and I can't afford to be slowed down. If you want to argue about it some more, we'll do it while we're riding, but I'll tell you right now, you'll just be wasting your breath. Now, let's get moving. We ain't got time to waste sitting around here, chewing the fat."

Chapter 9

Nellie sat silently beside Longarm as the buggy rattled over the rutted road in the deepening twilight. Her round chin was thrust angrily forward, and her rosebud lips were compressed into a straight line. Longarm glanced at her from time to time, but made no effort to begin a conversation. She'd been silent since they'd left, not even bidding Frank Turner goodbye when they turned off the road and he went on to Fort Supply.

Longarm was surprised when she said abruptly, "I'm very thirsty. Can we stop and get a drink of water at the first brook we cross?"

"They're called creeks in this part of the country, Nellie. And you don't need to wait till we get to one. Reach in back of you in the buggy-bed; my canteen's laying by my saddle, and it's full."

She knelt on the seat and stretched her arms to reach the canteen, which she swung by its strap onto the seat between her and Longarm. Then she reached back again.

Longarm asked, "What're you looking for now, something to eat?"

"No. A cup or a glass to drink from."

"The best way to handle a canteen's just to tilt it up and take a swig. But if you've got to have a cup, my coffee cup's in one of the saddlebags."

After another few moments of fumbling, Nellie found the cup. She settled down on the seat, with the cup in her lap, and took the cover off the canteen to pour. Just as she tilted it, the buggy wheel bumped over a rock, and water gushed out, wetting her skirt.

Longarm said mildly, "It'll dry. But the next time I tell you something, maybe you'll understand that I've got a reason."

"That was an accident. I'm perfectly capable of pouring myself a cupful of water."

"And wasting as much as you drink. There are times when all the money in the world can't buy a man a sip of water out here, Nellie. That's one reason we drink right out of the canteen, so we don't waste any. Try it my way, now."

Nellie made no reply, but she put the cup aside and lifted the canteen to her mouth. She swallowed several times, replaced the cap, and put the canteen back on the seat, still without speaking.

Longarm let a few minutes pass before he said, "Can't say I blame you for being mad. I came down pretty hard on you back there. In front of Frank, too, and I guess that made it worse."

"You certainly weren't very nice," she agreed. "Especially after I'd gone to such a lot of trouble to find you and bring you Short Bear's message."

"All right. I'll admit I was riled, but maybe I was thinking about what could've happened to you. I'd've blamed myself forevermore, Nellie, if a bunch of Indians like the ones that jumped Frank had taken out after you."

"I did have my gun, you know."

He smiled. "Are you sure you'd've remembered to use it? Or would you've tried to fight 'em off with your valise?"

"Now, that's not fair! I just got excited."

"What I'm trying to make you see, Nellie, is that you can't let yourself get excited when you're in a tight spot. You've got to think one jump ahead all the time, keep an edge on the other fellow."

"I won't forget again," she promised. "And I guess I did do a foolish thing, coming up here alone. But I got here safely, and there's no need for you to keep on being angry with me. Now, will you tell me what you've found out about the land-grab plan?"

"It's a bigger thing than I'd figured. Scott Forest—that's the fellow you heard talking on the train—has already done a lot of bribing to ease the way for him and his friends to take over the Indian range land in the Cherokee Outlet, and and I guess in the unallotted land south of it. To tell you the truth, I don't know how big it is, yet. I know there're army officers involved, and I guess there'd have to be a bunch from the Bureau of Indian Affairs and maybe some of the licensed traders, too."

"How can you go about finding out? It'd be harder to get them to tell you anything than it is to talk to an Indian."

"Frank Turner managed to get us on the inside, mainly because he heard about it when he was working for Forest, and between us, we got Forest convinced that we had to be taken in, too."

"How on earth did you do that?"

"Oh, just by letting Forest think I was a lot more important than I am, and that I've got a lot of cash that I can throw into the bribe pot, hid away in a lot of different banks."

Nellie shook her head. "You know, Longarm, your job's a lot like mine. We both get a hint that there's something wrong somewhere, and we start looking under carpets and behind doors until we bring it out into the open."

"There's one big difference, though."

"What's that?" she asked.

"You can print your story without having hard and fast evidence. If I spring mine before I've got proof that'll stand up in a court of law, somebody's going to peel my hide off me and nail it to a barn door."

"Well, I've got to be sure of my facts, too, before I write my story. There are libel laws, you know."

"Sure. But losing money and losing skin are two different things."

"Do you think you can get the evidence you'll need?"

"I intend to, somehow. After I find Eddie Boyle, of course."

They fell silent after that, lulled by the steady echoing of the horse's hooves on the dirt road and the swaying of the buggy as it rolled along. Once, out of the corner of his eye, Longarm saw Nellie sway and start to slide off the seat, fast asleep, He nudged her as though by accident, and she woke with a start, glanced at him, and sat erect for a while. Soon, though, she began, to doze again.

Longarm put aside the plans that had been occupying his thoughts and turned his mind to the immediate future. He kicked himself mentally for forgetting that Nellie had had no sleep the night before. He realized that he should have stopped to let her rest instead of pushing on, as he and Frank had decided to do the night before. Nellie's arrival with news that Boyle's woman was at the Pawnee camp had altered the situation completely.

Longarm changed his mind about pushing on through the night. It would be better, he decided as he glanced at Nellie dozing in the bouncing buggy seat, to stop somewhere while it was still dark and cool, so Nellie could sleep for the rest of the night. If they got started again before sunup, they'd reach Buffalo Creek in the late afternoon. With any luck, they'd sight the Pawnee hunting camp before dark. He began to watch the sides of the road—the land was as visible as by day in the bright moonlight—looking for a sheltered place where they could pull off and camp. It didn't have to be much of a place, he told himself, but they'd need water and maybe a little firewood.

Almost an hour passed before he saw a spot that looked promising. They crossed over a small creek, and when he slowed the buggy, he saw a pool of water gleaming brightly in the moonlight, sending silver reflections through the twigs of an encircling growth of sandplum bushes. At one side of the pool, a giant cottonwood tree spread its branches. He turned the horse, and the buggy lurched and creaked. Beside him, Nellie stirred and awoke.

"What's the matter?" she asked sleepily.

"Nothing's the matter. It's just time to give the horse a long rest. Us, too, as far as that goes."

"I thought we weren't going to stop until morning."

"I changed my mind," Longarm said, as he found a gap in the sandplum bushes and guided the horse through it. He reined in and the buggy's creaking ceased. The silence of the night was complete. "Come on, now," he told Nellie. "I'll spread out my blankets for you to rest on."

"What about you?" she asked.

"I'll use my groundcloth. That's all I need."

While Longarm was busy arranging the blankets for Nellie, smoothing a place on the ground, clearing it of stones and fallen cottonwood branches and bolls, she vanished for a few minutes behind the sheltering brush. When she returned, she watched him work in silence for a moment, and when he began spreading the stiff canvas tarpaulin for his own bed, a few feet distant from hers, she said, "The ground looks pretty hard. Are you sure you'll be comfortable?"

"More than you will, I'll bet. I'm used to this. You ain't."

"Funny, I don't feel at all sleepy, now that we've stopped."

"Don't worry. You will, as soon as you lay down. Come on, now. Settle in and get back to sleep. We've still got a lot of road ahead of us."

Obediently, Nellie lay down and stretched out. "The ground's not as hard as I was afraid it'd be," she told him. Then she yawned. "I guess I will go to sleep again."

Longarm was settling down on his own bed. He said, "Sure you will." He watched her for a moment, until her eyes closed and she relaxed, then he fished a cheroot out of his pocket and lit it. He took off his gunbelt and laid it beside his head, the bolstered Colt handy to a reaching hand, his hat covering the gun to protect it from the moisture that always condenses on metal exposed at night. He folded his vest for a pillow, but didn't take off his boots. Then he lay down and stretched, his cheroot clenched in his teeth, his mind busily perfecting the sketchy outline of the plan that had come to him a short time earlier. He was still thinking, his eyes slitted against the moonlight, when he finished the cheroot, stubbed its butt out in the gravelly soil beside the tarp, and drifted off to sleep.

A rustling, light and faint as a breeze, snapped Longarm awake. He lay unmoving long enough to identify the sound as being the whisper of cloth on cloth, not the heavier rasping of buckskin garments, then cracked his eyelids open just enough to confirm his impression. Nellie was standing at the edge of the tarpaulin, looking down at him. The moon was behind her, putting her face in deep shadow, and he was unable to see her expression. He lay still, thinking she'd gotten up to go again to the privacy behind the sandplum bushes, and not wanting to embarrass her if that was the case. She made no move to go on, though, but just stood gazing at him. In a moment, she settled down quietly beside him on the tarp.

Longarm kept his eyes closed, not even allowing himself to peer through his slitted lids now that she was so close. He felt the touch of a fingertip, as gentle as a butterfly's wing, pass along his cheek and explore the stubble on his chin. Another rustle of cloth told him Nellie was moving, and for a moment he thought she was getting up. The brushing of lips, hot on his, told him he was wrong. He did not pull away, but did open his eyes. Nellie's eyes were almost touching his; the closeness made him a bit dizzy until she lifted her head.

"You don't mind, do you?" she asked, her voice low.

"Mind what?" Longarm thought it wise to act as though he'd been awakened by the kiss.

"That I've come over to be with you. I woke up and lay there looking at you, and all of a sudden I wanted to be here beside you."

"No," he replied. "I don't mind. I ain't sure you know what you're doing, though."

"I know exactly what I'm doing," she contradicted him. "Goodness, you don't think I'm a blushing virgin, do you? Though I suppose you could, the way you've been acting, treating me like a little girl."

"Listen, Nellie, I'm a lot older than you are. Maybe you do seem like a little girl to me."

"Well, I'm not. I haven't thought of myself as a little girl for—for as long as I can remember, I suppose. And I haven't been a virgin since I was fourteen and started playing house with a boy from the neighborhood who was a few years older."

"I see. Or maybe I don't, yet."

"Let me show you, then."

Nellie bent to kiss him again. This time she thrust her tongue between Longarm's lips, and he knew at once that she was telling him the truth. She shifted a bit to lean heavily on him, crushing her small, firm breasts against his chest. He felt her hand moving down his belly to his groin, where it began exploring, squeezing, stroking. Longarm responded.

Nellie broke the kiss and raised her head above his. "That's better. But I'm not sure what I'm feeling down there is real."

"It's real enough." Longarm was almost ready to accept Nellie as a woman now, but he still hesitated, out of a lingering concern over her youth.

"I'm real, too," she said. She brought her hand up to grasp his, put his palm flat against her breasts, and then began to unbutton her bodice. "Find out for yourself."

Longarm slid his hand into the opening of her blouse and felt a breast, no bigger than an apple and as firm as one, with a budding nipple thrusting itself against his fingers.

"You see?" she asked. Her fingers were busy now on his jeans, unbuckling his belt, loosening the buttons of his fly. He felt her reach in and free his erection, still not full, that had begun to rise with his initial kiss. Her hands, soft and curious, stroked him gently. "Oh, my!" she breathed.

Longarm sensed her hesitation. "This is the time to stop, if you're not sure you know what we're heading toward," he said.

"Damn it, I don't want to stop! Quit treating me like a doll! Can't you get it through your head that I'm a woman and want to be loved like one?"

Suddenly, Nellie stood up and began dropping her clothes—blouse, skirt, chemise, pantaloons. At some point, she had shed her shoes, and she quickly pulled off her stockings. Then she stood above him, naked in the moonlight, a nymph of a girl-woman. Her body was at once slight and full. Longarm let his eyes travel from her smooth, round shoulders, over her pert, saucy breasts, and down to her spreading woman's hips. His gaze lingered on the fine, blonde fur of her groin, then continued down slimly tapering legs that might have been those of a boy.

"Look at me!" Nellie commanded. "Am I a woman, or not?"

"Oh, you are," he assured her. "There ain't any doubt a-tall."

"Then treat me like a woman!" she pleaded.

She dropped to her knees beside him. Longarm sat up, picking her up with strong, hard hands under her armpits, lifting her as he rose himself, and when he got to his knees, he swung her around to face him.

He lowered her to the rough tarpaulin, on her back. Nellie raised her legs and spread them, guiding him into her. Longarm lunged. She cried out when he entered her, a shriek of pleasure that held an overtone of pain. He fell forward heavily, sinking deeper, feeling her inner warmth increase wetly. Then he began to move, his hesitation gone now that he was buried in her. His thrusts were short, fast, and forceful. Each time he lunged, Nellie uttered a high, small moan of pained delight. She began to bounce beneath him, her slim hips and small, firm buttocks rising from the canvas with increasing speed until she started shaking uncontrollably. Her moans became an ecstatic sobbing as she shook with a final spasm and then went limp.

Her climax had come in minutes, and Longarm was still far from his. He stayed inside her, lying motionless now to let her rest, but pushing his hips hard against hers. Nellie lay back with her eyes closed and her mouth open, her white, perfect teeth glistening in the frame of her red rosebud lips. Longarm leaned forward to kiss her. She responded languidly at first, then her tongue grew busy, twining with his. She rubbed her upper lip against the bristles of his mustache, her small chin against the stubble of his square jaw, a bubbling sound of pleasure rising from her throat.

They broke the kiss, gasping, and when she'd taken a few deep breaths, Nellie whispered, "I still feel you inside me. Oh, God, but it's so delicious! When can we start all over and do it again?"

"Honey, we ain't stopped yet. That is, I ain't. But if you're tired out—"

"No, no!" she gasped. "At least, not too tired to want you to go on."

She stretched as best she could under the weight of Longarm's body. He felt her moving under him and raised himself enough to give her the freedom to choose the position she was seeking. She spread her legs more widely, opening herself to accommodate him.

Now Longarm began to move once more. This time he moved in slow-paced strokes, almost withdrawing from her, holding himself poised with hips raised for a moment before plunging deeply and steadily into her. Nellie lay supine for a few moments, unmoving, until she could no longer merely savor the sensations she was feeling, but needed to take part in them. She clamped her legs around Longarm's back. He was compelled to shorten the length of his strokes, but not their depth, and each time he raised himself, he lifted Nellie briefly with him and then fell on her with all of his weight as he lunged down into her.

She started to moan again, soft, throaty cries lost in the

vastness of the moonlit night. Beneath him, Longarm could feel her muscles tightening. He began moving faster, his own climax building. Nellie's body began quivering afresh. Longarm moved faster. He, too, was building to the bursting point, and when he heard Nellie's moans flow into sobs, and felt tremors rippling through her slight body almost without interruption, he speeded up involuntarily, then deliberately, timing himself, waiting to meet her explosion with his own. They came together, and Longarm's rasping breath softened as he fell forward and Nellie's cries died away.

He shifted to take his weight off her; Nellie clasped her arms around his torso and refused to let him move. "I like to feel your weight on me almost as much as I like feeling you in me. It's a good feeling. You're a strange man, Longarm. But a nice one, I guess."

Nellie tried to shift position, but his weight hampered her. Longarm raised himself and lay down beside her. He looked at her; in the soft light, she looked younger than ever. Somehow, Nellie read his thought.

"You're thinking of me as a little girl again, aren't you?"

"I guess. Sort of hard not to, you look so much like one."

"Didn't you find out that I'm not?" When he didn't reply, she went on, "Don't worry about me. I've been with—well, maybe not as many men as you have with women, but enough so that I know what sex is all about."

"It just seems funny."

She laughed huskily. "You don't know much about me, yet."

"You feel like telling me?" he asked.

"Why not? You know how old I am, I told you that when you bought me the little pistol. But—well, I guess I'm what they call precocious. Somebody who grows up fast. It seems that I knew what I wanted to do even when I was only ten or eleven years old."

He shook his head. "That's a mite younger than I was when I found out what I wanted to do. Of course, I started growing up fast when I ran away to go to war."

"How old were you then?"

"Just turned fifteen. A big, overgrown boy from West Virginia."

"Maybe that's why you feel so much older than you are. I've often thought that war makes a person grow up very fast."

He sighed. "It does that."

They were quiet for a moment, then Nellie said, "I don't know why I grew up so fast. Maybe it was because I was reading things that were too old for me, like *Woodhull and Claflin's Weekly*. Did you ever read that magazine, Longarm?"

Longarm shook his head. "I never heard of it before. But I'm not much for reading, Nellie. Never was."

"Two sisters put it out, Victoria Woodhull and Tennessee Claflin. They believed in women being equal to men in every way—being able to work at any job, to vote and run for office, to have lovers the way men have their women—a lot of things that aren't exactly popular."

"Well, I'll give you credit, Nellie. You've made a real good start at doing those things, if that's what you want to do."

Her violet eyes shone in the moonlight, and her voice vibrated with raw energy. "It *is*. Why, I'm just beginning to live! There are so many things I want to do! I want to be known as a good reporter, and I've made a pretty good start, I think. But I want to be a war correspondent when there's another war. I want to travel." She paused to think, then said, "There's a book I read not very long ago, by a Frenchman named Verne. He worked out a way that his hero could travel around the world in eighty days. Some day I'm going to do it in less time than that."

"I wish you luck. It doesn't look to me like you need luck, though, the way you've come as far as you have, and still so young."

"Damn you, Longarm, there you go again!" Nellie rolled over and straddled Longarm, her thighs across his stomach, while she pounded on his chest with her small fists. He kept himself from laughing, and captured her wrists. Holding them firmly, he pulled her to himself and kissed her. "You took what I said the wrong way," he told her when he let her go. "I was trying to pay you a compliment."

"All right. I'm sorry. I'm too sensitive about being young, I suppose, because I know I am. But not *too* young." Her hand crept behind her, feeling for him. She shifted her body down-

ward until she sat squatting on his thighs. Under the gentle
stroking of her hand, Longarm began to grow hard once more.
Nellie said, "Just the same, all men need a lesson now and then
about how women feel." She rose high enough to guide him
into her and sank down slowly. He felt her begin to twitch with
anticipation. Leaning forward, she kissed him lightly before
bringing her body erect again. "Now, then. How does it feel to
be on the bottom?"

Longarm didn't spoil her pleasure by telling her she wasn't
the first woman he'd known who enjoyed the sensation of
mounting a man. He said, "It feels real good. Go on, do whatever pleases you."

Nellie rotated her hips while moving her body up and down
on his rigid shaft. She began experimenting by varying the
speed of her movements and the angle of her torso.

"This pleases me," she panted. "Do you enjoy it, too?"

"Sure I do."

Longarm began caressing her breasts, which were so small
and firm that they didn't dangle forward and flop about, as did
those on fleshier and more mature women. Nellie gasped and
bounced faster, and small, urgent whimpers came from her
throat. Longarm rolled her over and took control again.

At his first deep plunges, Nellie cried aloud. Her spasm
began, and Longarm prolonged it by breaking his rhythm
now and then, holding her back until he saw she could wait no
longer. He took her through her orgasm with firm, easy thrusts,
but when her climax came and she sagged limp and unrespon-
sive, he did not stop. He slowed the tempo of his stroking, but
kept going into her without pausing until her muscles tautened
and she came back to shrieking, trembling life. Then, in a final
burst of passionate power, he drove faster and even more
deeply until his control gave way and he joined Nellie in a final
tremor that left them both gasping breathlessly, with muscles
like water, sprawled in a tangle of limbs in the warm night.

When she could speak again, Nellie breathed, "Oh, Longarm, I never dreamed it could be as good as this! I thought I'd
enjoyed it before, but I didn't know until now what it could be
like!"

Longarm softly kissed her puckered rosebud mouth. "I'm

glad you feel good, honey. Now, we'd better sleep some more.
We've got a lot of riding to do when it's daylight."

She cuddled against him, her head on his shoulder, her
body pressing close. He put an arm around her and smoothed
her cheek with his rough hand. She went to sleep almost at
once, and Longarm slept a few moments later.

Chapter 10

Longarm awoke first. There was a gray line cutting across the dark sky, a promise of sunrise soon to come. He disengaged himself gently from Nellie's arms and stood at the edge of the groundcloth looking down at her while he rearranged his clothing and strapped on his gunbelt. They'd shared his folded vest for a pillow, and he didn't disturb her by trying to move it. The horse whinnied gently, and Longarm took off its tether to let it move around, to graze and drink. He went into the sandplum bushes to drain his night-filled bladder, then came back and squatted at the edge of the pond to wash.

Shaking his hands dry, he looked around for firewood. There were sun-bleached limbs scattered generously under the great cottonwood tree, the deadfall of years past. He gathered enough to build a small, quick fire. While he worked, he found himself wishing that he'd been more sparing with the bottle of rye he'd bought at the sutler's in New Cantonment, but he and Frank had drained it during the long hours of the day they'd spent waiting for the gelding's leg to mend.

Moving as quietly as possible, he rummaged in his saddlebags for the packet of ground coffee that he kept in reserve against such times as these, when he didn't want to waste time pounding coffee beans. He filled the coffeepot with water, and set it on the fire to brew. Taking hardtack and jerky from the saddlebags, he sliced the jerky thinly, then dipped the pieces in the pond before putting them in the skillet. He laid the rounds of hardtack on top of the meat and covered the skillet with a tin plate before putting it beside the coffeepot on the fire. By the time the coffee brewed, the hardtack and jerky would have steamed soft enough to chew without the danger of breaking a tooth.

In the east, the line of gray had widened to a band that reached well up into the sky by the time Longarm's breakfast preparations were finished. Dawn light was filtering into the clearing. Longarm hunkered down on his saddle and gazed at the pleasant sight of Nellie sprawled naked on the tarpaulin, still deeply asleep. The small sounds he'd made preparing their food hadn't disturbed her.

That girl's a question inside of a puzzle, Longarm told himself. *She acts grown-up, but she really ain't. It'll take a few years before she gets as smart as she thinks she is, but for the rest of her life she'll never think she's as smart as she does right now.*

She's a woman in lots of ways, his thoughts ran on. *Except she's at the selfish age. She wants what she wants right off, and goes out full-tilt to get it. Only she ain't learned to give, yet, and folks who don't give as much as they get wind up making trouble for themselves and for lots of other folks, too.*

Last night was mighty nice, though. I've got to watch myself. If I get in too deep with her, my mind ain't going to be on what I've got to do here in the Nation. I ain't going to let her drag me into bed with her again. She just doesn't understand how things are out here. But then, most Easterners don't.

Nellie sat up suddenly. "You're doing some serious thinking," she said. "I've been watching you for the last minute or so. You look worried this morning, Longarm. Is something wrong?"

"Not a thing. Guess I was just busy planning in my mind what-all I've got to do next."

"I hope your plans include breakfast. I'm as hungry as a wolf."

Nellie stood up and stretched. Her slight figure grew taut, lifting her breasts and straightening her boyish thighs. Her flat stomach arced in below her ribs and swelled almost imperceptibly before it ended at her blonde pubic fringe. She saw Longarm watching her.

"Do you like me?" she asked.

"Sure I do. I've said it to you before, ain't I?"

"You're not feeling badly about last night?"

"There's no reason I should, is there? Like you told me, you're a full-grown woman."

She smiled. "I'm glad you think so at last." Her eyes caught the skillet. "What're you cooking? I hope it's good."

"It's nothing except what I carry—hardtack and jerky. Got 'em steaming so we can chew 'em easier. And the coffee's about made."

"I'll hurry and dress. I know you want to leave as soon as we eat. Don't worry, I'll only take a minute."

She was as good as her word. She disappeared briefly into the sandplum bushes, then came out to the pond to wash, walking with the tender soles of her feet turned inward on the rough ground to where her clothes were scattered. She dressed with a minimum of fuss and joined Longarm by the fire. He got up and motioned for her to sit on the saddle. He took the skillet off the fire and snapped away the plate that had covered it.

Nellie frowned. "Is that what hardtack and jerky are?"

"Best I can do. Don't run it down till you've tasted it. It's a lot better'n it looks."

After she'd taken a few bites she was smiling. "It is good. Or maybe I'm just too hungry to care. Do we have coffee cups?"

"Just one. We'll have to take turns drinking." He filled the cup and they passed it back and forth while they ate. Scouring the pan with earth, Longarm sloshed it through the water in the pond and held it over the coals until it dried. He replaced the breakfast gear in the saddlebags and threw them and the saddle into the buggy's bed.

"If you'll top off the canteen, I'll hitch up," he said. "If we don't run across a streak of the bad, we'll hit Buffalo Creek just before dark tonight."

"You said you were working up a scheme to get the Indian woman to help you find Eddie Boyle. You can tell me about it on the way."

"No, Nellie. I'll ask you to excuse me from telling you what I aim to try. You'll just have to wait, the same as I will, and see how it works out."

"Now that's just silly, Longarm. What are you afraid of? There's nobody I could possibly tell about it."

"Oh, it ain't that," he said vaguely.

"Don't tell me you're superstitious!"

"Maybe you'd call it that. I don't. But that's neither here

nor there. All I know is, I keep my schemes to myself until it's time to work 'em. That way there's nobody to blame but my own fool self if they don't pan out."

In spite of Nellie's intermittent prodding during the long day that ended just before sunset at the juncture of Buffalo Creek and the Cimarron River, Longarm kept silent about his plans. When he'd finished checking their location on his map, to make sure the stream was the right one, he said, "Now, Nellie, you listen to me real careful. I'm going to tell you what you've got to do to make this scheme of mine work, and you've got to promise me you won't go off on your own, or try to change anything I tell you to do."

Nellie had been somewhat subdued by the day's experience. She hadn't expected Longarm to withstand her persuasiveness; it had seldom failed her before. She said, "All right, Longarm. I get the feeling that this is important to you. I'll give you my word that I won't do anything you don't tell me to."

"It's important enough," he agreed. "I don't know how many Pawnee warriors are in this camp we're looking for, but if there're only a few of 'em, I'm still outnumbered. It might mean my scalp if my plan doesn't work out."

"I've promised. Go ahead."

While they traveled, Longarm had studied the countryside. It was more thickly wooded than the more southerly part they'd come from, though the distance between the Darlington agency and the Cimarron at that point was little more than a hundred miles. Trees were clumped thickly along the riverbank. Cottonwood, salt cedar, oak, and bois d'arc grew in mottes that began at the banks of the stream and extended for a wide belt on either side, as much as a mile in some places. As far as they could see to the west along Buffalo Creek, its banks shared the character of the valley of the bigger stream.

Longarm told Nellie, "I'm going to find a place where we can put the wagon, a place where it'll be hid so that nobody'll be able to spot it. After we do that, I'll tell you the rest."

He turned the buggy and guided the horse up the bank of the creek, moving very slowly and studying the terrain carefully.

Buffalo Creek was bigger than the small rills that pass for creeks, and often rivers, in the prairie country. Longarm followed the stream until he came to an almost-vanished trace made long ago by wagons and horses. The faint, overgrown ruts approached the creek at right angles, vanished in the water, and reappeared, equally faint, on the other side. Longarm turned the buggy onto the trace and urged the horse through the water. The creek was shallow here, barely covering the rims of the buggy's wheels. He let the horse pull up on the opposite side of the creek and reined in.

"What's the matter? Why are we stopping?" Nellie asked.

"You'll see." Longarm handed her the reins. "Now, you hold these, but let 'em slack when I tell you to."

He got out of the buggy and walked to the horse's head. Holding the cheek strap, he called to Nellie to let the reins slacken, and guided the horse backward into the creek, turning it so that the buggy's wheels stayed in the water and the horse stood in the middle of the waterway, heading upstream, Longarm splashed back to the buggy and got in. Watching the water carefully, he started the animal up the creek at a slow, steady pace. They covered a hundred yards or more before he found a turn-out to his liking, a rocky area that would show no trace of the wheels when he urged the horse up the bank to dry land.

Nellie nodded. "Anybody who sees the buggy's tracks will think we crossed the creek back there. Isn't that right?"

"Right as rain. I ain't sure it'd fool an old Indian, but a lot of 'em ain't the trackers they used to be. Even some of the older ones have kind of forgotten what they used to know. Anyway, for the time it took, it was worth a try."

"Exactly why did you do that, Longarm?" Nellie asked suspiciously. "You're not planning to start some kind of one-man war against that Pawnee camp, are you?"

"Why, of course not. Only as soon as it gets dark, I do aim to scout it a mite before we ride into it. If they catch on that I'm snooping and take after me, I don't want 'em to run across you and the buggy."

"You mean you're going to leave me by myself in this place? And at night?"

"That's the way of it," he told her curtly.

"I don't think I like that idea a bit."

"Nellie, I'll tell you this flat-out. It don't make no difference whether you like it or not. It was your idea to come along with me, and I don't aim to let you hold me back from what

I've got to do. As a matter of fact, this whole shenanigan is because I've got you with me."

She frowned. "I don't understand. How could my being here possibly make any difference to what you do?"

"I doubt that you'd understand if I was to try to explain, which I ain't got time to do right now. I've got to get this buggy hid and scout on upstream to get a look at that Pawnee camp before it gets too dark. But it ain't likely you'll be bothered while you're waiting for me to get back. Pawnees are like the Kiowas and Comanches. They don't fancy moving around much at night. It goes against their medicine."

Obviously unhappy, Nellie sat silently, a frown on her face, while Longarm held the buggy on its course along the creek. He almost passed the kind of place he'd been looking for, a motte of closely spaced trees growing out of a thicket of underbrush. He made the horse dance and the buggy swerve wildly as he urged the animal into the cover of the motte. Close to its center, he pulled up, wrapped the reins around the whip socket, and dropped to the ground.

"You just sit here a minute while I go see how good the buggy's hid," he told Nellie.

She heard him pushing through the brush. There was a long silence, then a loud splashing from the creek. After another spell of stillness, Longarm came back through the sandplum bushes and salt cedar growth, so silently this time that Nellie didn't hear him. She thought she was still alone until his form materialized beside the wagon. Startled, she leaped up with a cry of alarm.

"You did that on purpose!" she said accusingly. "You intended to scare me!"

"Yes, you're right, Nellie, I did. I wanted to show you how easy it is for somebody who knows how to move to take you by surprise. I want you to be extra careful while I'm gone. When I come back, I'll whistle like a meadowlark before I come up."

"What does a meadowlark sound like?"

Longarm demonstrated, then repeated the birdcall. "Now, you be careful," he cautioned her. "There's no way of telling how long I'll be gone, because I don't know how far upstream that camp is. But I've got to go right fast, because I want to look at it while there's still daylight left."

"Go ahead, Longarm." Nellie's voice was cool. "I'll be here when you get back, I promise you."

Longarm followed the north bank of Buffalo Creek, where the ground was a little higher than on the south side. He moved fast but with caution, dodging through the brush, stopping now and then to listen and to sniff the light twilight breeze. It was the wind that gave him his first hint that the camp was near. A vagrant gust brought him the scent of woodsmoke and cooking food. It was rapidly growing dark, and he approached the area faster than he should have. He saw the tipis, a score of them clustered in a bend of the creek, just in time to stop before he got too close.

Because the weather was still warm, the Pawnees' cooking fires had been kindled outside the tipis. In the waning light, details were difficult to see through the brush cover Longarm was using as a screen. After he'd watched a while, Longarm put the number of Indians at forty or fifty, almost equally divided among men and women, with a few older children. He saw no babies or crawling youngsters in the family groups that were clustered about their fires, eating.

On the prairie beyond the camp, he saw what he'd really been looking for: the Pawnee horses. There were more than a hundred animals in the herd. From the way they moved, he surmised that most of them were hobbled. Mustangs predominated among the horses, but there were a few, bigger than the rest, that displayed the results of crossbreeding the native mustangs with the bigger, heavier strains favored by the army and the ranchers.

Longarm looked for guards around the herd, but saw none. He smiled to himself. He hadn't expected the herd to be guarded. The Indians usually kept enough of their idle horses hobbled to discourage them from moving far, counting on the herd instinct to keep the others close by, and they'd gradually abandoned their former careful habit of setting herd guards because of the relative peace that was maintained between the tribes in the Nation. During the years when they'd moved freely and fought regularly, tribe against tribe, horse stealing had been an extension of their warfare, an honorable and planned activity. In pre-reservation days, no tribe would have left a herd unwatched, since fledgling warriors began their training by raiding the herds of enemy tribes.

Longarm started back to the motte where he'd left Nellie and the buggy. Before he'd covered the distance, darkness set in. The moon had not yet risen, and starlight did little to relieve the quickly descending blackness. When he finally reached the motte, he stopped at its edge and whistled like a meadowlark, then repeated the signal to be sure Nellie would be expecting his approach. His eyes had long ago become adjusted to the darkness, and his progress through the brush was silent. When the black silhouette of the wagon became visible, he signaled for the third time. Longarm didn't want Nellie to be startled into using her derringer. A yard from the buggy, he spoke in a normal tone.

"Nellie?"

"I'm here. And hungry. And tired. I tried to sleep, but couldn't."

"You could've eaten. You know where the grub is."

"I couldn't start a fire. I didn't have any matches."

"It wouldn't've made any difference. We've got to eat cold, anyhow. It's too near the camp to risk a fire. The Pawnees are sort of like the Comanches one way; they don't do much prowling at night, but there's always a chance that some of 'em might be going by late on their way back to camp."

"They wouldn't hurt us, would they?"

"I don't reckon the Pawnees would. Cheyennes or Kiowas or Comanches might. But don't let it fret you. I sleep light."

"Longarm, you've been so awfully mysterious about what you intend to do. Don't you think it's time to tell me?"

"No, not quite yet. You'll see, before too long."

He busied himself getting out food and showing Nellie how to eat cold jerky and hardtack. He shaved thin slivers from the rubbery sun-dried meat, crumbled the hardtack rounds with his knife butt, and taught her to hold a few slivers of jerky and some crumbs of hardtack in her mouth with a sip of water until they'd softened enough to be chewed. Nellie was so hungry that she ate without protesting the clumsy technique she had to follow. It took them a long time to finish their meal. The moon had risen, and to their night-dilated eyes, even the smallest details of their surroundings were clearly visible.

After he'd stowed the food away, Longarm told Nellie, "It won't be so spooky for you while I'm gone, now that the moon's up."

"You're not going off again?" she protested. "I thought we'd have the rest of the night together, like—"

"Nellie, honey, you know I'd enjoy that." Longarm realized with some surprise that he wasn't lying, in spite of the resolution he'd made earlier in the day. There was a strange little-girl quality in her eyes, and the moonlight gave her piquant face the same appeal he'd felt for it before. He went on, soberly and quietly, "I won't be away long. I know just where to go, this time."

"You're going back to the Indian camp, aren't you?"

"Sure. Where else is there to go?"

"What are you going to do, Longarm? Kidnap that woman?"

"Nope. I'm going to steal us a horse."

"But we've got a horse! And after you told me about horse thieves being hanged—"

"Let me try to get you to see it like the Indians would, Nellie. Men don't ride in buggies, they ride horses. Women ride in buggies. If I was to go into that camp sitting beside you in this buggy, the Pawnees would laugh me down. If I go in on a horse, they'll listen to me with respect. I ain't got a riding horse, so I've got to steal one of theirs."

"But aren't you afraid they'll recognize it?"

"I'll be real disappointed if they don't. I'm counting on 'em knowing I took it out of their herd, and me riding in on it'll make me a big man to 'em."

"That's just plain silly!" she exclaimed.

"No, it ain't. Indians respect a man with guts enough to take one of their horses, and if he's got gall enough to ride it into their own camp and face 'em down, they think he's about as big as a man can get. It's the way they are. You'll see, tomorrow."

Either Nellie was too tired and upset to argue, or she understood that nothing she said would change Longarm's mind. She sat silently in the buggy while he got his bridle and inspected his Colt and derringer closely in the moonlight. When he assured her again that she'd be perfectly safe while he was gone, her reply was curt and cold. Longarm wasted no time trying to soften her mood. He shrugged and started back for the Pawnee encampment.

This time, he moved along the south side of the creek and followed it outside the brake to the bend where the Pawnee herd grazed. He moved fast until he could see the animals ahead of him, then he stopped and examined the area around the horses. For all he knew, night guards could have moved into place while he'd been gone. He watched long enough to satisfy himself that there were none, then walked into the herd at an easy gait. Horses, he'd learned, weren't as likely to spook if a man approached them in a businesslike fashion instead of trying to sneak up on them.

A few of the animals shied away with startled snorts, but most of them ignored him. When they'd gotten used to his presence, Longarm began looking for the kind of animal he wanted. He ignored the roans and sorrels that made up most of the herd, and picked a roan-and-white paint, the kind of horse the Indians valued most, a showy animal. This one was beautifully marked. Its patches of color were defined sharply, it had a flowing white mane on a dark neck, and its forehead bore a distinctive blaze shaped like an arrowhead.

Moving quietly, he worked closer and closer to the paint. From a long stride distant, he spoke to it in low, persuasive tones. The horse ignored him. Longarm took a short step toward it and the horse took a step away. For several minutes, man and horse matched moves with the precision of dancers performing a classical ballet. Each of Longarm's steps had a purpose. He worked the horse through the herd, until it stood penned against the brush that enclosed the pasture area in a large natural loop. There the paint stopped, pawing the ground a bit nervously. Longarm stopped, too, and said soothing things in a low voice until the animal stood still.

Now Longarm moved closer. The paint walled its eyes, but let him come to its side. Longarm patted it on the shoulder. The horse stood quietly. Slipping the bridle from his belt where he'd been carrying it, Longarm made an open H-loop of the reins. He extended his patting from the paint's shoulder up to its neck. Whispering in its ear, saying nothing, but soothing the horse with his calm tone, Longarm caught its nose and jaw in the H-loop and pulled it tight.

Feeling the improvised halter, the pony tried to rear, but Longarm set his heels to its flanks and pulled its head down. The paint was also trying to whinny, but with Longarm's hand over its nose and the halter keeping its jaws together, the sound ended as a faint burble in its throat. Longarm waited until the horse had stopped struggling, took his hand off its nose, and bending down, cut the hobble free. The paint had been hobbled Indian-style, foreleg to hind leg, and a single slash freed its feet. With its feet free, the animal accepted the pressure of the halter.

Years had passed since Longarm had ridden bareback, but there was no other way to go. He knew that only a small number of Indian horses are broken to saddle and stirrups. He vaulted onto the paint's back. The pony reared, and he struck it sharply on the neck with his fist. The horse took off at a gallop, and Longarm let it run, hoping the noise it made going through the brake wouldn't arouse the Pawnee camp.

There was no pursuit. He let the paint run for three or four miles before bringing it under control with a relentless pressure on the reins. The paint was tiring by this time, and Longarm was far from feeling fresh himself. He turned the horse, and it accepted his pressure. He reined in and the animal slowed its pace. When Longarm guided it back toward Buffalo Creek, the paint responded readily. He kept it at a walk until he reached the motte where Nellie waited. At the edge of the brush, he pulled up and whistled the meadowlark call. Then he forced the animal through the growth; it pushed its way into the clearing without hesitation.

Nellie was standing beside the buggy when Longarm pulled the paint up. He sat on its back for a moment, then slid off. The pony, tired to the point of exhaustion, stood quietly.

"You really did steal a horse!" Nellie gasped.

"That's what I went to do," he replied evenly.

"I still don't understand why you took such a risk. Oh, I know, you explained how the Indians feel about it, but it just doesn't make sense to me," she pouted. The pout became a smile, and she added, "But I'm glad you got away with it."

"So am I. Now, let's get some rest. I don't figure on running into trouble when we go to the Pawnee camp, but I sure don't want to go there half asleep."

Longarm tethered the pony to one of the buggy's wheels and busied himself with the bedrolls. Within a few minutes they were asleep. Nellie did not come to his bed that night.

Chapter 11

Shortly before midmorning, Longarm and Nellie rode into the Pawnee hunting camp. Longarm had timed their arrival to take place when most of the men would be out on the prairie. Before they'd left the motte, he'd acted on a hunch and tried putting a saddle on the stolen pony. It had, he found, been broken to white men's riding gear.

Sitting erect on the paint, he led the way when they rode in. Nellie followed in the buggy, at a suitable distance behind. She had balked at first, wanting them to ride abreast, and it had taken a bit of harsh persuasion on Longarm's part to convince her how necessary it was to present the proper appearance. Even when she at last agreed, Nellie made it plain to him that she didn't relish the idea.

Their arrival created a stir. As he'd expected, there were no young men or youths in sight, just a few elders and a number of older children who were helping the women.

All the signs indicated that the hunt was going well. Strings of jerky were drying in the sun, there were hides stacked, waiting to be cured, and the women were busy at the stretching frames scraping other hides in the first step of curing them. The smell of rotting scraps wafted over the camp from the pile of bones that lay between the tipis and the creek. Longarm's stomach rolled in protest until he got used to the odor, and when he turned to look back he saw Nellie gagging into her handkerchief.

An oldster in deerskins came from between the tipis. He wore his hair in the old style of the tribe, a narrow, roached crest down the center of his head. Longarm didn't dismount, but made the peace sign, cupping his palms together at the level of his chin.

"You don't have to speak with your hands," the old Pawnee said. "I talk your tongue. But it is good to see a white man who knows the old ways. *Tura heh, idad.*" The old man made the peace sign himself, then told Longarm, "You are welcome. You can get off your horse."

Longarm knew only a word or two of Pawnee, but he'd learned that it was generally safe to repeat a greeting given by an Indian, no matter what language had been used. Echoing the old man's intonation as best he could, he said, *"Tura heh, idad,"* not knowing he was saying "It is good, brother." Then he dismounted.

"Why do you come here?" the old Pawnee asked.

Now, Longarm felt he was on safe ground. If he hadn't been welcome, he'd not have been invited to dismount. He began, "I come looking for—" but before he could finish, one of the young boys in the group that had assembled behind the greeter let out a shout and ran forward, pointing to the paint.

"Look!" he cried, "the *napi* rides Spotted Wolf's pony!"

An electric change took place in the Pawnees. They moved toward Longarm and the horse, talking excitedly in their own language, pointing and nodding agreement as one after another identified the horse. Longarm did not move, and he noticed that they did not crowd him too closely.

To the old man, Longarm said, "The boy might be right. My horse went lame, so I called for another one. If it belongs to one of your men, I'll give it back right here and now."

There was a brief flurry of chatter, louder than before, from the Indians. Longarm guessed that those who understood English were translating what he'd said for those who didn't. Then, with startling suddenness, the Indians fell silent.

"You called the horse?" the old man asked. Longarm nodded. The Pawnee asked, "Where were you?"

Longarm gestured vaguely to the south. A whisper ran through the crowd and the Indians started to back away.

"Tiwaruksti!" one of the Pawnee women called.

Turning to face his own people, the old man said a few words to them in Pawnee. Longarm could make out only the last one, which was repeated several times: *"Looah! Looah!"* Reluctantly, the Indians began walking back toward the tipis. They looked over their shoulders at Longarm as they went.

The old Pawnee stared hard at Nellie, in the buggy, then at Longarm. The faces of both men were without expression.

"You are a smart man, whoever you are," the old Pawnee said at last. "Maybe you do have big medicine, as Silver Cloud said, but I not think so. I believe the pony strayed from our herd, and you found it on the prairie. Will you tell me the truth about this?"

Longarm decided his position would be better if he did. "The truth is, I stole him out of your herd last night. My horse did go lame, and I knew what your people would think about me if I rode up in a buggy, with a woman."

"Hoh! Stealing a horse from a Pawnee herd so close to our camp is almost as much medicine as calling one to you!" the old man exclaimed. "You're right. We would have laughed at you if you'd ridden up like a woman, instead of on a horse, like a man should. Now. My name is Hawk Flies High. What's your name, and why are you here?"

"My name is Long. I'm a federal marshal, and I'm looking for a man who robbed a bank and did some murders in Colorado. I think one of your women knows where he's hiding. I have come to ask her."

"Who is the woman?"

"Her name is Late Morning Star."

"That one!" There was anger or disgust, Longarm couldn't decide which, in Hawk Flies High's tone. "She's not one of our people, but because her mother was Pawnee, we let her live with us."

"I heard she's here at the camp."

"You heard the truth."

"For all I know, the man I'm after might be here, too. Or he might have a hiding place close by."

"He is not with us. If he was hiding within a long day's ride of our camp, our hunters would have found him. They ride out every day."

"Has anybody else come asking for Late Morning Star?"

"No." Hawk Flies High was silent for a moment, then he added, "Late Morning Star doesn't usually come to our hunting camps. This year, she offered to come. Our women couldn't understand why."

"That gives me the idea that the man I'm after might be

planning to meet her here," Longarm said. "Will it be all right if I talk to the woman?"

"She is in the tipi of her brother, John Standing Elk. If you want to take your woman with you, the buggy will be safe. My people will fear your *tiwaruksti* too much to go near it."

"Thanks, Hawk Flies High. I'll get my saddle off your man's horse when I come back. I don't guess your people will think I'm a woman if I ride off in the buggy."

"You understand our people, Long. I wasn't wrong when I greeted you as a brother. You'll be welcomed at our camps any time."

The deputy touched the brim of his Stetson in salute. "I appreciate that. Now, I'd better tend to my business." Hawk Flies High nodded and turned to go. Longarm went over to the buggy, where Nellie had been watching with wide eyes.

She shook her head. "If I wrote this up as a newspaper story, nobody would believe it," she told Longarm. "I'm not sure I really believe it myself."

"I said Indians have got different ways from ours. That's why the government's had so much trouble with 'em. People back East have got the idea that Indians are just like us, but they're wrong."

"I'm beginning to see that." For the first time in almost two days, Nellie smiled at Longarm. "That's not all. The people in the East aren't like those out here in the West."

Longarm nodded. "I'll give you that. If you want to listen to what Late Morning Star says, come along."

"I certainly will. I'm curious to see what she's like."

Longarm asked a Pawnee boy to point out the tipi where Late Morning Star stayed, and he respectfully volunteered to lead them to it. The boy called her name, and added something in his own tongue that Longarm didn't understand. In a moment, Late Morning Star appeared in the open flap of the tipi. She looked curiously at Longarm and Nellie.

"What do you want with me?" Her English was good.

"All I want is to ask you a few questions," Longarm replied.

"About what?" The half-breed woman's straight, dark brows knit together. "Why should you come here to ask me anything?"

"Because I'm looking for Eddie Boyle. I know he's an old friend of yours. A real good friend, from what I hear."

While he waited for her answer, Longarm studied Late Morning Star. She was not as stocky as most Pawnee women, and her face was narrower than the average full-blooded members of the tribe. She wore the tribal dress, a shapeless deerskin garment that fell in a straight line from her shoulders to just below her knees. Her hair was long, and of a lustrous black, parted down the middle and gathered in two unbraided lengths that were draped over each shoulder down her breast. Her eyes were as dark as her hair, so dark that pupil and iris merged. Her nose was thin and flared at the nostrils; her lips were full and red, her chin broad.

She said at last, "Yes, I knew Eddie Boyle. A long time ago. Why do you want him?"

"I'm a deputy U.S. marshal. My name's Long. Boyle's wanted for murder and bank robbery up in Colorado."

"Why should you come to me with questions about him?" she asked with a note of hostility.

Longarm answered patiently, "Because Boyle was heading for the Nation. He told people he was going to join up with you here."

"Am I to blame for what other people say?"

The lawman held up a hand, palm forward, and waved the question away. "Nobody's blaming you for anything. Only if you do know where Boyle is, you can get in a passel of trouble if you don't tell me."

Late Morning Star said defiantly, "You don't scare me, Marshal. I haven't done anything to make me afraid of you. I don't know where Eddie is, but I'm not sure I'd tell you if I did. He hasn't done anything to hurt me."

"I'm not out to scare you," Longarm assured her, "and I didn't say you'd done anything wrong. There's a law against hiding a man who's wanted. The courts call it harboring a fugitive. Anybody who breaks the law's going to be in trouble."

"Your law doesn't apply to me," the woman said quickly. "I've answered your questions. If you don't want anything else, you can turn around and leave."

"If you hear anything about Boyle, will you send word to me?" Longarm asked. "I'll be at Fort Supply for a spell, and that ain't too far to send a message."

"I won't promise you anything." Late Morning Star turned abruptly and went back into the tipi.

Longarm had anticipated her answer. He turned to Nellie and said, "Well, I guess that's all she wrote. We might as well move along."

Walking back to the buggy, they were conscious of eyes staring at them. Nellie was doing some staring, too. Her eyes darted about like mice seeking a cat as she observed the busy camp. Everyone seemed busy at some kind of job. The children were bringing firewood from the brake along the creek, young girls were helping the women scrape hides or stretch skins between bowed frames made from green tree limbs. Halfway to the buggy, Hawk Flies High appeared from nowhere and walked beside them. The old Pawnee said nothing until they got to the buggy, then he asked, "Late Morning Star told you nothing?"

"Said she didn't have anything to tell me." Longarm started to take his saddle off the paint pony.

"Was she speaking straight?"

"Hard for me to tell, Hawk Flies High. But if she says she doesn't know anything, and if you say nobody's been hanging around or asking for her, I guess it's the straight truth."

"You don't think all our people lie to yours, then?"

"Nope. You've got some liars, so have we."

The old man sighed, and said sadly, "No one values or honors the truth as they did in the old days. It pleases me that you've made this thing only between you and Late Morning Star, and haven't accused all of us."

Longarm shrugged. "No need for that." He tossed the saddle in the buggy bed and said, "I haven't got a spare bridle, or I'd leave this one for your man, a sort of thank-you gift for the use of the pony."

"If you still need the horse, you can keep it a while," Hawk Flies High offered.

Longarm tried to keep his surprise from showing. "You'd trust me to bring it back?"

"Of course. What you did once, you'll do again."

"Well, thanks, Hawk Flies High, but I don't need him any more. I'll get my own horse back when I get to Fort Supply."

"I would like to ask you a question, Long."

"Ask away."

With a puzzled frown, Hawk Flies High indicated Nellie, who stood a few paces distant. "Is it a new custom for a man such as you to bring his woman on a journey like this?"

Longarm smiled. "Why, she ain't my woman. She's just riding around with me to learn something about the country. She writes stories for a newspaper back East."

"She will write about our people, when she goes back?"

"I guess. That's her business."

"See that she writes the truth, Long. Not all writers do."

"I'll tell her the truth. I can't guarantee she'll write it."

Hawk Flies High nodded. "You're not like other *napi*. You don't make promises you can't keep. I like you, Long. I say to you again, *tura heh, idad*." He held up his right hand, palm forward. Longarm pressed his own palm to the old Pawnee's. "I have told you, there is always a welcome for you in our tipis," Hawk Flies High said. He turned and walked back to the camp.

As they rattled across the prairie on a southwestward course that Longarm had calculated to bring them to Fort Supply, Nellie said thoughtfully, "You haven't asked my opinion, Longarm, but I think that Pawnee woman was lying to you."

"I sort of got that idea, too. She wasn't surprised enough when I trotted out Boyle's name, and she didn't ask enough questions about how I tracked her down."

"What are you going to do?"

He shrugged. "Nothing. How can I prove she's seen Boyle? Or even heard from him?"

"You're back where you started from at Darlington, then."

"It looks like it. Unless I pick up a trail at Fort Supply. There's got to be somebody there who'll know something, even if it's not any more than which direction he headed in when he left."

"Are you going to keep looking for Boyle, instead of working on the land-grab?"

"Boyle's the only reason I've got for being in the Nation, Nellie. Not that I aim to give up on Scott Forest and his scheme. The only one who can order me to come away is my boss in Denver, and I don't aim to report to him right away. Oh, I've got no idea of giving up. The land-grab scheme, with all its bribes and payoffs, makes Boyle look like pretty small potatoes."

Nellie nodded with satisfaction. "I'm glad you think so. Nobody in the East is interested in Boyle; there are plenty of bank robbers there. But a big scandal—one that might even reach to Washington—that'll make headlines, and headlines help make a name for Nellie Bly."

They talked very little after that. Nellie had gotten only a little sleep the night before, and she dozed now and then. Longarm's mind was busy plotting his strategy for pursuing Boyle. Late in the afternoon, they reached the road. Longarm reined in and looked in both directions along it, then took out his map and studied it.

"Don't you know where we are?" Nellie asked.

"More or less," he answered. "There's only the one road, and this is it. But we circled dry gulches so many times between here and the Pawnee camp, I can't tell whether we're north or south of Fort Supply. We'll take the road and go till I spot a landmark that shows on my map. I'm right sure the fort's north of us, so we might as well head out that way."

Longarm kept the horse to a walk while he studied the prairie on both sides of the road for landmarks. They were approaching a place where the road curved around a series of low bluffs when he looked back and saw a cloud of dust rising behind them.

"I'm real sure we're heading the right way," he told Nellie, "but whoever that is coming up on us will know for sure. We'll pull up and ask 'em when they come abreast."

They waited, growing warmer by the minute now that they no longer traveled in a breeze of their own making. The dust cloud came closer, and the figures of the riders and their horses grew more distinct. Longarm thought he recognized them when they were still nearly a mile off, and when they came within half a mile, he was sure. He turned back from scanning the road.

"Don't get upset, but trouble's coming," he told Nellie.

"Those two riders? Do you know them?"

"Unless I've lost my eyesight, it's that pair of bounty hunters, Brad Steele and Zelda Morgan."

"Why are they trouble, Longarm? Are they fighting you to get to Boyle first?"

"Oh, I don't mean *fighting* trouble. Just *talking* trouble. If they get wind of that scheme of Forest's, they're the kind who'd try to cut in and blackmail the ones who're handing out the palm-grease and the ones who're taking it, too."

"In other words, you want me to be careful of what I say to them?" she guessed.

He nodded. "That's the general idea."

"Don't worry. I've learned when to keep quiet."

By now, the pair was close enough for them to identify Longarm and Nellie. They pulled up, and their dust swirled and enveloped the riders as well as the buggy.

"Would you look who's turned up in the road, Zelda!" Steele said mockingly. "Our old friend, the marshal. He must've thought we weren't smart enough to pick up his trail after he skipped out." To Longarm, then, Steele said, "I guess you forgot about the promise you made us, to sit down and talk things over."

Zelda added, "That wasn't the right thing to do, Longarm. You did promise us, remember."

"I said we'd talk after I thought things over. Well, I'm still thinking," Longarm replied calmly.

Steele's normally high-pitched voice was even higher than usual when he said accusingly, "That's a damn poor excuse, and you know it! If it hadn't been for your little lady friend leaving such a wide trail, we might still be looking for you."

"Which you might as well be." Longarm was getting testy under Steele's prodding. "It sure ain't done you any good to catch up to me."

"You mean you're not taking our bid?" Zelda asked.

"I mean I hurried off to follow a tip that I hoped might lead me to Boyle. It didn't, so I'm still in the same boat you are. Nobody knows where he's got off to."

"I don't believe that!" Steele said hotly.

Longarm's gray-blue eyes glinted coldly from the shadow of his Stetson's wide brim. "I don't take kindly to a man that calls me a liar," he said quietly.

"You want to—" Steele began.

Zelda interrupted. "Don't start arguing, Brad! Longarm still hasn't said we can't agree on a deal. Just keep that temper of yours in hand, and let's the three of us talk sensibly."

"If you don't mind my saying so, Zelda, this ain't the time or the place for us to be talking," Longarm said. "You know who this young lady is, don't you?"

Zelda frowned. "I know her name. Cochrane, isn't it? Elizabeth Cochrane?"

"That's right, so far," Longarm agreed. "But do you know what her job is?"

"As far as I can see, her job's traipsing all over the Indian Nation after you," Steele broke in sarcastically. "Tell me, Longarm, are you nursing her, or is she nursing you?"

Longarm held back his temper. "Just in ease you're interested, Steele, Miss Cochrane's a reporter for a big newspaper back East. She's along with me because she's doing a story about how the law's enforced in the West."

"Oh, my God!" Zelda gasped. "Brad, that damned big mouth of yours has gotten us in trouble again!"

"What d'you mean?" Steele demanded.

"I mean that Longarm asked us to leave him alone a little while, and you had to talk me into chasing after him. Do I have to spell everything out for you?"

Nellie said, "I know who *you* are, of course. Marshal Long told me you're private investigators who have volunteered to help him find the man he's after. Is there something else he didn't tell me?"

"No, no," Zelda said hastily. "Not a thing."

Longarm took his cue from Nellie. "I told Miss Cochrane you'd suggested that we work together in trying to bring in Eddie Boyle, but that before I could give you an answer, I had to leave Darlington to run down a new clue. Then she unearthed some information which she brought me, and we've been checking on that."

Steele asked suspiciously, "What'd you find out?"

"Nothing," Longarm said. "You know how these cases go, Steele. You run down a dozen rumors, and maybe one is worth following up."

"We know," Zelda said. She turned to Steele. "Well, Brad, we'd better go on. We'll talk to Longarm in Fort Supply."

She looked pointedly at Longarm and asked sweetly, "Won't we, Marshal?"

"We sure will," Longarm replied, just as sweetly. "We'll see what we can work out about sharing information."

"We'll be looking for you," Steele said dourly. He didn't add, *if you don't look for us,* but he left no doubt as to what he meant. Turning to Zelda, he jerked his head to the north and said, "Come on. I hear, they've got ice in Fort Supply, even at this time of the year. Maybe we can get cold beer there."

He spurred his horse, and Zelda followed his example. Longarm and Nellie sat watching the cloud of dust disappear. Longarm said, "Well, at least we're sure which way to turn, now."

"Did I help you stall them off all right?" Nellie asked.

"You did fine, Nellie. Now all I've got to do is figure out how to dodge 'em in Fort Supply, and keep an eye on 'em at the same time. That won't be so easy." He sighed and picked up the reins. "We might as well move on, too. They're far enough ahead now so we won't have to eat any of their dust." Then he added ruefully, "I wish I was as certain of not having to eat their dust in chasing Boyle." He slapped the reins and turned the horse onto the road.

Chapter 12

"I thought this was going to be just another dinky little camp like New Cantonment," Nellie said. Her voice showed her surprise.

"I guess that's how it started out," Longarm replied. "But it's sure grown into a lot more than that, now."

From the top of the slope where Longarm had reined, in, the ground dropped gently into the shallow valley through which the north fork of the Canadian River flowed lazily. The river's waters, now at their pre-winter low, arced around the settled area. From the ridge where they sat in the buggy, Longarm and Nellie saw Fort Supply almost as it would have looked to a bird winging overhead.

There was no mistaking the fort itself. A stockade made by imbedding big cottonwood logs vertically in the ground was at its center; at two corners of the stockade, square redoubts of logs laid horizontally rose above the walls. Field guns were mounted on the redoubts. There were other buildings, most of them wooden, but a few constructed of red brick or fieldstone, spaced around the inner perimeter of the stockade, leaving the center bare to serve as a parade ground. The fort had spilled over outside the stockade, though. There were almost as many buildings bearing the unmistakable stamp of army construction hugging the outside of the outer walls as there were inside them.

Longarm ticked off the buildings with an eye sharpened by long practice; his cases had taken him to forts in most of the Western territories, and wherever he'd gone, he'd found army buildings constructed according to the patterns taught by Corps of Engineers instructors at West Point. Long barracks made of wood housed enlisted men; smaller rectangles were for noncommissioned officers; there were cottages for married officers, and more elaborate barracks of brick for the commissioned bachelors. At one side of the parade ground stood an imposing two-story building with white columns along its front that he'd have identified as the headquarters even without the flagstaff in front of it. A long, narrow brick building had to be the dispensary and hospital, and a smaller brick structure with high, small windows could be nothing except the guardhouse. There were warehouses with blank faces, stables with open sides, a big sutler's store, and ammunition sheds like low, square mushrooms hugging the ground.

Forming a belt around the army buildings, and separated from them by a broad road, were still other structures. These did not conform to the army's patterns. They were predominantly of wood, with a few scattered ones of brick or fieldstone. Even from a distance, they could be distinguished as stores, saloons, hotels, livery stables, blacksmith shops, and dwellings.

"It's really quite a good-sized town," Nellie remarked. "I hope there's a hotel with a bathtub, and a laundry. I must be carrying several pounds of the Indian Nation on my body and clothes."

"You'll have a chance to rest up, too," Longarm told her. He started the horse moving down the grade. The sun was low enough now to shine in their faces as they rode. "Once I pick up Boyle's trail, I'll take off after him, and you and Frank can stay here and keep your eyes open while we're waiting for Scott Forest to get back."

"Do you think two weeks will be enough time to find him, Longarm?" Nellie sighed. "Everything out here is so far from everything else. And there are no railroads to get you where you want to go."

"With a good horse under me, I can cover a pretty fair amount of ground in two weeks," Longarm told her. He stated it as a fact, not a boast. "Don't worry. There'll be plenty of time."

There were three hotels—one of them more a boarding house than a hotel—in the settlement that fringed the fort. Longarm and Nellie stopped at two of them before finding accommodations at the third. The Outpost Hotel was better than Mrs. Murray's establishment in Darlington, but not by a great margin. It did, however, boast a bathtub in its own room, with water piped from a cistern on the roof.

"I'm going to soak for an hour," Nellie told Longarm. "After that, I'll feel more like myself."

"Well, while you're' soaking, I'll go looking. We'd better connect up with Frank before we do anything else. Maybe I can find him before supper, and we'll have a confab while we're eating."

Sunset had brought a little relief from the autumn heat wave. Longarm began looking for Frank Turner in the places he'd learned that single men in a strange town usually seek: the saloons, of which there were a half dozen. He went from one to another before he found the one favored by cowhands and cattlemen—the Star. From the bar where he'd stopped for a glass of his usual, Longarm saw Frank across the room, sitting alone at a table near the faro layout. The young cowhand was so interested in watching the players buck the tiger that he didn't look up until Longarm sat down in the chair beside him.

"Longarm! I didn't expect you'd get here so fast."

"That Pawnee breed woman didn't know where Boyle is— or said she didn't, anyway. Wasn't much use wasting time out on the prairie, so we come on in. You had time to do any asking?"

Frank shrugged. "Some. There's a liveryman over on the north side of the fort who sold a horse to somebody who sounds like your man. He didn't remember much about the fellow, except that he paid the asking price in gold without stopping to dicker."

"That sure sounds like him. Maybe we'll walk over after a while and I'll see if I can jog his memory a mite. Right now, I aim to sit here for another glass or two. My throat's caked with dust clear down to my belly button."

"There's no sign of Forest yet," Frank volunteered. "Still too early."

"We'll be here when he is. Or at least, you and Nellie will be."

"I was wondering about her. A right pretty girl, ain't she?"

"You noticed that, did you? And a smart one, too. Maybe a little bit too smart to suit me."

"How's that?" Frank asked.

"I don't know whether you've run into it or not, Frank, but folks who're smarter than the usual run sometimes feel like they've got to be the boss."

"Nellie didn't strike me as being that way."

"You weren't with her the last few days. But I've got to give her credit—she pulled us out of the fire when we ran into that pair of bounty hunters on the way here."

"I guess that's something I missed out on. You mean there're bounty hunters after Boyle, too?"

"A man and a woman. Brad Steele and Zelda Morgan, by name. Only they don't have to bring Boyle in to collect, just kill him."

"If he's a murderer, he'll be hanged anyway, won't he?"

Longarm fished out a cheroot and clamped it between his front teeth.

"More'n likely. But he'll have a trial if I bring him in, and a judge and jury'll sentence him according to law. Now, if Boyle draws on me when I'm arresting him, and I beat him out and kill him, then that's legal, because I'm an officer and he's resisting me. But this pair they'll draw and shoot first."

Frank scratched his jawline, a gesture Longarm had come to recognize as characteristic of him. "It's a pretty fine point, I guess, but I see what you're driving at."

Longarm struck a match on the underside of the table, and lit his cigar. "And there's more to it than that," he said, shaking out the match. "If—" he stopped short and jerked his head toward the bar. "Now, speak of the devil!"

Turner looked in the direction Longarm indicated. "Is that one of the bounty hunters?"

The deputy leaned back and exhaled a large cloud of blue smoke. "Sure is. Brad Steele, he calls himself."

Steele was more than a little bit drunk, Longarm judged, although he showed few outward signs of it. Longarm wondered where Zelda Morgan was, and decided she must be following Nellie's example and soaking off the road dust in a bathtub full of hot water. Steele was pounding on the bar, arguing with the bartender. Longarm and Frank were too far away to hear what was being said, but they finally saw the bartender shrug and pour Steele a drink from a different bottle than the one that sat on the mahogany in front of him. Steele swept the old bottle to the floor, where it smashed with a tinkle that caused those in the saloon to fall silent. All eyes turned to see what was going on. In the silence, the bartender's voice could be heard even at the back of the saloon where Longarm and Turner were sitting. He said, "That was a damn near full bottle, mister. I'll expect you to pay for it."

Steele fumbled in his pocket and tossed a gold eagle on the bar. "Here. That'll pay for the one I broke and this bottle of good whiskey, too." He picked up the unbroken bottle in one hand, and his glass in the other, and turned away from the bar. As he started toward the back of the big room, Steele saw Longarm and headed for the table where he was sitting. He stopped a pace away and said, "Well, if it ain't the big lawman himself! I'll join you and your friend, Longarm. I don't enjoy drinking by myself."

Longarm said quietly, "We're talking business, Steele. You're welcome to sit with us later on, when we're finished."

"I've got some business to talk over with you, myself," Steele said. "Business you never did find time to finish. Suppose you get this fellow to wait while we get ours settled."

"Don't get anxious," Longarm advised the bounty hunter. "I'm not in any special hurry to settle what you're talking about."

"Well, I am," Steele snapped. "I'm tired of waiting on you."

"I think we'd better wait. This ain't the place to talk, and I want your partner to be in on whatever we say."

"Don't worry about Zelda. She'll do what I tell her to."

"If you say so. But I still say we'd better wait till we're in a more private place and I can talk to the two of you at the same time."

Steele scowled. "Damn it, you're putting me off again! I told you, I'm tired of it! Now, tell your friend goodbye, and we'll go find Zelda and whatever kind of private place suits you, and get things worked out."

Longarm was losing his temper under Steele's prodding. "As soon as I get through here."

"That's not good enough! If you're going to take our deal up, I want you to say so right now! Shit or get off the pot, Longarm!"

"You're too drunk to know what you're saying, Steele." Longarm kept his voice level. "I don't talk business with any man unless he's sober. Now, take your bottle and get out of here, before I lose my temper with you."

"Damn it, I don't take orders from anybody!"

"I don't either," Longarm replied quietly. "But I've got sense enough to know when I've had a few too many."

"Are you saying I'm drunk? Well, by God, drunk or sober, I can take you and a dozen like you!"

Steele let the bottle fall to the floor and groped for his gun. Longarm had started moving the instant he saw Steele's grip on the bottle relax. He was out of his chair cat-quick. He covered the few feet between himself and the bounty hunter while Steele's hand was moving to draw. Before the bottle had thudded to the floor, Longarm had grabbed Steele's wrist and was clamping it in his muscular hand. He tried to pull free, but couldn't break Longarm's grasp.

"Turn me loose, damn you! Let go my wrist, and I'll show you which one of us has got the best gun hand! We'll go outside and match up, man to man!"

"We won't do any such thing," Longarm said around the cheroot that was still clamped between his teeth.

He slid Steele's pistol from its holster and shoved it into his own belt. He didn't relish humiliating the man, and realized he was making an enemy, but so far Steele hadn't done anything to justify shooting him. Twisting the bounty hunter's arm up into the small of his back, Longarm frog-marched him to the batwings and shoved him through them. One of the swinging doors hit Steele's face and his nose spurted blood.

"Let go of me, damn you!" he sputtered. "I'm bleeding!"

"Not bad enough to hurt. It'll stop after you've soaked your head a while."

Standing on the board sidewalk, holding Steel immobilized, Longarm studied for a way to solve his predicament. He had no idea where the man was staying, and Steele was too drunk and angry to give any answers that made sense. If he let go of Steele's arm, the man was sure to swing, and Longarm had no taste for battling drunks.

He tried persuasion. "All right, now, Steele. Tell me where you're stopping at, and I'll see you get there. Tomorrow, when you sober up, we'll talk things over."

"I'm not drunk, Longarm! Turn me loose, and I'll prove it!"

"For God's sake, don't turn him loose!"

It was Zelda Morgan's voice. Longarm looked around, and saw that she was standing in front of the saloon next door to the Star. She hurried toward him.

"I've been looking for Brad for the past hour," she said breathlessly, as she reached the two men. "He left while I was in the bathtub. Said he was going after a fresh bottle of whiskey. I—well, I know what his weakness is, so when he didn't come back right away, I came out to try and find him. Did he give you a bad time, Longarm?"

"Not as bad as he tried to. You think you can handle him, or do you want me to march him to your hotel?"

"I can take care of him." Zelda patted Steele's cheeks with a series of short, sharp slaps. "Brad! Pay attention to me! We're going now. Do you understand?"

"I got to take care of this damned marshal, Zelda! He made me look a fool, and you know I don't stand for that!"

"He was just trying to help you. Now, straighten out, Brad! You know you promised me you'd be careful, after that last time."

"You're going to be mad at me, ain't you? Don't be mad, Zee." In the unpredictable manner of drunks, Steele's mood had shifted suddenly. "If you won't be mad, I'll straighten out. Look."

Steele tried once more to free himself, and failed. Zelda nodded to Longarm, who released him. She took a handkerchief from her jacket pocket and held it to Steele's nose; the bleeding had almost stopped by now.

"Come on, Brad," she urged. "Let's go fix up your nose."

"It hurts, damn it! Longarm hurt me!"

"He didn't mean to." Aside, she whispered to Longarm, "Go back inside, please. I can handle him when you're gone."

Longarm took the cheroot from his mouth, and noting with a shake of his head that it had been broken in the scuffle, he crushed it beneath his boot heel as he asked her, "Are you sure?"

"Yes, I'm sure. Go ahead. Tomorrow, he'll be all right. Can we talk then?"

"I don't see why not. I'm staying at that hotel right there, the Outpost. I'll be there, or in the Star, here."

"I'll find you," Zelda promised. "Hurry up, get out of sight. He'll come along with me as soon as you're gone."

Longarm was glad enough to get back into the saloon. He picked up a bottle of Maryland rye from the bar and rejoined Frank Turner.

"How'd you get rid of your friend?" Turner asked with a smile.

"Turned him over to his partner. That came close to being real trouble, Frank." As Longarm sat down, the revolver he'd taken from Steele nudged his stomach. "Damn. I forgot I had his gun. Well, he's better off without it right now. I'll give it back to him tomorrow."

Frank grinned. "I felt a lot better when I saw you take it away from him. I was about ready to duck. There wasn't much I could see to do to help you. You had him well in hand, and I don't like to butt into another man's affairs."

Longarm had downed his first shot of rye faster than was his custom. He poured another, topped up Turner's glass, and lighted a fresh cheroot. "Nellie ought to be ready to eat supper by the time we put these drinks down. We'll have ourselves a pow-wow while we eat, and see if we can figure the best thing to do."

Their discussion over the supper table brought no clear-cut decision except an agreement that Longarm should begin at once to try and find Boyle's trail. Frank and Nellie could do nothing except wait for Scott Forest to arrive.

Longarm felt peevish; waiting was not his favorite pastime. When Nellie said she wanted to go and inspect the fort, and Frank agreed to go with her, he excused himself and went back to the hotel. He found a barbershop and treated himself to a hot bath while waiting to be shaved, but aside from the relief of getting rid of an accumulation of trail dust, he felt no better about the dead end that his search for Boyle seemed to have reached. Fort Supply did not interest him.

Longarm remembered the bottle of rye in his hotel room, and returned there. One swallow tasted good, the second tasted better. After the third, he decided a good night's sleep was what he needed to improve his outlook. He went through his bedtime preparations with swift efficiency, and blew out the light and was asleep two minutes after his head hit the pillow.

* * *

A tiny tick of metal against metal brought him instantly awake. He had no idea how long he'd been sleeping or what the time was. He lay quietly for a moment. The tick was repeated. Noiselessly, Longarm slid his Colt from its usual bedtime position, dangling in his gunbelt from the head of the bed, and padded on bare feet to the wall beside the door. When the tick sounded the third time it was followed by an almost inaudible grating sound as the doorknob slowly turned. The door swung silently open. A woman's silhouette showed against the faint glow of a lamp far down the hallway. Longarm relaxed, but not totally.

He said, "I wasn't expecting you tonight, Zee, but do come on in, even if I ain't exactly dressed for company."

"I must be losing my touch," Zelda Morgan sighed.

She started into the room. Longarm reached for the bath towel that hung on the nightstand near the door and wrapped it around his waist. He said, "I imagine you came to get your partner's gun. Sorry I disremembered to give it to you to keep for him. It's laying there on the nightstand. How come he ain't along to collect it himself?"

"You know perfectly well why not. Brad's sleeping it off. He was drunker than hell."

"I know it, and you do too, but I doubt that he did." He indicated the chair, the only place other than the bed to sit down. "Well, since you're here, I guess you want to talk about the deal you and him put to me?"

"No. I want to talk about a deal I'm going to put to you myself. I've been thinking about it ever since I met you, and after seeing how Brad acted today, I guess you'll understand why."

"Does he do that often?" Longarm's vest hung at the head of the bed opposite the gunbelt. He produced a cheroot, then slid his gun back into its holster and sat down on the bed. Flicking a match into flame with his thumbnail, he lighted the cheroot. He took a quick look at Zelda Morgan before blowing out the match. She'd settled down into the chair, and was looking at him intently. The light from the match was kind to her. It softened the angles of her face and took a few years from her age.

"Not too often. Enough so that it keeps me feeling nervous. Damn it, Longarm, you're in the business. You must know how I feel, having an unreliable partner, one I've got to look after."

"I don't work with a partner, except now and again. But I can see how you'd feel, sure." He waited for what he knew was coming next.

"Now, if I had somebody like you to work with . . ." Zelda let her voice trail off into silence.

"Sorry, Zee. I've got a job. I like it, and I don't feel like I'd want to change."

"You'd make ten times as much as you're making now. And you wouldn't have to resign your job. Longarm, think what we could do, with you on the inside and me working the outside! We could clean up!"

Longarm knew what she wanted, but said, "I guess I don't follow you."

"Why, the money, Longarm, the thirty thousand Boyle's got—or what's left of it, maybe twenty, twenty-five. We'd only have to return a few thousand to the Warde brothers. We'd just say the rest was hidden where we couldn't find it, or that Boyle had spent it."

"Boyle'd take the starch out of a yarn like that," he pointed out.

"Not if he was killed when he tried to get away from us. The reward says dead or alive, remember?"

"How many jobs like Boyle do you get in a year, Zelda?"

"Three or four. I'll tell you, it's a rich gravy train."

"I suppose so. What about Steele, though? How'd he act if you told him you wanted to split up?"

"He'd have to be put with Boyle," she said coolly.

"And that'd be my job?" Longarm asked the question even though he already knew what the answer would be.

"You can take him without any trouble. Brad's slowed down a lot in the past couple of years, since he started drinking so much."

"Zelda, I draw the line at murder."

"Don't act holy with me. You've killed before, plenty of times."

"Sure, but not for money, not even in the War. To uphold the law. I never took a man down in cold blood. I ain't sure I could."

"You can do anything you make up your mind to." She was moving restlessly in her chair. Longarm puffed the cheroot vigorously; he wanted light to see what she was doing. He blinked. She'd begun to discard her clothes; already she was naked to the waist.

Zelda recognized the trick he'd used and said, "That's not fair."

"It's fair when I don't know what you're up to."

"I thought you understood what I was saying. I go along with the deal. And I can be more woman than you've ever known before in your life, Longarm. Did you know I grew up in Europe, and that my first husband was a French count?"

"No. I never gave it any thought, whether you were married or not."

Zelda rose and stepped to where Longarm sat. She put a hand on his bare chest and pressed him down across the bed. With her other hand she pulled away the towel he'd draped around his hips.

"Etienne taught me a lot of things," she said, her voice a sultry whisper. "Things most women in this country don't know and are afraid to try. Like this."

She leaned over and Longarm felt the soft, gentle pressure of her full breasts against his groin, Zelda's fingers were busy. They found Longarm's still-flaccid shaft and he became aware that it was being engulfed in the satiny smooth warmth between her breasts. Her hand moved in a subtle massage. He could feel himself getting hard. The pressure on his hips increased. Zelda was resting her full weight on him now, while her lips and the tip of her tongue traced moist paths across his belly. The tip of her tongue explored his navel briefly before she shifted on the bed to lean across his thighs.

Longarm was totally rigid, now. In his varied experiences with women, he'd encountered some—not many, but a few— who'd preferred the variations of sex to its more conventional expressions. Most of them had been novices drawn by curiosity to experiment with pleasures about which they'd heard shocked whispers. Others had already discovered what they liked, or what they thought gave men pleasure, and took their enjoyment with great gusto. As Zelda's tongue dragged in a wet line down his belly he sensed that she was one who knew.

She was cooing softly to herself as she fluttered the tip of her tongue along his upstanding penis. Her mouth seemed to take on a life of its own, nibbling upward, then down, then up again. She wrapped both hands around his erection and turned her head slowly while she rubbed its tender tip over her cheeks and eyes and chin. The darkness was too deep for Longarm to see her face, but when she spoke, he heard that sensual smile in her voice.

"I hoped you'd be big. I got a lot more than I hoped for."

Longarm felt her mouth engulf his shaft. Her tongue was busy as she twisted her head from side to side and up and down. A great deal of time had gone by since Longarm had enjoyed the kind of skilled caresses Zelda was giving him. He felt himself losing control, and wanted to tell her to stop while he got it back, but couldn't bring himself to speak.

Zelda had learned to read signs, he discovered. She lifted her head long enough to say, "Don't hold back, Longarm. And don't be afraid to let go. I want to drink your juice. I love a man's come, it tastes like honey to me."

Her interruption, brief as it was, had given Longarm time to regain command of himself. He felt her lips go around him again, and farther down on his shaft than she'd gone before. She was kneeling beside him now, her head bobbing up and down, her lips slackening and compressing in turn, her tongue in constant motion inside her mouth. Zelda's frenzy transmitted itself to him. Longarm wanted to hold on, but he also wanted to let go. Within a few moments, Zelda gave him no choice. Her insistent lips and tongue imprisoned his senses. For a few seconds he relaxed. His hips heaved up and he began pumping his juice down Zelda's throat.

With a humming murmur like a huge, contented cat, she gulped and swallowed and gulped again and again. Even after Longarm lay completely drained, her lips still persisted. What had been pleasure took on an overtone of pain. Longarm arched his back and tried to roll aside, but Zelda was pressing him down with a hand on each hipbone, and he was unable to get away from her still-demanding mouth. He stood her tongue's rasping pressure as long as he felt he could, and pushed her head away.

"Not yet!" she insisted. "It'll be even better, next time."

"Next time, wouldn't you like to—" he began.

"To fuck?" she broke in. "Longarm, you won't be able to fuck when I've finished with you. Oh, I enjoy fucking for a change, but this is what I love, Right now, I want to feel you getting hard inside my mouth."

She slid her head along his thighs, her lips reaching to engulf him again. Before she succeeded, the door banged open. The tall, thin figure of Brad Steele was silhouetted in the dim light of the hall.

"Zelda!" he grated. "I see you in there with that son of a bitch Longarm! Get to one side, while I take care of him for keeps!"

In a flash, Longarm recalled that he'd been draping himself with the towel when Zelda closed the door, and he'd forgotten to lock it. With her weight on his legs, he was unable to move quickly. He tried to roll and grab for his Colt, but he was lying slantwise across the bed. His holster dangled from the headboard, out of reach.

Zelda moved like a striking snake. She grabbed Steele's pistol from the nightstand, and the room was illuminated as if by bolts of lightning as she pumped two slugs into her partner. By the time Longarm came to his feet with his own weapon in hand, Steele was crumpling to the floor of the hall.

"Jesus!" Longarm blurted, as the ringing echo of the shots in the confined space died slowly away, "You didn't have to kill him!"

"Yes I did!" she retorted. "I've put up with that drunken bastard too long! I couldn't take any more from him!"

Excited voices floated up from the floor below and footsteps began pounding up the stairs.

"Don't let them catch me, Longarm!" Zelda pleaded. "They'd hang me! Besides, if I hadn't shot him, he'd've killed both of us!"

Longarm doubted that Steele would have been able to do that without a weapon, but he didn't say so. He felt he owed Zelda something. It had been his fault that he hadn't given her

Steele's gun on the street, and his fault that the door had been unlocked. Even if he owed her nothing else, she'd saved him from having to kill Steele in a shoot-out.

"Get under the bed," he commanded. "Take the pistol with you."

Zelda obeyed without question. Longarm reached for the towel she'd dropped on the bed and wrapped it around his hips in time to step into the hallway as the first of the inquisitive townspeople arrived.

"You men stay back, now!" he ordered. "I'm a federal officer, and I'm taking charge until the town marshal gets here,"

A man in the group called out, "There's no town marshals in the Nation. It'll be the provost's police from the fort that'll straighten things out."

Within a few minutes the military patrol arrived, consisting of two privates commanded by a sergeant. The sergeant looked at Steele's body. "Who shot this man?" he asked. Only then did he see the gun in Longarm's hand. "You! Hand over that weapon!"

"Now, wait a minute!" Longarm protested. "I didn't shoot him. I'm a federal marshal, and if you look at my gun, you'll find out it ain't been fired."

He handed the Colt to the sergeant, who swung out the cylinder and ejected the cartridges, then sniffed the muzzle. "I'd say you're telling the truth," he said, handing the weapon back to Longarm. "I don't see another gun around here, though."

A man in the crowd saved Longarm from answering. "Whoever done it must've run down the back stairs. They're just down the hall."

"I suppose so." The sergeant frowned at Longarm. "Did you see anybody running toward the stairs?"

Longarm was glad he could answer truthfully. "I sure didn't. I didn't know there were stairs back there. And there wasn't a soul in the hall when I came out of my room."

"You're alone in the room?"

"Look for yourself," Longarm invited the sergeant. "If you want to search it, I'll light the lamp for you."

"No need. I can see from here that nobody's in there," the sergeant said after a quick glance. "I guess you can prove you're who you say you are?"

"I'll get my badge." Longarm went into his room, and came back with his wallet. He closed the door carefully, then showed the sergeant the badge pinned in the wallet's fold.

"It looks all right to me," the sergeant said. He handed the wallet back. "I'd guess somebody followed this fellow in here. Might have been somebody with a grudge against him. All right, men. Pick him up and carry him down to the undertaker's. We'll let the day squad find out who he was and whatever else they can about him." He asked Longarm, "Will you be around tomorrow, if there's any questions?"

"I'll be right here," Longarm promised. He watched the soldiers carry Steele's body down the stairs, with the small group of onlookers following. After the hall was empty, he went back into his room. This time, he was careful to lock the door.

In a low voice, he said, "All right, Zelda. You can come out now." When there was no reply, he repeated, "Zelda. Come on out."

Still getting no answer, Longarm bent down and looked under the bed. Zelda was not there. He gazed around the bare little room. It had no closet, no place where she could have hidden. Then he noticed that the window had been opened full. He leaned out. In the light that splashed up from the street, he saw a narrow ledge, the width of a single board, which ran along the face of the building. The ledge was just wide enough for Zelda to have worked her way along it until she found an open window, or perhaps reached the safety of the back outside stairs.

Well, old son, Longarm told himself, *she must've been spooked right bad. She might've figured I'd turn her in to save my own skin, if push came to shove.*

He had a feeling he'd seen the last of Zelda. With a murder charge hanging over her, she wasn't likely to stay in the Nation, especially now that Steele was dead. He took a healthy swallow from the bottle and lighted a fresh cheroot. It didn't taste as good as he'd thought it would. He stubbed out the cigar, took another swig from the bottle, lay down, and went back to sleep.

Chapter 13

"And the provost marshal's men haven't figured out who shot Steele, or why?" Nellie asked.

"Not up to now," Longarm replied. "But maybe they figure one more civilian gunhand ain't worth wasting time on. From the way they talked, they get two or three killings a week around here."

Longarm, Nellie, and Frank Turner were eating their noon meal at the little dining room just down the street from the hotel. Nellie and Frank hadn't gotten back from their sightseeing trip to the fort until after the excitement that followed Steele's killing had died down. Longarm had an idea the pair had done something more than just inspect the fort, but he figured that wasn't any of his business.

He'd spent most of the morning at the fort, invited firmly by a messenger from the provost marshal to give them more details of the shooting. He hadn't mentioned Zelda; he'd simply let the young lieutenant questioning him draw his own conclusions, based on the report made by the sergeant who'd been at the hotel. Longarm had impressed on the lieutenant the importance of keeping his name out of the official report; he'd convinced the young man that the case he was on in the Nation might be jeopardized if his presence there leaked out. Back at the hotel, he'd given Nellie and Frank the same carefully edited version of the affair that would appear in the official report.

Frank asked, "What're you going to do now?"

"Just what I planned to do. Except that I've got to make up half a day that I lost answering those damn fool questions. You and me better go talk to that livery-man you told me about, the one you think sold Boyle a horse. He's about the only lead I've got."

"I'm ready whenever you are."

Longarm stood up. "The sooner we get at it, the quicker we'll have some answers. Let's go."

"What about me?" Nellie asked.

"I just figured you'd come along with us," Longarm replied.

Outside, they found the street in front of the restaurant almost deserted; earlier, in the cool of the morning, it had been bustling with activity. Soldiers, civilians, and Indians had been hurrying to get their business completed before the heat of the day reached its peak. There were only a few people walking along the sidewalks now, and three or four horsemen, a wagon or two, a buggy, and a buckboard occupied the middle of the thoroughfare. Longarm's horse stood at the hitch rail; Frank Turner's was still at the livery stable behind the hotel. Longarm turned to suggest that Frank and Nellie take the buggy, and was standing with his back to the street when Nellie put a hand on his arm.

"That looks like the old Pawnee man and the woman we saw at the hunting camp the other day," she said.

Longarm turned around. Hawk Flies High and Late Morning Star, riding Indian-style on unsaddled horses, were coming along the street, moving slowly, searching the faces of the people they passed. Longarm stepped out into the street, and they saw him. They rode up and reined in their ponies.

"*Idad*," Hawk Flies High said. "We were looking for you." He was not wearing the buckskins he'd had on at the camp. Today, he wore a white man's suit of dark serge, a white shirt—though he'd left off the customary starched collar—and a high-crowned felt hat. "This one"—he jerked his head to indicate Late Morning Star—"has things of importance to tell you."

"I'm sure ready to listen," Longarm said. "If you're hungry, we can go in there and you can eat while we talk."

"We have eaten," the old Pawnee replied. "And what she wants to say is better told where no one can overhear. Do you have your horse now? Or are you still riding with the woman?"

"I've got my horse right here." Longarm pointed.

"*Tura heh.*" Hawk Flies High nodded. "Ride with us outside the town, then. The trees and grass have no tongues to repeat what is said in front of them."

"What about my friends?" Longarm asked.

Hawk Flies High shook his head, "We should go alone."

Longarm told Nellie and Frank, "I guess that's how it'll have to be, then. I'll be back as soon as I can, and we'll go ahead with what we were going to do. You can keep each other company a while longer, I guess, without it hurting your feelings."

He unhitched his horse. The Pawnees started down the street. Longarm swung into the saddle and caught up with them. When he joined them, Late Morning Star checked her horse so that Longarm could ride beside Hawk Flies High, while she followed behind them, in the proper place for a Pawnee woman.

Hawk Flies High remained silent during the short ride. He led them away from the fort and its ring of buildings, apparently sure of where he wanted to go. They rode three-quarters of a mile onto the prairie. The sun beat down on them from a sky that showed no trace of cloud. They reached a small knoll, where a lone bois d'arc stood like a sentry, and Hawk Flies High reined in. Longarm and Late Morning Star did the same. They dismounted and Hawk Flies High sat down in the scanty shade of the tree, with his legs folded under him. Longarm managed to bend his booted legs into almost the same position. Late Morning Star did not sit down. She stood by the tree, waiting patiently.

"I sent for this one after you left our camp," Hawk Flies High told Longarm. "I don't like it when our people speak with twisted tongues, even to a *napi*. Now you will hear what she told me." He looked at Late Morning Star. "You can speak now, woman."

"I can tell you where Eddie Boyle is," she said. "He came to find me while I was on the reservation, before we went to the hunting camp. He needed a place to hide. He had a great deal of money that he'd gotten from the bank in Colorado, but had spent a lot getting to the Nation. I had him taken to a place where he'd be safe."

"Where?" Longarm asked. "Is he still there?"

"It is a place near here, in the Antelope Hills. He's still there, I'm sure. If he'd left, I would have heard."

"This place she speaks of is not far from here," Hawk Flies High put in. "Before I let her tell you about it, I must have your word that you will not lead the soldiers to it. There would be a lot of trouble for all our people if you did."

Longarm frowned. "What kind of place are you talking about? Sounds like it's right important, if the army'd be interested in finding it."

"Before I tell you more, do I have your word?" the old Indian insisted.

Longarm turned his gaze to the ground in front of him. After a moment, he raised his eyes to meet those of the old Pawnee. "I ain't sure I can guarantee you that, Hawk Flies High. Not unless you want to tell me a lot more than you have so far."

Hawk Flies High seemed to ponder this. Finally, he said, "Tell me this, *idad*. How much do you know of the way things are now, in what you call the Indian Nation? Do you know of the troubles we Pawnees are having with the Cheyennes and Arapahoes? Of the greed the Cherokees are showing toward their brothers of other tribes? Do you know that your army is trying to take our land away, and that the men your government has sent to feed us are helping the soldiers? Because unless you know all these things, you will not understand."

It was Longarm's turn to sit and think for a while, What Hawk Flies High had asked him indicated that there was a lot more going on in the Nation than he'd imagined. The Pawnee's last question hinted that Scott Forest's land-grab scheme wasn't the only one in the making, perhaps not even the biggest. He had a feeling Nellie had uncovered only the tip of what was beginning to look like a damned big iceberg.

He said, "I ain't sure I know too much, Hawk Flies High. I know I don't know as much as you do. Suppose you start at the beginning and tell me about it."

Hawk Flies High spoke slowly and thoughtfully. "The Cherokees and Creeks and Seminoles came to the Indian Nation first. Your people promised them the land would be theirs as long as the sun shines and the grass grows. Then the land of other tribes was taken by your settlers, who made forests into farms and drove away the game, and because our people were poor and starving, they brought other tribes to share what had been promised to the Cherokees and Seminoles alone. But there was room, as long as you *napi* stayed on the sunrise side of the big river."

"That was a long time ago," Longarm observed. "Way before the War."

"True, And when your people divided and fought, some of ours joined them. They thought if they helped your soldiers, they would be given back their land. But the Cherokees couldn't decide which of your soldiers would win. Some went north, some went south."

"I know that. Hell, everybody's heard about Stan Watie and his Cherokee army."

"He was not the only one," Hawk Flies High said. "But when your people made peace among themselves, and began to take more land on our side of the big river, there were more of our people's tribes sent to the Nation. They were given land the first tribes to come here had been told was theirs. I know this, because we Pawnees were among the first to make peace with your pony soldiers and agree to move here. And we were told there would be hunting grounds where we would always find game. We weren't told that the hunting grounds had already been given to the Cherokees and Creeks and Osages and Chickasaws and even more. So there was a time when we were at war with our own brothers, because the men your people sent to give us the beef we'd been promised were taking it for themselves."

"That didn't last long," Longarm said, finding himself on the defensive and not liking the feeling. "As soon as we found out what was going on, we stopped the stealing."

"Perhaps. They still steal, sometimes. But we saw that if we were to live, we must have our own beef, since by then your hunters were wasting buffalo. We started herds, small ones, with cattle we took as payment from the big herds driven across our land."

"And a lot that your people stole from ranches and farms, too," Longarm reminded him.

"That is true. We stole the cattle because we had no buffalo to hunt, Your hunters had killed all of them. Today, we keep our herds on the land that was promised to the first tribes. You call it the Cherokee Outlet. It is the only land with grass and water that is left in the Nation for us to use."

"Don't the Cherokees still claim it?" Longarm asked.

"Yes. So do the Creeks and Seminoles, and so do we Pawnees. But now, to keep the land from being stolen by your army and your agents to be sold to white men, the Cherokees say they will share it with the rest of us." He turned to Late Morning Star. "Now, woman, you tell him the rest."

"What my uncle hasn't explained is that before our Indian herds were grazed in the Outlet, outlaws—white outlaws—hid in it when they were running from their own people. Even then, there were some who brought stolen cattle there, to keep until they had enough for a herd to sell at Dodge City or Abilene or Wichita."

"I hear there's a lot of that still going on," Longarm put in. "Not just white outlaws, either."

"Yes. Our own people use it for the same reason," Hawk Flies High agreed. "But before you turned our men into cattle thieves, your own people were there. Not only cattle rustlers, but robbers and killers like Eddie Boyle. The men who make whiskey for the whiskey ranches used it, too. After a while, there were so many that they built a big camp in a hidden valley in the Antelope Hills. They call it Outlaw Valley."

Longarm nodded. "I've heard about a lot of places like that." He didn't list the more than twenty similar spots in the Western Territories: the Hole in the Wall in Wyoming, Robber's Roost in Utah, Brown's Hole on the Green River, the Buzzard's Roost in the Big Bend of the Rio Grande, and others less notorious. All of them lay along what in an earlier time had become known as the Outlaw Trail, which stretched from the border of Canada to Sonora in northern Mexico. There were other Outlaw Trails, too, offshoots from the central stem, almost as well-known to lawmen as to the bandits who had created them.

"I don't know of other places," Late Morning Star said. "I do know this place. Our cattle rustlers use it and so do yours. It's a place where men like Eddie Boyle go to hide."

"Are you telling me Boyle's there now?"

She shrugged. "I suppose he is. He expects me to meet him there. He wants me to go to Mexico with him, where he can start fresh."

"Using the money he stole from that bank in Colorado?"

"Of course. Why else would he have stolen it?"

Longarm asked Hawk Flies High, "How come you're letting her tell me all this?"

"You spoke to me as man to man. You didn't look at my skin, but into my eyes. I told you her words were true. Even though I didn't know then that she talked with twisted words, I must save my honor now by making her tell you the truth."

"You knew about this Outlaw Valley, though, didn't you?"

"Of course. If you wonder why I didn't tell you, even after I called you *idad*, you must try to understand our way. The outlaws of the valley are from our people as well as yours. We only punish our people when they break our tribal laws; we don't call it a crime to break *napi* laws. And we need the help those men in the valley give us."

"That's why you wanted me to promise I wouldn't show the army where it is? You're afraid they'll go in and bust it up?"

"Yes."

"Don't you understand that if the white ranchers get ahold of the Outlet land they're after, they'll bust up Outlaw Valley? They won't let a bunch of rustlers stay where they can raid the herds."

"I thought of that. I'm afraid the valley will go, no matter what happens." Hawk Flies High smiled sadly. "It seems that when we go against your people, we lose even when we win."

Longarm shook his head. "I can't give you the kind of promise you asked for, Hawk Flies High."

"His promise doesn't matter, Uncle!" Late Morning Star said. "He can't go in alone and bring Eddie out. He won't leave that valley alive!"

"Do you understand this?" Hawk Flies High asked Longarm.

"Sure. It's a risk I get paid to take. I'll tell you what, Hawk Flies High. You people like to gamble. You let Late Morning Star take me into that valley, just her and me. If I come out alive, I win. If I don't, I lose, and it's my fault, not yours."

Late Morning Star spoke angrily to Hawk Flies High, in Pawnee, and he replied in the same language. They argued for a few moments, until Longarm could tell by the old man's tone, even without understanding the words, that the woman had lost.

"I'm more sure than ever that I was right when I called you brother," Hawk Flies High said to Longarm. "A man who gambles his own life to win what he wants is an equal to our own bravest warriors. We have made a bet, you and I. This one will take you to the valley."

"When do we go?" Longarm asked Late Morning Star.

"That's up to you," she told him. "If you want to go today, we can start now."

"I can't leave without telling my friends not to worry about me. They know I left the fort with you two, and if I don't show up back there, they're liable to send the army out looking for me."

"Tomorrow, then?" she suggested,

"Make it the next day. How much of a trip is it?"

"Two days from the fort to the valley."

"All right. You come on to the fort, day after tomorrow. I'll have the grub we'll need, and be ready to travel. You'll find me at the Outpost Hotel. It's just up the street a ways from the place where we met today."

"I know where it is," she replied quietly.

Longarm couldn't tell whether or not Late Morning Star was angry. Her face showed no emotion; her voice was level and unconcerned.

"You can trust her to lead you there," Hawk Flies High assured him. "I've told her what will happen to her if she breaks her word, or lies again."

"I ain't taking her word, Hawk Flies High. I'm taking yours."

"And I have given it to you."

"That's all I need, then. Come on. We might as well get back to Fort Supply."

"We won't go that way, I think," the Pawnee said, "It's shorter if we follow our own hunting trail back to our camp." He stood up and extended his arm, big hand raised, the palm toward Longarm. "*Tiwaruksti tura, idad.*"

Longarm put out his hand and pressed it to the hand of Hawk Flies High. "I hope you're wishing me good luck."

"I am."

"Thanks. I've got a feeling luck's something I might need plenty of, before this thing's all over."

Longarm watched Hawk Flies High and Late Morning Star ride off, the woman a yard or so to the rear of the old man. Then he got on his own mount and headed for the fort.

He rode slowly, to give himself time to think. He wasn't quite sure what kind of mess he'd gotten himself into, but he figured it would be something worse than a cactus patch and not quite as bad as a prairie fire. He didn't see any way to plan in advance, because he hadn't any way of knowing quite what to expect. The more he thought about it, the less he seemed to know. Having reached that conclusion, he stopped trying to plan, and decided to play the cards the way they fell. During the rest of the ride to town, he felt better.

Chapter 14

"Are you sure you'll be back by the time Forest gets here to put the finishing touches on the land-grab?" Nellie asked. Her rosebud lips were pursed in a thoughtful pout. "You know how important that is to me, Longarm."

"I set just as much store by it as you do," Longarm reminded her. "But like I told you before, my first job's catching Eddie Boyle."

"If he's in that hideout the Pawnees told you about, why not let him stay there until after we break up Forest's scheme?" she insisted.

"Because I can't be sure that's what he'll do. I ain't sure right this minute that the Pawnee woman ain't figured out some way to warn him."

"Suppose she has?" Turner asked. "What good would it do you to go and wait for her? She'd just never show up, and you'd be left holding the bag."

"I'm betting she won't dare go against her tribe," Longarm said. "If you'd seen Hawk Flies High's face when he promised the tribe'd take care of her if she didn't take me to the hideout, you wouldn't be too worried about it, either. If Boyle's gone when I get there, I'll guarantee to find out which way he headed."

"That's what bothers me," Nellie said. "You might be gone a lot longer than you're planning."

"Well, if I am, then you and Frank'll just have to figure out a way to make Forest hold things up till I get back. Now, I've said all I intend to say."

They were sitting in Longarm's room at the Outpost Hotel, since it was too early for supper and Nellie couldn't join them in any of the saloons. Longarm and Frank were sitting on the bed, with a fresh bottle of Maryland rye on the floor between them. Nellie sat in the room's only chair, beside the narrow window. When Longarm delivered his ultimatum, she stood up and turned her back to him. The room was silent for a moment. Then, over her shoulder, Nellie said, "I think your timetable just got broken up, Longarm. Look out on the street."

Longarm stood up and gazed out, over Nellie's head. Scott Forest, on his black stallion, was reining in at the hitch rail in front of the Star.

Longarm frowned. "Now, what in hell's he doing here? He ain't supposed to be back for another two weeks!"

Turner joined Longarm and Nellie at the window in time to see Forest go into the Star. He said, "I don't know, but if he's back here, it's for a good reason. He's supposed to be getting his friends together to wind up their deal."

"Whysoever he's here, we can't let him catch sight of Nellie. I've got a hunch that fellow that tried to get her in Darlington was sent by Forest."

"Do you really think so?" Nellie asked. "You didn't mention it before."

"I didn't know what you'd gotten into before. Afterward, when it occurred to me that that might be it, I didn't want to spook you."

"You know by now that it takes more than that to spook me, I hope," she said dryly. "Well, what are we going to do now?"

"First thing we'd better do is find out why he's here so far ahead of time," Longarm said, thinking aloud. "I guess that's up to us, Frank. We sure don't want him to know about Nellie."

"If you show up, Forest's going to want to know why you're not off on that trip you let on you had to make, getting your money together," Turner pointed out.

"That's something I can figure out an answer for. There hasn't been enough time go by since I was supposed to leave for him to get suspicious about that."

"I could handle him alone, I guess," Frank suggested. "Let him think you've already left."

Longarm shook his head. "No. If we did that, I'd have to hole up and stay out of sight. It'd be real hard to do in a little place like this. If you told him that, and he caught sight of me, he'd really start wanting to know why."

Nellie said, "You could tell him you got a touch of—what kind of sickness is common here? Ague? Dysentery? Something that would keep you from traveling, but wouldn't stop you from going out. But you'd have to be sure Forest doesn't see you when you ride off with that Pawnee woman day after tomorrow."

"That sounds like the best idea," Longarm agreed. "Maybe you'd better feel poorly, too, Nellie. Stay in your room. We'll see that you get fed as long as Forest stays around." He looked from Nellie to Frank. "All right, if we've got our stories straight, let's see what your old boss has got to say."

They found Forest standing at the bar in the Star. He gave a start when he saw Longarm.

"Long! What in hell are you doing still in the Nation? You said you were leaving to—well, never mind that right now. Let's go back to a quiet table where we can talk." Forest picked up the bottle of whiskey that stood in front of him and led them away from the bar. When they'd settled in a far corner of the saloon, he said to Longarm, "I didn't expect to see you still here. Did something go wrong?"

"Nothing but a case of the squats. I guess I got ahold of some alkali water. I'm just about over it now. I'll head out tomorrow or the next day."

Forest was obviously relieved. "I'm glad that's all it is."

"Well, my sore butt sure ain't," Longarm frowned. "What about you? You ain't supposed to be back so soon, yourself."

"Oh, these damned nervous-Nellie army officers! Now they've picked up some kind of rumor that Washington's sent some Pinkerton spies to nose around. Estes sent me a wire—caught me at Fort Elliott, where I'd stopped for the night on my way home. I rode my horse's back raw getting back here."

"You lost me there," Longarm said. "Who's Estes?"

"He's the colonel commanding Fort Supply. I can't afford to have him panic. He's one of the keys to keeping the rest of the army people in line."

"How many of them is he speaking for?" Turner asked.

"All of them," Forest said. "After Rogers brought him into the plan, Estes pretty well took over the leadership."

"How many are tangled up in this now?" Longarm asked.

"That's not important, there're enough to make sure it'll

work," Forest replied. "But Estes and Rogers are the important ones."

"How about the Indian bureau men?" Longarm asked. "Are they getting jumpy, too?"

"I don't know, yet," Forest answered impatiently. "Damn it, Long, I just rode into town. I haven't seen Estes yet, and I don't want to go to the fort until the end of the day, when he'll be out of his office and in his private quarters. We can talk there without being interrupted. But all these damn government people are like a herd of cattle. If just one of 'em gets locoed, the whole damn bunch is likely to stampede."

"Amen," Turner agreed sagely, "I've seen it happen."

Longarm decided it was time to muddy the waters a little bit. He said thoughtfully, "There was a killing over at the Outpost Hotel the other night. I heard that the man who got shot was some kind of investigator, but I never got the straight of it. Heard a woman was with him, but it looks like she flew the coop. Nobody's seen her since the killing. You think they're the ones who've got your army friends worrying?"

"I don't know, I tell you," Forest retorted peevishly. "And I won't know until I talk to Estes." Then, frowning, he said, "This fellow who was shot—was he a Pinkerton man?"

"I never did hear," Longarm replied with a casual shrug. "It happened in the hall close to my room, so the provost's men from the fort talked to me about it, but they weren't saying too much."

"Look here, Long, why don't you come to the fort with me when I go to talk to Estes this evening?" Forest suggested. "Maybe after he finds out that we've got you with us to pull strings in the government it'll cool down his panic."

Longarm had been hoping for just such an invitation, but he didn't want to seem too eager. He said, "I guess I can, if you think it'll help things along. Just sort of soft-pedal what you tell Estes about me, though. I don't want any tales getting back to my boss."

"Estes is in this thing too deep to back out now," Forest said grimly. "He'll change his tune after I talk to him tonight, I'm sure of that. If he doesn't, he can kiss his pension goodbye."

*   *   *

Forest was still in a grim and angry mood when Longarm met him at the Star after supper. During the short ride to the fort, the cattleman told Longarm, "I sent Estes a note to let him know we were coming to see him. There's always a bunch of flap-ears hanging around at a place like Supply, and I wanted to make sure we'd have a private talk, in his quarters instead of his office."

When they reached the fort, Forest, with an air of casual familiarity, reined in before the white two-story structure with a colonnaded front that Longarm had identified as the post's headquarters. It stood out like a marshmallow in the middle of a freshly iced chocolate cake. A sentry was on duty at the door to take the reins of their horses and lead the animals to the hitch rail that stood on one side of the headquarters building. The colonel's orderly was waiting for them at the door.

"Colonel Estes is expecting you," he told them, leading them past busy offices to a stairway at the end of the hall. "Go right on upstairs."

Colonel Samuel Estes might have been a commanding figure on horseback, Longarm thought, after introductions had been completed and the colonel was settling them down in his sitting room. But the C.O. of Fort Supply was a small man when he stood on foot. He was growing pudgy around the middle, and bulgy in the seat. He wore his beard in the style prescribed officially for the U.S. Cavalry in a service manual that was obsolete long before the Civil War. The beard didn't hide the fact that Estes's lips were pursed and pudgy, like those of a wax-faced doll. His movements, as he bustled around providing drinks and cigars, showed that he'd knocked back a few while waiting for Longarm and Forest to arrive. He finally sat down himself, facing his guests.

"Now, gentlemen," he announced, "we can begin."

Forest lost no time in cutting to the bone of the matter. "What in hell did that wire mean, Sam? Damn it, man, we've gone too far with this thing for you to get cold feet now."

"My feet aren't cold, as you put it," Estes said primly. "I took the risk of sending you a private message over army wires because I thought it was important for you to know there's apparently been some kind of leak in our plans."

"What do you mean, 'apparently'?" Forest demanded. "I

understood from your wire that you were sure there was one. Now I'm ready to hear the facts. Who's responsible? How far has the leak gone?"

Estes looked questioningly at Longarm. Forest said, "He's not to blame. He doesn't know enough, and he's just as open to job trouble as your men or the Indian bureau people are. Now, let's get down to cases."

"There was a man murdered in town the night before last," Estes said. His manner of speaking was precise, even fussy. "My provost people found that he'd come here from Fort Reno by way of New Cantonment. There was a woman traveling with him, but she's disappeared. They were investigators, Scott. I suspect they were Pinkerton spies. The Pinkertons still handle a great deal of confidential investigation work for the government, and they don't always identify themselves as being from Pinkerton, you know. There are a lot of other agencies in the Pinkerton system that don't carry the Pinkerton name. But I remembered that Pinkerton favors using women as investigators, and woman-and-man teams. That's what aroused my suspicions."

"You mean you've got nothing but suspicions to go on?" Forest flared.

"My provost men are still trying to connect the agency these people worked for with Pinkerton," Estes replied. "They just haven't had time to do it, yet. They have to be careful, too, you know."

Forest was compressing his lips, holding back an explosion, Longarm noted. The cattleman kept the suppressed anger from his voice as he asked Estes, "Sam, did you drag me back here from Fort Elliott, damn near twenty hours in the saddle, because you think you see a ghost under the bed?"

"That's unfair, Scott," Estes protested. "I just took what seemed to me to be a sensible precaution."

"Sensible precaution, my ass!" Forest snorted.

Longarm was having trouble keeping a straight face. He liked to see crooks quarreling among themselves. Arguments opened gaps through which he could reach for evidence. He sat quietly, watching and listening.

Estes said angrily, "There's only one thing a Pinkerton spy team could have come to the Nation to investigate. That's this scheme you've got me into, Scott. I think we'd better hold things up until we find out exactly where we stand."

"Like hell!" Forest snapped. "I might listen to your fool ideas if you had anything but imagination to back them up. Damn it, Sam, you're not even sure those two spies were working for Pinkerton; you don't know what they were looking for; you don't know how long they've been here; you don't know whether they've turned up anything. Come back to earth, man! We've got a deal to push through before somebody really *does* find out what we're planning, and tries to stop us! This isn't the time to slow things down!"

Estes appealed to Longarm, who'd been very careful to stay out of the dispute between the two conspirators. "What's your opinion, Mr. Long? Scott says you know your way around in the federal government. Would you push ahead and take an unnecessary chance? Or would you exercise due caution?"

"I'm afraid I'd have to agree with Mr. Forest, Colonel. From what you said, you can't be sure those investigators weren't here to look into something else." Longarm paused, trying to decide whether it would be wise to climb out on a limb. Then he said, "I think if there were any suspicions, I'd've got wind of 'em."

"Really?" Estes almost quivered with eagerness to be reassured. "You're in a position to hear things like that?"

"Mr. Long's with the Justice Department," Forest said. "He'd know."

Estes sighed. "Well. That makes me feel better. You know why I'm worried. General Pope's a straitlaced man. If he got any idea, even a hint, that I or my fellow officers were thinking about breaching the army's code of conduct, we'd be cashiered and our pensions would be taken away from us."

"Pensions!" Forest snorted. "You work a lifetime, and get put on the shelf with a picayune sixty dollars a month. Or was it eighty you said you'd draw when you retire next year? You stick with us, Sam, and you'll have a good nest egg when you go out."

"That's what I'm counting on," Estes replied. He sighed. "I guess I was being overly cautious, Scott. I'm sorry I brought you back, but you can understand why I was worried."

Having won, Forest could afford to say, "It's all right. This just delayed us a week or so. Now I'm heading back to Texas to get on with the job I'm supposed to be doing. Long, you'll be ready when it's time, I suppose?"

"Sure." Longarm didn't say he'd be ready before then, now that he had some idea how basically weak Estes was, as well as a few more ideas about how to use that weakness. "When you get back, I'll be all set." As an afterthought, he added, "If something else comes up to bother the colonel while you're gone, Forest, why can't he ask Frank Turner for any advice he might need? If Frank couldn't handle it, he'd know enough to get hold of you. It might save you a trip back."

Forest hesitated. "I still don't like the way Turner shoved in on my deal. If it was you, I wouldn't worry, but—"

"I wasn't aiming to be pushy," Longarm broke in. "It just struck me that as long as Frank's here, he might as well be doing something."

"There shouldn't be anything for any of us to do except wait," Forest said. "But maybe you've got an idea, at that. He'd at least be able to judge whether one of Sam's crazy scares is something I ought to know about."

Longarm nodded, keeping a straight face in spite of his disappointment. He'd hoped to get Frank Turner deeply enough inside the scheme to learn the names of most of those involved. He told Forest, "You're dealing this game. Whatever you say, that's how we'll do it."

When Late Morning Star arrived as she'd promised, at noon on the following day, Longarm was waiting. He'd held a faint doubt that the Pawnee woman would show up, but he betrayed no surprise when he greeted her. She had no saddle or saddlebags on her pony, just a blanket rolled behind a pad.

"You got everything you'll need?" he asked.

"Yes. There's a roll of pemmican in my blanket. I know where the water holes are. I'm ready, if you are."

"Just point the way. No reason I can see to put off leaving."

Late Morning Star pointed to the road south. "I'll tell you when we must turn off."

From Fort Supply, the old wagon road to Fort Elliott followed the twisting course of Wolf Creek, a tributary of the

Canadian River's north fork. Late Morning Star ignored the road after the first few miles, and when it curved along a loop in the creek, she cut straight ahead. They crossed and recrossed the creek a dozen times during the first hours of their ride. They talked little. At first, after she started them across the prairie on the occasions when they left the road, she dropped back to ride behind Longarm, At last, he insisted that she move up so they could ride abreast.

"I ain't an Indian," he pointed out. "If they want their women to hang back, it's their right. I like to see whoever's riding with me and not have to twist my neck to do it."

She didn't argue, but moved up to keep abreast of him. The change in position didn't seem to increase her loquacity, however.

As every trailwise man crossing strange country does, Longarm looked back often. Landmarks often look different when approached from the opposite direction. If he had to find his way back alone, Longarm wanted to know the signs he'd need to follow. In the late afternoon, he saw a bank of low-hanging clouds behind them that promised some overdue autumn rain, if the clouds moved in the right direction and weren't burned away by the broiling sun. He pointed out the clouds to Late Morning Star.

"Looks like rain clouds. You figure we're going to get wet tonight?"

"Does it matter?" she said stonily.

He shrugged. "I reckon not. Just making conversation."

She was silent for a moment, then seemed to soften a bit. "I'm sorry if I'm dull company. I suppose I'm thinking about other things."

"You don't feel right about taking me to Eddie Boyle," he said. "I could tell the other day you didn't cotton to what your uncle told you to do."

"Hawk Flies High isn't really my uncle," she replied. "He's just one of our oldest and wisest chiefs. All young Pawnees call him 'uncle' to show respect."

"I didn't realize that. Well, I guess I ought to feel sorry for making you do something you don't want to do, but I've got a chief, too, and he tells me what I've got to do."

"I hadn't thought of white men as having chiefs over them," she said. "To me, they've always seemed so free, with no tribal laws to follow."

"Seems to me everybody's got laws that make 'em do things they don't really want to," Longarm observed. "At least, part of the time."

"You talk like you're no more anxious than I am to go to Outlaw Valley."

"I didn't mean it that way. But I guess I'd feel better about going if you hadn't been pushed into showing me the way." Longarm hesitated before asking the question in his mind. "You still got a lot of feeling for that Boyle fellow?"

Late Morning Star shook her head. "No. I was a very young girl when I met him for the first time. I thought I was in love with him. I still didn't understand what being half white and half Indian means when you get to be a woman."

"Is it because you're half white that Hawk Flies High gets so rough with you sometimes?"

"Yes. He's just following our custom, and I've almost gotten used to it by now. Any child of mixed blood born to a Pawnee woman learns that he has to pay for what his mother did when she took a man from outside the tribe. It was worse, years ago. There are so many mixed-blood Pawnees now that the custom's dying, The only ones who pay much attention to it are the old men, like Hawk Flies High."

"Why do you stay with the Pawnees, then? You're half white."

"The whites are worse. All I could expect if I went to them would be a job as a servant, or as a whore. I tried living away from the tribe once. I worked for an army wife, then for a trader, I was never a whore. I saw your people treat mixed-blood whores a lot worse than they do white ones."

"I see."

"Maybe you do, at that. At least you're treating me like a human being. That makes taking you to the valley a little easier." She looked curiously at Longarm. "Tell me, Marshal—you're not part Indian by any chance, are you?"

"If I am, I don't know about it. When I was a little tad down in West Virginia, folks didn't waste much breath telling youngsters about their family history. Maybe it was because most families back there didn't have much history to tell. Mine didn't, as far as I know. We were just ordinary, hard-scrabble-poor farm folks."

Longarm turned for one of his habitual looks behind them. The clouds that had been a narrow line just above the horizon were towering into the sky now, and moving toward them rapidly. The quality of the sunlight had changed subtly.

"Looks like we're going to get that rain," he told the woman.

She shrugged. "It won't be the first time I've been wet."

"Nor me. The only reason I said anything is because you know the country and I don't. I figured you might want to head for someplace where there's shelter."

Late Morning Star looked back at the clouds, then scanned the terrain ahead. "We'll be getting back to Wolf Creek before the rain gets here, if it's going to rain at all. There are trees there, and a few sand caves in the brakes. There'll be wood for cooking, if you've brought something to cook."

"Nothing except beans. We can boil 'em tonight so we'll have a hot breakfast tomorrow. And I've got hardtack and jerky, if you'd sooner have that than pemmican. I don't fancy pemmican much; it's too sweet for my taste."

For the first time, Late Morning Star smiled. "Don't take this as an insult, Marshal, but I'm sure you've got Indian blood now. Most white men take enough food on a trip like this to feed an army, even if it's summer. And half of it spoils in the heat before they get a chance to eat it."

It was Longarm's turn to smile. "I started out that way. Found out there's nothing like a saddlebag full of putrid meat to learn you not to let your eyes outrun your gut."

Late Morning Star looked back again and smelled the air. "It is going to rain."

Overhead, the sky was still clear, but the cloud bank was now scudding toward them rapidly. Below it the air was blue, the blue of chilled steel, like Longarm's eyes. Behind the blue they could see the leaden sheen of falling rain.

"Can we still make it to Wolf Creek?" Longarm asked.

"We've been easy on the horses. If we let them run, we might be able to get there."

They kicked the animals into a lope that looked easy, but covered the ground fast. Behind them, the rainstorm continued its steady advance. Jagged streamers of white lightning slashed from clouds to earth occasionally. These were the killers of prairie storms. In such a flat, treeless land, the highest point to attract lightning was the wet peak of the hat worn by a man on horseback.

Three or four miles after they'd started the horses running, the storm caught them. It was preceded by swirls of blowing dust that whipped the dead stems of dry prairie grass around them in a series of miniature whirlwinds and turned their faces brown. Then the rain caught them. Longarm had untied his slicker when the wind began. He offered it to Late Morning Star, but she shook her head. He wrapped the oilskin around him, but the wind was carrying raindrops parallel to the ground and sent them trickling under it and down his collar.

Ahead, a line of green, looking almost black in the dark, rain-filled air, marked the creekbed. Late Morning Star called out, "The place I'm thinking of is a little way farther along the creek. The bank's high, and a sand cave goes back into it. We can ride right on into it."

Longarm nodded and motioned for her to lead the way. He followed her as she skirted the line of trees, slowing her horse, looking for the cavern. She turned suddenly and splashed across the creek, with Longarm close behind her. He saw the cave's opening then, wide enough and high enough to admit a man on horseback if he ducked his head just a little bit. Late Morning Star rode into the dark opening, and Longarm followed her.

Chapter 15

For several moments, blind in the sudden darkness, Longarm sat on the gelding. As vision returned, he could see that the cavern went back more than twenty feet into the porous limestone of the bluff. Late Morning Star had dismounted at once and led her pony to the back of the cave. Longarm swung down and unsaddled. Late Morning Star had disappeared, but in a few moments she came back through the cavern's opening, dragging a huge cottonwood branch with each hand. Longarm hurried to help her.

"Don't spoil me, Marshal. I'm used to this," she told him. "Making the fire's a woman's job, where I live."

Longarm stood aside. Late Morning Star quickly broke twigs off the deadfall and snapped them to expose dry inner wood. She made a small cone of twigs just inside the cave's opening. Wordlessly, Longarm handed her one of his waterproofed matches. In equal silence, she took it and scraped it into flame on a rock. The twigs caught at once, and she began breaking larger branches to feed the fire. When it was crackling brightly, she took one of the large branches and walked back to the far end of the cavern.

"Rattlesnakes," she explained tersely. "They come into places like this to stay cool when the weather's hot." Carefully, she circled the back area, then came back to the mouth of the cave and tossed the branch on the fire. "We don't have to worry. There aren't any. If you've got coffee in your saddlebags, Marshal, it'd taste good right now."

Longarm, used to doing his own camp chores, had the small coffeepot out, with coffee from his reserve packet and water from the canteen poured into it, before Late Morning Star realized what he was doing. She took the pot and arranged two large branches across one side of the fire to set it on.

"You said you had hardtack and jerky?" she asked.

"In the saddlebags. You want me to get 'em?"

"Unless you object to a glue-fingered Indian prowling in your belongings, I'll do it."

Longarm nodded and watched her idly while she went through his saddlebags. She set aside the bag of beans and the small skillet, found the jerky and hardtack rounds, reached in to rummage again, and brought out his telegraph key. She held it up.

"It's not any of my business, but why do you carry this?" she asked. "All I can see that it does is add weight."

"It's come in handy a few times," he said. "I'm just in the habit of having it along, I guess."

She put the key back and said, "I can only find one cup."

"That's all I tote. We'll share it."

Late Morning Star came back to the fire, and put the beans and the skillet beside it. "I'll start these cooking after supper so they'll be done in time for breakfast. Here," She held out the jerky and hardtack. "Go ahead. I'll wait."

"Unless we're breaking some sort of Pawnee law, we'll eat together," he told her. "The way I was brought up, ladies go first."

"You're spoiling me again. I can't get used to the way you seem to trust me. For all you know, I might be planning to cut your throat while you're asleep."

"I'm a light sleeper. The only Indian who ever tried that trick on me wound up real dead." Only after he'd said them jokingly did Longarm realize that his words weren't funny.

Late Morning Star looked at him soberly, took the jerky shavings she'd whittled off for herself, and sat down on the opposite side of the fire. Longarm couldn't think of anything to say. They are in silence. Outside, the rain kept spattering down. When the coffee was done, she filled the cup and handed it to him. He drank, sipping carefully, and held the cup out to her. Late Morning Star shook her head. He didn't pull the cup away.

"Take it and drink it, damn it!" he told her angrily, then

softened his tone. "I didn't mean what I said to come out the way it did."

Slowly, she extended her hand and took the coffee cup. After a sip, she said, "I guess you hit too close to home. A white buffalo hunter killed my oldest brother with a shot from his blankets. My brother was fourteen."

"What I said wasn't very funny, anyhow," he admitted.

"You didn't know, about my brother. I'm sorry. I shouldn't take out old, dead sorrows on you."

Late Morning Star stood up. She filled the skillet with water from the canteen, poured the dry pinto beans in it, and placed it at the edge of the fire. Longarm lighted a cheroot with a flaming twig, and refilled the coffee cup. Late Morning Star walked to the mouth of the cave and stood listening to the rain. It was no longer coming down in sheets, but in a dying spatter. She disappeared outside.

Longarm got busy spreading his bedroll. He didn't try to do anything about Late Morning Star's blanket, which was still tied to her saddle pad. She came back in, her deerskin robe dark with the rain, and began untying the blanket. Longarm went outside and found a sheltered spot close to the wall of the bluff. He let a stream of steaming urine splash to the ground in company with the raindrops.

Late Morning Star was sitting on her blanket with her legs folded under her, when he came back into the cave. She said nothing to him, and he did not speak to her. Longarm lay down on his blankets after arranging his gunbelt close to his head and working off his boots to serve as a pillow. He'd hung his hat on his saddle horn to dry when they'd first come inside. He stretched, wriggled his hips to find a spot where they rested comfortably, then lay back and closed his eyes.

Late Morning Star finally broke her silence. In a completely matter-of-fact tone she said, "I feel empty tonight. I need a man to fill me. Would you like for me to sleep with you?"

Longarm was too surprised to answer at once. Finally, he said, "If it's something you want to do."

She answered by coming to stand beside his bedroll, where she slipped her deerskin dress over her head; She wore nothing under it. The shapeless robe she wore had given no hint of the contours of her body. It was not squat, with the elongated torso common to most of the Indian women Longarm had seen naked. Instead, her form was slender and symmetrical. Her breasts were high and small, with long, dark nipples that were erect and protruding. Her stomach was flat and her waist full, but not so full that it concealed the spread of her generous hips, Her legs were symmetrical, long, and firm, tapering down from a black thatch of pubic hair that veiled her crotch with mystery.

When she'd pulled off her dress, Late Morning Star had let her braids fall down her back instead of bringing them over her shoulders. The freeing of her face from its black frame made the Pawnee woman seem younger and somehow more vulnerable. The reflection of the dying fire flickered on her high cheekbones and shadowed her eyes, which glinted from deep caverns. The firelight accentuated the redness of her full lips and softened the width of her chin.

She stood quietly while Longarm inspected her. "Do I please you?" she asked.

He smiled. "You look right pretty."

For the first time that he could remember, she spoke to him in Pawnee. "*Tura heh.*"

Late Morning Star lay down beside him then, and Longarm shifted a bit to make room for her. He was surprised that he was not getting an erection. That was usually an automatic response with him when he saw a naked woman getting ready to come to bed with him. Even now, when he could feel her warmth and inhale the musky strangeness of her woman-scent, Longarm wasn't aroused.

Late Morning Star asked, "Aren't you like other white-eyes? Doesn't the idea of sleeping with an Indian woman make you eager? Or do you have to rape her to be interested?"

He shook his head.

"I was wondering why you wanted to sleep with me."

"I told you; I need a man inside me." She stroked his crotch, then began unbuckling his belt and unfastening the buttons of his fly. Longarm eased his weight off his hips to let her pull down his trousers, and felt Late Morning Star's warm hands lifting and cupping him, but her caresses brought him only half-erect. He reached out a hand to stroke her breasts, and rolled her elongated nipples between his fingers. She gasped and began to breathe more rapidly, and her hands moved faster, trying to bring him to a full erection.

"You're hung like a bull elk," she told him, her voice a husky whisper in the semidarkness. "But not as hard as one, yet."

"Maybe I've just been put to stud too many times," he suggested.

"No. Not you. Not with all this?"

Late Morning Star pulled herself closer to Longarm and threw a leg over him. Her hands kept busy, and he began to be aware of the warm moisture of her juices, the subtle scraping of her dark, thick brush. She managed somehow to tuck him inside her, still half-flaccid, and began squeezing with her inner muscles in a rhythmic massage that soon brought him fully hard. Longarm rolled over to lie on top of her and plunged deeply. She sighed contentedly under his slow, measured strokes.

Longarm didn't hurry. He thrust deliberately, in a slow rhythm, almost languidly, pushing hard for several seconds at the end of each downward plunge before beginning another, equally slow. Late Morning Star began responding with upward heaves of her hips. She was breathing heavily, and in the dim light Longarm could see that her head was bent backward, her neck arched, lifting her shoulders off the blanket. He did not change the tempo of his thrusting until she started to tremble and he could hear her breath rasping in her throat. Then he moved faster, striking deeper, pounding harder, until the Pawnee woman began pulsing under him, her muscles trembling, her arms flailing. Deep sighs that were almost grunts poured from her throat. She shook wildly in her final, tearing spasms, then relaxed and lay limply beneath him.

Longarm waited for a moment before moving to leave her. Late Morning Star clasped her legs around his hips and pulled him back into her. "Don't," she commanded. "Stay in me. Keep filling me. I can feel that you're still hard. Didn't you come?"

"No. Not yet."

"Then don't move. Just lie on me. I'm not tired, and I like to feel full, with your weight on top of me."

Longarm lay quietly as the minutes flowed by and the supper fire died to a red glow of coals. Late Morning Star held him firmly with her legs, now and then straining to pull him into her more deeply. He felt her beginning to work her inner muscles again, a slow pressure that became a firm squeezing, followed by a quick relaxing. Her movements continued until he stirred restlessly and tried to lift his hips.

She released the cage of her legs when she felt Longarm stir. Stretching upward, she grasped a hand around each of her ankles and pulled her legs downward until her knees rested beside her ribs. Her hips lifted high with her movement, and Longarm felt her opening to him even more widely than before. He was still completely erect, kept so by the warmth of her depths and the massaging of her inner muscles. He raised himself and almost left her, then pounded back with a long, deep thrust. Late Morning Star gasped as their bodies met, and the next time Longarm plunged, she pulled her feet still farther down and brought her hips up to meet him. When their bodies collided, her breath exploded in a shuddering whimper.

Late Morning Star's response triggered a reaction in Longarm. He braced his knees on the blanket and started to hammer into her with the fierce speed of a racer nearing the finish line. Caught up in the frenzy she'd generated in Longarm, Late Morning Star writhed and quivered. Her hips rolled under his swift, full strokes as she joined Longarm in the race, The fever that had galvanized them was too great to be prolonged. Longarm's back heaved in a final, exhausting lunge as he went into orgasm, and Late Morning Star's breasts quivered with expiring sighs as the strength flowed from their bodies and they collapsed in a loose entwining of arms and legs, wet with sweat, gasping for breath.

Late Morning Star was the first to move. She stood, with a single, lithe unfolding and stretching of her legs, and went to put fresh wood on the fire before its last coals died completely. Longarm studied her swift, economical movements as she broke cottonwood branches into burning-lengths and placed them on the coals. The fire blazed again, bringing light back into the cave. Late Morning Star came back to the blanket and looked at him, a question in her eyes.

"Is it all right if I sleep by you? Or do you want me to go to my own blanket?"

"I'd I feel funny if you did that. What makes you ask such a fool question?"

"Pawnee men believe that when a woman sleeps beside a man, she drains his strength away in the night."

"Well, now, I can see how they'd feel like that. I'm a little bit winded right now, myself."

"No, not from fucking. Just by sleeping beside him."

Longarm shook his head. "I guess everybody's got their own notions. You come on here to bed with me. It won't make me any weaker tomorrow. At least, it never has before. Besides, there're some questions I need to ask you about this place we're heading for."

"I thought there might be." She settled down by him, and they lay side by side, gazing up at the flickering shadows on the ceiling of the cave. "What do you want to know?" she asked.

"How many owlhoots am I likely to run into there?"

She shook her head. "I don't know. Men come and go in the valley. Sometimes there'll be only eight or ten, sometimes twenty."

"Make a guess."

She thought for a moment. "Ten, at the most. This is the time of year when the herds are driven north to Abilene and Wichita. They wait until the Texas trail herds have passed, and stay a day or two behind them."

"These steers," he said. "Are they rustled, or what the Indians own legal?"

"They're mixed. All the cattle the whites bring are stolen. They change the brands in the valley before driving them north. Our people take stolen cattle there to have the brands changed, too, but some of those that go to be sold belong to us."

"How come this valley's been let go all through the years? It seems to me your Indian policemen ought to know about it."

"They do. They leave the outlaws alone because our police don't feel it's up to them to help yours bring in men who haven't done anything wrong here in the Nation. And also because the outlaws help us by changing brands. I suppose there's money paid, sometimes."

This was about what Longarm had expected to hear; Hawk Flies High had told him much the same thing. He asked, "How big a place is this Outlaw Valley?"

"It's big. Big enough for the horse and cattle herds, and for the stills run by the men who sell liquor to the whiskey ranches. It's hard to find, too, and even harder to get in after you know where it is. There's always a guard at the gorge that's the only way into it."

"I'll bet it's as hard to get out of it as it is to get in."

"Yes," she confirmed. "You'll be searched when you go in. If I were you, I'd hide any spare money you've got, your badge, and anything else that might give you away."

"What about my guns?" he asked.

"They've got rules about that, after you get in. I don't know very much about them. I never carried a gun in there, of course."

Longarm turned his head toward her. Her fine-boned profile was silhouetted against the fire's orange glow. "How come you know so much about this place, Late Morning Star?"

"I told you, I lived away from my tribe for a while. I don't guess I have to tell you the whole story. I took up with a man who used the valley for a hideout. There aren't any women allowed in the valley, not even those with their own men, but I could go and stay a day now and then. And I've taken supplies to our men there."

"This man you took up with—was it Eddie Boyle?"

"No. He was killed before I met Eddie. And you already know I took Eddie there." She sighed. "I don't know much more."

"I'll find out what else there is to know, after I get inside." Longarm yawned. He listened to the rain, still pattering gently outside. "We'd better grab some shut-eye. We've still got a lot of traveling left to do."

Morning brought a clear sky and a bright sun to the freshly washed prairie. Longarm and Late Morning Star wasted no time getting back on the trail. By midmorning, they'd passed over the area the rainstorm had covered, and for what seemed like endless hours, their horses struggled through soft, yielding sand dunes. The orange earth was bare of vegetation except for clumps of sandgrass. Eventually, the dunes gave way to hard-baked red dirt, thinly covered with prairie grass. They rode steadily, stopping only to rest their horses, and early in the afternoon, they ate a scanty lunch while they took shelter from the sun under an overhanging ledge in a dry gulch.

Toward early evening, Late Morning Star pointed ahead. Longarm squinted through the heat haze and saw in the distance a dark, wavy line.

"It's the middle fork of the Canadian River," the woman explained. "The Antelope Hills are just beyond it. But it's too far away for us to reach tonight."

"We'll make a dry camp, then," he said. "I guess you know a good place along here, too?"

"We won't have a cave, or even a tree. But it won't rain, either. We can stop here, or go on for a while; it doesn't matter. There won't be any wood for a fire, but if we go on to a buffalo trail that's a little way ahead, we can build a chip fire."

"Let's do that," he decided. "I always sleep better if I have a cup of hot coffee to finish supper with."

Darkness was near when they reached the buffalo trail, now almost hidden by the prairie grasses. Beneath the curling grama stems, the crescent-shaped tracks cut by the hooves of the migrating beasts showed plainly in this land of infrequent rain. Their droppings, bleached almost white and dried bone-hard, each one as big as a pie plate, lay everywhere. The trail covered a swath half a mile wide on the flat plain, impressive enough unless one realized that the herds had once blackened the prairie from horizon to horizon.

"There's a wallow just ahead," Late Morning Star told Longarm. "We'll be sheltered from the wind there, if a blow comes up tonight, and our fire won't be so likely to be seen by anybody riding this way."

At the bottom of the wallow, a saucerlike depression that lay six feet below the surface of the surrounding plain, they made camp. While Longarm hobbled the horses, Late Morning Star collected buffalo chips and lit a small fire that burned fast and hot and without smoke, just long enough to brew a pot of coffee. They ate jerky and hardtack again, and washed the dry meal down with strong, black, unsweetened coffee. Late Morning Star went to her horse and started to undo her rolled blanket.

"I'll ask you this time," Longarm said. "I'd feel right lonesome if you didn't stay with me again."

He couldn't see her smile in the early darkness, but there was a lightness in her voice. "Of course I will."

Later, after they lay exhausted following an hour of easy, relaxed lovemaking, she said to him, "I wouldn't have come to you if you hadn't invited me."

"I sort of had an idea you wouldn't't," he admitted. "Anyway, it was my turn."

She rolled over to face him and he turned to her. He went into her, and she thrust her pelvis forward to meet his deep penetration. There was no hurrying or hesitation now. They matched rhythms, prolonging their pleasure. Their sighs were carried away by the soft night wind sweeping across the endless prairie. Then they slept, quietly at peace.

While the sun was still reaching for noon the next day, they splashed across the middle fork of the Canadian. Late Morning Star rode ahead; she knew the locations of the quicksand beds for which the river was notorious. The stream was low, a sheet of water only inches deep, spreading in ripples across a bed of orange-yellow sand a quarter of a mile wide, bordered by brakes in which wild grapevines and sandplum bushes grew between thin stands of salt cedar and cottonwood.

Until they'd crossed the river, the Antelope Hills had been visible, but obscured by heat haze. When they came out of the brake on the Canadian's south bank and mounted the bluff of gravelly sand that divided the river from the plain, they could see the hills clearly. Longarm, who compared all high ground to the majestic Rockies, wasn't impressed by the miniature range that lay ahead. The hills rose abruptly, an island of steep, seamed slopes and bare ochre bluffs in a land that stretched flat to the horizon in all directions. They were notable only because wherever else Longarm looked, there was nothing except bare, rolling prairie, as featureless and unbroken as an expanse of windless ocean. A lone bois d'arc tree two or three miles ahead was the only other vertical object visible.

Longarm pointed to the tree. "If I'm going to hide my badge so I can find it, guess it'd better be by that tree yonder."

"It's as good a place as any," Late Morning Star agreed. "And there's one more thing we'd better settle before we get to the valley. What am I going to call you there? I can't call you Marshal Long."

He said, "Just use my first name, like it's the only name you know me by. That's worked before."

"What is your first name?"

"Custis."

She tried the name experimentally a time or two and nodded. "All right. I won't forget, or make a slip."

At the bois d'arc, Longarm wrapped his badge in a clean bandanna from his saddlebag and gouged out a hole in the baked earth at the base of the tree trunk. He dropped the badge in, scraped the dirt back in the hole, and pressed it firm. Then he smoothed it so the disturbed ground was almost unnoticeable from a few feet away.

"There's one more chore I've still got to take care of," he said. "Didn't want to do it till the last thing, and I guess this is about as last as we'll get."

He picked up a windfallen twig from beneath the tree and shaved its end into a ruff of wooden curls, then lighted the dry wood. It caught at once and burned quickly. When its end was a glowing coal, Longarm stepped over to the gelding, blowing on the branch to keep the coal alive. Working carefully, blowing on the end of the branch often, he traced a curve to close the top of the "U" on the horse's cavalry brand. Then he connected the ends of the "S" with a slant stroke. He stepped back and looked at his work. Instead of the brand reading "US" it now showed as "O8".

Late Morning Star had watched him in silence. Now she frowned and said, "That won't fool anybody who looks at it closely."

"I don't expect it to. But I'll be a lot better off riding into that place we're headed for with a 'Circle 8' that doesn't look right than with a government brand that ain't been changed."

He mounted and they rode on. Late Morning Star led the way to the hills, and around the first of their low humps. Ahead, a bluff of solid rock towered abruptly. As they neared it, Longarm saw that it was split by a crevasse that parted the bluff from top to bottom, forming a narrow passageway with sheer, vertical walls. He followed Late Morning Star into the split. They rode in single file between the sides of the crevasse until the passage took an abrupt turn. Just before they reached the jog, a man holding a rifle stepped seemingly from nowhere to block their way.

"That's far enough," the man said, holding the rifle poised at his shoulder. "If you don't know where you're going and who you're looking for, you're at the end of the road."

"It's all right," Late Morning Star told him. "There's a man named Eddie Boyle in the valley that we've come to see. I guess you know who he is." When the rifleman's expression did not change, she went on, "If you don't know Boyle, I'm sure you know Cass. Go ahead and signal that we're on the way. Cass will vouch for us when we get to the valley."

For a moment, Longarm thought the sentry's face was frozen and could not change. Then the man gave what was supposed to be a smile and said, "If you know about Cass, I guess it's all right. Go on. I'll signal 'em that you're on the way." He stepped aside to let them pass.

Late Morning Star nudged her horse ahead. Longarm followed. They'd gone only a short distance when a rifle shot rang out behind them, the report echoing and reechoing off the steep rock walls. Longarm drew as he twisted in his saddle. The sentry's rifle was pointed to the sky. He fired a second shot.

Late Morning Star said quickly, "I should have told you what to expect. He's signaling that we're on the way in. Two shots, two of us."

Somewhat sheepishly, Longarm holstered his Colt and followed her on through the gorge. For some reason, he thought about his badge, hidden at the bois d'arc tree, and suddenly Longarm felt as if he were riding naked, but the sensation soon passed. He looked back once. The sentry stood watching them. The narrow passageway looked even smaller than it had before when Longarm turned back around and followed the Pawnee woman into Outlaw Valley.

Chapter 16

A reception committee waited for them at the end of the narrow passage, which ended abruptly. The valley spread out in front of them. Two riders sat near the passage, and when they saw the newcomers, they moved forward, their hands on their gunbutts.

"Don't argue with them," Late Morning Star warned Longarm in a low voice. "Just do what they tell you. It'll be all right."

Longarm studied the riders as they approached. The one in the lead was a bulky man, not tall, but deep-chested and wide, with a belly that pushed forward to touch his saddle horn. He wore a blue serge vest over a butternut shirt, and Levi's jeans that barely came over his hips. Under a low-crowned hat with a battered brim, his face was covered with a half-inch of gray beard. His nose had been mashed flat more than once. His small eyes were deepset, heavily lidded, and a pale, nearly gray shade of blue.

Something about him was familiar, Longarm thought, but he couldn't bring it to mind, and put it aside while he studied the second rider. This one was angular, all arms and elbows and thin legs in stovepipe twill pants and knees that stuck up higher than his saddle skirt. His chest and arms were bare under a calfskin vest. His hat was a roll-brimmed derby, incongruous above his cadaverous face, which narrowed to an outthrust jaw that came to a point nearly as sharp as a steer's horn.

"Hell, I know you," the wide man said to Late Morning Star. "You're Eddie Boyle's girl. Who's your friend, though?"

"His name's Custis. He's looking for a place to stay for a while."

"A friend of Boyle's?" the big man asked.

Longarm decided to speak for himself. "No. I've heard of him, but I've never seen him."

"Who wants you?" the man asked abruptly.

"What's that to you? And who in hell are you, to go asking that kind of question?" Longarm shot back.

"The name's Cass Sterret. I sort of run things here. If I say you can stay, you stay. If I say you can't, you can hightail it back outside and go to hell, for all I care."

Sterret's companion idly swung his rifle muzzle to cover Longarm. His hand was convenient to the trigger. Longarm didn't have to wonder whether there was a shell in the rifle's chamber; he knew there was.

He said, "No offense, Sterret." Then he frowned. "Wait a minute! You can't be Cass Sterret. He's been dead ten years or more."

Sterret chuckled lustily, "You're looking at a mighty active corpse, then. You cross me, and you'll find that out."

"I'm not looking to cross anybody, Sterret," Longarm said evenly. "Just a place to rest a while, till things in Nebraska settle down."

"You're a long ride from home," Sterret observed.

"Not because I had much choice. And that's all I aim to say about Nebraska, or anyplace else. Now, do I stay here, or don't I?"

Again Sterret chuckled. "You stay. If you can pay your way, that is."

"Say that in figures," Longarm told him.

"If you're busted, being pushed, you can work for your keep. If you're loaded heavy, sixty a month for your grub and a bunk. If you're light, a dollar a night for a place to spread your bedroll, and you scramble up your own grub."

Longarm nodded. "Sounds fair. What about the woman?"

"She don't figure in it," Sterret said. "She knows she can't stay longer than tomorrow morning."

Late Morning Star said quickly, "I guess I forgot to tell you that he won't let women stay in the valley."

"Too much trouble," Sterret growled. "These bastards get horny, they can go find their own piece. No women, Custis; that's the rule here."

Longarm nodded slowly. "All right. Even if I was inclined

to argue, which I ain't, I guess I ain't got much of a place to stand on."

"You got nothing here that I don't give you," Sterret said brusquely. "You staying, then?"

"That's what I came for," Longarm replied.

"All right. Hank, look over his saddlebags. Custis, give Hank your gunbelt and rifle." Sterret saw the look on Longarm's face and explained quickly, "They'll be kept safe for you; you'll get 'em back when you ride out. You got my personal word on that, Custis. I make the rules here, and my first one is no guns except the ones me and Hank pack. And you know why that's the rule. I run a hangout, not a graveyard."

Hank pulled his horse up beside Longarm. He opened the flaps of the saddlebags, and rummaged through them. Jerking his head toward Longarm's pistol, the outlaw held out a hand. Longarm unbuckled his gunbelt and passed it over. Before hanging the belt on his saddle horn, Hank swung the chamber open and let the shells fall in his hand. He asked, "You got a sleeve gun on? Or one in your belly-band?"

Instead of answering, Longarm lifted the bottom of his vest. "Fan me for one, if you want." Hank ran his hands around Longarm's waist, and passed a hand down each arm.

"All clean," he told Sterret. Then, turning back to Longarm, he said, "I'll take your Winchester, now."

Without hesitating, Longarm pulled his rifle from the saddle scabbard and surrendered it. Hank wheeled away.

Sterret said, "All right. You can pay me when we get to the bunkhouse. Let's go." He led the way into the valley, with the others following him.

From the sketchy description of the place given him by Late Morning Star, Longarm hadn't really expected as much as he now saw. He'd been prepared to see a shacktown, and there were some shacks among the buildings that were scattered without order or planning around the valley floor. They were crude, makeshift affairs cobbled up from bits of tin and timber. In addition to the shacks, though, there were some neat, small houses built of adobe or native stone, and three quite large structures, one of fieldstone, the other two of wood. The buildings followed no plan, either in style or placement. They centered roughly on an open area where a well stood, its wooden casing rising to a crossbar from which a pulley and bucket dangled.

Other buildings, even more widely spaced, stood at a distance from those clumped around the well. The valley itself formed a rough oval. Longarm judged it to be nearly three miles long and more than a mile wide. A rough corral fence stretch across the farthest end; behind the fence there were perhaps fifty steers and a half-dozen riders working them. Longarm recalled that Late Morning Star had said there would be fewer men around at this time because there were so many away on trail drives to Abilene and Wichita.

Along one side of the valley, silhouetted against the high cliffs that enclosed it, stood several closely grouped adobe buildings. Tall chimneys towered over all but one of them, trickling thin smoke trails that dissipated before the smoke reached the upper air. Longarm saw a man step out of one of them and walk to another. These buildings, he thought, must house the whiskey stills. On the other side of the oval-shaped area enclosed by the cliffs, there was a small log cabin with a shed tacked onto it. A short distance from the cabin there was a small pole corral that held a number of horses. An open-sided stable with its stalls clearly visible stood near the corral. There was a haystack at one side of the stable.

Cass Sterret had led the little procession from the valley's opening, and he headed for the big fieldstone house. In front of it, he reined in. Longarm saw that the house stood nearer the well, and closer to the two wooden structures than any of the other buildings. The fieldstone house, with its two stories and its full-length veranda, actually dominated the valley floor.

"Light down and come on in," Sterret invited. "I always give a stranger a drink to make him feel at home. After that, whatever liquor you want you get from the store, or buy it off the whiskey cookers, if you don't give much of a damn what you pour into your guts."

"I'll go over to Eddie's cabin," Late Morning Star announced. She looked at Longarm and added pointedly, "I won't tell Eddie I rode here with you, that would make him jealous. If you want to get acquainted with him after a while, I guess it'll be all right for you to stop by his cabin."

Longarm read her meaning, and nodded. He followed Sterret into the fieldstone house. Hank dismounted but stayed outside, taking a seat in one of the chairs that stood on the veranda. Inside the house, it was dim and cool. Sterret crossed the big room to a tall cabinet and threw it open.

"What's your pleasure, Custis?" he asked. "Don't be bashful about naming it. I got just about any kind of stuff a man could ask for here, and none of it was made in them stills out there. Fine bourbon, brandy, rum, rye, even got some of that funny-tasting stuff made in Scotland, the kind them Britishers over in the Texas Panhandle likes. What's yours?"

"I favor a good Maryland rye, myself."

Sterret smiled, obviously pleased with himself. "And I've got it. Told you I could pour whatever you asked for."

Sterret took out bottles and glasses and put them on a large round table in the center of the room. Longarm joined him, and poured himself a drink of rye while the outlaw filled a glass with brandy. For the first time, Longarm noticed that Sterret's right arm hung limp and useless at his side; while riding, the old outlaw had kept it propped against his saddle horn. The big man caught Longarm's look.

"That's why you thought I was dead," he said. "The last job me and my old gang pulled—a bank out in Utah Territory—I took a shotgun blast in my shoulder. Couldn't get to a doctor. It festered up till I was like to die. My boys was getting itchy to move on, so I give 'em their split and let 'em go. Took a long time for me to heal up, and my arm wasn't no good when I did. I figured it was time to quit. When a man gets over a killing wound, he's a damn fool if he pushes his luck any further."

"And you wound up here in the Indian Nation."

"Right in this very spot. Nothing here, then. All there was in the Nation was them reservations over east. Never figured they'd go and crowd the Comanches and Kiowas and Cheyennes and 'Rapahoes in at my back door. But I learned to get along with 'em. Something I never managed to do with my own kind." Sterret raised his glass and Longarm followed suit. They drank.

Longarm said, "I never figured I'd ever be raising an elbow with Cass Sterret. I guess there're damned few who've forgot you, Cass. Lawmen, especially. Even if they have got you tagged as dead."

"I want 'em to keep me tagged that way, too. That's why I never go out of the valley no more. When a man can't draw a Colt or put a Winchester to his shoulder, he ought to either be dead or smart enough to quit." He drained his glass and put it down. "All right, let's get on to business. How long you figure to stay?"

"Now, how in hell do you expect me to tell you that?" Longarm asked. "Two weeks, a month. When I think it's safe, I'll stick my nose out and sniff the air. If it smells clean, maybe I'll move on. If I don't like it, I'll duck back in. Like a woodchuck does when winter's getting over."

"I don't give a shit how long you stay, Custis. All I want to know is, can you pay me for as long as you're here?"

"Let's say I pay you for a month, bunk and grub. At the end of a month, if I stay, I'll keep on paying. I've got it, if that's what bothers you."

Sterret gave a peculiar, one-shouldered shrug. "Suit yourself. Long as you follow the rules. No guns, no gambling, no women. Buy whatever you need at the store. For cash, no credit. You can sleep in the bunkhouse or one of the shacks; I got room in both places, Eat in the cookshack, back of the store, breakfast and supper."

"You said grub," Longarm protested. "I took it to mean three squares a day, not two."

"If I'd meant three, I'd've said three. You don't like it, move on," Sterret replied.

"I'll put up with it," Longarm said. He kept his voice mild. Fishing in his pocket, he selected three double eagles by feel and put them on the table. "I'll pay again when this is used up."

"Long as you're prompt," Sterret said, as he swept the gold coins up in his good hand and dropped them in a pocket. Raising his voice, he called out, "Hank!" When the lanky man came in, Sterret said, "Custis says he'll stay a month, maybe more. You can take his guns over to Dutchy now."

"Wait a minute," Longarm protested. "If I'm going to give up my guns, I want to see how you'll look after 'em. I don't guess there's anything in your rules against that, is there?"

The old outlaw nodded. "Now, I respect you for that, Custis, I like a man who looks after the tools of his trade. You go on with Hank, and ease your mind." Then he added, "Hank, you might as well show him the ropes, as long as you're outside. Save me doing it."

Longarm rode with Hank to the log cabin that snuggled up to the valley wall. The lanky man was apparently in no mood for conversation. When they dismounted at the cabin, Hank took Longarm's guns and started inside. Longarm followed.

At first glance, he thought he'd walked into a gun shop. After a second look, he was sure he had. A balding man bent over a workbench that spanned the cabin's end; the bench was littered with guns and parts of guns being repaired. A loading press occupied one end of the bench, with its dies racked neatly on the wall beside it. A cabinet stood against the back wall, an iron grill forming its door. Rifles were racked closely along the back of the cabinet, and pistols hung on pegs on each of its end walls. The door leading to the shed was in the back wall; it stood ajar, and Longarm could see kegs and canisters of powder stacked inside it. The man at the bench finished the adjustment he was making to a rifle action and looked up.

"Got a new boarder, Dutchy," Hank said. "This here's Custis. Here's his guns."

Dutchy bobbed a nod to Longarm and took the guns with a lover's hands. He levered the shells from the rifle and peered at its action. Then he put the Winchester on the bench and gave the Colt a minute inspection. He smiled at Longarm. "You vas a careful man, Herr Custis. But more careful of der pistol, *ja? Sehr gut*, I clean der rifle."

Dutchy stood up and Longarm saw his legs, which had been hidden under the bench. The right leg ended in a stump at mid-calf, and the gunsmith's knee rested in a wooden peg strapped to his thigh. He hobbled to the cabinet and unlocked it, and after wiping Longarm's weapons carefully with an oiled cloth, he affixed a small brass tag to each of them. He hobbled back to Longarm and handed him a third tag, Longarm looked at it; it bore an engraved number, 26, on its face.

"Dis vay, you are chure I don't get der guns mixed up," Dutchy explained. "Ven you go, you gift me der tag, I gift you der guns."

Hank had already started for the door, and Longarm hurried

to catch up with him. They mounted up, and started back toward the buildings that clustered around the well. Halfway there, Hank pulled up.

"Cass said show you the ropes," he told Longarm. He pointed as he spoke. "Bunkhouse yonder. Store and cookshack's in back of it. Breakfast's at sunup for an hour, supper's from sundown till everybody's ate. Card game in the cookshack most nights. No bets, though. Take any bunk that ain't claimed, or pick you a shack nobody's using. That'd be them two 'dobes past the well or them cruddy ones further on. Anything else you wanta know?"

"I guess not." Longarm surveyed the empty shanties. "If it's all the same, I'll take that middle 'dobe."

"Good enough. Might be a bucket in it, or you can buy one at the store. Shithouse is in back of the bunkhouse."

"I'll find it when I need it," Longarm assured him.

"Turn your horse in the corral when you're unsaddled. Nobody's going to bother it. Was I you, I'd get one of the boys at the stock corral to fix that brand up, though. It wouldn't fool nobody that looked at it close."

"I was in a hurry when I got this nag," Longarm explained. "It was the only one I could lay hands on. And I don't carry a running iron; that ain't my type of work."

"Sure. Well, you take him over tomorrow or the next day and tell Pete or Charlie what you want. They'll take care of it for you."

"Thanks, I'll do that. But I don't expect I'll be going outside for a while."

"If you do, let Cass or me know. There's a guard out at the passway day and night, and nobody gets in or out unless Cass or me says so," Hank said. "Well, I guess that's all. See you at supper."

Longarm watched the lanky rider stop at the hitch rail in front of Sterret's house and hurry inside. He'd noticed the old outlaw's eyes squinting at the US brand on the horse, and had been ready to repeat to him the story he'd just told Hank.

So far, old son, he told himself, *it's working out all right. So far.*

Late Morning Star's horse stood outside one of the adobe huts about two hundred yards from the one Longarm had selected. He started to pull up and see how she and Boyle were getting along, but decided he might walk in on their reunion when it was in an embarrassing stage, and went on to the one where he'd be staying. He took off his saddlebags and bedroll and dropped them on the dirt floor of the hut. The hut was eight feet on a side, its only furniture a narrow bunk and a three-legged stool. If it had held any more furniture, time and hard use had removed it. Longarm shrugged and went back outside.

He looked around the valley. There was no activity visible at Sterret's big house, or at the bunkhouse or the store. The wranglers at the cattle corral were still visible, and smoke still trickled from the buildings that housed the whiskey stills, Longarm realized that somebody in Sterret's house might be keeping an eye on him. His movements had to be those of a man settling in for a long stay. He led his mount to the horse corral and unsaddled it. There were other saddles on a rail in the open-sided stable, and Longarm added his to the lineup. Then he started walking back to his adobe.

Halfway there, he changed his mind. If Late Morning Star and Boyle hadn't finished celebrating their reunion by now, it was time they did. He strolled to the hut where the Pawnee woman's horse stood tethered. The door was closed. He knocked.

"Who is it?" Late Morning Star called.

"Custis. Mind if I come in?"

"Just a minute."

He waited. After a few moments, the door opened and Late Morning Star held it ajar.

"Come on in," she invited him.

Longarm stepped inside. He squinted in the dimness. He could see the form of a man lying on the bunk, a single bunk like the one in his own hut. He supposed it was Boyle, but couldn't yet make out any details of the recumbent man's appearance. He turned to speak to Late Morning Star, who was still standing by the open door.

Suddenly, the door slammed shut. A shadowy figure stepped from the shadows. Longarm couldn't see the figure clearly, any more than he could see Boyle, but the trickle of light that filtered through the small dirt-encrusted window of the hut glinted on the blue steel of a pistol, pointed at him.

Longarm wouldn't have tried to draw, even if he'd been wearing his gunbelt. He extended his arms, hands open. "All right," he told the shadowy man. "You got me cold, Now maybe you'll tell me why."

"Just make sure you behave yourself, Marshal," the man said.

Longarm looked questioningly at Late Morning Star.

She nodded. "Yes," she said. "He knows who you are. I didn't tell him; I didn't have to. He already knew. He was waiting for me when I came in."

Longarm's eyes were adjusted now to the dim interior of the hut, and he could see details. The man was an Indian. He wore the blue uniform, the wide-brimmed black hat, and the badge of the Nation's Indian police.

"I'm Black Horse," the Indian said. "And I think you'd better go sit down, Marshal Long." He flicked the pistol in the direction of the cot where Boyle lay. "I don't guess it'll bother you to sit by a dead man."

"Boyle?" Longarm asked.

"He'd already killed Eddie when I came in," Late Morning Star told Longarm. "He was waiting for you to get here—Black Horse, I mean, not Eddie."

"Boyle didn't want to help us," Black Horse said casually. "The only thing I could do was put my knife in him."

"I'm trying to figure out what all this is about," Longarm said. "Late Morning Star, why's this fellow here, anyway?"

"If you'll do what I told you to, and sit down, you'll find out a lot quicker," Black Horse said. "She doesn't know the whole story, anyhow."

"All right." Longarm stepped to the bunk and sat on its edge. He glanced at Boyle, saw the blood-soaked shirt that the dead man wore, and turned back to face the Indian policeman. "I'm ready to listen, and I hope you've got a good story."

"It's good enough for us. It'll have to be good enough for you, whether you like it or not." Black Horse hunkered down, leaning easily against the wall. He gestured to Late Morning Star with his gun, and she sat down on the floor, her legs folded under her.

"It's a real quick story to tell," Black Horse said. "We want the money Boyle stole, and we want the reward that's offered for him. We've got the money; that's in a sack under the cot there. But there's only a little over twenty thousand left, and that's not enough. We need the other ten thousand, the reward. You're going to help us get it, Marshal."

"Do you mind telling me who you mean when you say 'we'?" Longarm asked.

"Now, that's not quite as easy to explain, but I'll try to make you understand," the Indian said. "I don't know how much the woman's told you about us, or what old Hawk Flies High told you, either, but we Pawnees are tired of being one of the poor tribes. We see the Cherokees getting rich, and the Comanches and Kiowas still taking just about anything they want. Even the damned Creeks are getting ready to take part of what the Cherokees and Cheyennes will get for letting white-eyes keep cattle on our land. We're going to see that the Pawnees get a share, too."

"Hold up," Longarm protested. "You're talking way past where I sit. I've got to catch up to where you are, Black Horse."

The Pawnee nodded, took a breath, and continued more calmly, "Our hunting grounds in the Outlet will be ruined soon. The Cherokees sold land to the railroad, and already the trains go through where we once went to hunt. Now, both the Cherokees and the Cheyennes are going to lease the rest of the Outlet and unallocated land to white ranchers. We will have no place to hunt, so we must have part of that land to begin cattle herds."

Longarm cut in, "If you're talking about Scott Forest's scheme, I know about that, all right. I didn't know about the railroad, though."

"Trains have just begun to run on the new tracks. But do you think Forest is the only one who wants the Outlet land? That is not true. The Cherokees and Cheyennes themselves are planning to lease it to other ranchers than the ones with Forest."

"If it makes you feel any better, I aim to squash Forest's scheme to get that land."

Black Horse said thoughtfully, "That won't stop the Cherokees and Cheyennes. How do you plan to handle them? You must, to help us."

"You still ain't told me who 'us' is," Longarm reminded the man.

The policeman slapped his chest with his free hand, and said proudly, "We're the young Pawnees. We're like the Cheyenne Dog Soldiers. We don't agree with the old men of our tribe, who want us to keep on taking whatever scraps the army and the agents toss to us."

"Where does Hawk Flies High come into this?"

"He doesn't," Black Horse answered. "He's one of our old men. We respect him because he used to be a great leader of our tribe, but we don't listen to him any more."

"It might be a good thing if you did," Longarm suggested. "He struck me as being a pretty wise old man."

"His wisdom belongs to another time!" Black Horse said, with contempt in his voice. "Hawk Flies High was a young man when our tribe was the most powerful on the prairie. He saw our young fighting men killed by the pony soldiers and the Comanches and Kiowas and Sioux, and by your smallpox. And then we were nothing. We were beggars—starving because your agents didn't feed us like they were supposed to. That's when we young men decided things had to be changed."

"How are you aiming to change things?" Longarm asked.

"If the Cherokees and Seminoles and Creeks are going to let others use their land—or what they claim is their land—we think it should be us, and the Arapahoes and the other hunting tribes. Let the Cherokees and Chickasaws and Wichitas keep their farms." He spat out the word "farms" with loathing. "We want the range land, where we can grow cattle. Why should they let your people have it, when it belongs to all of us?"

Longarm nodded. "I guess I can see how you'd feel. But what's all that got to do with me?"

"We need money to pay the Cherokees and their friends, to replace the money they'd be getting from your ranchers. We don't want to rob our people, Marshal. We're willing to pay for what we want, but we Pawnees are a poor tribe."

"I'm getting the idea now," Longarm said. "You need Boyle's cash, and the reward money the bank's offered for him, to close up your deal with the eastern tribes."

"Yes. But Boyle's money's not enough. We've got to have the reward money, too."

"And that's where I come in?"

"You can arrange for the reward to be paid to one of us.

Why not? There's Boyle's body, right behind you. I killed him—me, Black Horse, a Pawnee. The reward poster says 'dead or alive.' Why shouldn't I get what's due me?"

"I'd say you've got the reward money coming," Longarm agreed, "even if I was on the way here to take him back, which would've been alive, if you hadn't butted in." He looked at Late Morning Star. "How do you feel about this scheme Black Horse has got going?"

"I didn't bring you here for a reward. I did it for Hawk Flies High. But I don't have anything to say about what the tribe does. You know that."

Black Horse broke in, "You're stalling, Marshal. I want you to say right now that we get the reward and the money Boyle stole."

Longarm had made up his mind. Casually, as though impelled by habit, he brought up a hand and began fingering his watch chain. He said, "Black Horse, the stolen money's not mine to give away. I'd be stealing it myself if I let you have it. I'll try to see that you get the reward, though."

Black Horse stood up. He shifted his revolver to his left hand and slid a long knife from his belt sheath with his right. "Then you'll have to die, too. The reward money's not enough."

Late Morning Star gasped loudly and Black Horse glanced at her involuntarily. Longarm tugged his watch chain and the derringer leaped into his hand. He fired. Black Horse crumpled to the floor while the flat report of the derringer was still echoing in the little hut.

Chapter 17

"Is he dead?" Late Morning Star asked. Her voice was cool and matter-of-fact; she might have been asking the time of day.

"Dead as anybody'll ever be," Longarm answered tersely, as he dropped the derringer back into his vest pocket. "No way to miss, from only six feet away." Longarm indicated the body on the bed. "You'd better catch me up on how all this happened."

"All I can tell you is what Black Horse told me," the woman replied. "He knew I was bringing you here, so he came in last night, climbed up and came in at the side of the valley. I don't suppose Sterret worried too much about the old Indian trails that go through the hills, so Black Horse got in without anybody knowing he was here."

Longarm said with some relief, "Well. That makes me feel considerable easier. I half-suspicioned that he and Sterret were in cahoots."

"No. It was Black Horse's idea, his and his friends. He'd already killed Eddie when I got here, and was hiding in the house. He knew that sooner or later you'd come here, so all he had to do was wait. And that's as much as I know."

"It's enough. At least I know Sterret won't be looking for Black Horse. Or Boyle, either, as long as you're here."

"He'll expect me to leave tomorrow," Late Morning Star warned Longarm. "When I brought Eddie in here, Sterret let me stay the night because it was too late for me to start back. I suppose he'd do the some thing this time."

"That'd figure." A plan was forming in Longarm's mind. It was still incomplete, and he needed time to round it out. He asked the woman, "That railroad Black Horse said something about. How come we didn't cross the tracks on our way here?"

"Because it's west of the trail we took. We came straight south from the fort."

"How far is the track from the place where we came into the valley?"

"Fifteen miles, more or less. Why?"

"Never mind why, right now. I've got the start of a plan, and if I can work it out, we might be able to get through this mess with whole skins." Longarm spoke confidently, but he wasn't certain that he could pull all the strings of his idea together, and tie them into a knot tight enough to hold.

Late Morning Star sat quietly while Longarm lighted a cheroot to help him think. After a few moments he stood up and started pacing. The hut was so small that he could only take two steps in each direction, but by the time the cigar was reduced to a stub he had the plan in fairly good shape.

He asked bluntly, "You think you can stay in this place by yourself tonight? With these two bodies?"

"Why not?" she said, and Longarm noticed with some surprise that she was actually smiling. "I'm not afraid of the dark, or of dead men, either."

"All right. I can't work my plan until tomorrow night. There's too much to do to make it go, and I've got to show up at the supper table this evening, or Sterret and his bunch might start wondering about me. I need to look his crew over, anyhow. I'll tell 'em Boyle's feeling poorly—which'll be the truth, in a way—and that you're looking after him. I'll bring you some supper, too."

"You don't have to do that. I can miss a meal without it hurting me."

"If I don't behave like Boyle's still alive and there's nothing wrong with him but a gut ache, my plan might fall apart. You just sit tight. You know how to handle a pistol?"

"Yes."

Longarm gave her Black Horse's revolver. "If anybody but me tries to get in here, use it."

"Is that part of your plan?"

"No. But if anybody gets inside this shack before tomorrow night, my plan's busted before it even gets started." He went to the door. Before leaving, he said, "I'll be back in a while. Don't be afraid to do what I told you, now."

"I'm not afraid," she said, without a trace of quaver in her voice. "But I hope I won't have to use the gun."

Longarm walked to the dining room. There were eleven men at the table, counting the wranglers and the whiskey cookers he'd noticed during the afternoon. Sterret wasn't at the table, and Longarm guessed that he ate by himself, in his own house. Dutchy, the gunsmith, was also missing. Hank was there, and so was the man who had been guarding the valley entrance earlier in the day. Hank made perfunctory introductions, which the others acknowledged in offhand fashion, between bites. Longarm didn't try to remember all the names, but concentrated on sizing up the men he hadn't seen before, while he ate steak, fried potatoes, beans, and biscuits, and washed his food down with coffee.

Halfway through the meal, Hank remarked, "I guess Boyle's too busy making up for lost time to come eat tonight."

"I nearly forgot," Longarm said. "I stopped by his place to pay the Pawnee woman for bringing me in here. She said Boyle's got a gut ache, and she's going to stay to look after him. I told her I'd bring her a dish of food on my way back."

"Gut ache, my ass," one of the men said with a rasping chuckle, "Eddie's just got a hard-on he can't work down with one shot at her."

"Can't say I blame him," another grinned. "I get mighty horny when I been here a long time, myself. I wouldn't mind having a while with that woman, even if she is a breed."

"Well, he better enjoy it tonight," Hank observed. "Him and the woman both know Cass's rules. She's gotta get out of here before noon tomorrow."

"All I know's what she said," Longarm volunteered. "Sort of surprised me. The way Cass was talking this afternoon, I thought she'd have to go tonight. That's why I stopped by to pay her off."

"Tell Sally," Hank said. "He'll fix you up something to take 'em."

"You going to set in on our game?" asked one of the wranglers.

"What's the use of playing cards if a man can't make a bet on what he's holding?" Longarm asked. "I ain't fond of dry runs."

"It's better than just sitting with your finger up your ass," another put in.

Longarm grinned. "Maybe, but not much, No, I've done a lot of riding today. I'll save your game till tomorrow. Right now, bed looks pretty good to me, and I'm heading to crawl in."

He stopped in the store and bought a bottle of Maryland rye, then went to the kitchen to ask Sally—all rangeland cooks were called that, even though virtually all of them were men—to fix a plate of food for Eddie Boyle. With the bottle under one arm, and the plate held in both hands, he walked to the late Eddie Boyle's cabin in the darkening twilight. Late Morning Star had the door open, waiting for him.

"I was watching for you," she said. "Or for anybody who might decide to come and ask about Eddie."

"I don't think you've got much to worry about," Longarm assured her. "The way Hank talked at supper, Sterret's looking for you to stay tonight. But he says you've got to be out by noon tomorrow."

She nodded. "I know. Is that going to give you enough time?"

"Plenty." Longarm wasn't certain, but he wasn't going to sow any doubts in her mind. "If you stayed to go out with me, it'd be twice as hard for both of us to get clear. There're some things I'll ask you to help me do tonight, though."

She indicated the bodies. "These?"

"Yes. I can't take a chance on somebody coming to see Boyle after you go." Stepping to the cot, Longarm worked the blanket out from beneath Boyle's stiffened corpse. "While you can still see, cut a set of muffles out of this. You can get your horse to wear 'em, can't you?"

"I've never tried. But he's pretty manageable."

"If we have to, we'll do without 'em, but I'll feel better if we can move him around real quiet."

"All I can do is try," she said with a shrug.

"That's all any of us can do. All right, I got to get to my own place, now. Are you going to be all right till I come back? It'll be late."

"What if somebody comes? Do you still want me to shoot?"

"Only if you have to. I doubt you'll be bothered—I sort of hinted that you and Eddie were busy. I'll keep an eye out, and

try to head off anybody who looks like he's coming this way."
He peered out the window to make sure no one was watching,
then realized that he had a perfectly legitimate reason for
being there, and went to the door. Just before he left, he said,
"I'll tap, around midnight."

Back in his own small adobe hut, Longarm stretched out on
the bunk with the bottle on the floor within easy reach. He lay
there while the first hours of the night dragged by, getting up
now and then to step outside and survey the valley. He let the
cabin stay dark, and when he moved outdoors it was like stepping from the midnight black of a shut closet into a candlelit
room. The quarter moon beaming through the clear night air
gave him enough light to see clearly from one end of Outlaw
Valley to the other.

Threads of smoke still ribboned from the whiskey stills,
though the stillhouses were unlighted. He concluded that the
cookers left their mash to bubble without attention through
the night. There were no guards at the stillhouses, the corral,
or the stable. Dutchy's light went out early. The lights in the
store and cookshack burned latest, until almost midnight. The
bunkhouse lights were extinguished soon after that. Sterret apparently retired early; his big house was dark by ten. Only two
of the cabins had occupants, Longarm concluded, and they
went to bed soon after the store closed. Long before moonset,
the valley lay quiet and dark.

Even so, Longarm waited until an hour after the last light
had vanished before he decided it was safe to make a move. He
walked quietly to the cabin where Late Morning Star waited
and scratched at the door. She opened it and he slipped inside.

"You got the muffles ready?" he asked her.

"They're already on the horse. I risked walking him around
the cabin. He'll be all right."

"Good." Longarm went to the bunk and lifted Boyle's body.
The period of rigor mortis had passed, and the corpse was limp
now. He hefted it over a shoulder and carried it outside, where
Late Morning Star helped him drape it across her pony's back.
They went inside again. Black Horse's body was stiff, its limbs
set in the position in which the Pawnee had fallen. It was a
hard job for both of them to lift and carry the ungainly burden

outside, and a bigger job to get it balanced beside Boyle's body on the horse's back.

Longarm said, "You lead the horse over to that haystack by the stable. I'll walk along and hold the—hold the load on."

Its hooves muffled by the layers of blanket wound around them, the pony walked silently under Late Morning Star's guidance. At the haystack, Longarm groped until he found the pitchfork; it was leaning against one of the timbers that supported the stable roof. He opened a trench in the middle of the haystack and he and the woman put the bodies in it. Then Longarm replaced the hay he had removed.

"They'll stay hid for as long as we need 'em to," he told her. "Now let's get on back."

Their return to the cabin was as silent as their departure had been, and as uneventful. Longarm said, "You take off the muffles while I step inside and pick up Boyle's loot. With any luck, it'll all go with me back to Colorado, if I get back. And I'll see that you get the reward money, Late Morning Star. You've more than earned it."

She shook her head vigorously, with a grimace of distaste. "I don't want it."

"Give it to your people, then. I'd trust old Hawk Flies High to see that it was put to good use." Longarm took her silence for assent.

"What about Black Horse's gun?" she asked. "I haven't any place to hide it when I ride out."

"I'll take it; I might need it tomorrow night."

"Will I see you tomorrow before I go?"

"Not unless I'm just standing around when you pass by. I aim to keep out of everybody's way as much as I can tomorrow."

"Will you come to the reservation before you leave? We'll only be at the hunting camp a few more days."

"If I get time, Late Morning Star. If I don't get to, you know I'm real grateful to you for the help you gave me."

"I think I owe you more than you owe me. You've made me feel like a whole woman again." She pulled Longarm's head down and kissed him. While still holding him close, she whispered, "I wish we could be together again tonight, but I know it wouldn't be safe."

"I'd like it, too," he agreed with a sigh. "But you're right. It wouldn't be safe or smart."

"Goodbye, then, Custis Long."

"Don't make it sound so final, damn it!" Longarm tried to be casual, but he knew their parting was more likely than not to be a final one. "I'll be in the Nation awhile. We'll meet someplace."

"Yes, of course."

Longarm slipped out and heard the door of the shack close behind him. He went to his own shanty and undressed in the dark. He knew the nights ahead might be sleepless, and he intended to make the most of this one.

He went in for breakfast at the latest possible time. Except for the night guard who'd just gotten back from watch duty at the valley entrance, he was the only one at the table. The guard was sleepy and grouchy, and not much interested in talking. The meal was a silent one, and Longarm went back to his shack at once.

In midmorning, a time when he thought busy men would be apt to pay the least attention to him, Longarm saddled up and rode around the valley. While he was adjusting the saddle on the gelding, he inspected the haystack. As nearly as he could tell, it hadn't been touched; at least the pitchfork was still where he'd left it.

He rode across to the stillhouses first. A hundred yards away from them, the sour smell of cooking mash struck him like a wall, and seemed to grow stronger as he got closer. The whiskey cookers had apparently grown used to having new arrivals in the valley visit them. They paid little attention to Longarm, and did nothing to keep him from wandering around, watching them at work. The wood-fired stills were bubbling in three of the four houses. They were big metal vats, from the tops of which long coils of copper worms protruded. From the open ends of the worms, thin but steady streams of clear distillate dripped into collecting barrels. The smell of raw alcohol was overpowering inside the houses, stronger even than the prevailing aroma of the cooking mash.

Curious about the fourth building, Longarm went into it,

after he'd seen that what was happening in the others was pretty much the same. Here two of the cookers he'd met at the supper table were dipping the raw liquor out of kegs and transferring it to wicker-covered gallon jugs.

"That your aged stuff?" Longarm asked.

One of the perspiring cookers snorted contemptuously. "Aged, shit! We don't do nothing fancy like that. This is the stuff we sell to the whiskey ranches. It's—well, hell, take a taste for yourself." The man passed his dipper over to Longarm.

Overcoming his scruples, Longarm took a small sip from the dipper. The liquid seared his lips and tongue like liquid fire. He was unable to swallow it, but spat it on the floor. The two cookers guffawed.

"Jesus God!" he exclaimed hoarsely. "How can anybody swallow this stuff?"

The cooker who had handed him the dipper stopped laughing long enough to say, "Why, nobody does. This here's a hunnerd-'n-forty-proof dynamite. The whiskey ranchers cuts it half or more, and puts in a little sugar and a squirt or so of tobacco juice, and a good wallop of red pepper before they puts it in bottles. A gallon of this cuts down to five or six gallons of what they sell for whiskey."

To take the taste of the uncut spirit out of his mouth, Longarm produced a cheroot and was about to flick his thumbnail over a match when the man slapped the match out of his hand. Seeing Longarm's anger, he quickly apologized.

"Sorry, friend. I forgot to tell you we can't have nobody light a match in here. This stuff'd go up like coal oil. Faster, even. Can't you smell them fumes?"

Longarm could not only smell them, he could almost see them. He said, "My fault. I didn't know it was that bad." Then he asked, "How do you get what you need for the mash, away from everything this way? Seems to me you'd be better off with your still close by a road somewhere."

"Oh, it ain't too hard," the cooker answered. "Less'n ten miles from the entrance to the road that runs from Fort Supply down to Fort Elliott, there's always loads of corn for the cavalry and sugar for the mess halls being hauled over it. The army pays teamsters worse'n privates. Some of 'em don't balk at saying that a bunch of Indians jumped 'em and stole their load. And not too far up north, in the river brakes, there's plenty of wood."

"Seems to me like a hell of a lot of work," Longarm observed.

"It ain't, though. We only run off a batch every three or four months. That keeps the whiskey ranches in business."

Longarm smiled. "I think I'll stick to banks. Guess I better get out from under foot now and let you men work. See you at supper."

He rode back across the valley to the gunsmith's shop. Dutchy was hard at work, this time on a pistol. He paid little attention while Longarm, making conversation all the while, wandered around the shop, looked into the powder storage shed, and generally made himself at home. He visited with the gunsmith for nearly a half hour before he led his horse the few hundred feet to the corral, unsaddled it, and walked to the store.

"Didn't think I'd be hungry after all that breakfast I had so late," he told the storekeeper. Like Dutchy and Sterret, the man behind the counter was a former outlaw who been crippled in some foray that had ended badly. The storekeeper's injury was a mangled right hand.

"I'll sell you some cheese and crackers," the man offered. "Or some airtights, if you want. I got peaches and figs and greengage plums in airtights—all of 'em mighty tasty."

"Now, I sure don't figure on ruining a good knife, opening airtights," Longarm said. "But if you've got one of those patent cutters they've come out with, and you'll make me a loan of it, I'd relish some peaches with my crackers and cheese."

"I got one I'll sell you for a dime. Handle's a little bent, but it won't be much of a trick for you to straighten it out."

"I'll just take it. Since I'm going to be here a spell, I'll get my dime's worth out of it." Then, as if it were an afterthought, Longarm added, "And I've got to have some of that light rope they use to hold the canvas in those bunks. One side of mine busted out last night. The rope rotted through."

"I know what you want. Damn it, I keep telling Cass he oughta string them bunks with rawhide, but he don't listen.

Nobody pays much attention to me around here. You'll need about eight feet of that stuff, if you only got to fix one side."

"Better give me enough for both sides. And I don't aim to pay for it; you charge that to Cass. I'll fix the damn bunk myself, but it's his bunk, and I won't buy the rope to fix it with."

The storekeeper scratched his grilled chin with his scarred and twisted hand. "Well—I'll tell Cass I give it to you, but don't you be surprised if he says you got to pay for it."

"If he tells me that, I'll straighten him out about it," Longarm assured him.

Longarm took his purchases back to the shack and made a quick meal. He forced himself to eat all the peaches, but poured most of the juice onto the ground outside the door. Then he washed the can with water from his bucket, dried it well, and sat down to untwist the strands of light rope he'd gotten. The roper was made of cotton, and the cords were loosely twisted. He stretched the three lengths that the untwisting had produced, and coiled them in the empty can. He poured most of the kerosene from the shack's lamp over the coils, and put the can in a corner to let the cotton soak up the kerosene, Then he lay down and catnapped until dusk.

A roar of laughter from the dining room greeted Longarm when he entered the store. He found Cass Sterret presiding at the supper table. The old outlaw's plate was empty, a bottle of whiskey stood in front of him, and he was laughing harder than anybody else. Sterret saw Longarm and waved him in.

"Plenty of room, Custis, and plenty of grub left, too. Most of us has ate; we're just swapping lies and wasting time."

Longarm ate slowly, listening, while the role of storyteller passed from one outlaw to another around the table. He told no yarns himself, but made a point of laughing at the right time, or shaking his head soberly when the tale was a serious one. The card game started, but again he excused himself from joining the players. He stayed until the men began to drift away, and chose a time to leave when his own departure would attract the least attention. A lot of night lay ahead before he could start his work. Never a man to waste time, he slept again, lightly, until he judged that the hour was late enough for him to put his plan into operation.

When he looked out the door, all the buildings were dark: the headquarters, the cabins, the store, the bunkhouse. The quarter moon hadn't come up yet, and the valley was in the ghostly shadow of a night lighted only by stars.

All of Longarm's preparations had been made. He'd worked out the timing of his improvised fuses before going to supper, and cut the kerosene-soaked strands of rope into the proper lengths. Carrying the strands coiled in the can to keep them wet, he walked across the level valley floor to the still-houses. Their doors had no locks. Longarm laid a soaked strand in each stillhouse in turn, running them in straight lines from the doorway to the open barrels that caught the first-run liquor as it dripped from the copper worms. In the bottling house he breached several of the kegs to form puddles on the floor, and stretched his fuse into one of the puddles.

Laying the fuses had taken less time than he'd thought the job would, but staying ahead of schedule would do no harm; it was falling behind that worried him. Longarm lit the fuses, one match to each fuse.

Two of the four sputtered and spit before catching, then settled down to burn with a tiny flame that consumed two inches of cotton strand per minute. Having lit the final fuse, he hurried to the gunsmith's cabin. He tapped lightly but insistently until Dutchy's sleep-blurred voice called, "Who is dere? Go avay und come back yen it is daytime."

"It's me," Longarm said, making his voice as unrecognizable as possible. "Hurry up, Dutchy. Cass needs you to help him, right away."

There was a long silence, then a light appeared beneath the door, and soon the thudding of the gunsmith's wooden leg sounded as he crossed the floor. The door opened and Dutchy's china-blue eyes blinked and squinted at Longarm.

"*Was ist los?*" he asked. "Vot does Cass vant?"

Longarm shoved Black Horse's pistol into the man's ribs. "Sorry to get you out of bed, Dutchy, but I need my guns."

"*Nein!* For me to give dem to you—"

"I know," Longarm interrupted. "You've got to have Cass's say-so. He ain't here, but this talks louder'n he can." He emphasized his words with sharp, repeated prods of the revolver muzzle, backing the gunsmith into the cabin. "Now open that cabinet, and move fast!"

Dutchy, slow to awaken, finally realized what was happening. Muttering under his breath, he moved slowly to the chair on which his trousers were draped, produced his keys, and unlocked the cabinet. Before he could turn around, Longarm stunned him with a tap of the pistol barrel on the side of his head. Dutchy sagged to the floor.

Longarm quickly doused the lamp on the workbench before dragging the unconscious man outside. He half-hauled, half-carried the smith the short distance to the stable, and grabbed the handiest bridle to lash him to one of the roof posts. With quick efficiency, Longarm saddled his gelding and led it back to the gunshop.

There was one more length of fuse in the peach can. Longarm groped through the darkness and found his guns. He risked lighting a match and then another while he scooped up handfuls of ammunition and stuffed the cartridges in his pockets. He propped his rifle against the doorjamb, his gunbelt hanging from its muzzle. Now he turned his attention to the powder shed. He rolled out three full kegs of powder, breaching their tops with the butt of Black Horse's pistol before tossing the weapon aside. One of the kegs he rolled to the gun cabinet, with powder sifting from its top to lay a train to the second keg, which he left in the center of the cabin. He rolled the third keg into the storage shed, again letting a line of powder spill along the floorboards. Finally, he ran his last length of fuse from the center keg to the door and touched a match to it.

Running back to the corral, strapping on his gunbelt as best he could with one hand, Longarm removed the gate bars of the corral and tossed them aside. He jerked the gelding's reins free from the corral fence and led the horse back to the shack he'd occupied so briefly. His saddlebags were packed, heavy with the gold from Eddie Boyle's hut. He fastened them behind the saddle and mounted.

Resisting the temptation to hurry, he walked the gelding to the bluff where the passageway leading to the outside opened into the valley. Pulling the horse into the deep blackness at one side of the narrow slit, he sat and waited.

Though Longarm had known that the timing of his fuses was a long way from being exact, he waited so long that he began to wonder if the damned things had sputtered and gone out. He was thinking of going back to check on them when the first stillhouse exploded with a muffled boom and burst into blue flames. The other two stillhouses went up seconds later, followed after a short pause by the bottling house. The first explosion had brought men tumbling out of the bunkhouse. Longarm could see them silhouetted against the dancing fires that now lighted the side of the valley. The door of Sterret's headquarters swung open and Hank's unmistakable lanky frame appeared. Cass Sterret was at Hank's heels.

Men were running in and out of the bunkhouse, getting boots and pants. A few of them were already on their way to the stillhouses on foot, and others were running to the horse corral. Longarm saw Hank heading for the corral, and saw Sterret's arms waving as the old outlaw urged him to hurry. Before any of the runners reached the corral, the gunsmith's cabin blew up. The first blast was light, more a puff of blinding flame, as the loose powder in the kegs flashed. Then the storage shed exploded with a boom that shook the ground and sent bright sparks arcing into the sky. The men who'd been running toward the corral stopped when they saw the horses, spooked by the explosions, stream out and scatter over the valley floor.

Longarm had counted on the explosion to open his way out of the valley. He sat watching, his lips set grimly, as the flames danced higher. In a few moments the sentry guarding the passageway galloped past, drawn by the noise and fires. He dashed by Longarm without seeing him, all his attention concentrated on the havoc that engulfed the valley floor.

Longarm's mouth relaxed into a smile, He nudged the gelding with his toe and guided it into the narrow passage. He let the horse walk until he reached the end of the slit, then bounced his heal lightly into its belly to start it loping. Behind him the red glow brightened, lighting the sky and silhouetting the low humps of the Antelope Hills as Outlaw Valley surrendered to the flames.

Chapter 18

As they headed northward through the night, Longarm held the gelding to a walk, though it was well-rested and wanted to run.

There's time, he kept reminding himself. *It'll be a spell before things simmer down back there and they take out after me. They've got to put out fires and scrabble for guns and gather the horses up. And Cass Sterret's too cagey an old coon to start out in the dark. He'll wait for light so he can follow my tracks. It'll likely be noon before they get away. But from what I heard about Cass, he's a mighty vengeful man. He won't let something like what I just did to him pass by without trying to get even.*

When he got to the Canadian, Longarm pulled the gelding up and dismounted. *The horse doesn't really need the rest,* he thought. *Even with almost a hundred pounds of gold coins added to the weight it's carrying, it ain't a bit winded. And it had a breather when I stopped to dig out my badge. I'd play a fool's trick, though, trying to cross that river in the dark, what with all that quicksand in the bed just waiting to swallow a man up.*

With his back propped against a cottonwood tree on the bluff overlooking the Canadian, Longarm smoked a cheroot and waited for dawn. He sat quietly until the gray dawn light was bright enough to let him pick out the landmarks Late Morning Star had used when she'd led the way across the stream on their way to the valley. He let the gelding highfoot through the shallow water, ready to pull back on the reins if one of its feet should drop into a pocket. With the stream safely behind them, he let the animal lope part of the time after he turned west to look for the railroad line.

Dawn's gray had been washed from the sky by bright morning sunshine before he saw the tracks. They were so new that their tops hadn't yet been polished by the friction of steel wheels, and the ties still glowed bright yellow, unstained by oil and soot. Longarm angled to the tracks, and meeting them where a telegraph pole stood, he wrapped the gelding's reins around the pole while he fished the telegraph key out of his saddlebag. Dropping the key in his pocket, he stood on his saddle, balancing carefully while the horse stirred as it got used to the change in the weight it bore. He swung free of the saddle and shinnied up to the top of the pole.

There was no crossbar for him to hook a knee over. Longarm had to cling by clamping his thighs tightly around the pole while he opened his knife and scraped the single wire the pole supported. He twisted the lead wire of his key around the bright area of copper his scraping had created, then he had to rest his legs a minute by wrapping his arms around the pole. When he could hold himself in place again just by the pressure of his legs, he began tapping the key, Slowly at first, then faster, as the code came back to him.

— • — • — — • —

He tapped in the telegrapher's shorthand: "CQ," meaning "I'm calling."

After he'd sent the two-letter message several times he let the key rest, waiting to see who might answer. He had no idea to which railroad the tracks and telegraph wire belonged.

A reply came almost at once:

• — — • — • • • —

Longarm translated the dots and dashes as they came through. "W R U," the unknown operator at the other end of the line was asking: "Who are you?"

"L-o-n-g U-S-M-a-r-s-h-a-l," he tapped. "W R U?"

"FT W DE," the reply ticked out on his key. Longarm allowed himself a smile. He was in direct touch with the Denver office of the Fort Worth & Denver Railroad.

Picking up speed as he regained his feel of the key, what telegraphers call their "fist," Longarm sent: Official business. Get Chief U.S. Marshal Vail there fast."

"Why?" the inquiry came back.

Nettled, Longarm sent, "None of your damn business. Get Vail in your office on the double."

"You in trouble?" the Denver operator asked.

"Yes. Need Vail quick."

"Where are you?" Denver asked.

"Between hell and breakfast someplace in Indian Nation. Get Vail in your office and hurry up."

After that, Longarm stopped sending, though the key kept tapping, bringing questions from the railroad telegrapher in Denver. Longarm surmised that silence from his end would be more effective than words, and his hunch proved correct. A few minutes after he'd sent his last message, the key clicked and the Denver man sent, "Call-boy gone after Vail. Will you be there to answer?"

"Sure," Longarm transmitted. "CQ when Vail gets there."

Wedging his telegraph key between the porcelain insulator and the pole, Longarm let himself down. His legs were aching, and when his feet touched the ground he had to sit down for a few minutes and lean against the pole. The angle of the sun warned him that he was running out of time. By now, the uproar in what was left of Outlaw Valley had died down, and Cass Sterret was more than likely leading his gang out of the valley in pursuit. Every minute he sat waiting for Marshal Vail to answer cut Longarm's margin of safety thinner. He tried to make the minutes pass more quickly by getting out his military maps and studying them, looking for an area that might provide a hiding place in the flat, generally featureless land.

What he needed, Longarm thought after he'd examined the best map he had, was a hole he could crawl into and pull shut over him, and there wasn't any such place. Water was the one thing he couldn't do without, and the only water hereabouts was Wolf Creek, which didn't leave him a hell of a lot of choice. Without water, his horse would go down, and he wouldn't last long on foot, with Sterret's crew riding on his tracks. *Keeping a horse hid in this damn country*, he thought, *is just about like hiding an elephant on a pool table: no place to duck into in the middle, and the pockets around the edges are too damn little.*

Longarm's impatience increased as the sun climbed and the telegraph key stayed silent. At last it gave a preliminary clatter, as though clearing its throat, then tapped out: "Long. Vail here."

Longarm wasted no time getting back on top of the pole and grabbing for the key. The Denver operator was repeating his first call, and Longarm had to wait before he could reply. He tapped out, "Billy. Going to need some help."

Vail's answer came back, "What the hell kind of mess are you in now?"

"Not my mess. Got Boyle and bank money. Need help to handle graft in army and Indian bureau," Longarm explained.

For several seconds the key was silent, then it clicked, "Let army and bureau clean up their own mess."

"Can't," Longarm clicked back. "Too many big wheels in it."

"Get help from Fort Dodge," Vail suggested.

"Too big for Dodge. Needs Pope to handle it."

"Which Pope? Rome or General?" Vail asked.

"Stop fooling. You know who. General Pope," Longarm sent.

"You sure it's that big?" the key spelled out.

"It's that big. Get me Pope and a cavalry platoon." Longarm could almost see his chief's face getting redder and redder as the railroad telegrapher in Denver handed him the flimsy on which he'd copied that message.

After a few seconds the key clattered again, and when he spelled out the words its dots and dashes formed, Longarm grinned in spite of the cramps that were catching his legs. The message said, "See doctor. You got brain fever."

He suddenly realized that Vail's message wasn't very funny. He hunted for words that would convince his chief of the urgent need for the presence in the Nation of the West's highest-ranking military man and a small force of men responsible to him and not to a local commander. Longarm shorted his key with its sliding knife switch while he thought over his next message. When he opened the switch again, the key was tapping out the last few words of a transmission from Vail: "—got to know more about it before I stick my neck out."

Longarm waited as long as he thought safe before fingering the key again. "Being chased," he sent. "Can't argue any longer. Get Pope and platoon here on special train from Leavenworth. I'll meet them at Wolf Creek railroad bridge in four days." He was reaching for the key's lead wire to disconnect it when he saw the riders.

His height on top of the pole gave him the advantage. He hoped that to the approaching men he'd look like part of the pole itself. They were still distant, almost at the limit of his vision, but Longarm had no doubt as to who they were. He counted eleven of them, and even at this distance he was sure the wide, bulky figure on the first horse was that of Cass Sterret.

Longarm wasted no more time. He jerked the lead wire off the telegraph line and dropped the key in his pocket. He let himself down from the pole, and when he hit the ground and unwrapped his arms from the pole, his legs gave way under him. Cramps caught his thigh muscles, strained from their long period of being clamped on the pole, supporting his entire weight, during the long exchange with Vail. The cramps tied his muscles into knots. He tried to get up, but his legs would not respond. Ignoring the pains that stung like needles and set his legs twitching, Longarm reached up and got hold of the gelding's reins. He maneuvered the horse around until he could reach a stirrup. Then he used the stirrup to pull himself up until he could grab the saddle horn and lever himself into the saddle.

There wasn't any doubt in Longarm's mind as to what he had to do; he didn't have many choices. The flat prairie was no place for him to take on Sterret's gang single-handed; he had to keep away from them. For that, he needed broken country and the only place fitting that description was the strip of sand dunes—or hills, as the map described them. The map bore a note of warning to army teamsters and cavalry commanders: "bad sand hills."

Longarm remembered that when he and Late Morning Star had gone across the dunes on their way south he'd thought to himself that finding a fugitive who'd taken refuge in them would be a real job for a posse. It hadn't occurred to him then that he'd be a fugitive running from a gang of outlaws who were rougher than any posse, and would show him a lot less mercy.

As long as Sterret and his crew could see him, they'd dog him to exhaustion, then close in for the kill. Rough as the sand hills would be on his horse, their humps would hide him and their shifting, soft soil wouldn't hold hoofprints that trackers could follow. The dunes covered a crescent-shaped area nearly fifteen miles long and five miles across at their widest point. That was enough to give him running room as well as chances to hide and rest the gelding.

Longarm nudged the horse's ribs with his toe, urging it ahead, up the railroad embankment. The animal shied at the rails. When Longarm finally got it to step between them and turned it north, the gelding danced in protest against the unfamiliar footing offered by the wooden ties and ballast. Longarm kept the horse moving, and after a while it accepted the strange surface and settled down. Longarm's trail now dead-ended at the railroad. When Sterret's men got there, they'd be forced to split up and search in both directions until they found where he'd left the printless roadbed.

Even after they split, though, Longarm thought, there would still be five or six of them following the rails north. If they caught up with him, they could split up again, two or three men in each group. Experience had taught him that a single rider had little chance of escaping two pursuers, and practically no chance at all of getting away from three. He'd seen too many posses box their quarry and force a lone rider into a trap. Cass Sterret had seen that, too, Longarm knew, and he wasn't going to make the mistake of underestimating the wily old outlaw.

He kept the gelding on the roadbed for five or six miles before letting the horse step off. He picked a spot where the gandy dancers who'd laid the rails had worked down a carload of gravel ballast. For a hundred yards, the ground on both sides of the tracks was covered with spilled gravel and rutted with wheelbarrow tracks. The gelding crossed the area without leaving a telltale trail. Longarm headed east and entered the sand dunes at about the middle of their crescent-shaped expanse. Now he could circle and angle as much as he needed to. The only way Sterret's outlaws could flush him out would be to form a single line and sweep the dunes from end to end, and there weren't enough of them to do that effectively.

For the past hour, Longarm's stomach had been sending him signals. He'd had no breakfast, and the gelding hadn't grazed or been watered since the Canadian River crossing. On their way to the valley, Late Morning Star had mentioned that even the Indians avoided the sandhills because they had no springs or streams in them, He'd known all along that he'd be limited to the water his canteen held, and that he'd have to manage to get to Wolf Creek or go back to the river to refill it. He'd calculated the risk, and taken it, because he'd have to be at Wolf Creek to meet the army contingent at the railroad bridge, even though he wasn't certain the troops would be there in four days—or ever.

Longarm found a shallow gully between two undulating ridges of sand where sandgrass grew in a narrow strip that caught and held water after one of the infrequent rains. There was no water there now, but the grass would provide grazing for the roan. Before he let the horse eat, he poured water from his canteen into his cupped hand and splashed as much of it as he could into the animal's mouth. Then he reached into his saddlebag for jerky and hardtack, and found that he had something else to think of besides water.

Haste had made Longarm careless. He'd neglected to replenish his rations before leaving Fort Supply. Always, he carried a foot-long chunk of jerky and a dozen or so rounds of hardtack. He'd used his reserve more than usual, though. He and Nellie, then he and Late Morning Star, had fallen back on the hardtack and jerky several times. He now had a two-inch stub of jerky and a single hardtack round. There were a little bit of rice and a small handful of beans, but both were useless to him in the waterless, woodless dunes. Longarm took the jerky and broke off a quarter of the hardtack round and sat down on the side of the dune to eat.

Nibbling at shavings of the jerky, he watched the roan grazing. "Damn me for a constipated jackass," he said aloud to the empty air. "Looks like that horse is going to be better fed than I am for the next couple of days."

Longarm's offhand observation turned out to be remarkably accurate. The sandgrass wasn't plentiful, but it grew abundantly enough in scattered patches for the gelding's hunger to be satisfied, as long as it was moved from one patch of sandgrass to the next. For the first two days, Longarm moved only enough to provide for the horse's grazing, His own hunger remained, a constant gnawing that the few shavings of jerky and the crumbs of hardtack he allowed himself did very little to ease. To make matters worse, he'd smoked his last cheroot. By midmorning of the third day, the horse showed signs of suffering from lack of water. The small quantities that Longarm could splash into the animal's mouth were never enough to satisfy its thirst. Now the canteen was nearly empty. Both he and the horse needed water.

During the long, hot hours while the sun beat down and sucked the moisture from both animal and man, Longarm tried to put himself in Cass Sterret's boots. He decided that if he were the outlaw chief, he'd first have sent one group of his men south along the railroad tracks, and the others to the north, to find out where Longarm had left the railbed. That, he thought, would use up the better part of two days. By the third morning, Sterret's crew would have found the place at which Longarm had entered the sandhills. With no trail to follow in the shifting sand, Sterret wouldn't be able to tell whether Longarm had moved directly across the dunes or had stayed among them. Cass would have split his bunch, Longarm decided. He'd have sent one man across the sand to see if he could pick up a trail where the prairie began beyond the dunes. At the same time, he'd probably have sent two parties out, one to start from Wolf Creek, the other from the Canadian, to zigzag through the dunes and try to flush Longarm out, if he'd taken refuge in them.

About the most unlikely place Sterret would expect him to come out of the dunes, Longarm decided, was the same place he'd gone in. As the sun dropped low on the afternoon of his third day in the sandhills, Longarm swung onto the back of the weakening gelding and started the animal at a slow walk back toward the west edge of the wasteland.

He saw the glow of the campfire while he was still deep enough in the dunes to avoid it. Longarm turned the gelding's head north. Wolf Creek was a more logical place to head for than the river. He rode parallel to the edge of the sand, the gelding plodding wearily up over the small round humps, until the fire's glow was a faint yellow line behind him. Then he headed for the prairie to the west.

He hadn't counted on Sterret posting guards along the edge of the sandhills. Longarm swore at himself for having failed to spend the time and energy required to scout the campfire, and count the number of men around it. The outlaw sentry saw Longarm before Longarm saw him; he'd been lying on the ground, his horse tethered away from his lookout post. The outlaw got off the first shot but Longarm's return fire was more accurate. The guard didn't shoot again. Longarm didn't know whether he'd killed the man when he drew and fired at his muzzle flash, or had just wounded him. All that mattered was that there had been shots, and the men in camp were close enough to have heard them. In a half hour or so, they'd be at the spot where the guard he'd shot was posted. With a tired horse, that was little enough time.

Longarm didn't dare to run the gelding, and the horse wasn't in any condition to struggle through the dunes again. All he could do was to move away from the scene of the shooting, nursing the gelding's remaining strength, and hope the outlaws wouldn't take after him in the darkness. He headed the horse away from the dunes, holding it to an easy walk, reining in when the animal's legs began to grow unsteady, and straining his ears during the stops for sounds of pursuit.

He heard them soon enough—the drumbeat of hooves on the hard ground. He'd covered less than a quarter of a mile, and the still night air carried every noise to him distinctly.

"Smoke oughta be someplace around here," a man said as the hoofbeats spaced out and stopped. "Spread out, and see can you find him."

"Maybe he's took off after that Custis fellow," another said.

Cass Sterret's unmistakable growl replied, "Not Smoke. Not after I told him to stay put and watch which way the son of a bitch headed, if Smoke didn't bring him down."

A shout, then a call. "Here's Smoke. Stiff as a three-day-old cow turd."

"That's another score against Custis," Sterret grated. "Damn him, anyhow! And that Pawnee bitch that brought him in! Boys, we're going to finish both of them off before we quit!"

"Well, which way had we oughta head?" asked the man who had spoken first.

Longarm, hearing the voice for the second time, was pretty sure the speaker was the one named Hank.

Sterret said, "We ain't heading noplace. How in hell're we going to read trail in the dark? We stay here and take off after Custis when it's light."

"He'll get too much of a start," Hank objected.

"Can't be helped. It won't do us no good to go riding ass-over-appetite, not till we're sure which way to head. Gordo, you ride on back to where we was camped and tell Pete to bring up the buckboard. He can haul our bedrolls along with the water barrel. The critters are going to need to drink good before we set out in the morning."

Longarm had heard enough. Sterret had come prepared for a chase. He sighted on the North Star, and turned the gelding's head in that direction. The slow steps the weary animal took didn't sound enough like hoofbeats to be heard a dozen yards away. He tried to forget his own growling stomach as he nursed the exhausted gelding in the general direction of Wolf Creek.

Though Longarm had guessed correctly that the stream was only seven or eight miles north of his starting point, the night was almost gone when he sighted it. A quarter-mile ahead, a belt of brush showed dark against the brown-burned prairie in the faint streaks of dawn light that were breaking on the eastern horizon. By the time the gelding's fading strength allowed them to reach the water itself, the sky was gray and growing brighter. Longarm sighted along the prairie, up and down the creek. There was no sign of a gully or a rock outcrop that would hide him or give him a protected place from which he could stand off Sterret's outlaws. He had two hours at the most before the gang found his tracks and started after him.

He led the horse to the creek, through the brush and scattered small trees. *No cover here*, he told himself soberly as he let the horse drink sparingly. For all he knew, he'd need the animal for quite a while, and a foundered horse was worse than useless. He was wrestling the gelding's head up from the water when a family of jackrabbits hopped out of the brush across the stream. Longarm drew fast and shot three times. Two jackrabbits jumped up and flopped dead to the ground. A third struggled to move, its back broken. Rather than waste a shot, Longarm waded the horse across the stream and tethered it to a tree away from the water before he finished off the wounded rabbit.

He gathered twigs and built a small, hot fire, letting it burn to smokeless coals while he skinned the rabbits. He looked at the stripped carcasses with disgust. The long, hot summer had caused the jacks to develop warbles—big maggots that burrowed beneath their skins. Swallowing his distaste, Longarm flicked the grubs out with the tip of his knife and cut away the flesh around the holes they'd made. Then he spitted the carcasses and propped the rabbits over the coals.

While his own meal sizzled, Longarm led the horse through the brush on the north side of the creek and let it graze briefly. He inspected the prairie on that side while the animal fed. It was as bald and bare as that on the south. Long before the gelding was ready to stop eating, Longarm decided it had had enough. He led it back to the creek and allowed it to drink sparingly once more. When he led it up the bank away from the creek, the horse walked more easily, but he could tell it was in no shape to run, or even walk more than a mile or two.

By now, Longarm's mouth was watering from the smell of the cooking rabbits. He tore into one, and had eaten half of its stringy flesh before remembering the salt in his saddlebag. Seasoning helped him choke down the other two but he still told himself that jackrabbits would never be fit meat, even for a hungry man. He felt better for the food, though, as he buried the skin and skeletons under the dirt he piled over the ashes of his fire.

A double gamble lay ahead. Half of it was a sure thing; the other half was chancy. Longarm started leading the horse west, just outside the swath of brush that bordered the stream. His almost-sure-thing bet was that the railroad bridge was upstream. The chancy half was that he'd find a place where he could hold off Sterret's men long enough to give him a chance to survive while he waited for the army train to arrive, or that the train would even be sent.

He made no effort to hide the tracks he and the horse made as they crossed the baked earth. Less than a mile from where he'd stopped to eat, he came to the railroad bridge. The creek was narrow at the point where it crossed, and the bridge was no more than thirty feet long. It had no center pier: big dressed-stone abutments bordered by gravel formed its support at each side of the stream. Longarm studied the bridge and a lopsided grin grew on his face. He'd found the fortress that he needed.

Mounting the gelding, he persuaded it to walk up the embankment and step between the rails. The job was easier than it had been the first time he'd tried it. He tried to persuade the horse to walk the bare ties across the bridge, but the animal balked. Longarm dismounted, and with a lot of patient persuasion, led the gelding onto the ties. He took his time, even though he knew time was precious. A single misstep, one slip of a hoof between the unballasted ties, and the gelding would almost surely break a leg. It was slow going, and when the animal stepped safely onto the ballast again, Longarm let out the breath he'd been holding.

Keeping to the gravel that bordered the bridge abutment, he led the horse down to the water's edge. There wasn't room between the surface of the water and the bottom of the bridge timbers for him to ride into the creek. With a sigh, Longarm took off his gunbelt and looped it around his left shoulder, with the butt of his Colt just below his chin. Then he backed into the cool, shallow water of Wolf Creek, leading the horse.

As best he could, Longarm kept an eye on the creek bottom as he backed under the bridge, wading in the gentle current of the waist-deep water, until he and the gelding were pressed against the stone abutment. He'd reached the shelter just in time. Downstream, he heard the thudding of hoofbeats. He took his Winchester out of its saddle scabbard and cradled it across his arm. Then he waited for Sterret's men to approach.

His wait was not a long one. The hoofbeats stopped. Their sound was distorted by the echoes that the water's surface created under the bridge. The outlaws had pulled up just short of the railroad tracks.

Cass Sterret said, "We got the son of a bitch for sure, now. Only two ways he could've gone, north or south on the tracks."

"Makes two times he's tried that dodge." This time it was Hank's voice. "You'd think somebody like Custis'd know it wouldn't fool a ten-year-old kid."

"Hank, you take two of the boys and try the north," Sterret ordered. "Pete, you was bitching about the buckboard man never getting in on nothing. You and Gordo and Tom see if you can pick up his tracks to the south."

"He can't be too far now," Hank reminded his companions. "That fire he tried to hide back along the creek wasn't an hour old."

"Well, get moving, damn it!" Sterret rasped. "When you find where he's gone back on the prairie, one of you come back here and tell me. The other two, keep after him."

Longarm heard hoofbeats start up and fade out.

"Damn it, Pete!" Sterret growled. "What's holding you back? Get on across the fucking creek and start looking! The sooner we start, the quicker we'll catch that tricky bastard."

"All right, all right, we're going," the outlaw replied. "Come on, Gordo, Tom. You heard what Cass said."

Under the bridge, Longarm tried to pull back farther against the stone abutment. It didn't give an inch. He started feeling naked and exposed the minute he saw hooves of the horses ridden by the outlaws heading south dip into the surface of the creek.

Chapter 19

Pete and his two companions had waded the mounts halfway across the stream, and Longarm was beginning to think his hiding place wouldn't be discovered, when the last rider in the line leaned forward in his saddle and peered curiously under the bridge.

Longarm knocked the man off his horse with a slug from the Winchester before the surprised outlaw could move to draw. He shifted his rifle to take out the man ahead of the one he'd shot, but only succeeded in wounding his horse. The animal reared and thrashed in the shallows, unseating its rider and sending up sheets of water that kept Longarm from sighting on the floundering man. By the time he'd swung the rifle to get its sights on the leader, the third outlaw had spurred out onto the far bank and was hidden by the bridge timbers.

"He's hiding under the bridge!" one of the men yelled.

"I can see that myself, you damn fool!" Sterret replied. "One of you give Gordo a hand getting outta the creek, before Custis gets another chance at him!"

Longarm snapshot at the outlaw who spurred into the shallows downstream to help the one who'd fallen in, but the wounded horse was still plunging around in the creek. It got in the way just in time to take a second slug. Whinnying shrilly, the horse got halfway up the bank, where it collapsed and thrashed for a few moments before it died.

"Damn you, Custis!" a voice called from the bank. "That was my best trail horse! I'll take a patch outta your hide for killing him!"

"Shut up, Gordo!" Sterret snorted. "Don't you see Pete's got his? No, you asshole! Don't go in the creek after him! You stay on the bank. Tom! You go down the side you're on, and when you're sure that fucker under the bridge can't get a shot at you, fish poor old Pete out!"

A flurry of hoofbeats told Longarm that the men were following their boss's orders. Fresh hoofbeats pounded up before those near at hand faded out, and he heard Hank call, "What in hell's the shooting about? Did you flush Custis out close by someplace?"

"He's under the goddamned bridge!" Sterret replied. "Last place anybody with any sense'd pick to hole up. There ain't a way in this world he can get away from us now!"

"If he's under there, let's get him out!" Hank exclaimed.

"Whoa, now!" Sterret commanded. "Let's figure how to do it, and not go off half-cocked. He's already killed Pete. Slim, you ride over to the upstream side of the bridge and keep an eye out. Don't let him pull a sneak while all of us are on this side. Then we can take our time and get the bastard out without anybody but him getting killed."

Longarm heard hoofbeats pass over the tracks just behind his head and knew that the upstream side of the bridge was now being guarded. *Old son*, he told himself, *it looks like Wolf Creek's turned into shit creek, and I sure don't have a paddle that'll get me out of this one*.

For several minutes there was silence from the outlaws. Longarm could hear an undertone of voices, kept purposely low, he was sure, to prevent him from overhearing their plans.

Finally, Sterret called, "You, Custis! You hear me?"

"I'd have to be deaf not to."

"You're a dead man, you know that, don't you?" When Longarm didn't respond, the veteran outlaw went on, "Now, I look at this thing thisaway. We got you cold. There ain't a way you're going to get past us. Come on out and give up, and you'll die quick and merciful. I'll do it myself, one shot through your brain. You'll never know what hit you. And we'll bury you decent, too, not leave you for the buzzards and coyotes to gnaw on."

"That offer don't tempt me a damn bit, Cass. You'll have to come up with a better one," Longarm replied.

"Um. I sorta had an idea that's what you'd say. Guess I would, too, in your place." Sterret waited for a moment. "Looks like we'll have to come in and get you, then."

"Come ahead. I got plenty of shells. I'll guarantee I won't be the only one carried away."

"You're just making it hard for yourself," Sterret called. There was anger in his voice now. "You ruined my valley, and you killed two of my men. I figured I'd stretch a point and let you die easy, but if you make us take you, I'll see to it that you'll take a long time. By God, Custis, you'll be begging me to shoot you by the time I get through."

"There's some real good reasons why I don't figure to take you upon any deal you drag out, Cass," Longarm called back. "One of 'em is that I don't think your word's worth a kangaroo's bean-fart. Another one is that you only got half of my name; I disremembered to tell you the rest of it when I got to your place the other day."

"Hell, I didn't expect you'd be using your real handle. Who d'you claim to be now? Mysterious Dave Mather? Billy the Kid growed up? Or maybe General Custer, come back from the dead?"

"You're going the wrong way, Sterret. They're all dead men. I ain't dead yet, and I don't plan to be. The other half of my name's Long. Custis Long. Deputy U.S. marshal. And the other reason I don't aim to take up any offer you throw me is because I got a lot of good help on the way here right now."

There was a moment of silence from the creekbed, then Longarm heard Hank say, "Jesus, Cass, he's the one they call Longarm!"

"Ah! He's lying!" Sterret rasped.

Longarm's suspicions had been increasing as Sterret dragged out their conversation. A scraping, no louder than a whisper, alerted him. He turned his head and looked up into the muzzle of a shotgun. There was just time to throw his body to one side before the gun went off, its report deafening him, buckshot pellets churning the water inches away, in the spot where he'd been leaning a second ago. Longarm had no target in the narrow space between the railroad ties, He whipped out his Colt and fired at the muzzle of the shotgun just as it was disappearing. A yell rewarded him.

"Somebody help me!" the voice of one of the outlaws came from above the bridge. "The son of a bitch damn near took my arm off!"

"You know, Cass, that bastard down there just might be Longarm," Hank said, his voice audible under the bridge even when filtered through the scuffling of boots on the bridge abutment made by the men helping the wounded outlaw back to the group.

"He can't be!" Sterret replied.

"I ain't so sure." Hank insisted. "That bank Boyle robbed was up in Colorado, and everybody knows Longarm's working outa Denver. And Boyle didn't show up when all that ruckus broke out the other morning."

"Longarm wouldn't be fool enough to get hisself caught in the kinda trap that sucker under the bridge is in," Sterret objected.

"Maybe he would," Longarm called. "Maybe I got a reason for wanting to hold you and your crew right where we are, Sterret. I told you I had help on the way."

"He's bluffing," Sterret said, his tone obviously designed to reassure his men. "Anyhow, whoever's down there, we're going to wind this up right now!"

Once more there was silence. Longarm made use of the time. He reloaded his Colt and refilled the magazine of the Winchester. Then he began wondering if there wasn't some last-minute scheme he could come up with to give him a fast, clean shot at Sterret. Picking off the outlaws' veteran leader would take a lot of the starch out of those who were left, Longarm looked around, upstream and down, along the creekbank. There were still no signs of movement, and practically no sounds at all from above him.

He counted the number of men Sterret had left. Eight. Four on each side. He frowned. *Maybe if I duck underwater and don't let 'em see me right off, I can bob up quick from in back of the gelding's rump and get that shot I need,* he thought. *But I've got no time to look for him; one shot, and then I've got to get back underwater faster than I think I can. There'll be eight of 'em looking for me.*

Seconds dragged into minutes, and still the attack didn't begin. Straining his ears to catch any telltale noises the outlaws might be making, Longarm gradually realized that a strange sound was reaching his ears. It was a low-pitched, singing hum, a noise he knew he ought to recognize, but couldn't place.

He shook his head, trying, to sharpen his ears. The source of the noise burst on him in a flash of memory. Groping underwater with his foot, he found a stirrup and lifted himself up until he could reach through the ties and take hold of the rail over his head. The noise was instantly translated into an almost imperceptible vibration.

"Sterret!" Longarm shouted. "Hold up whatever move you got planned! I want to give you one last chance!"

"You're locoed!" Sterret jeered. "You can't give me nothing, Longarm, if that's who you really are. And I ain't giving you no more. We'll be coming after you when we get ready. All we're doing now is giving you a chance to get shaky, waiting for us!"

"I told you I had help on the way," Longarm called. "You take a minute to look and listen. You'll find out there's a train just up the track, heading this way. That's what I've been waiting for!"

Sterret guffawed. "That's too big a bluff for anybody to swallow! Nothing but work trains runs on this track yet! We been watching it!"

Just then, the faint wailing of a locomotive's whistle cut through the afternoon air. The rail above Longarm's head was singing louder now. He began inching along the abutment in the direction from which Sterret's voice had come.

"What've you got to say now, Cass?" Longarm called. He said the first thing that came into his mind, any words to keep the outlaws thinking of the train instead of whatever move they'd planned.

"By God," Hank said loudly, "it is a train, Cass! Listen, that jayhawker under the bridge has got to be Longarm! From what I've heard about him, he'd be one to order up a trainload of help, if he took a mind to."

Again, the whistle sounded. It was louder now. Longarm had almost reached the edge of the abutment, and was crouching down to keep the men on the bank from seeing him. He waited for the whistle to sound a third time, counting on its blast to make the outlaws turn their heads and look up the track. When the whistle blew, he stood up, Colt in hand.

Sterret turned around too late. He held a pistol in his left hand, but Longarm's slug knocked the old outlaw off his horse before he could fire. Longarm ducked, and the slugs from the other outlaws' guns whistled through the air above him or ricocheted off the stones of the bridge abutment.

A thudding of hooves indicated to him that the outlaws were scattering. The train was only a short distance from the bridge, its brakes screeching as the engineer brought it to a stop. Longarm waited until he was sure the coast was clear, then waded out on the bank. He was just in time to see an officer in army blue, his blouse thick with gold braid, swing off the single coach the engine pulled. The entire train consisted of two baggage cars, a coach, and a tender. Soldiers began leaping from the baggage cars, lowering ramps. Longarm's eyes goggled as Marshal Billy Vail got out of the coach after the army officer.

Vail walked along the track to where Longarm stood. He looked at his deputy for a moment without speaking, then turned his eyes to survey the scene. Cass Sterret's recumbent form lay by his horse. The other dead outlaw lay a few yards distant. The slain horse lay beyond the corpse. Vail turned back, gazed at Longarm, and cocked an eye at the deputy's dripping clothes.

"I see you've been working," the chief marshal said calmly. "And I guess a man needs a bath after he's done a job. But, damn it, Longarm, ain't you got sense enough yet to take your clothes off first?"

"I do remember to do that most of the time, Billy. I was in a smidgen of a hurry to get wet today." Longarm frowned. "How come you're here, anyway?"

"I got tired of riding a desk chair and shuffling papers. So I hopped a train to Dodge and met the army special when it switched."

"Did you, now? I figured it'd take a stick of dynamite to get you out of that office."

"Well, damn it, you set the dynamite off."

"How do you figure that, Billy?"

"In all the years you've been my deputy, you've never asked for help before. This is the first time I thought if you needed the army, you might need me, too. I can pull more rank than you can on those gold-braid dudes, which is all they understand."

"I won't say I ain't glad to see you, because I am."

"You feel like telling me what's happening?" Vail indicated the figures on the ground.

Motioning for his chief to follow, Longarm walked over to where Cass Sterret lay. He said, "Billy, you ain't going to believe who this is." He poked Sterret's recumbent form with the toe of a boot. "All right, Cass, you can quit playing possum now."

Reluctantly, the veteran badman sat up. "God damn you, if you ruined my only good arm, I'll have your balls. And that goes whether you're Longarm or Judas Priest hisself!"

"Who is this old booger?" Vail asked.

"Billy, you're looking at Cass Sterret, in the flesh."

Vail shook his head. "Can't be. Cass Sterret's been dead ten years or more."

"In a pig's ass I have!" Sterret grunted. "I'm a mite shot up right now, but I'll get over it, and I'll ride again!"

"If you're really Cass Sterret, I don't imagine you will," Vail told him. "There's three hanging eases you're wanted for, and if one judge don't stand you on the gallows, the next one will."

"Seemed sort of like it'd be better if he hung than if I killed him," Longarm said. "He'll likely feel a rope more'n he would a bullet, so I just knocked him off his horse instead of aiming to kill."

"Did you have me get the whole damn Department of the West out on his account?" Vail asked. "What about that yarn you spun me on the telegraph, about the army and Indian bureau all wound up in graft and corruption? I had to get a direct telegraph wire to General Pope and spend two hours making him believe the army was in a mess and the army had to clean it up."

Longarm smiled broadly. "Seems like you managed, though. Where is the general, by the way? Still in the day coach?"

Vail winked. "You didn't think Pope would come himself, did you? I had to settle for a colonel. But he's Pope's personal aide, and he's got the general's direct authority to do anything in reason to clean up whatever mess the army's in."

"It might take some doing. These men he brought—are they all pencil pushers, or are there some real soldiers among 'em?"

"You'll find enough for whatever soldiering's needed," Vail

assured him. "While I think about it, this is still your case. I didn't come to boss your job. I'll just butt in when you ask me to."

"You might have to start right now. That young colonel's got his men formed up, and I guess he's ready to go to work."

"Put him to work, then," Vail said. "His name's Manley, by the way. I haven't figured out yet whether he can live up to it or not."

Colonel Manley walked up to Vail and Longarm. He looked somewhat disapprovingly at Longarm's unshaven face and soiled, soaked clothing. "Is this the man you were telling General Pope about?" he asked Vail. "If he is, I'm ready to find out what we're here for."

"Colonel, this is Custis Long, my deputy. Long, Colonel Manley," Vail said.

Longarm nodded. Manley didn't offer to shake hands, but gave Longarm the kind of stiff half-salute that he and his colleagues of the military profession reserved for civilians of the second rank.

"Well, Long?" Manley asked.

"Your real job's at Fort Supply, Colonel. And New Cantonment, and Fort Reno, and Fort Elliott, I suspect, and a few other places. But there's a side job that needs cleaning up right now, if you'll take it on."

Stiffly, Manley replied, "General Pope's orders are to place myself and my men at your disposal for any reasonable task within the scope of this assignment." He hesitated before adding, "sir."

"I call it reasonable." Longarm pointed to Sterret. "That old buzzard's been running a rustler's nest and an outlaw hideout a ways south of here. I busted it up pretty good, but it needs a few touches to finish it off. It's part of this case, because everybody connected with it is on one side or the other of the cattle-stealing business."

"I see," Manley replied, frowning.

It was clear to Longarm that the colonel didn't see, but that he didn't want to start rocking the boat so early. He went on, "Now, if you'd have your boys toss these bodies on the train, and have this fellow here show you where his hidey-hole is, you can finish tearing it up, and collect the rest of the gang as they straggle home. They can bring whoever they grab, and the bodies they'll find in a haystack there, on up to Fort Supply and report in to you."

"Very well, I'll detail a squad," Manley said, still mystified.

"You do that, Colonel. Then you and me and Marshal Vail will set down and go over the rest of it," Longarm said soberly. "I'll guarantee you there's a bigger mess to be cleaned up than you ever dreamed of." As Manley turned to go, Longarm added, "Oh, yes, Colonel. There's a horse under the bridge there. It's army property, and it could stand some looking after." Longarm started for the creek.

Vail said, "You don't need to wade in after that horse, Longarm. Let a trooper do it. I've got a bottle of Maryland rye in my bag, and you look like you could use a drink."

"No, sir." Longarm shook his head stubbornly. "I borrowed the horse, and I'll hand it back on dry land. Anyhow, I want my saddle and gear." He waded under the bridge and came out leading the gelding.

"Now, then," he told Vail, "I'll let the trooper handle it from here. What was that you said about a drink?"

Side by side, the two men walked toward the coach.

Manley joined Longarm and Vail before they'd finished their first drink. Vail shoved the bottle toward the young colonel, who shook his head.

"Thank you, Marshal, but I don't indulge." Turning to Longarm, he asked, "Well, what's our first move? Or I suppose I should say our *next* move, since I've started a detachment to that valley you told me about."

"What comes next ain't going to be quite so easy," Longarm said. "Are you acquainted with the man in charge at Fort Supply?"

"Colonel Estes? Of course. A very free officer. And a gentleman, I might add. I'm sorry I can't say the same about some of the other officers left in the service after the War."

"He's a crook who's sold out to a bunch of land-grabbing cattle ranchers," Long said bluntly.

The colonel's eyebrows shot up, and he stared at the deputy for a moment before he recovered from his shock enough to say, "That's completely incredible, sir. I suppose you have facts to back up your statement?"

"I've got a lot of facts, but they ain't going to do no good if you won't believe 'em when you see 'em," Longarm replied. "If you mean have I got law-court facts—no, I ain't. That's part of your job, Colonel."

Manley frowned. "I'm afraid I don't follow you."

Longarm sketched the meeting he'd sat in on between Scott Forest and Estes. He concluded, "Now, Forest's going to be getting back to Fort Supply real soon. He's going to be ready to close up his deal, meaning he'll pay Estes off. I don't know who else at Fort Supply's mixed up in this with Estes. It's part of your job to find out, seeing as how Billy and I've got no standing on army property."

"How do you expect me to find out?" Manley asked.

"That ought not to be too hard. You've got authority from General Pope to do just about anything. Colonel Estes is bound to have some kind of papers—notes, letters, or telegrams— that'll show what he's cooked up with Forest—"

Manley broke in, "He wouldn't be foolish enough to keep the kind of documents you're talking about in any of his official files!"

"I don't expect so, Colonel. You're going to have to get hold of his personal letters. He's got an office in his quarters upstairs in the headquarters building. I'd expect you'll find what we're after up there."

"I can't invade the private quarters of a fellow officer," Manley protested. "It wouldn't be proper."

Longarm's patience was growing thin. His eyes glinted a warning as he said, "Now, you listen a minute, Colonel. Your ticket from General Pope doesn't draw lines between what's proper and what's necessary. I don't give a damn whether it's proper or not, I just know it's got to be done that way if we're going to find out who-all's mixed up in this scheme. And we need evidence that'll stand up in court."

"Court?" Manley echoed. "Are you talking about a civilian trial for an army officer?"

Longarm slapped a large palm down on the table in front of him. "I don't much care whether your men are tried by a fed-

eral judge or by an army court-martial," Longarm told him.
"The bureau men who're in with the army—they'll go to federal court, the agents and the traders. And I guess the Indian
police who're in it will go to federal court, too. We need hard
evidence against them, and I figure it's got to be someplace in
Estes's stuff."

Manley still seemed undecided. "Suppose I agree to sieze
Colonel Estes's private correspondence, Marshal Long. Do
you expect me to hand it over to you?"

"Either to me or a federal prosecutor, if it's got anything to
do with the case we want to make against the agents and the
other BIA men. I doubt whether we'll get much help from
them."

Manley exhaled loudly. "I'll have to consider your request.
Let's put that aside for the moment. I've got men outside who
have either got to be moved out or bivouacked. We've got
nothing but field rations, so I need to get an idea of what you
and Marshal Vail plan."

"Don't look to me," Vail said quickly, gesturing broadly
toward his deputy. "It's Long's case."

Longarm said to Manley. "I'll leave that for you to decide,
Colonel. Was it me, I'd bivouac right here tonight, and start out
early tomorrow for Fort Supply. There's where it all centers.
But there're officers like Captain Rogers at New Cantonment
and some at Fort Reno and I'd guess at Fort Elliott over in the
Texas Panhandle who're mixed up in this scheme."

"I didn't have any idea that this affair was so widespread."
Manley's forehead was deeply furrowed. He sat silently for a
moment, then, surprisingly, he said crisply, "Very well. We'll
bivouac here and move out at first light. Fort Supply's a six-
hour march. We'll be there by noon, or shortly after. I'll take
over the telegraph room and put my own signalman in charge.
No word will get through to New Cantonment, Elliott, or Reno,
or any other installation, for that matter, until we've learned
who's involved. After we know that, we can do whatever else
seems called for." He stood up. "I'll see to my men." Then he
said hesitantly, "If you gentlemen don't have rations, my quartermaster will see that you're provided." Then Manley hurried
up the coach aisle and swung to the ground.

Longarm looked at Vail. "You know, I didn't have much

hope for that fellow. But it looks like he might shape up into a pretty good man, after he gets dried behind the ears. Come on, Billy. It's been four days since I had anything to eat except a couple of mangy jackrabbits and a bite of jerky. My belly thinks my mouth's on strike. Even army bully beef's going to taste good to me right now."

Chapter 20

Nellie Bly said somewhat tartly, "That's all very good, Longarm, but when do I get my story?"

"Whenever you can talk Manley into telling you the army's side of it."

Longarm, Nellie, and Frank Turner were sitting in the restaurant down the street from the Outpost Hotel. It was the first chance they'd had to talk with each other since Longarm had ridden in with Manley's special detachment. Longarm had to give him credit; once Manley had made up his mind to act, he'd acted quickly and decisively.

Estes had been placed on house arrest within minutes after the army detachment reached Fort Supply. He'd been confined to his bedroom while Manley, Vail, and Longarm searched the study upstairs. In a locked steel box in a drawer of Estes's desk, there had been papers, letters, memoranda of payments made, and notes of conversations with Scott Forest, other army officers, Bureau of Indian Affairs employees, agents, and traders. The documents gave the whole story of the conspiracy. In return for bribes by Forest and his group of cattlemen, the white government officials and a handful of Indian police had agreed to secure the consent of the Indians to the opening of the Cherokee Outlet and unassigned lands to the ranchers' cattle herds. Or if not their consent, at least their silence. This was to have been achieved by means of promises, payments, intimidation, or coercion.

Manley, Longarm, and Vail had worked three days and most of three nights, sorting the documents and making lists. The ornate French clock on the mantel in Estes's study had chimed three o'clock before they'd finished the night before.

Longarm had leaned back in his chair. "Well, Colonel," he

said, stretching, "that looks to be it. I guess you've got enough men to go out and bring all these people in?"

"Bring them where?" Manley asked. "There aren't any civilian courts in the Outlet. The army can take care of its own officers, of course. I'm sure General Pope will convene a court-martial at department headquarters to handle their cases. What do you expect me to do with the civilians? I can't put them in our guardhouses; they've broken no army regulations."

"If you'll bring 'em in, we'll find a way to handle 'em," Longarm promised.

"Very well. It's irregular, but this entire matter is unlike anything I've encountered before." Manley ran his hand over his forehead. The room was close, the night was warm, and he was sweating. "I'll detail detachments to start this morning for New Cantonment, Fort Reno, and Fort Elliott. That's as far as I'm prepared to go until I've made a full report to General Pope and have gotten further instructions from him."

"When's that going to be?" Longarm asked.

"I'll telegraph my report this morning. I won't try to guess when the general will reply." Manley began gathering up the papers that were strewn over the desktop. "I'll need these for my report, so I'm taking custody of them for the present."

Longarm and Vail exchanged questioning looks. Both knew that technically they had no standing on a military reservation. Vail said, "Maybe you'd better have your clerks begin making copies for us, Colonel. It'll save time later on. Now that this case is finished, we'll be leaving for Denver as soon as we can."

"General Pope will see that you're provided with copies of everything pertinent to the civilians, when the time comes," Manley told him.

"We'll need the material about the army, too," Vail said. "If we don't have all the evidence, we might have trouble making a case."

"I'm sure the general understands that," Manley replied. "Now, gentlemen, if you'll excuse me, it's late, and I have a lot of work ahead."

"So," Longarm concluded his story to Nellie and Frank, "that's where things sit. Till General Pope makes up his mind, all we can do is wait."

"How long will you wait?" Nellie asked. "I want to get started on my story."

"If the colonel doesn't send word for us before evening, Billy and me are going to see him."

"Take me with you, Longarm!" Nellie pleaded excitedly. "The public's got a right to know about graft and bribery in the Indian Nation, just like they have if it happens in New York or Pennsylvania, or anywhere else in the country. I'm going to force the colonel to give me my story."

Frowning, Longarm rubbed the back of his neck. "I ain't so sure the chief's going to cotton to that idea," he said dubiously.

"Where is Marshal Vail? I'll talk to him if you won't," Nellie persisted.

"Well—" Longarm nodded. "I owe you for tipping me off about this thing first. I guess I can talk Billy into letting you come along. You be in your room about four. I'll tap on your door."

Vail protested at first, but only mildly, and at last agreed with Longarm that Nellie was entitled to go along. They reached Fort Supply shortly before five, after the short walk from the hotel, to find the headquarters in a hubbub. Small mountains of paper-stuffed manila envelopes were piled on every desk, spilling to the floor. The men of Manley's special detachment were opening the envelopes, examining their contents, and extracting a document now and then. Manley kept them waiting only a short time. An aide showed them into the office that had been Colonel Estes's. Manley nodded at the men, then saw Nellie and stood up.

"I haven't had the pleasure of meeting this young lady," he said.

"Miss Elizabeth Cochrane, Colonel," Longarm said. "She's a reporter for a big newspaper back East. She signs herself Nellie Bly in her pieces for the paper, though."

Manley bowed. "Miss Cochrane. Are you here on behalf of your newspaper, or just as a friend of the marshal's?"

"In your terms, Colonel, my business is official." Nellie's tone was cool. "You see, I'm the one who uncovered Scott Forest's plan to steal Indian land by bribing your fellow officers and others. I've been working with Marshal Long in finding out more about it."

"It's odd that Marshal Long hasn't mentioned you before," Manley said.

"He didn't have any reason to before," Vail explained. "Now, can we get on with this? I suppose you've heard from General Pope?"

"Within the last hour." Manley looked pointedly at Nellie. "But I'm not sure I'm prepared to read his message to anyone except you and Marshal Long."

"Is that your idea or the general's?" Nellie demanded. "Because if it's his idea, I intend to get on the telegraph and tell him I mean to get all the facts, one way or another. If it's your idea, I doubt that General Pope will support it."

Manley sat for a moment without speaking. Finally he shrugged. "I'm sure your friends would give you the details if I didn't, and I'd prefer you got them straight." He took a sheet of folded foolscap from the desktop. "I'll read you the pertinent paragraphs."

Nellie sat down and took out pad and pencil. Many started to object, but changed his mind. Longarm and Vail sat down, uninvited.

Unfolding the paper, Manley began to read aloud. It was obvious to all of them that he was skipping portions of the message. "This matter must be kept confidential," he read, "not because of the disrepute it might bring to the Service, but because of the possibility that it could have serious consequences which could bring open strife back to the Indian Nation.

"I have decided to allow the officers involved to resign instead of bringing them before courts-martial. I cannot answer for the action the Bureau of Indian Affairs might take relative to its people, but am recommending to Washington that a similar course be followed. We cannot afford the risk that disclosure of this effort to transfer Indian lands to whites might create widespread discontent, and might even lead to outbreaks of violence by the tribes.

"I cannot allow the army to take responsibility for this, if it should follow. Too many of our men have given their lives in pacifying the tribes to let such a relatively trivial matter undo what they have accomplished. You will therefore impound all documents pertaining to this matter and will make no disclosures." Manley laid the paper down. He said, "There's more, but it's confidential army business involving the procedures I'm to follow in changes of personnel at the forts affected by the resignations."

In the silence that followed, Nellie's voice rang loudly. "That is disgraceful, Colonel! The army's trying to hush up a scandal on the flimsiest grounds I've ever heard of!"

"I'm afraid I must disagree with you, Miss Cochrane," Manley replied in a toneless voice. "At any rate, I must follow my orders."

Longarm and Vail exchanged glances. Both knew that technically they had no jurisdiction over army officers on their own posts.

Nellie appealed to Longarm. "Do you agree with the colonel?"

"Can't say I do," he answered evenly. "The way I look at it, anybody who breaks the law had better be punished. Otherwise, people get the idea they can do just about anything they please from then on, and go scot-free."

She turned back to Manley. "What about Scott Forest and his friends? Aren't they going to be punished at all?"

"They're civilians, Miss Cochrane," Manley pointed out. "The army has no jurisdiction over civilians."

"Marshal Vail?" Nellie asked.

Vail leaned back in his chair, folding his pudgy fingers across the front of his vest. "General Pope's ordered the colonel to impound all the evidence we've got. I don't see how we can make a case against Forest and his bunch, unless the general lets us have the papers we found," Vail explained. "And his message gave me the idea he won't do that."

Nellie stood up and stamped her foot. "It's disgraceful! I don't intend to let the army get away with it! When I get back to Pittsburgh and tell my chief editor about it, he won't stop short of the President in forcing you to release the whole story!"

"That's his privilege, Miss Cochrane. And yours," Manley told her. "Now, I see no reason to discuss the matter any further."

As they walked the short distance back to the hotel, Longarm and Vail were silent, but Nellie fumed. She said to Longarm. "After all the time you spent on this case! The risks you took! Doesn't it infuriate you to see it all wasted?"

"I'll get paid for my time. The risks go with my job."

"Marshal Vail, is that how you feel?" she asked.

"When you come right down to hard cases, I don't have much grounds to raise a fuss," he said. "Longarm was sent to bring back a bank-robbing killer, and he closed out his case. All this other stuff never was part of his assignment."

They were passing the Star at the time. Nellie saw the saloon's sign and said, "There are times when I wish women were allowed in saloons. If they were, I'd go right in there and have myself a drink."

Longarm smiled. "Guess that's what Billy and me are going to do, as soon as we see you to the hotel. Too bad you can't come along."

"Go have your drink now, if you want to," Nellie told them, a bit peevishly. "I can certainly go on by myself. It's just a few steps, and Frank will be waiting for me. We're going to have supper together."

"You sure you don't mind?" Vail asked.

"Certainly not. Go ahead."

Longarm and Vail had little to say until they'd had two drinks in quick succession. Finally, Longarm asked, "You mad at me for butting in on that land-grab deal?"

"No. You closed your case. The other was just something you got dragged into." Vail grinned. "Anyhow, you got me out of that damned office for a while. You know, I feel ten years younger."

"Only one thing bothers me," Longarm said. "I sort of wonder if Forest and his rancher friends are going to try the same thing again."

"Sure they will," Vail said with complete assurance. "This mess was hushed up, it wasn't cleaned up. Now the little dogs at the bottom will have a chance to move up and be big dogs at the top. You'll have the same mess to clean up all over again, in a few more years."

"Do me a favor and send somebody else next time," Longarm said. "I feel—" The blast of a shot on the street outside interrupted him. He started for the door, drawing his Colt as he ran. Vail was slower to start. He lagged several steps behind Longarm.

Two doors from the saloon, in front of the Outpost Hotel, Frank Turner lay on the board sidewalk. Scott Forest stood a dozen feet away, with a revolver in his hand. Nellie stood between Forest and Longarm.

Forest was shouting, "And you're as much to blame as he was, you nosy bitch! Too bad my shooter missed you in Darlington! But I'll finish the job myself!"

Forest was bringing his gun up as Longarm fired. The rancher crumpled, and his gun fell from a hand gone limp. Nellie stared at the two bodies. Longarm was at her side in seconds.

"You all right, Nellie?" he asked, putting an arm around her trembling shoulders.

"I—I guess so."

"What happened? Where'd Forest come from?"

"He was riding along the street when he saw Frank and me. We'd just come out of the hotel. We were going to supper, you know. He jumped off his horse and started swearing at Frank. From what he said, he'd been to the fort and talked to Manley. He was wild, almost insane—no, I guess he really *was* insane. Before I knew what was happening, he'd shot Frank. I guess he'd have killed me, too, if you hadn't gotten here."

Vail had beaten the gathering crowd of curious onlookers to the scene. He was bending over Turner. He looked up and said, "He wasn't even wearing a gun."

Nellie said in a strained, small voice, "Frank didn't think it was polite to wear a gun when he was taking a lady to supper."

Keeping his voice low, Vail said, "This whole place is on army ground. I've got a buckboard and driver. The Santa Fe's going to make a flag stop for me and Longarm at midnight. That's how long it'll take us to get to the rail line. You'd better come along with us, Miss Nellie, or Cochrane, or whatever you want to be called."

Nellie shuddered. "Yes. I guess I'd better." She shook her head. "I've seen dead men before, you know, Marshal Vail. But—I guess it makes a difference, doesn't it, when it's somebody you know?"

Vail nodded. "Yes. I guess it does."

*   *   *

Longarm looked across the aisle of the railroad coach as the train swayed across the flat prairie. Nellie Bly was sitting beside Vail, leaning forward, listening intently while he talked. Her violet eyes were wide open, her rosebud lips parted. From time to time she nodded at something Vail said.

Longarm's grin wasn't quite wide enough to be seen under his mustache, which had grown a bit since he'd last had a chance to visit a barber. He settled back against the plush seat and fingered the envelope in his vest pocket. Vail had given it to him shortly after they'd boarded the train, saying, "Messenger boy brought this to the office for you a day or so before I left. Clean forgot about it until now."

Taking out the envelope, Longarm opened it and removed the folded label that had been carefully soaked off a bottle of Maryland rye. On the back of the label, in bold feminine script he'd never seen before, but which he recognized at once, was written: *Windsor Hotel, Suite 425. J.B.*

Longarm closed his eyes. His grin grew wider as the train rattled through the night on its way to Denver.

NOVEL 6

———◆———

Longarm
and the
Loggers

Chapter 1

Longarm paid the barber and stepped out through the shop's open doorway onto the sidewalk. The big lawman was restless, his dark eyes gloomy, as he looked across the crowded street at the recently completed Windsor Hotel.

By his own reckoning, he had tarried too long already in the Mile-High City and had spent too many evenings in the hotel's ornate taproom. Perhaps it was the gaudy floor—studded with three thousand silver dollars. The evening before, the son of one of Denver's wealthiest men had stayed in a game too long with nothing in his hand but two pair—seven high. The bluff had not worked. Longarm's full house had taken everything the man had—which was much more than he could afford, as it turned out. A few moments later there had been a scuffle in the gent's room. A shot rang out, and it soon became common knowledge that the young heir had tried to shoot himself.

The memory was not a pleasant one. Longarm didn't like playing poker with men who couldn't lose with dignity. He didn't like those flabby, suet-faced wastrels who had hung about that poker table, either. Longarm was still as lean and as hard as he had been at the end of the War, some fifteen years ago. If he hung around this place much longer, he was afraid he might soon come to resemble that crowd in the hotel. He was eating too much and was sure as hell smoking too much. It was a simple matter to quit smoking, he reminded himself bleakly. He had done it countless times.

Longarm took out a cheroot and stuck it into the corner of his wide mouth, then turned up the street and headed for Colfax Avenue and the federal courthouse. It was almost eight o'clock. He knew it would be well past eight by the time he reached Marshal Vail's office. He didn't care. Let Billy blow his stack. Maybe it would goad the fellow into digging up an assignment for Longarm that would send him out of this Sodom. Wallace and Grenoble had been getting all the juicy assignments lately; now it was Longarm's turn.

As he strode along, he was a study in gunmetal blue and saddle-leather brown. His hair and his John L. Sullivan mustache were both brown, as was the Stetson he was wearing, whose crown was telescoped flat on top. Longarm's tweed suit and vest were also brown. His shirt was blue-gray. He wore a black shoestring tie knotted at his neck. His boots, fashioned of cordovan leather, were low-heeled army issue.

Longarm moved with a swift, catlike stride. Those who saw him coming made no effort to dispute his progress as he cut a path through the early-morning tide of humanity now surging along the sidewalk. The curbing was lined with unharnessed trucks. Hesitant, unhappy people peeked out from between them, awaiting their chance to make a dash for it across the traffic-clogged streets. In contrast, street urchins ducked swiftly across, weaving among the thundering carts and ducking deftly in front of the horsedrawn streetcars to burst with cheerful shouts onto the sidewalks.

Longarm was approaching one corner when a small lad— his begrimed face round and impudent with the energy of youth—ducked onto the sidewalk just in front of him and slammed full-tilt into a drummer, sending the salesman back against the wheel of a parked brewery truck. As if on cue, one of the truck's huge stallions began to void a thick steaming gout of urine. The drummer found himself being spattered from head to toe as the heavy yellow stream pounded into the steaming mash of manure and mud swirling about the horse's fetlocks. Jumping quickly away from the horse, the drummer uttered a startled cry of dismay and took off after the urchin. He might as well have tried to overtake yesterday.

Smiling slightly at the sight of the two antagonists disappearing into the crowd, Longarm turned the next corner onto Colfax and started up the slight hill to the courthouse.

Ignoring the clerk playing on his typewriter in the outer office, Longarm pushed past him and stepped into Marshal Billy Vail's inner sanctum. His superior looked up at Longarm's entry. One bushy eyebrow was cocked upward. As usual, the pink-cheeked, balding official was making an effort to shovel his way out from under a blizzard of dodgers and official communiques from Washington.

"Sit down," he growled. "I'll be with you in a minute—as soon as I dig myself out of this mess. I'm not going to bother telling you you're late."

"You just did," Longarm said, slumping into the chief's red leather armchair. He chewed impatiently on his unlit cheroot, his eyes on Vail. As he watched Vail, he was reminded that here was a man who had ridden over half of the Southwest after assorted bandits and hoodlums in his time—but who was now reduced to the role of a flabby bureaucrat chasing paper over a desktop. The thought of all that lean muscle turning to fat troubled Longarm deeply.

At last Vail found the dodger he had been looking for. He pulled it toward him with a grunt and glanced up at Longarm. "I understand you got young Tobin between a rock and a hard place at the Windsor last night. What were you holding, to beat him?"

Longarm never revealed a hand when he didn't have to—but this was a little different. He took the cheroot out of his mouth. "Fours and tens, full house."

"Ten high!" Vail's eyes lit up.

Longarm nodded. "And three fours."

"What did Tobin's kid have?"

"Two pair. Sixes and sevens."

"Jesus." Vail spoke softly, shaking his head.

"The kid asked me to hold off on his IOUs. They'd better be good."

"Old man Tobin'll see to it," Vail assured him. "Hell, this isn't the first time. But you're not getting too popular in Denver, beating young Tobin like that. Don't forget, his old man's helping Flannigan to finance that new opera house. That makes him a big man in town."

"Opera house!" Longarm snorted, shaking his head.

"That's right, Longarm. Culture. It's on its way. Yes, it is. Hell, we're all going to have to start taking a bath once a month, whether we need one or not, I swear." He sobered, and glanced significantly at the banjo clock ticking on the oak-paneled wall.

"What kept you? I've got some action here—what you've been howling for—but I almost gave it to Wallace."

"I'm here now. What action have you got?"

Vail tapped the dodger in his hand with a finger. "I want you to take Blackie Bolen to St. Louis. The extradition papers are on the way. You can leave with Blackie on the afternoon train. They'll be right pleased to get the sonofabitch, I can tell you."

Longarm nodded. Deputy Wallace had brought Bolen in a week ago, after the outlaw had messed up a bank job north of Colorado Springs. In St. Louis they wanted him for everything from murder to armed robbery to kidnaping. But Longarm did not want to go to St. Louis. He was sick of traffic, smells, and the swarm of overfed townsmen. "Send Wallace," he said.

"I thought you wanted action. You've been grousing now for two weeks."

"Send Wallace. He brought Bolen in; I didn't."

"I was going to send him on another job—to Nevada."

Longarm nodded. "Nevada sounds fine. Send me."

Shrugging, Vail put down Blackie Bolen's dodger and poked into the pile of envelopes and folders on his desk. He pulled forth a new manila folder and opened it. Glancing through its contents silently for a minute or two, he looked up at Longarm. "Ever hear of Silver City, Nevada?"

Longarm shook his head.

"It's smack dab in the middle of nowhere—Digger land, the Great Basin, as hot and dry as Hades, only not nearly as interesting."

Longarm's eyes glinted. "Go on, Chief."

"The Silver City sheriff telegraphed the War Department about three weeks ago. It seems he spotted an army deserter in a logging town well up on the headwaters of the Humboldt. He was on other business at the time and couldn't chase him. Besides, he didn't have the authority."

"You know that area?" Longarm asked.

Vail nodded, arching his eyebrows demoniacally. "Like I said, it's high, dry, and dusty—a godforsaken patch of alkali basins and black rock populated by bush Indians and a few damn fool settlers. You'll have a long, miserable ride on a livery horse to get to that logging town north of Silver City—and after you get there, most likely you'll find out the poor bastard you're hunting is long gone. You still want the job?"

"I want out of Denver, Chief," Longarm replied wearily. "And St. Louis sounds like more of the same—only worse. Let Wallace have it."

Vail sighed. "Okay, Longarm. Here's the background. The fugitive is a Mountain Man, name of Ned Shortslef. He deserted to the enemy while he was scouting for the cavalry during the Rosebud campaign four years ago. He was married to a Cheyenne squaw and is known to have had a son by her. He's a big fellow, better than six feet—almost as tall as you, I reckon. Hair on his face—plenty of it, in fact. Blue eyes. That's all it has here. Whipsaw's the name of the logging town where the sheriff spotted him."

"That must mean the sheriff knows this jasper pretty well," Longarm guessed.

"He scouted with him during the Rosebud campaign. Yeah. He knows him very well."

"What's the sheriff's name?"

"Martin Tanner. See him first in Silver City. Maybe you can get a better description of the scout."

"I'll need it."

Vail closed the folder. "Be on that train for Silver City tonight. Get your expense vouchers and your railroad pass from my secretary on your way out." He grinned suddenly. "I'll send Wallace to the fleshpots of St. Louis. And I'll just let him think it was all my idea."

Longarm got up and walked to the door. As he pulled it open, he glanced back at Vail. "I've got to shake the smell of this city, Chief. Seems to me the West is filling up too damn fast."

Vail nodded, smiling slightly. "It's all that damn Greeley's fault."

Longarm left the office.

Two days and some seven hundred miles later, Longarm waited for the baggage master to drag his saddle across the baggage car floor to him. When he did, Longarm hefted the

army-surplus McClellan saddle onto one shoulder, and with
the rest of his gear draped over his other shoulder, he went
looking for the hotel.

It didn't take him long to find it. There was only one in Silver City—an unpainted two-story building with the one word
HOTEL painted across the front. The whitewash used to paint
this message had almost faded away in the blistering sun.
Flanking the hotel were the town's livery stable, a blacksmith shop, a barbershop, and a general store. The town's best
saloon, the Silver City, sat facing the hotel from across the
wide, dusty main street. After this, the false fronts petered out
swiftly; the remaining frame shacks, small and nondescript,
seemed to be cowering visibly under the merciless sun.

Longarm mounted the hotel's porch steps and entered the
building. An ancient cowpoke came to his feet behind the front
desk. A room off the lobby containing about six tables served
as a dining room, Longarm noted as he put his saddle and gear
down.

"Got a nice room on the second floor, front," said the desk
clerk. "And Jim Powers next door in the barbershop has some
tubs in back if you're wanting to wash off that railroad grime."
The clerk looked hopefully past Longarm. "Anyone else get
off the train with you?"

"Nope," Longarm replied, signing the register.

"We don't have a bellhop," the clerk told Longarm unhappily.

"That's all right," Longarm said. "Maybe you can tell
me where I might find Sheriff Tanner?"

The old man glanced down at Longarm's signature. "The
sheriff's office is four buildings down on the other side of the
Silver City Saloon, Deputy Long," the clerk replied, dropping
the room key and tag into Longarm's waiting hand.

"That's right. I'm Deputy Long," said Longarm, hefting his
saddle and the rest of his gear onto his shoulders. "I hope you
ain't a flannelmouth, mister."

"No, sir," the old man said with some pride. "I keep it shut
as tight as a burro's ass, and that's a fact."

"That's fine, mister," Longarm said, starting for the narrow
stairs to his room.

* * *

A small, pudgy fellow wearing a black derby hat and a dark brown suit was sitting on a kitchen chair on the board sidewalk in front of the sheriff's office. The chair was tipped back on its two rear legs, the back of the chair resting against the building, the man's crossed ankles resting on the hitch rail. He kept this position until Longarm reached him, then pulled his legs off the hitch rail and let the chair tilt forward.

"I'd like to see Sheriff Tanner," Longarm said.

"Who the hell are you, mister?" the fellow asked Longarm lazily, a slight smile on his round face.

"Deputy U.S. Marshal Custis Long. And just who the hell are you?"

"Oh, I'm Constable Seegar. Pete Seegar." The fellow was too ill-mannered to offer his hand. Longarm didn't mind at all.

"I asked you a question, Constable," Longarm reminded him. "How long before you expect the sheriff to return?"

"You planning on waiting for him?" the constable asked laconically.

Longarm nodded, his irritation growing.

"You better take that chair over there. You got a long wait, I'm thinking."

Longarm took the chair, then pulled out a cheroot and lit it. His bath had been a long, steaming delight—and he had treated himself to a shave and a haircut as well, since the prices in this lonely outpost were very reasonable—two bits for the shave *and* the bath. He hoped the smoke would restore his spirits to the even temper they had enjoyed before he had started this conversation.

"Sheriff Tanner left about a week ago," the constable finally said. "Told me it wouldn't take him long to get to Whipsaw and finish some business he had."

"Some business?"

The fellow nodded. Parts of him seemed to be trying to ooze out through the weak points in his vest and over his belt. His brown suit and vest were lightly checked. They were filthy. He wore no collar with his striped shirt, and his black bowler carried a thin patina of dust.

"That business he wired the government about," the constable went on, "and what you're here for, I suppose—that renegade Mountain Man what ran off in battle and joined his Indian buddies. That turncoat."

Longarm had half expected this. The sheriff had gotten tired of waiting for the government to send someone and had gone off to track the man before he got out of reach once again. This Tanner was not the usual sheriff, it seemed, one content to sit back and wait for the plums to fall into his lap. Longarm decided he liked the man. Still, there was one thing about all of this that bothered Longarm.

"Say there, Constable," Longarm said. "How is it that Tanner didn't send out his deputies? How come he's not back here tending to the paperwork, like most county sheriffs I know?"

"Tanner don't have no deputies. And he said I could handle the paperwork. He's right; there ain't nothing to it."

Longarm frowned. "No deputies, Constable?"

"You gotta have money to pay deputies. Now, ain't that so?"

"I can't argue with that."

"And this godforsaken pasture in hell ain't got no money, Deputy—at least not any it wants to spend lining the pockets of deputy sheriffs, not when the Western Lumber and Land Combine provides us with their own company guard. Hell, we got all the law we need in this county provided free by them."

"You mean the Western Lumber and Land Combine *is* the law in this county."

"And there ain't nothing wrong with that, neither. Slade Desmond—he's the company manager—him and Bat Lawson keep the lid on things real nice."

"And Bat Lawson's the man in charge of the company guards, I guess."

The constable smiled his agreement. "You know what I was before I got appointed town constable?"

Longarm waited; he was certain the fellow would tell him.

"I was one of Slade's bookkeepers at the mill in Whipsaw." The fellow smiled, tipped his chair back against the wall, and stuck his feet back up onto the hitch rail. "But I hated that, so he let me try this job. I been doing fine. I always wanted to be a lawman. Hell, that's what I came out West for in the first place—for some adventure."

"Maybe you've been reading too many dime novels."

The man smiled. "Just got the latest adventure of Deadwood Dick back in the office—*Deadwood Dick's Home Base*. It's a corker. That Bob Wheeler is some writer. He sure knows a lot about Calamity Jane and how the West really is."

"You're sure of that, are you?"

The constable looked at Longarm with suspicion. "You're damn right I am."

Longarm didn't want to argue with the man, even though he knew Calamity Jane as Jane Canary, a broken-down old ex-whore. When Longarm had last heard, she was spending most of her time cadging drinks at whatever bars still let her inside. Longarm puffed on his cheroot, turning over in his mind what the constable had given him: this Tanner was sheriff only on the sufferance of that logging company operating out of Whipsaw; the logging company's operation was under the control of Slade Desmond; one of Desmond's lieutenants was a man called Bat Lawson, who bossed the company's private guard; further, this Constable Seegar was here to keep tabs on Sheriff Tanner as well as on the town of Silver City and its new inhabitants. Not a sparrow fell to the ground, it appeared, without this Slade Desmond knowing all about it. He ran a tight ship.

Longarm glanced at Seegar. "You say Sheriff Tanner's been gone about a week?"

The fellow nodded and pushed his bowler down over his forehead to shield his eyes from the sun's glare.

"Just one thing more, Constable. What did the sheriff tell you about this deserter?"

"Not much. Said he was a big son of a bitch—favored a bushy beard and mustache." Seegar laughed suddenly as he remembered. "Said there was one time on the Snake when this Mountain Man came up to their camp at night and one of the Shoshone scouts thought he was a grizzly. Tanner said the Mountain Man was all dressed in his furs, and with that beard of his, the only things that looked human were them two blue eyes peering out from behind all that hair. After that, the Shoshone scouts called him 'Man Who Moves Like Bear.'" Seegar nodded again as he thought over what Tanner had told him. "A real big man, I guess. Like most of them Mountain Men."

"They weren't *all* that big," Longarm said quietly. He was

thinking of Joe Meek, who had been just a little over five feet tall. The little Mountain Man had fought and killed grizzlies hand-to-hand. Once he had used a coup stick on one grizzly and killed another with his hatchet. He'd been in real close and had buried the hatchet's blade in the grizzly's brain.

"What do you mean?" the constable demanded. "They sure as hell *were* big men—*all* of 'em. What do you think they called them *Mountain* Men for?" He squinted at Longarm suddenly, almost losing his bowler in the process. "How long you *been* out West, Deputy?"

"Long enough," Longarm replied.

The fellow grunted. "Don't sound like it. Don't sound like it a-*tall!*"

"Maybe so, Constable. Now, is that all the description of Shortslef you can give me? Is that all Tanner told you?"

"That's all. Tanner ain't all that chock-full of information— not when I'm around, that is. He's a little suspicious of me because I'm such a good friend of Slade."

"Thank you, Constable."

Longarm got up, touched the brim of his hat to Seegar, and started back to the hotel. He figured now might be a good time to catch some shut-eye before supper. He was still weary from his long train ride—and even wearier from talking to the town's well-read constable.

He was about to enter the hotel when the sound of hoofs and the jingle of harness caused him to pause and look down the street. Riding into town from the north were at least six horsemen and a small coach. The coach looked quite elegant, with red trim, red wheel spokes, and gilt edging around the two side windows. Three riders rode in front and three in the rear. For a county with the lid on nice and tight, this was a most formidable guard.

As the coach pulled up in front of the hotel, the six riders dismounted noisily, loudly proclaiming their thirst. They paid scant heed to their weary, lathered mounts, which they left at the hitch rails in front of the hotel, and crossed the street to the Silver City Saloon. All but one. This fellow went straight to the coach's door and pulled it open. A buxom, handsome woman got out—and one look at the lovely chestnut curls coiled on her shoulders and the wide, generous portion of her neck and bosom open to view told Longarm all he needed to know about her. Perhaps she *was* worth this much protection.

The fellow who escorted the woman from the coach was a dark-visaged man with a hooked nose and a strong, prominent chin. His shirt was of crisp, white linen and he was wearing an immaculate black string tie. His black hat was flat-crowned, his six-gun gleaming, his expensive, finely tooled boots shining despite the dust. As the man escorted the woman past Longarm into the hotel, the lawman caught a flash of her brazen eyes and gleaming teeth as she saw him standing there.

Abruptly, she turned in the doorway and called back across the street to the other riders in a strident, brassy voice: "Don't you bozos get too tanked, now! That train's due in pretty soon and those girls are going to be mighty tired."

"Hell, Ruby," one of the men called out, his hand on the Silver City Saloon's batwing door, "we're just going to wet down all that alkali. Come on over and join us—less'n you got *other* business!"

The rest of the men with him roared at that, then followed him into the saloon. Ruby laughed, herself. "You heard what he said," she told her escort. "Is that the kind of discipline you have over those bohunks?"

"You want me to discipline them or take you up to your room?" the man asked in reply.

"Now what do *you* think, Bat?"

He reached down for her canvas gladstone and led her into the hotel lobby.

Following them into the hotel, Longarm looked over the man she had called Bat. This was the leader of Slade Desmond's company guard, and those men who had ridden in with him were part of that guard—what amounted to a private army. In this case, a small company delegated to make sure the shipment of new girls arrived safe and sound. Those loggers in Whipsaw were waiting anxiously, no doubt.

As Ruby and her escort neared the desk, Longarm moved past them and up the stairs to his room. The matchstick he had left wedged between the door and the jamb was undisturbed. He unlocked his door and walked in, pocketing the matchstick for future use. He was taking off his hat when he heard the clatter of hooves and the rumble of a wagon's big wheels. He stepped to the window and looked down.

Loggers—evidently tardy members of the same party escorting the madam—were piling out of a wagon in front of the saloon, filling the air with the hearty shouts of big men intent on slaking prodigious thirsts. They had come to help Ruby greet the new girls.

Longarm turned from the window, carefully removed his Ingersoll pocket watch from his left-hand vest pocket, and placed it on the top of the dresser. The gold-washed chain attached to the watch was clipped to the butt of a double-barreled .44 derringer. A potentially fatal surprise for any of Longarm's enemies, it fit snugly into his right vest pocket, the bright chain dangling across the front of his vest between his derringer and his watch. Next, Longarm unholstered his double-action Colt Model T .44-40. The barrel had been cut down to five inches and the front sight filed off. Placing the Colt under his pillow, he removed his cross-draw holster and gunbelt and hung them over the bedpost, after which he unbuttoned his vest and shirt front and flopped onto the bed without bothering to kick off his boots.

Longarm had trained himself over the years to be able to sleep instantly anywhere—while at the same time retaining a catlike ability to awaken on a moment's notice. Longarm's hand snaked under his pillow and came to rest beside the butt of his Colt. He closed his eyes and was asleep almost at once.

Longarm awoke to the sound of booming laughter and the clash of silverware, coming from the dining room beneath his room. Swinging off the bed, he stood up and consulted his watch. It was a little after five.

Swiftly he buttoned up his shirt and vest, replaced his watch and derringer, and strapped on his rig. The holster was open-toed, fashioned of waxed and heat-hardened leather. He wore the rig high, adjusting the Cordovan belt to ride above his hip bones. Withdrawing the Colt from under the pillow, he swung it out over the bed and emptied the cylinder, then dry-fired a few times to check the action. After examining the five cartridges, he reloaded and dropped the revolver into the holster, resting the firing pin on an empty chamber.

He settled the snuff-brown Stetson onto his head and left the room, ducking slightly to clear the door frame.

Entering the dining room a moment later, he considered himself lucky to spot an unoccupied table, and headed for it. The small room was crowded with loggers, all of whom had eyes only for the three fetching young ladies sitting at the table with Ruby. The girls had arrived safe and sound. As Longarm sat down, he noted with some amusement that Ruby's girls were doing their best not to show how pleased they were by all this attention.

Two of the three were pretty only in that they were young and fresh-looking and were neither too fat nor too slim. The third girl, however, was more than just youthful—she was very pretty. She had glanced up at Longarm when he had entered the dining room. She did not know Longarm, and he did not know her, yet an awareness had passed between them in that instant; a feeling both of them immediately responded to and understood. The girl had dark auburn hair. She wore it combed out boldly, in thick curls. Her face was not heavily rouged like the faces of the others, and her eyes—a dark, emerald green— dominated her pale, freckled face.

As Longarm turned his attention to the menu, he could feel her eyes on him. After he gave the waitress his order, he glanced at her again. She was looking directly at him. As soon as their eyes met, she looked hastily back to the other girls at her table and launched into a highly animated conversation. It did not fool anyone, however. Longarm saw the madam turn curiously and look boldly at him. She smiled. Longarm nodded at her, returning the smile. Turning back around, the madam said something to the girls, causing them all to break into delighted laughter.

Longarm's meal arrived and he tore into it. It had been a long day and he was famished. He was reaching for his second cup of coffee when he heard tables scraping the floor and looked up to see three hulking loggers approaching the madam's table. The one in the lead had obviously been selected as their spokesman. He was the tallest and roughest-looking, with a patch over one eye and shoulders wide enough to use as a gallows. He cleared his throat while his huge hands twisted his stocking cap. The madam waited. He cleared his throat again.

In exasperation, one of the men behind him prodded him angrily in the back.

"Ruby," the fellow faltered, ". . . we was wonderin' . . . I mean, what we was hopin' was that . . ."

From the other loggers in the room there arose a sudden howl of protest that shook the small dining room. These three loggers were jumping the gun, moving too soon! The uproar was terrific. Ruby waved the room to silence and then looked up at the logger wearing the eyepatch. She obviously knew him.

"Now, Gus," she told him, "you know full well what these girls here have been through—a long, hard ride all the way from San Francisco. Now, why don't you fine gentlemen give them a chance to rest up—at least one night?"

"Aw, Ruby!" the logger replied, no longer tongue-tied. "They been resting up since they got on that train!"

Ruby shook her head. "Gus, you are no gentleman."

"That's right, Ruby!" cried a logger standing beside Gus. "He ain't no gentleman. None of us is. And these here ain't no ladies!"

A roar of agreement seconded that assertion. With a massive shrug, Ruby turned to the girls as if to say *What can I do, girls? It's up to you!*

At once, the first three were joined by other loggers. Surrounding the table, they beamed down with grimy, bewhiskered faces at the young girls. It didn't take long for two of the girls to make then choices. The third girl—the auburn-haired one with the green eyes—seemed undecided. This was the girl Gus wanted.

He reached down, took the girl by the wrist, and pulled her gently but firmly toward him. The girl left her chair and moved around the table toward Gus, still obviously reluctant. Abruptly, she leaned down and whispered something in Ruby's ear. Ruby listened attentively.

"Never you mind about that, Alice," Ruby boomed when the girl had finished. "Why, Gus here will be real gentle with you. Won't you, Gus?"

"As gentle as I can be," admitted Gus, pulling the girl roughly against himself. The other loggers laughed. Evidently, Gus was not considered the gentlest of men. This laughter—and the girl's reluctance—angered Gus.

The girl saw this. At once, her tactics changed. She wrapped her arm around the big logger's arm and smiled up into his face. "That's all right," she told him. "I don't want no trouble. If you promise to be nice to me, Gus, I'll be nice to you. Real nice."

Gus's capitulation was awesomely complete, his anger vanishing instantly. With an almost grateful glance down at Ruby, Gus left the dining room with the girl—to the jealous hoots and ribald jibes of the loggers remaining behind.

Longarm finished his coffee. Leaving a silver dollar to cover his meal and a generous tip for the waitress, he stood up and started from the dining room. He was almost to the door when Constable Seegar entered, nodded curtly to Longarm, and went directly to the madam's table. Ruby made him warmly welcome. The two, it seemed, had business to discuss.

Longarm continued on out of the hotel and made directly for the livery, where he proceeded to examine the horses. Ordinarily, if Longarm needed a mount for field work, he would borrow one from the nearest army post or remount station. Neither accommodation existed within miles of Silver City, however, and Longarm had decided to leave for Whipsaw the next day.

The deputy was a keen judge of horseflesh. Though he appreciated a good horse, he was not a sentimentalist. A horse is just about as bright as a cat—no brighter. Its one mental ability is a good memory. Usually that was enough for Longarm. There was no sense in expecting anything more than that from a horse, and he didn't. Usually, Longarm preferred an army mount over a cow pony because of its size. A good bay gelding was what Longarm was looking for at the moment—until he spotted the Morgan.

She was a tough, long-winded, all-purpose saddle mare that still had some good miles left in her. Longarm listened closely to her breathing, then carefully checked all four feet. One hoof would need a fresh shoe; the frogs of all four hooves would have to be cleaned as well. Longarm went to find the owner of the livery.

"Yep, best saddle horse I got here," the old cowpoke said, when Longarm told him of his choice. "'Course, everyone complains because she's a mite old and not as sassy as the younger mounts. But she's a Morgan." He shook his head. "Some people just don't know nothin' about horses."

"She'll do fine," Longarm told the man. Then he mentioned the shoe and asked him to clean out the frogs thoroughly.

"You didn't have to tell me," the man protested. "I wouldn't let a horse leave my stable what wasn't in perfect condition."

Longarm smiled at that, and was about to go back to take another look at the Morgan, when he heard shouts erupting suddenly in the darkening street. He stepped out through the stable door and saw four mounted men dragging four Indians at the ends of ropes. The men were riding at such a brisk trot that the Indians were unable to keep their feet for any length of time. They were, in fact, almost totally exhausted. Their appearance was wretched. Their hair was matted with sweat-caked alkali and their knees and elbows were raw and bleeding.

The horsemen pulled up in front of the Silver City Saloon with guns thundering into the sky. The Indians collapsed forward onto their knees. Longarm shook his head in disgust as loggers and gunmen poured out of the saloon to dance in glee around the sullen, prostrate Indians. With some satisfaction, Longarm noted that not one of the Indians had uttered a single cry. They were as silent as vengeance as they lay sprawled in the dust, looking up at their tormenters.

"Now that's real excitement, ain't it?" the old man said, his tone betraying the contempt he felt for those four riders.

Longarm glanced down at the old cowpoke. His hair was almost gone, and what was left was fine-spun cotton. He had the squinting look of men who have spent too many years looking long distances under a glaring sun—and the bulbous, cherry-red nose of the inebriate. The bulge of a flask was clearly visible on his hip.

"You don't approve?" Longarm asked him.

The man thrust his chin forward indignantly. "No, sir. I don't. After all, them Indians is just Diggers—poorest damn excuses I ever saw for a red man. They ain't no bother. All they do is kill jackrabbits and eat pine nuts." Then he shook his head. "But there ain't nothing I can do about it. If I was to go agin' that bunch, they wouldn't pay me no more heed than a steer does to a cobweb. I'd have as much chance as a wax cat in hell."

He turned and started back into the livery. Longarm looked back and watched as the four men dragged the Indians—still roped—into the saloon. Abruptly, Longarm started across the street. He worked for the federal government. These Digger Indians were wards of that government. It was part of his job to see to their safety.

Chapter 2

Only a few men paid attention as Longarm entered the saloon. He moved to the wall, well behind the circle of men, and slumped into a chair behind a small table. One logger was already standing on top of a table, dropping ropes over a beam that ran the length of the ceiling. Another logger was busy fashioning hangman's knots in the ropes, while others were cheerfully tying the hands of the four Diggers behind them.

Once the nooses were ready and the Indians were securely bound, they were unceremoniously lifted up onto the tables—each Digger standing on a separate table. Standing on a chair behind each one, the fellow who had made the hangman's knots dropped the nooses over the Diggers' heads, then pulled them snug. Stepping down at last, he surveyed his accomplishment with some satisfaction—if not outright glee.

Longarm took out his Colt and placed it on the table in front of him, resting his hand lightly on its grip. Those closest to Longarm's table became aware of the exposed gun almost instantly. In a matter of seconds, the word traveled. The place quieted ominously. All eyes turned to Longarm—and to the dark bore of his Colt yawning at them from the table.

Through the crowd toward Longarm bulled the same fellow who had escorted Ruby from the coach earlier that day—Bat Lawson. He planted himself firmly in front of Longarm and looked angrily, insolently down at him.

"My name's Bat Lawson, mister. This here business ain't none of your concern."

"Maybe it is," Longarm said quietly. "I'm Deputy U.S. Marshal Custis Long."

The man's hawklike face darkened. He did not appear surprised, however, at learning Longarm's identity. The constable must already have gotten word to him of Longarm's presence. "I don't care who you are, Long, or why you're here. I take my orders from Slade Desmond."

"And he wants you to hang these four Indians, does he?"

"That's right."

"Why?"

"As a warning to other Diggers. It's the only kind of warning they understand. They been giving us trouble lately. Now, you can watch if you want. But I advise you not to interfere."

While Lawson had been talking, Gus had entered the saloon. Out of the corner of his eye Longarm saw how dismayed—at least for an instant—the man was at the sight of the four Indians standing on the tables with nooses around their necks. Now Constable Seegar entered the saloon looking a mite winded. He slunk over to the bar and tried to become invisible. Longarm anticipated no help from that quarter.

He got up with his gun leveled at Bat and said, "Cut them down, Bat. Now."

He thrust the barrel of his Colt deeply and firmly into Lawson's midsection before the man had time to draw his own Colt from its holster. Longarm prodded him with such sudden violence that Bat almost stumbled in his haste to get back.

But Longarm kept after him, increasing the pressure. "Do it, Bat! If anything happens to any one of those Indians, this gun is going to go off—and most likely it'll cut you in two at this range."

"Everyone stand back!" Lawson cried, his face ashen. "I'm doin' what this here crazy lawman says to do. We'll settle up with him later! Now get back! All of you!"

The men crowded hastily back. Longarm kept his Colt's barrel pressed into the small of Lawson's back while Lawson reached up and lifted the nooses off the shoulders of the four Diggers. Longarm stepped back a little as Bat untied their hands. Considering the sorry state of Lawson's nerves, the Indians were free in a surprisingly short time. As each one was freed, he jumped down and disappeared through the door. At last, the fourth Digger was gone, the sound of his bare feet pounding down the street, the batwings thumping slower and slower.

Bat turned to face Longarm. "You ain't heard the last of this, Long."

"Maybe neither of us have. Those Indians are wards of the federal government. I don't know just how big this lumber company of yours is, Lawson, but it sure as hell ain't big enough to outlaw the constitution, due process, and a few other such items."

"You'll see," the man said meanly, still confident. "We got friends in Washington. Big friends."

It was pointless to continue the debate. Holstering his gun, Longarm left the saloon and crossed to the hotel. He was weary. It was late. Men like Lawson made him sick to his stomach. He would be glad to shake the dust of this town the next morning, but he knew he would most likely have to deal with Bat Lawson one way or the other before he left these parts. *Men like that work awful hard not to learn*, he thought.

Nodding absently to the desk clerk, Longarm mounted the stairs and turned down the hall to his room. His practiced eye caught the absence of the matchstick from its spot in the doorjamb. Someone was waiting inside. Longarm unholstered his Colt, slowed down, and placed his back gently against the door, then pushed slightly. The door gave just enough to tell Longarm that it was not shut tight.

Longarm stepped past the door and flattened himself against the wall. With the barrel of his Colt, he gently pushed open the door. As it began to swing into the room, he gave it a final shove. When he heard it slam into the wall, he sprang into the room, crouching low, his six-gun in front of him, waist-high, his elbow bent. Nothing. No flash of gunpowder lancing through the dark.

He heard the bedsprings creak—and a girl's voice, low and seductive, laughing softly. Waiting a moment for his eyes to adjust to the sudden darkness of the room, he saw something long and pale stir on the bed.

"My, my," the girl said. "You must be awful nervous to enter like that all the time."

Longarm straightened, feeling a mite foolish, and kicked the door shut. By this time, he was able to recognize the girl. She was Alice, the one who had caught his eye in the dining room. She was lying on his bed, wearing a long silken nightgown. He glanced swiftly around the room to make sure there were no other surprises, then holstered his Colt, chucked his hat back from his forehead, and started for the dresser.

"Don't do that too often, Alice," he told her, lighting the lamp on the dresser. "I almost blew a hole in your pretty face."

"Well, I *did* do it and I *am* here. So what are you going to do about it?"

"Do I have any choice?"

"No," she said, a devilish gleam in her eye. "You don't. And it won't cost you one penny."

"I don't usually pay for it, Alice," he said evenly.

"I didn't think you did."

Longarm looked down at the slim, lovely girl. He was not exactly in the mood for playing with her. His adrenalin was still kicking up a fuss from that business in the saloon—and the manner of his entry into his room had done little to quiet him down. He was tempted to slap the girl on her fanny and send her packing. But he didn't.

"Please," she said, "take off your boots. I know men don't usually do that in sporting houses—but I would appreciate it."

"Would you, now?" Longarm slipped out of his coat and vest, placing his watch and derringer carefully on the top of the dresser, working swiftly enough to keep the small gun hidden from her. As he unbuckled his gunbelt and hung it over the brass bedpost, he saw the girl shudder just a little. He withdrew the Colt from his rig and tucked it under the pillow.

She watched him with widening eyes. "Do you always make love with a gun under your pillow?"

He smiled at her without replying, sat down on the edge of the bed, and tugged off his boots.

"Thank you," she said softly.

Peeling off his shirt and longjohns, he turned to her—almost grimly.

"Could you—turn down the lamp some?" she asked. "There's . . . so much of you. It kind of unnerves a girl."

"You do it," Longarm told her quietly. "I like to watch you move. Besides, this was all your idea."

She looked at him for a long moment, her green eyes wide at his curt manner. He thought she might get up and leave. Finally, with a shrug, she got up and turned down the lamp.

It was worth the wait. The sight of a woman's body moving under a silken nightgown was a rare one for Longarm, of late. He enjoyed himself very much as he watched her return to the bed and coil softly beside him.

The softer light was an improvement. She cuddled playfully for a moment, then rolled onto her back and began to unbutton all the buttons that ran down the front of her nightgown. He watched her. When she was finished, she rolled out of the nightgown like a large glowworm out of its cocoon, and thrust herself delightedly against him. She had been wearing nothing under the gown, not even a shift. This was unusual. Working whores almost never stripped. They plied their trade with their shifts on, and kept their long stockings and high-heeled footgear firmly in place, just as their customers traditionally retained their boots.

This young whore was evidently a new breed of cat. As he looked at her long figure beside him, the ugly feeling left over from that ruckus in the saloon slipped slowly from him.

"What are you up to, young lady?" he asked.

"The question," she replied, glancing significantly down at him, "is what are *you* up to? Is there something the matter?"

"Alice," Longarm said quietly, folding his arms under his head and gazing up at the ceiling, "if a man's been lost on a desert for a spell, you don't let him drink a gallon of water all at once. You let him work up to it. Do you get my meaning?"

"Oh, I see!" she laughed. "You've been deprived."

"'Disciplined' might be a better word." He turned to look at her, allowing himself to enjoy the view.

The nicest thing about her—besides her catlike eyes—was her long, curling hair. It reached to her waist, and as she reclined beside him, she contrived to let the long tresses spill over her full breasts, all the way down her slim body to her thighs. She had the delicacy to keep the hip closest to Longarm slightly upraised, preserving that much mystery, at least. Longarm liked a little modesty on the part of the women he bedded—if only because it gave him pleasure to make it vanish in the heat of passion.

"Ah, Mr. Long," she said, "I see you are doing much better now."

"Who told you my name?"

"Ruby—when she warned me to stay away from you." She seemed delighted with herself.

"I'll ask you again. What are you up to, Alice?"

She looked at him, her face suddenly grave. "I am up to enjoying myself," she said simply. "Is that such a crime? Men do it all the time."

"You enjoy yourself, working for Ruby?"

"I didn't want to marry some clod and have to put up with his miserable lovemaking, his beatings, and his kids, for the rest of my life. I have been lucky to find out in time what loving a man—a *real* man—could be like." She smiled at him. "My parents had money. Too much perhaps. They hired a French violin teacher for my two sisters and me. He gave me private—very private—lessons."

"Is this the story you tell your customers?" he asked bluntly.

"Heavens, no! Most of them would be shocked to hear such a thing. I tell them what every whore tells them—what they want to hear. How I was destitute, miserable, and lonely after my fiancé jilted me and left me penniless on the streets of San Francisco, where Madame du Roch found me—little better than a beggar—and took me in. I was a stray cat, grateful and willing to do anything to help my benefactress. Only too late did I learn the real business of Madame du Roch's salon—and what was expected of me in payment for her kindness. Alas! What was I to do? Return penniless to the streets?"

Longarm laughed. He could almost see her, bathed in the white, unnatural glow of footlights, declaiming this melodramatic speech, with the back of her hand against her forehead.

Alice laughed too, then looked seriously at him. "I saw something in your eyes," she told him, "when you walked into the dining room. And you saw something in mine. Didn't you?"

He nodded.

She moved closer. He gave up trying to figure her out and let his hand drop lightly onto her bare shoulder. Suddenly, her lips were on his, her mouth opening, her tongue darting—while her hands moved down his chest, all the way to his loins. He came alive under her caresses. He strained toward her. The girl laughed and moved her lips down his chest, nuzzling the wiry hair on his rock-solid chest, and moving on down almost to his crotch. Fire enveloped him as her tongue explored his pelvis, then moved up his back. Her hands touched him boldly, measuring his potency with an eagerness that caused him to sweep her under him.

She cried out softly, her head flung back, at the force with which he entered. She turned her head, her eyes wide, her teeth clenched. "Oh," she gasped, "there's so *much* of you!" It was not a complaint. Her legs rose behind him to lock fiercely around his thrusting buttocks.

Their first climax came quickly, more quickly than Longarm wanted. He stayed up and kept himself in her. Taking his time now, he grabbed both of her buttocks in his big hands and hauled her in closer under him. Each stroke brought a feverish, shuddering response from the girl. Alice dug her nails into his back and crossed her heels tightly behind him. Longarm was reaching bottom with almost every thrust. When he tried to pull back a little to make it easier on her, her face became a naked mask of fury as she lifted her pelvis and jammed upward to get the full impact of each stroke.

"Damn you, Mr. Long!" she cried. "Deep! Go deep! I want *all* of you!" Then she began to gasp, her face and neck growing scarlet "Now! *Now!*" she cried exultantly. "Yes! Oh, Jesus!"

Her fingernails were like bear's claws now, as they raked down his back. She shuddered once, twice, and then Longarm climaxed himself, joining her with one last, deep thrust, expending himself with involuntary ejaculations that left him— finally—soft and warm and exhausted.

She had gone limp under him. He rolled off, satisfied. She turned to face him and rested her cheek on the palm of her hand. "Mmmm," she murmured contentedly. "That *was* nice. I feel warm—all the way down to my toes."

Longarm said nothing, just watched her.

"You are all I thought you would be, Mr. Long."

"Call me Longarm," he said quietly.

"Oh, that's much better. Yes. Longarm," she said, leaning close and kissing him on the lips, softly. He could smell the sweetness of her perspiring body. There were tiny beads of sweat on her upthrust breasts. "Take a nap," she told him softly. "Maybe afterward . . ."

"Just what I was thinking."

She got up and pulled down the sheets. Bouncing lightly back down beside him, she pulled the blankets up around both of them. She snuggled against him, fitting herself into his back. He felt her warm body relax, and closed his eyes.

She dropped off to sleep, or appeared to. Her breathing became regular. For a while he was certain she was asleep. Still he waited, allowing his own breathing to grow heavy. It was difficult not to fall asleep. Once or twice he almost drifted off, the warmth of her body lulling him.

She sat up slowly, waiting for some sign that her movement had disturbed him. He lay still. She lifted back the covers and was on her feet, moving swiftly around the bed, as silently as falling snow. Longarm was facing toward the dresser. He opened his eyes just enough to see what she was doing. He saw her reach into his inside coat pocket and remove his wallet and papers. She took the papers over to the lamp—the warrant for Shortslef, the notes on his physical description, a copy of the telegram Tanner had sent Washington—and read them swiftly by the lamp's light.

Satisfied, she folded the papers, replaced them in his wallet, and tucked it back into his inside pocket. As she started back around the bed, he sat up, withdrawing his Colt from under the pillow. She froze in her tracks as he leveled the gun at her pale, almost luminous breasts.

"My God," she breathed.

"Who put you up to this?" he asked, without a trace of emotion.

"Ruby. She told me I had to do it," she answered quickly.

He smiled. "And I thought it was all because you couldn't wait to pleasure a real man."

"That was part of it, honest. Ruby asked which one of us new girls wanted to do it. I volunteered because I liked you."

"What were you looking for just now?"

"They want to know what you're really doing here."

"Who are 'they'?"

"Constable Seegar and Slade Desmond, his boss. Seegar works for Slade. He's suspicious of you. He told Ruby she had to do it or he would tell Desmond she had refused to help."

Longarm believed her. He had been suspicious the moment

he found her in his bed. No madam would allow herself to be this careless concerning the whereabouts of one of her girls, and certainly not for this length of time.

Still standing before him, Alice ran a nervous hand through her long hair. "You never believed anything I told you," she said softly. "Did you?"

"No, Alice, I didn't."

"Can I leave now?"

"Of course."

Longarm put the Colt down and watched her as she swept up her nightgown and let herself out. He listened to her bare feet running from his door and down the hall. When he heard a door open and close at the other end of the hall, he threw back the covers and dressed rapidly.

A thin, freckled-faced man in steel-rimmed glasses was behind the front desk as Longarm strode through the lobby and started for Sheriff Tanner's office. The uproar in the Silver City Saloon was still in progress. As Longarm walked along the boardwalk, he saw an occasional logger stagger drunkenly from the place and reel off into the night, like a wagon with its wheels coming off.

Entering the sheriff's office, Longarm found it empty. A kerosene lamp on the sheriff's desk was lit. The desk had obviously gone unused for some time. A smaller desk in the corner—most likely Constable Seegar's—was littered with old dodgers, official correspondence, dirty cups, and an old coffeepot with a broken spout. A cot along the far wall sat next to an open door that led to the lockup. Glancing into it, Longarm saw four empty cells. He returned to Seegar's desk and eased himself into the constable's swivel chair. Propping his boots up on the desk, he listened to the drone of the horsefly convention being held on the ceiling and prepared himself for a long wait.

That silly constable was most likely questioning Ruby or Alice at that very moment—and might even be staying for a while.

The sound of horseshoes striking stone alerted Longarm. He pulled his feet down and stood up. Someone was riding into town. Blinking the weariness out of his eyes, he stepped outside and peered into the darkness. A horse and rider were angling onto the town's main street. The rider, slumped well over the saddle horn, seemed dangerously close to falling off.

Longarm left the frame shack and hurried out to meet the rider. Once he got close enough, he reached up and grabbed the horse's bridle, pulling the animal to a halt. Longarm reached up and steadied him. Peering carefully up at him through the darkness, Longarm saw that his eyes were closed. His tan shirt front contained two large, irregular dark patches—and a sheriff's badge.

Sheriff Tanner had returned.

Both of Tanner's hands were clasped tightly about the horn. The man did not seem aware of Longarm's presence. Longarm led the horse down the street to the sheriff's office. Dropping the reins over the hitch rail, he reached up to pull Tanner out of his saddle. For a moment, the sheriff clung obstinately to the horn. When he did let go, Longarm found himself hefting a surprisingly light burden across the walk and into the office.

Longarm carried Tanner to the single cot against the wall and eased the sheriff's bird-frail body gently down upon it. Tanner could not have been more than five and a half feet tall. Soaking wet, he must have weighed a hundred and fifty pounds. His face was small. The boy that used to be Tanner stared up at Longarm—an old, wrinkled boy. The skin on his face was as weathered as old boot leather and drawn tightly about the skull, causing his cheekbones to stick out prominently. His closed eyes rested in dark hollows. The thin line of his mouth was drawn straight and grimly down. The man was obviously close to death. Only a fierce instinct had kept him on that horse.

Longarm leaned close. "Tanner! What happened? Who did this to you?" he asked.

Tanner's eyes opened and the expression on his face grew terrible. The sound of Longarm's voice had aroused him, but he had not understood the words. He reached up, grabbed Longarm's vest, and pulled him closer.

"That you, Seegar?" he gasped.

"Never mind Seegar," Longarm said. "Was it Shortslef? Did he do this to you?"

"Illegal!" The man raved, wide-eyed. "Wrong place! Settlers—right. Stop him! Stop. . . !"

"Tanner!" Longarm said, leaning still closer. "Where's Shortslef? Is he the one who shot you?"

The man's eyes focused on Longarm for the first time. "Shortslef? You want Ned Shortslef?"

"Yes," Longarm replied. "Is he the one who bushwhacked you? Where is he?"

"Who are you? Where's Seegar? That idiot, Seegar!"

"Never mind him. I'm here to get Shortslef—Ned Shortslef. I've got a copy of your telegram to Washington."

Tanner laughed, and his skull-face turned hideous. As he laughed, his eyes closed and his boy's fist relaxed, releasing Longarm's vest. Martin Tanner's hand dropped to the cot. His shrunken head sank deeper into the pillow. His eyes remained open only because there was no force still left in the man capable of closing them.

Longarm pulled a blanket over the dead man's face and stood up. He looked down at the quiet form for a moment, then turned and walked out of the office. A couple of loggers stumbled out of the saloon. Longarm took out his Colt, stepped into the middle of the street, and pumped two slugs into the night sky. The detonations reverberated thunderously throughout the sleeping town. The tumult inside the saloon quieted instantly. The two loggers halted in confusion and looked down the street at Longarm. A second later, those still in the saloon charged from the place. Some of Bat Lawson's men had their guns drawn.

As they came to a halt in the middle of the street, Longarm called out to them, "Sheriff Tanner's dead! Someone find Constable Seegar—and get an undertaker!"

Longarm holstered his weapon and went back into the late Sheriff Tanner's office.

As the coach carrying Whipsaw's fresh supply of girls and the wagonload of loggers left Silver City the next morning, Longarm climbed to the crest of the hill that was the town's graveyard and saw to the burial of Sheriff Tanner. Town Constable Pete Seegar, the owner of the livery, and the bespectacled hotel night clerk were the only ones besides the gravediggers who joined Longarm at the grave site. Longarm had selected what he felt were appropriate verses from a hastily procured Gideon

Bible and read them over the body of his fellow lawman, then stood back as the cheap, hastily constructed pine coffin was lowered into the ground.

The rest left hastily after that. Seegar looked furtively back at Longarm, while the tall deputy remained behind at the grave, hat in hand, contemplating the small rectangle of ground it had taken to cover a man's life forever. It was true that there were never many tears shed at a boot-hill burying, but that didn't make it any easier for Longarm to accept.

Like Longarm, this lawman had known the loneliness of long days in the saddle, of dry camps and dark nights with the yapping of the coyotes as his only lullaby, his only comfort. Tanner had exhibited a rare tenacity of purpose shown not only in his determination to bring in a man he had once called a friend, but also in the way he had ridden for a day, at least, with two bullet holes in his back. When Longarm thought finally of the size of the man in contrast to the fierce spirit that must have driven him, he felt peculiarly close to him. He wished he could have met the sheriff while he had still lived and shared a glass of rye with him, perhaps, or a game of poker.

Longarm took out the man's badge, buffed it on his trouser leg, then drove its pin into the top of the rude wooden grave marker. In the bright early morning sunlight, the badge gleamed brilliantly. Longarm stepped back. The badge would soon be dusty. The wind and the rain would tear it loose. Perhaps then it would become buried in the shifting sands of the gravesite, resting at last with the man who had worn it with such dedication.

Longarm put his hat back on and pulled it down snugly. The dry wind whipped and bellied the tails of his Prince Albert coat as he turned and started down the hill. He had a score to settle with that weasel, Seegar. He was anxious to see to it and ride north to Whipsaw, for he rode now with a renewed purpose—to find Ned Shortslef and bring him in. Not only for desertion, but for the backshooting of Sheriff Martin Tanner.

Longarm found the constable waiting for him behind his desk. The man was sitting bolt upright. His desk top had been cleared off somewhat—as if he wanted a better view of Longarm as the man approached him. For the first time since Longarm had

known him, Seegar was wearing a huge old Remington six-gun
that tugged heavily on the man's gunbelt and was worn ludi-
crously low on Seegar's hip. If Seegar got up suddenly and
started running, he would most likely trip over it and break
a leg.

Longarm pulled out Tanner's chair and sat down beside
Seegar's desk astride the seat, his arms folded on the back. He
chucked his hat back off his forehead and smiled at the town
constable.

"Why in blazes did you send that girl to my room last night,
Seegar?"

"I don't know what the hell you're talking about."

Longarm didn't say anything for a moment or two, then
repeated his question a second time, a bit more softly. "Why
did you send her, Seegar? What were you expecting to find? I
told you what I was doing here."

"Hell! I didn't send no girl to your room. Why in Hades
would I do anything like that?" He smirked. "You're just popular with whores, Longarm."

Longarm stood up, kicking his chair halfway across the
room, reached over and grabbed Seegar by his checked vest.
He snapped a few buttons as he hauled Seegar out of his chair
and dragged him across the top of his desk. Black ink spilled
over the desk top, smearing a dark stain over the front of
Seegar's checked trousers. Longarm lifted Seegar until both of
his heels were off the floor, then flung him after the chair.
Seegar came to rest against the overturned chair, spraddled
as loose as a rag doll. He seemed not entirely conscious but as
Longarm approached he clawed for his Remington. Longarm
waited until the hog leg was clear of its holster, then kicked it
out of Seegar's hand.

"All right!" Seegar cried raggedly. "I sent her! I just didn't
believe you was only after that army deserter is all."

"What else *would* I be after? Why didn't you believe me,
Seegar?"

"I . . . I just didn't, that's all. Who the hell cares about
something that happened so long ago? Them Indian Wars is
over now. Why should Washington send a guy all the way up
here for a turd like that?"

Longarm considered the trembling man sprawled at his

feet. His naked fear was like a stench in Longarm's nostrils. The constable got his picture of the West out of the books he was always reading, only this wasn't a book—and if it was, it sure didn't read like all the others. Longarm realized then that there was really no way he could make this poor excuse for a lawman tell the truth—even if the man knew what it was.

He took out a cheroot, lit it to clear out his nostrils, and left the office. Longarm had already checked out of his hotel. Soon he would put the dust of this town behind him. And he would make damn sure he didn't return to it the way Sheriff Tanner had.

Chapter 3

The rough wagon road Longarm followed north to Whipsaw took him through a bleak, rocky, alkali wilderness. So deceptive were distances in the clear, high air that rock formations on far distant ridges appeared to leap into view as he rode toward them. At times Longarm felt he could reach out and pluck a giant cottonwood from the bluff it was sitting on, even though it was maybe five miles away.

The mountain barriers hemming in this bleak hinterland were hazy escarpments lost in the distance. Longarm was continually surprised by the sudden green valleys he came upon. They had the impact of mirages. Riding through them, he found them to be cool, meandering belts of green vegetation following the banks of streams, most of which fed the Humboldt, many miles to the south. Cottonwoods, quaking aspen, and fragile willows grew in abundance in these valleys. Longarm was always sorry to ride out of the cool, whispering fragrance of these valleys into the denuded passes that led from them.

Well past midday Longarm found himself riding through deep draws and canyons, putting him almost constantly in the shadow of towering ridges spiked with pinyon and juniper. The sharp, medicinal tang of pine resin filled the air. Soon he was climbing past gaunt, wind-blasted bristlecone pine, their indomitable roots clutching at the rocky cliffsides, their branches reaching out like the gnarled fingers of an arthritic.

The road kept to a ridge for a long while, then dropped gently to the floor of a canyon. Longarm rode for close to a mile along the canyon floor, until the wall to his left dropped away, and he glimpsed the heavy, shouldering peaks of the Santa Rosa Range, its flanks clothed in pine. Below its foothills Longarm saw the beginnings of another broad, fertile valley with a river snaking through it. It was, as usual, a beautiful sight. Longarm pulled up to drink it in.

A rifle shot shattered the silence.

The bullet ricocheted off the trail just in front of Longarm's horse. It had come from the top of the ridge to his right. Even as Longarm yanked his Winchester from its boot and rolled off the Morgan, a second slug—this one much closer—sent rock splinters into the air just beside him.

A fusillade of rifle fire followed him as he dashed to the foot of the ridge and flattened himself against the rock face. He looked around for a trail that would lead to the top of the ridge. He spotted what he hoped was a way to the ridge and looked back at the Morgan. The animal was in among some rocks, casually cropping the sparse grass. Longarm crouched low and raced up the broad slope of a boulder into a cover of juniper. As he reached the timber, three more shots poured down upon him, each round shearing through the branches, sending pine cones flying. He left the shelter of the junipers and raced about ten feet along a steep-sided gully that led up among the rocks. Once inside, he found the draw widening and followed it for a couple of hundred yards until he caught sight of a game trail that led up a steep incline.

The loose gravel made the footing treacherous as he raced up the slope. More than once he had to slam the butt of his rifle into the ground to keep himself from sliding back down on his belly. Close to the top of the ridge, he found himself clinging first to one pine and then to another as he hauled himself up hand over hand, the toes of his boots finding precarious purchase on the thin limestone ridges that poked out of the almost sheer wall. He almost lost his rifle at one juncture and thought seriously of abandoning it. Instead, he carefully kept it ahead of him, sometimes wedged into crevices and at other times snugged under the exposed roots of the scrub pine that clung to the side of the mountain.

At last he pulled himself after his rifle over the lip of the ridge and found himself on a large, flat caprock that was as gouged and weathered as an old man's face. About thirty paces from where he lay grew a thick stand of pine. About a hundred yards down the ridge, partially hidden by the timber, three men lay flat on a rock as they peered over its edge at the canyon floor below. Scrambling to his feet, Longarm raced swiftly across the caprock. He was almost to the pines when one of the men turned and caught sight of him. The fellow's shout of alarm echoed along the ridge.

Longarm kept on into the pines. Once under their cover, he headed toward the spot where he had seen the men. After twenty paces or so, he ducked back toward the open ledge and flung himself down behind a pine at the edge of the stand. One of the bushwhackers had mounted and was just galloping past where Longarm lay. The two others were racing through the pines behind Longarm, their spurs clinking heedlessly.

Longarm waited until they were past his position before he opened fire on the rider. He tried to bring down the horse, aiming at the base of its tail, hoping for a spine shot. The round carried high, however, and caught the rider in the shoulder. The man reacted as if a two-by-four had slammed into him. He was flung sideways off the horse, landing on the rock face and skidding a good distance on his belly. His nose made a poor rudder. For a moment he lay still; then—moaning in pain—he began to crawl toward the pines.

The downed rider's cries brought the others to the edge of the pines. They were well past Longarm. As they left their cover to aid their fallen comrade, Longarm got to his feet and stepped out of the pines, pointing his rifle at the sky. He fired. The two men halted in their tracks and whirled. As Longarm lowered his rifle, training it on them, both men quickly— almost eagerly—dropped their six-guns.

They were *too* eager, and something in their faces warned Longarm. He flinched to his right. A slight *thunk*, followed by an agonized gasp, came from behind him. He spun and saw a thin shadow of a cowboy slumping forward onto his knees. There was a small arrow lodged in his back above one shoulder blade. The gun in his hand clattered to the ledge. He sagged over onto his side, careful not to fall back on the arrow, looking up at Longarm, his eyes filled with surprise and pain.

Longarm swung quickly back around to face the others. They were crouching, their hands only inches from their six-guns. Longarm fired. The Winchester's round sent one of the six-guns spinning across the rock. Both men sprang erect without their guns, their hands jerking upward as though pulled by strings, as Longarm reflexively levered another round into the rifle's chamber.

"All right, Tigbee!" one of them cried. "All right, goddammit! You got the drop on us! Now call off your damn Diggers!"

Without a word, Longarm moved back behind the downed cowboy, his rifle still leveled at the two bushwhackers, and kicked the man's six-gun off the ledge. "You two better split up," Longarm suggested, "and see to these men."

As the two uninjured men hurried to the aid of their stricken partners, Longarm kicked their dropped weapons over the edge of the rock into oblivion, then scouted about the ledge and into the pines for any sign left by the Indian who had sent that arrow. He saw nothing and heard nothing. He was not surprised. When an Indian puts his mind to it, he can be as quiet as a cheating woman—and just as cold-blooded. But why had a Digger Indian saved *him?* Why were they *his* Diggers?

And who the hell was this fellow Tigbee, for whom these bushwhackers had evidently mistaken him?

Longarm returned to the ledge and found the four in a miserable, huddled group. He almost felt sorry for them. The fellow with the arrow in his back had had it pulled out. It had left a large, ragged hole. The wound had been plugged with a sweaty bandanna, but was still leaking badly. The fellow with the gunshot wound in his shoulder was just hunkered down and trying to stay quiet, his mouth a straight line, his eyes closed. The man's shoulder appeared to be broken.

The two healthy ones stood up to face Longarm. The fellow who had called him Tigbee looked to be about forty-five. He had a long, narrow face and a lantern jaw covered with white stubble. His eyes were gray, frank, and, at the moment, alight with indignation. The other man, considerably younger, had light blue eyes, a wide face, and round cheeks, reminding Longarm of a squirrel with its cheek pouches full. Both men wore the dress of working cowpokes; their hats and boots were as weathered and as dry as the country.

"Who are you?" Longarm asked the older one.

"Lyle Butts," answered the man, "if it's any of your damned business."

"Mighty perky for a bushwhacker on the wrong end of a rifle barrel, ain't you?"

"I ain't crawling for no damn gunslick." The anger in the man's eyes kindled to a brighter glow. He appeared ready to leap at Longarm—despite the obvious foolhardiness of such a move.

"Mind telling me who this fellow Tigbee is?"

Butts frowned angrily. "You trying to deny who you are, Tigbee?"

"Let me tell you something, Butts. You better thank that Digger Indian, if you ever find him; he saved your friend from killing me. I'm a deputy U.S. marshal; my name is Custis Long. If I'd been just a mite unluckier, you would pretty damn soon have found this place crawling with federal marshals."

"Hell, you ain't no federal marshal," the younger one said. "You're Clyde Tigbee, the gunslick Slade sent for!"

"Now, just how the hell do you know that?"

The two men exchanged quick, apprehensive glances. It was Butts who swore softly, his narrow face darkening. "Jesus, Billy. Tim Caulder! *That son of a bitch!* He was lying!"

"Hey, mister," Billy said, grown suddenly sheepish. "You got any identification?"

Longarm reached into his breast pocket, withdrew his wallet with its badge, and flipped it to the cowpoke. Billy looked it over and passed it to Butts without comment. Butts sighed deeply and handed the wallet back to Longarm.

"Tim Caulder's one of Slade's men," Butts explained. "We thought he was on our side. He sure wanted us to think so, anyway. He reached Whipsaw a few hours ago, riding a lathered horse, and ran into us at the Paradise Valley. He told us Tigbee was riding in. That's the gunslick we've been waiting for—the one Slade's bringing up here to keep us cattlemen in line. You've heard of Tigbee, ain't you?"

"No, I ain't heard of Tigbee," Longarm replied wearily, "There's a new gunslick popping up every week. Looks like they just want to get into Buffalo Bill's Wild West Show before it closes. This one's probably some flannelmouth wearing a load of hay on his skull and packing enough artillery to make his horse swaybacked. Hell, you men ought to know the type. Usually those characters are as yellow as mustard, only without the bite. But what's Slade bringing in a hired gun for? What are you cattlemen up to, anyway?"

"It ain't us!" Butts exclaimed. "It's him—and that company of his. They're ruining the valley—cutting and slashing the pines off the ridges and the mountainsides, chewing up everything till there ain't no place left to graze a single cow. The water's either running off or standing in ditches, instead of going into the ground. Some of us cattlemen are already losing water in our wells. Hell, even the sage on the desert floor is drying out. If they don't stop cutting the way they're doing, there won't be nothing left but tree stumps and mud-holes. And then that damned company will move on to tear some other valley up, leaving us with homesteads not worth a plugged nickel."

"This *is* federal land, Butts," Longarm said. "This lumber company must have rights to the timber on it. You can't go against that."

"You watch us."

"That's right," Longarm snapped, glancing down at the two wounded men. "That's just what I'm doing right now—watching. What I see is four damn fools who just threw down on a stranger—and lost. Maybe you better go talk to Slade. You couldn't do any worse than this. And he just might listen to you."

Billy shook his head. "You don't know Slade Desmond, Mister Long."

Longarm shrugged. Satisfied that the two men were no longer a threat to his life, he put down his rifle and helped them gather their horses, after which he did what he could to make it easier for the two wounded men as they mounted up. Once they were in the saddle, Longarm felt only pity for them. Both were as white as new-spilt milk and were hanging on with guts alone, bowed over their saddle horns—coffin fodder on their way to hell. If they didn't get to that home spread of theirs pretty damned soon, they would likely never get to choke on the alkali dust of another roundup.

Longarm looked up at Butts as soon as the older man had mounted. "Just one thing, Butts. Did this Tim Caulder give you a description of the hired gun?"

Butts smiled bitterly. "The son of a bitch did, all right. It was a good one, too. He did a fine job of describing you and what you was wearing—in detail."

Longarm stepped back. The four men rode back down the long slope of the ledge, heading west, away from Whipsaw.

Bat Lawson had known Longarm was riding to Whipsaw.
Pete Seegar had told him that much, at least. So it could simply
have been Bat Lawson's idea, his way of squaring accounts
with Longarm. On the other hand, if Slade Desmond was having trouble with the local cattlemen, what better way to put
them on the defensive—to discredit them entirely—than to
trick them into killing a deputy U.S. marshal?

Neat. Very neat indeed, he thought, as he thumbed three
fresh rounds into the Winchester's magazine.

Longarm reached Whipsaw close to four o'clock that same
afternoon. It was Longarm's first glimpse of a logging town.
He didn't much like what he saw—here or in the countryside surrounding it. From a mile back, the valley floor and the
mountain slopes had resembled a torn, muddy wound extend-
ing as far as the eye could see; and now, in the midst of that
desolate, stump-filled landscape, sat this raw, unpainted logging town, both sides of its main drag lined with wooden
shacks and tents of varying sizes, selling whiskey, gambling,
or women. The larger tents provided all three.

Railroad tracks snaking alongside a sluggish, silted river
led directly to the sawmill and lost themselves behind a mountain of sawdust. Sitting on a side spur were several triple-
decker bunkhouses-on-wheels. These rolling bunkhouses had
probably been used once in the construction of this railroad,
and now served as living quarters for the loggers.

In sharp contrast to the ramshackle impermanence of almost everything else were three large, substantial frame buildings at the end of the town farthest from the sawdust and
whining screech of the mill. They were the first buildings
Longarm approached on his way into Whipsaw. One was the
Paradise Valley Saloon, the building next to it was the Western
Lumber and Land Combine General Store, and the third building was a three-story hotel set back on a slight rise.

Riding past the hotel, Longarm glimpsed a girl sitting in a
window. She waved to him. Longarm knew at once that this
was where Ruby's girls held court. Longarm rode on into town
past the mill, until he found the livery stable. It was a sprawling collection of tents, corrals, and wooden barns constructed
crudely of unpeeled logs. Longarm dismounted in front of the

largest barn and was giving the Morgan a drink at the trough when a shout, followed by a string of magnificent oaths, pulled him up short. A wagonload of recently cut logs was on its way past to the sawmill. It was the driver—a powerful, raw-faced logger—who had warned Longarm. As the man's whip cracked over the backs of his horses, Longarm pulled the Morgan out of the way and entered the livery.

He emerged a moment later, having learned from the liveryman that Ruby's place was indeed a hotel—for those who had the money to patronize what the man told him—with some pride—was probably the most famous establishment of its kind in northern Nevada. It was also owned, lock, stock, and roulette wheel, by the Western Lumber and Land Combine, like everything else in Whipsaw.

There were no sidewalks. Longarm slogged through the muck, doing his best to avoid the constant stream of huge logging wagons and their massive workhorses. His tall, lanky, obviously well-muscled figure did not go unnoticed. He recognized some of Bat Lawson's men; he could tell they remembered him as well. Those of Bat's men whom he did not recognize from Silver City he knew by their flashy dress and their willingness to freight themselves down with artillery. Many fancied double rigs and ivory-handled six-guns, with cartridge belts worn lower than good sense would dictate. They swaggered.

As Longarm neared the Paradise Valley, an obviously disgruntled Bat Lawson stepped through the batwings with one of his lieutenants to watch Longarm walk past. He was not dismayed, it seemed, only resigned to the necessity of having to cook up another scheme to rid himself of Longarm. Longarm nodded solemnly to the man. Lawson turned and disappeared back into the saloon.

The lobby of Ruby's hotel was expansive and, considering its clientele, not at all what Longarm had expected. Its decor was subdued, even prim. Well to the right of the front desk, however, a short flight of red-carpeted stairs led up to an ample archway. Beyond this, Longarm glimpsed a wall hung with gilt-edged mirrors, fleshy portraits, and over it all, the soft glow of pink lamps. The tinkle of women's laughter and the occasional bellow of some early celebrant having a good time came clearly to Longarm. Yet the laughter, the click of poker chips, and the rattle of dice all were kept to a soft, barely audible level. It was most civilized, indeed. Ruby—and the Western Lumber and Land Combine—ran a disciplined house.

"A room for the night," Longarm told the desk clerk.

Abruptly, Longarm felt someone plucking gently at his sleeve. He turned to see a brilliantly liveried bellhop pointing at Longarm's boots.

"Please, mister," the boy said, "you got to take them off in Ruby's place." The bellhop indicated a wall alongside the entrance where at least ten pairs of boots were already lined up.

"Okay," Longarm said. "But I'm taking them up to my room with me."

The boy offered no objection, and while Longarm signed the register, he lifted first one foot and then the other as the bellhop tugged off his boots. Longarm carried his boots up to his room while the bellhop carried the rest of his gear. Longarm tipped the boy, and as soon as he had closed the door behind him, went to the window and looked down at Whipsaw.

The logging town was obviously a gut-it-and-get-out operation. From the look of things, the logging company was doing a lot of gutting, not only of the land but of the loggers as well. The company probably charged the loggers outrageously for their miserable accomodations in those railroad bunkhouses, and then saw to it that wherever in Whipsaw they spent their wages, most of the money found its way back into the company's coffers.

But the loggers probably didn't mind as long as the booze hit hard enough and the girls were plentiful. It was the settlers, the cattlemen mostly, who would find it impossible to live with this operation. At the rate the Western Lumber and Land Combine was going, the valley and the ridges and mountainsides flanking it would soon be a wasteland. Longarm knew with some certainty how long it took high desert land like this to regain its cover and survive the ravages of a one-purpose company town like this one. The West was pockmarked with abandoned mining towns and railheads, and the ruined landscapes that surrounded them.

It was still light. Bands of loggers just quitting work were gathering to begin their night's carousal. The loggers crowded first into the company's general store, where they were probably paid their day's wages, then left to drift up and down the line. A few headed directly for the hotel. Longarm could hear their heavy boots mounting the low porch, then their booming voices—almost immediately silenced—as they entered the lobby. He could imagine the bellhop hurrying among them, removing their brogans with swift dexterity.

His attention was suddenly drawn to a brawl in front of one of the tents. A floozy had been on a logger's arm and been about to entice him into her place of business when another logger with a thick mane of silvery hair rushed up and pulled the floozy away. At once the two men started clobbering each other. The first fellow, smaller by a foot at least, had enormous shoulders and the biggest head Longarm had ever seen. Big Head seemed to know precisely what to do with it. Tucking in his chin, he rammed Silver Hair repeatedly, at last catching him amidships and sending him sprawling backwards into the mud.

As the crowd that gathered cheered him on, Big Head took a running jump and came down with both of his calked boots on the man's chest and face. Treating the downed man as if he were a log running downstream, Big Head began to birl him, driving Silver Hair's head and shoulders down into the muck and then up again and around—faster and faster, to the delighted shouts of the onlookers—until Silver Hair was little more than a mud-caked, bloody torso. Only then did Big Head cease his logrolling and jump off.

The crowd broke up. A large contingent led Big Head into the Paradise Valley. Only the floozy remained. She sat back on her haunches in the mud beside her fallen champion. But not for long. Soon she left the still figure on the ground, caught hold of a little fellow in a red stocking cap, and drew him into her tent.

Longarm turned from the window. He was weary and needed a bath, but he knew he would have to wait until the next day. Not until the loggers drifted off to their bunkhouses for the night would there be a place in town safe enough for a quiet bath; booze would be the only liquid allowed to flow, until then.

Longarm saw to his gear, then went downstairs to the lobby. It was crowded with bootless loggers, all of whom seemed strangely subdued without their boots as they filed up the low stairs past Ruby, who was greeting her favorites at the arch. Her ample figure was poured into a long red dress agleam with sequins. Her thick curls crowded her pale shoulders and broad bosom. She was being welcomed by everyone and seemed genuinely pleased to be back in harness. The day's exhausting journey seemed to have left no mark on her.

The dining room was at the end of a long hall that led off the lobby. There were chandeliers and liveried waiters. The silverware gleamed brilliantly on white, freshly ironed linen. Despite himself, Longarm found himself comparing its quiet elegance with one of the many fine restaurants in the Windsor hotel back in Denver.

Just as Longarm finished ordering, Bat Lawson walked into the dining room with a companion. From the deference Bat showed the man, Longarm surmised that he was Slade Desmond. The two men approached Longarm's table, Bat Lawson hanging back a bit. The dining room grew silent. Knives and forks froze in midair or were put down carefully as all eyes followed Slade Desmond's progress to Longarm's table.

"I'm Slade Desmond," Bat's companion introduced himself. "I'd like a word with you, Mr. Long. May I join you?"

Slade Desmond was almost a foot shorter than Bat. He was barrel-chested and stubby-limbed. He held a chocolate-brown derby in one hand, revealing a domed, hairless cueball of a head. His jaw was forward-thrust, his nose was small, and his eyes—set wide in his round face—were cold and humorless and deadly, reminding Longarm of spent buckshot.

Assuming that Longarm would have no objection to his request, Slade started to pull out a chair for himself at Longarm's table. Longarm smiled coldly at the man and shook his head. "I like to eat alone," he said, "or at least choose my own company, and that lackey behind you is sure as hell not welcome at any table of mine."

Slade Desmond pulled back and glanced with surprise at Bat. When he looked back at Longarm, his buckshot eyes had narrowed dangerously. "You and I *should* talk, Long."

"At your office, Desmond."

Slade nodded curtly. "It's in the company store, in back. I'll be waiting for you." The man turned and strode out of the dining room with Bat Lawson on his heels.

The dining room was small enough for everyone in it to have heard the exchange. From the glances that came Longarm's way, Longarm realized he had created a sensation by treating Slade Desmond that curtly. The tone of their meeting would be common knowledge throughout the town before morning. But what bothered Longarm was that someone like Slade Desmond should have this much power. Desmond had entered the dining room and strode out of it again like an absolute monarch.

The frown on Longarm's face left the moment his steak arrived.

Slade Desmond rose to his feet as Longarm entered his office. Bat Lawson stood up also. The deputy ignored Lawson as Slade walked around his desk and shook Longarm's hand. The handshake was firm, even hearty. There was a slight, approving smile on the company manager's face.

"I like a man who says what he thinks, Long. Bat, here, has been filling me in on a few details. It seems you and he had a little misunderstanding in Silver City."

"I don't think 'misunderstanding' really catches the gist of it, Desmond."

"Call me Slade, please. And do sit down. No need for us to stand on ceremony. I am sure we can all work together nicely."

"I don't mind standing," Longarm replied. "Been using my bottom most of the day. My feet could stand the straightening." That was not the reason and Slade knew it, but it preserved some civility.

Slade nodded curtly. "I am afraid Bat is somewhat over-zealous at times. He's sorry for any trouble he might have caused you. Isn't that right, Bat?"

"Sure. I'm sorry, Long. I just got carried away," Lawson said.

"And later? When you sicked those four cowboys on me?"

"That was Tim Caulder's doing. I never could hold him down. He has all kinds of crazy ideas sometimes."

"This one almost worked." Longarm had no intention of telling Bat that two of the men had been wounded in the encounter.

"Yeah." Bat glanced nervously at Slade. "Well, that's the way it is. You win some, you lose some."

Longarm pointed a calloused finger in Slade's direction. "I'll tell you this once, Slade. Then I'll just figure you've got it straight so I won't need to repeat it. Leave the Indians alone. They are wards of the federal government. You are working on federal land. I am an officer of the federal government and I will enforce its laws. And if anything happens to me, there will be other federal marshals along right soon to take up where I left off."

"Them Diggers are causing us real trouble," Lawson protested. "We sent a wagonload of supplies to Cedar Ridge two weeks ago for the few loggers we got working up there. The little bastards killed the driver and made off with most of the supplies. Are we supposed to just stand by and take that? Like I told you once, I wanted to set an example with them four Indians."

"Don't set any examples," Longarm said. "Report what's happening and let the proper authorities take care of it."

Lawson snorted. "By proper authorities, you mean Digger-lovin' federal marshals."

"Bat!" Slade said sharply. "That's enough!" Slade turned back to Longarm. "There's no calculating the mischief those little devils can accomplish, Marshal." Slade's voice was filled with sweet reason. "I'm logging this land under a tight schedule. I can't afford to pussyfoot around when armed heathens attack my men and carry off my supplies."

Longarm nodded. "I'll check around and file a report. If action is to be taken, the army will see to it. I repeat, Slade, this is federal land—not yours or your company's private little kingdom."

"I appreciate that, Marshal, I can assure you."

"Good."

"Now, what brings you to Whipsaw? Since we've cleared the air, Marshal, I am sure Bat will be more than willing to cooperate in your—investigations. It would be surprising if there weren't one or two renegades among those loggers out there. They're a hard bunch. They work hard and they play hard. Whatever they call themselves, whatever deeds their past may be filled with, I don't pry into—not as long as they pull their weight."

"I'm looking for an army deserter—name of Ned Shortslef.

A big guy with bushy hair and a beard. He's a squaw man—or was. An ex-Mountain Man. He may not be using his own name, of course. Sheriff Tanner spotted him working up here."

"Yes, so I understand. I was sorry to hear of that man's death. He was a good lawman, Marshal. We all respected him. Do you think this Shortslef is the one who killed him?"

"Seems likely, if Tanner was getting too close to him. Did you give Tanner any help in locating Shortslef when he came to bring him in a couple of weeks ago?"

"We gave him the run of Whipsaw, let him ask all the questions he wanted. It seems he spent considerable time at one of the cattle ranches, too." Slade turned to look at Lawson. "Isn't that right, Bat?"

Lawson nodded. "Yeah. When he wasn't nosing around here, he was out there."

"Which cattle ranch?"

Slade glanced at Bat.

"The Flying T," Bat replied. "You should know them fellows pretty well by now." He could not keep the smirk off his face.

"Did Tanner have any contacts among the loggers?" Longarm asked, ignoring the smirk.

"Gus Dodds," Bat said. "He went straight to Gus when he got here."

Longarm nodded, remembering the one-eyed logger from Silver City. "What's Gus's job in this camp?" he asked.

"A chopper. And he's one of the best. Averages close to sixty a day. You could see Fitz about him."

"Fitz is the chief foreman," Slade put in. "His full name is Arnold Fitzpatrick."

Longarm nodded. "Thanks. I'll talk to him."

The two men, obviously relieved by this time at Longarm's reasonable manner, expected him to take his leave now and go about his business. Longarm could feel them waiting for this, and said, "I understand you're sending for a gunslick to keep the ranchers in line, Slade."

The man's buckshot eyes grew cold, and his bulldog chin became more set. "Who I bring in is my business. If you are referring to Clyde Tigbee, he's a fine, experienced lawman who has worked for me in the past as a sort of town marshal.

He may have killed a few men, but only in the line of duty. He's not a gunslick." Slade smiled then, somewhat sardonically. "If you'll walk around Whipsaw tonight, you'll see we could use a town marshal capable of banging a few heads."

"What's wrong with Bat, here?"

"Bat has other, more important business to attend to. He's in charge of the security of this entire operation. Him and his men."

Longarm could see Bat swelling up as Slade sang his tune. Slade, of course, was lying, but he was doing a fine job of it.

"You don't expect any trouble with the cattlemen, then."

"Didn't say that, Deputy. But any trouble they and their vigilantes can stir up, Bat and his men can handle."

"Vigilantes?"

"Yes, Marshal, vigilantes. These ranchers have been doing some night riding. They threatened one of my crews at Elk Springs. They were pretty rough on my men. Said they were logging on their homesteads. It was a lie, of course."

"I guess that means you got a federal land survey to prove that."

Slade smiled. "The men from the Bureau of Land Management were here from the Department of the Interior less than three months ago to extend the area allotted to us. We're waiting now for their map to get here from Washington. If you have had any dealings with that city, you know how long it will most likely take for it to get here."

"Those men saw the way your loggers are tearing up the land around here?"

"I must confess, they were not happy about it. But we're cutting timber, not digging gold or silver out of a few holes in the ground. In either case, Marshal, there has to be some damage to the land. As it is, we are turning what amounts to scrub pine into wealth. Furthermore, we have many friends—and I might add, powerful friends—in Washington, who have a stake in our operation here. I repeat, Marshal—we are creating wealth where there were only alkali sinks, rock, and desert. This is progress, Marshal, and I do not need to apologize for our role here."

Longarm had no urge to dispute with the man. Slade had puffed himself up like a bullfrog in a hog wallow as he had delivered that spiel. Longarm had heard potbellied bankers in barber chairs in Denver spouting the same bilge. He had no doubt that the fat cats in Washington felt the same way. They were perfectly capable of aiding and abetting this plundering of the West, now that robbing the Indian on his reservation was no longer as profitable as it had once been. A list of the stockholders of this lumber company would prove most interesting, but it would be worthless. Everything would most probably be set up legally, with no loopholes. Longarm shrugged slightly. It was not his concern. He was after that deserter and murderer, and he thought he'd best keep his mind on that.

Longarm nodded curtly to the two men. "Guess I'll be thanking you for your time, Slade."

"I hope we've been of some help, Marshal," Slade said, leaning back in his chair, his tiny black eyes gleaming. He was obviously pleased that Longarm was proving so easy to get along with, and he had apparently defused a potentially explosive situation between his lieutenant and Longarm.

"You have helped," Longarm assured him. He turned and walked back to the door. Pulling it open, he glanced back at Bat.

"I'm going to find Tim Caulder now, Bat," Longarm said. He smiled slightly. "If that bit of tomfoolery was his own idea, I'll take it out of his hide. If it was your business to begin with, I'll be back to see you."

He stepped through the doorway and closed the door firmly behind him.

A moment later, leaning back casually in the shadow of the building, Longarm watched Lawson leave the general store and plunge headlong into the traffic of the main drag. Longarm followed. In the night, dodging among the crowds of loggers in and around the tents and shacks, Longarm almost lost sight of Bat. He stayed close to him however, and saw him duck into the rear of a larger-than-usual shack at the far end of town.

As he reached the door, he paused. From within, he heard Bat's rough voice: "I'm saying it was your idea, Tim—and I'm telling you to get on your horse and vamoose, if you know—"

Longarm pushed open the door and strode into the room.

The small, smoke-filled place went silent—except for the continued clicking of the roulette wheel along the far wall.

Three poker games were in progress; the games were being played on surprisingly bright green felt-topped tables. At the table closest to Longarm, the man Bat had been talking to when Longarm had entered was sitting with his cards down, his face turned upward as he looked at Bat.

He was a slightly built fellow with a weasel face—long nose, receding chin, and gray, furtive eyes that now shifted in sudden panic from Bat to Longarm.

"Are you Tim Caulder?" Longarm asked.

"Yeah." Caulder glanced at Bat, his tongue flicking out to moisten his upper lip. "That's me. So what?"

"So your boss just told me it was your idea to sic those cow-punchers on me this afternoon."

Slowly, and as silently as possible, the loggers at the other tables began sliding their chairs back. The men at Caulder's table seemed prepared to dive under it. Tim Caulder's face had gone gray with Longarm's words.

"Hell," Caulder managed, "it was all Bat's idea. He sent me on ahead because I knew the punchers. I been keeping on the right side of them."

Longarm believed Caulder. Bat's story had sounded phony from the start, but he wanted Caulder—and as many others as possible—to know who had tried to put the finger on him. Longarm turned his attention to Bat. The man took a step back. Longarm faced him squarely.

"Sure is nice, Bat, to see a man who'll stand up for his own riders. I guess these men would follow you straight into hell, now, wouldn't they?" Longarm smiled. He was deliberately goading the man and knew he should feel ashamed—but he didn't.

"Damn you, Long!" Bat hissed. "I ain't afraid of you!"

"'Course you ain't," Longarm said softly. "I never thought you were yellow. And now you're going to prove that, ain't you?"

The men at Caulder's table—including Caulder himself—dove under it as the others in the room broke for the walls, out of the line of fire. Bat slapped leather. Longarm strode quickly toward him, his Colt appearing in his hand as if by magic, its muzzle trained on Bat's startled face. Bat's right hand froze on his gun, halfway out of its holster. Before he could take an-other step back, Longarm moved closer, and with one brutal swipe, he brought his gunbarrel down on the crown of Bat's head. The man's hat was driven from its perch. Bat, his eyes closed, dropped to the floor with all the grace of an empty grain sack.

With the toe of his right boot, Longarm nudged Bat's shoulder. The man groaned and opened his eyes. Longarm kicked Bat's gun the rest of the way out of its holster. It skittered across the floor and came to rest against the wall with a solid clunk. It was the only sound in the place. Longarm returned his own gun to its holster.

"Now, you listen to me, Lawson," Longarm said. "Two damn fools are hurt pretty bad because you had some idea you could get them to bushwhack me. They weren't very bright or they wouldn't have listened to Tim, here, and I suppose they deserved what they got. The thing is, I just figured it wouldn't be fitting if I let you walk away scot-free."

"My head," Bat muttered, reaching up to feel the bump rising on the top of his skull. "It's bleeding. It must be bleeding. I can feel it!"

There was muted laughter at this. No blood was showing at all. Bat, in a kind of panic, kept feeling about his head.

"You'll be all right," Longarm told Lawson, "as long as you keep your nose clean. I don't hold grudges."

He turned and left the shack. His anger at the attempted ambush had been building steadily since that afternoon. He felt much better now. Despite the late hour and the fact that the loggers would have to be busy with their axes come morning, the town was still jumping. Kerosene lamps had been hung on posts almost everywhere along the line of shacks and tents. The lamps glowing from inside the tents cast a pale, feeble glow over the men roaming past in the street. Horsemen were still riding and carts were still being driven through, as small gangs of drunken men roamed back and forth across the single wide street. The place was noisier than a Mexican revolution, Longarm reflected as he sidestepped a drunken logger who had just reeled out of a small shack. The man disappeared past him into the night, zigzagging dangerously.

Longarm had about decided to go back to his hotel room when he caught sight of the logger Gus Dodds. Remembering what Lawson had told him, Longarm halted and changed direction, following Gus into the Paradise Valley. The saloon—obviously a company run operation—showed considerably more class than any of the other watering holes in Whipsaw. The dark mahogany bar ran the length of the saloon and was easily forty feet long. The rear of the saloon was given over to roulette and poker. As Longarm stood for a moment in front of the flapping batwings, the place quieted noticeably. He could hear clearly the ticking of the roulette wheel, the croupier's droning voice, and the clicking of clay chips between the fingers of the dealers at the tables.

The bar was crowded and most of the tables were taken. The brass rail seemed to bend under the weight of so many calked boots. The floor was at least an inch deep in clean, recently spread sawdust. Over it all hung stratified layers of tobacco smoke, the clouds changing and swirling with each movement of the men.

Gus was at the bar, his big shoulders hunched as he leaned on it, giving his order to the barkeep. The bartender said something to Gus, then ducked to get a glass. Gus turned and looked directly at Longarm with his one good eye. The place was a lot quieter now. The clicking of the roulette wheel in back had ceased. Longarm walked across the slippery sawdust and pushed up to the bar beside Gus.

"Join me in a drink, Gus?" Longarm invited him.

Beneath a bushy eyebrow, Gus's eye focused unwaveringly on the lawman. "I'd let the devil himself buy my booze, if he's of a mind to," said Gus.

The marshal chuckled. "He's of a mind to."

Longarm glanced over his shoulder and spotted an empty table against the far wall. He turned back around, paid for Gus's whiskey, and ordered his own.

"Since you're paying," Gus said, "we'll just take this here bottle with us." As he spoke, he took the whiskey from the barkeep's hand.

Longarm shrugged and dropped three silver dollars onto the polished mahogany. The barkeep said, "Four dollars."

Longarm was a little taken aback. He saw the broad smile on Gus's face, shrugged, and paid the ransom. "Let's go over to that table," Longarm suggested.

Gus voiced no objection and followed Longarm across the

saloon floor, clutching the bottle of whiskey in his hand tightly about its neck. Longarm took the chair against the wall. Gus sat beside him, facing the door. The level of noise and activity in the saloon gradually returned to its former level. Gus finished his glass and poured himself another. Longarm sipped at his whiskey.

"I remember you from Silver City," Gus said. "You freed them Diggers, and I was glad you did. What do you want with me?"

"You knew Tanner."

"So?"

"He was bushwhacked."

"I knew that, too, mister."

"Call me Longarm."

Gus downed another shot of whiskey. His eye reddened slightly as tears crowded into it. He coughed, then cleared his throat. "I don't know where the company gets this tonsil varnish, Longarm. It sure enough tastes like it was brewed in one of them circles in hell I hear tell about."

"I'd like to get the man who did that to Tanner," Longarm said quietly.

Gus pondered this for a moment, then looked squarely at Longarm. "I suppose I would, too. I liked Tanner. For a lawman, he was pretty square with us when we got in a jam."

"Maybe you can help, then," the deputy suggested.

"Sure."

"I'm looking for the same man Tanner was after."

"The deserter?"

Longarm nodded.

"Well, I helped Tanner all I could on that. I got to know a logger pretty good who fit that deserter's description. He lit out of here just after Tanner rode through on his way to collar a horse thief." Gus paused to pour himself another jolt. "A week or so later, Tanner came back asking about him, then took after him. Now Tanner is dead. I guess all I can do is give you the same information I gave Tanner."

Longarm sipped the low-grade rotgut. "I want a better description of Ned Shortslef than I got from that constable in Silver City."

Gus frowned thoughtfully, pushing his glass in small circles over the damp tabletop. "You sure he's Ned Shortslef? He called himself Tom something-or-other. I never got the last name and I never asked."

"Why don't we call him Ned? Nothing like thinking positive. That's the name of the deserter, and if Tanner went after him, he's Ned Shortslef. But like I said, I need a better description than the one I've got now that Tanner's dead."

The logger shrugged massively.

"How do you describe a guy? I don't remember nothing special about the way he looked. He was big, is all."

"Lots of hair? The color of his eyes?" Longarm prodded.

Gus shrugged again. "He wasn't bald and he had a full beard. I don't guess I ever really looked at his eyes to tell what color they was. He wasn't no girl I was romancing."

"Any limp or scars? He was supposed to be a Mountain Man at one time. Maybe he got into a rasslin' match with a bear or something. I understand he lived with an Indian woman for a time. Is that right?"

"Yeah. But that didn't leave no scars that I could see." Gus grew thoughtful. "Ned loved her quite a bit, as a matter of fact; her and the boy. He used to talk about them a lot."

"What happened to them? The squaw and the breed?"

Gus looked at Longarm sharply. "He never liked anybody to call her a squaw, or the boy a breed. That used to get him real mad."

"What else, Gus?"

"How's this going to help you? You said you wanted a description of Ned."

"Just answer my questions. You'd be surprised. It'll all fit in somewhere when the time comes; it usually does."

Gus went back to his whiskey glass, again pushing it about before him, tracing the wet circles, the patterns of which seemed to fascinate him. "She was a Cheyenne woman. Tall, and as graceful, he would say, as a flower in the wind. Fact is, that's what her Indian handle was. Black Flower Woman."

"What did Ned call her?"

Gus smiled. "Ned called her Muddy Face."

"Muddy Face?" Longarm echoed, a mite surprised.

The logger nodded.

"She worked so hard on the hides and stuff during their first months together, trying to impress him, that all he seemed able to remember of her was her dirty face at night when she poked her head in through the door of their lodge."

"And the boy?"

"Ned Flower Shortslef, he was called." Gus spoke somberly now.

"What happened to them?"

"Dead. Both of them. They died on the way to the reservation after the Rosebud Campaign. Probably froze to death. Ned wasn't sure what really happened—not that it makes all that much difference."

"Where was he during all this?"

"Running, I guess. The Cheyenne had made him a brother of the Dog Soldier Lodge, and he had taken an oath to defend the camp alongside the Dog Soldiers while the other warriors were away doing battle. When Custer's men stumbled on the camp, he sided with his wife's people. That was when he was spotted by one of Custer's lieutenants. So after the campaign, he lit out. He knew that if he hung around he'd only cause more trouble for his wife and her people. And his son."

"And Tanner was at the Rosebud, too."

Gus nodded.

"So now Tanner's dead. Do you think Ned killed him?"

Gus stopped fiddling with his glass. "How the hell should I know?" he muttered, as he tossed the glass of whiskey down in one gulp and reached for the bottle.

"It's just that you seem to know so much about this jasper," Longarm persisted. "Maybe you could tell me if he was the sort of man who could shoot Sheriff Tanner in the back—twice."

Gus kept his eye averted from Longarm. His shrug was elaborately casual. "I only knew him for a few months while we bunked together. He was good with an axe, so after a while we teamed up. He was a quiet one and kept pretty much to himself. When he saw Tanner, he knew he'd have to make tracks. So he did."

"Where did he go?"

"He didn't want to leave this area. His people are still up north, cooped up inside a reservation near the Snake. He went north, to work on one of the ranches."

"Which one?"

"Biggest one around—the Flying T."

Longarm considered this. He was going to have to pay that outfit a visit, it seemed. There wasn't any way around it and he wasn't looking forward to it—but everything so far pointed in that direction.

"I wish you could have given me a better picture of Short-slef, Gus."

"Just look for a big man—a *very* big man. Moves like a cat." Gus looked appraisingly at Longarm. "The way you do. And he's a man who don't smile often and likes a goodly distance between himself and the next guy."

"And I can find him at the Flying T?"

"I didn't say that. I said he went to them looking for work. I didn't say he found it. He might just have gone on north into Snake River country. Could be he's back with his people."

Longarm nodded a bit wearily. If this logger was giving him help, he was also making it seem as though the apprehension of Ned Shortslef was going to be a damned sight more complicated than he had anticipated.

A loud crash startled Longarm and caused him and Gus to turn in the direction of the noise. A logger had just gotten to his feet in a hurry and overturned a poker table in the process. The chips were rolling over the floor, the cards scattering in every direction. The two other loggers at the table were backing away. Everyone else, including those men at the bar, was cautiously moving away from the overturned table. The outraged logger was standing over the wreckage of the game, his chair lying on its back behind him. The house dealer was facing him from the other side of the overturned table, a Smith & Wesson pocket .38 in his right hand.

The dealer—in white shirtsleeves, a black vest, and a black, wide-brimmed, flat-crowned hat—smiled a reptilian smile. His mouth moved, while his eyes remained coldly amused. He had a pale, almost greenish face with a pencil-thin mustache on his upper lip, giving him the look of a stage villain. But there was nothing stagey about that Smith & Wesson in his hand.

"Put that gun down!" the logger said. "I ain't armed. And you been cheatin'! I saw you dealin' from the middle of the pack!"

"You ain't armed, mister. But you're a couple of feet taller than I am. I figure this here revolver makes us even." The dealer smiled and straightened.

"I saw you cheat!" the logger shouted. "I want my money back!"

"That's a libel, mister, and you know it. I don't have to cheat to outplay you. And if I did cheat, you'd never see a thing."

Abruptly, one of Slade's men broke away from two of his companions at the bar and, coming up from behind the logger, brought the barrel of his six-gun down hard on the top of the logger's head. With a barely audible sigh, the logger sagged to the floor, his face sliding through the muddy sawdust.

At once, the place exploded. Every logger in the place—including Gus—swarmed toward Slade's men and the house dealer. There were five dealers in all, along with two bartenders and three of Slade's men against about nine loggers. Calculating swiftly, Longarm joined the loggers. Under the circumstances, the tall lawman would have avoided a donnybrook like this, but he decided that he might need the loggers' help someday against Bat's men. Shouts and threats rent the air. Someone leaped onto the bar, a chair in his hand, and hurled it at one of the barkeeps. Longarm saw one of the leaders industriously hammering with the barrel of his six-gun on the skull of a logger. Longarm waded toward the dealer, ducked a chair that whistled just overhead, then brought his own Colt down across the dealer's wrist, sending his gun flying into the milling crowd.

The logger whose head was being pounded so diligently blinked once, straightened, and swung a roundhouse right, catching the dealer on the side of the head. The dealer went spinning backward into the melee. The logger, a broad crimson slash running down the side of his head, grinned widely and waved at Longarm, then turned and set off after another dealer. Almost knocked off his feet by a tumbling body, Longarm turned and was able to regain his balance just in time to duck under a wide, sweeping blow from one of the barkeeps. He was using a sawed-off peavey that just caught the crown of Longarm's hat, knocking it off. This upset Longarm. He kicked the fellow in the groin, and when he doubled over, brought his

knee up into the barkeep's face, permanently altering the shape
of the man's nose. His eyes snapped shut, and with a solid left
jab to the chin, Longarm sent him flying backward over one of
the few tables still upright.

Before Longarm could look around for his hat, a chair
crashed down on his head and shoulders. He blinked, and staggering under the impact, he went down on one knee, shaking
his head in an effort to clear it. It cleared just in time for him
to dodge a fellow lunging at him with eyes as wild as a spooked
steer. It was one of Bat Lawson's men, thinking only of getting out of the saloon. Longarm stuck out his boot. The fellow
left his feet and went sailing into a wall, head first. Longarm
straightened up then to ward off a clumsy attack from a dealer.
Longarm reached out, grabbed the fellow's vest, and yanking
him toward himself ducked aside, flinging the fellow across
the bar. The man, his arms and legs flailing willy, crashed into
the shelves of bottles.

Surprisingly, this living projectile was the first missile to
hit the bar's stock of firewater. The crash of breaking bottles
seemed to alert the surging mass of bodies to the damage
they were doing to their favorite watering hole and at once, it
seemed, the mayhem quieted remarkably. Longarm looked
quickly around and saw that the loggers had matters well in
hand. Gus was in a corner with a dealer, the joyous look on his
face in sharp contrast to the bloodied, glazed look on the face
of the fellow he was holding up by the vest. Gus let go of the
dealer, who sagged unconscious to the floor. A logger on top
of the bar hurled one of the barkeeps in the general direction of
the door.

The other loggers scrambled out of the way. The barkeep
landed on his knees and then lunged frantically for the batwings. He was assisted by several well-aimed boots in his
wide rear, and was airborne by the time he got to the door.

"Let 'em go, boys!" said one logger standing on the bar.
"We don't need them anymore tonight."

With that he dropped down behind the bar and started placing fresh bottles and glasses upon the bar.

"Drinks are on the company!" he yelled.

With a roar, the loggers bellied up to the bar while someone
stepped outside to announce the news to the rest of Whipsaw.

Longarm spied his hat and hurried over to it. It was scuffed a little, but it would do. He clapped it on and caught Gus's eye.

The logger smiled at him and saluted. Longarm nodded back and left the saloon along with those dealers and company men who were still conscious. Once outside, he had to sidestep quickly to avoid the stampeding mob of loggers hurrying toward the Paradise Valley to share in the sudden wealth. Glancing across the street, Longarm saw a sullen crowd of battered men reporting to a now fully conscious Bat Lawson.

Bat was evidently trying to decide whether or not to try and take back the saloon. He evidently thought better of it and stalked off into the night with his unhappy band of enforcers. Longarm chuckled. The man would have a difficult time explaining this to his boss. This had not been Bat Lawson's night.

Chapter 4

Longarm spoke softly to the Morgan and pulled up. It was early in the morning. He was on his way to Wolf Creek to interview the foreman, Arnold Fitzpatrick, and found himself on a ridge overlooking Whipsaw. He dismounted, walked to the edge, and looked down.

From this height, he saw how the river lost its gleam as it neared Whipsaw and became only a dirty, sluggish moat looping halfway around the town. Great, misshapen clods of earth, composed of tree stumps and roots with ridges of mud and sand piled up behind them, dotted the mountain slopes on both sides. Those that were nearest the ridge were large enough to block Longarm's view of much of Whipsaw. Long, raw scars—skid marks from logs that had been snaked down the slopes—ran down both mountainsides, some leading into the river, others disappearing into the town. Whipsaw, the source of this spreading blight, festered just below—the bright, clean yellow of the mill's growing pile of sawdust reminding Longarm of the pustulous core of a boil that needed lancing.

He turned away from the sight and mounted up again.

On the rest of his ride to Wolf Creek, he found the same desolation. Slope after slope was denuded of all but the stumps of trees, littered with branches and other discarded portions of trees, all of it ground into the soil, obliterating what little vegetation had managed to grow in the rocky, inhospitable soil before the logging. When he reached what had been described to him as Wolf Creek, he found the waters muddy, but a significant number of pinyon and juniper still crowded the surrounding slopes, and there was considerable grama grass growing on the flats alongside the stream. The smell of pine resin hung heavy in the high, clean, bracing air.

As he rode up the stream, he could not help comparing this sudden explosion of green and standing pine with the country he had just ridden through. It was with a keen sense of disappointment that he watched the waters of Wolf Creek grow muddier, and saw the traces of broken branches and bark caught in the shallows along the shore. Crossing a low flat, he topped a rise and looked down on sudden desolation. Closest to him was a small camp made up mostly of tents for the men, and barns and corrals for the wagons and the horses. Beyond the camp, both slopes leading down to Wolf Creek were swarming with loggers. The crests had already been shorn. Now the loggers were busily chopping down the pine on the slopes. Tiny figures straddled the downed trees, swiftly hacking off the branches. Here and there on lower portions of the slopes, he saw loggers building neat skidways of gleaming, freshly peeled pine logs. Wagons piled high with logs were moving off along a heavily rutted road that followed the creek and then cut south toward Whipsaw, following a longer but less arduous route than the one Longarm had taken.

Longarm rode into the town and asked the cook, scouring out a pot in front of the huge eating tent, where he could find Fitzpatrick. The cook pointed with his scrub brush to a slope on the other side of the creek. "Halfway up," he said, then went back to his scrubbing.

Longarm nodded and rode down to the creek, searching for a place to ford it. As he started across, the cook poked his head out of the large pot and yelled something to him about Fitzpatrick wearing a green jacket. Longarm waved his thanks and a moment later gained the far shore.

The cook's directions had been clear enough, but Longarm had difficulty finding the foreman. Finally, he came across a crew chief in a red-checked shirt standing apart from a crew of loggers. His arms were akimbo as he angrily supervised the building of a fresh skidway. As Longarm rode up the slope toward him, the foreman turned to look at him.

Longarm nodded. "Howdy. Maybe you might be able to

help me." Out of courtesy, the lawman dismounted to face the man on foot.

"Do I know you?" the crew chief asked.

"You will. Call me Longarm. I'm a deputy U.S. marshal. Right now I'm looking for your foreman, Arnold Fitzpatrick."

"You are, are you? Well, you'll just have to wait, Marshal. These so-called loggers are messing up this here skidway something awful."

The crew chief turned away from Longarm then, shouting, "Keep that log even! You'll never have a smooth deck less'n you keep them logs moving even!" he cried.

There were six men in all. Using a kind of four-foot-long pointed stick with an iron hook swinging from a socket near one end, the men were jacking logs up onto the skidway, which was a neat pile of recently cut logs kept in place with chains. The slopes were dotted with these skidways of fresh logs waiting for the wagon that would eventually transport them to the sawmill in Whipsaw.

The loggers appeared to be quite skillful with those hooked sticks, called peaveys, and Longarm found it difficult to understand why the crew chief was so critical of the loggers' performance. He watched as the crew chief snatched one of the peaveys from a logger and showed the fellow how to use it in jacking the log up the pole ramp onto the skidway. Longarm had to admit, the crew chief indeed knew how to handle a peavey. There seemed to be some kind of dispute raging in the camp as to which was more effective: the small, mean-looking peavey—the tool preferred by the younger loggers—or a much longer pole called a pike pole, which a few of the old-timers carried about with them much as shepherds carried their staffs. From the manner in which this crew chief in front of Longarm used the peavey, Longarm found it difficult to imagine a more efficient tool.

The crew chief returned the peavey to the chastened logger, then stepped back to join Longarm. The loggers worked even harder than before as they jacked the logs up the ramp onto the deck of the skidway, and now Longarm saw what the crew chief was after. The logs were falling into place neatly, seeming to slide up onto the skidway in a steady, effortless flow.

Satisfied, the crew chief turned to Longarm. "All right, Marshal. You say you're looking for Fitz."

Longarm nodded. He realized abruptly that the foreman was nervous—perhaps trying to stall.

"I just want some information," Longarm said.

"Just information, eh?"

"About a logger who used to work for him."

Obviously relieved, the fellow grinned slyly. "Nothing at all to do with last night, eh?" He broke into a broad grin. "Thought maybe Slade might have sent you. But then, you was pitching in along with the rest of us."

Longarm smiled. The crew chief must have been one of the loggers he had battled beside the night before. "That's right. Nothing to do with last night. I just want to talk to Fitzpatrick."

"Fitz is through that pass somewheres, checking out the log scale on what pine we got left on that slope."

"Thank you."

"That's all right, Marshal. Glad to help. If you see Fitz, tell him Jock's almost through here."

"I'll do that," Longarm said, swinging into his saddle.

He headed for the low, wooded pass Jock had indicated and was beyond it about a half hour later, approaching a small clearing, when he caught sight of Fitzpatrick on the far side of it. The green jacket stood out clearly as the foreman, standing on what appeared to be a small stump, spoke to some ten or twelve loggers gathered around him. He appeared to be excited about something, waving his arms as he talked.

But Longarm was too far away to hear the words spoken by the foreman, and before he could get close enough, a shot echoed from the hillside to Longarm's right. He pulled up at once and looked in that direction. When he glanced back at the group in the clearing, he saw the loggers moving off into the pines, their axes over their shoulders. The foreman was walking across the clearing to meet Longarm.

Longarm rode closer, then dismounted. That shot, he realized, was a signal.

"Are you Arnold Fitzpatrick?" Longarm asked.

The fellow nodded. "That I am. And you'd be that federal marshal."

"I'm Deputy U.S. Marshal Long. You can call me Longarm; it's easier to remember."

"Call me Fitz, then. What can I do for you, Longarm?"

"Slade said you might be able to help me. I'm looking for an army deserter who used to work for you."

"If Slade says I got to talk to you, then I'll talk." Fitzpatrick's white teeth gleamed in a sudden smile. Like the crew chief back at the skidway, he seemed to be relieved to learn what Longarm wanted.

The foreman looked to be in his late thirties. He was of medium height, thick about the chest and arms, with a gut only just beginning to strain against his belt. He wore a red cotton shirt under his open jacket, and heavy pants of a coarse woolen material tucked into his laced boots. A narrow, flat-crowned hat covered most of his thick, dark hair. His face was full and his dark, handsome eyes peered alertly out at Longarm from under jet-black, bushy eyebrows.

"This fellow I'm looking for, Fitz, worked for you until a few weeks ago. His name is Ned Shortslef, but I don't expect he'll be using that name. Like I said before, he's gone now—but I thought you might have some idea where he went. Anything you could give me would be a help."

"You got more than his name? A description, maybe?"

Longarm described Shortslef as best he could, relying on Seegar's and Gus's descriptions. By the time he had finished, he realized how inadequate his description was. The foreman's dark eyes reflected Longarm's misgivings.

"Well, now," the foreman began, "I suppose you might think that to be a fine description, but it don't tell me much. You say this bucko is tall. We got plenty of tall loggers, Longarm. He has a beard, has he? Look around you. My men don't have time to shave—not out here, they don't. Moves like a big cat, you said. Well, these loggers better move like a cat or they'll get flattened in no time at all by some falling tree or by a load of logs breaking from a skidway. Longarm, you just about described most of my loggers."

"This one was a good friend of Gus Dodds."

The foreman arched an eyebrow. "Gus Dodds, you say?"

Longarm nodded.

"Gus Dodds is a loner," Fitz told him. "A fast man with an

axe, make no mistake about that. One of my best. He can drop a tree on a stake already set in the ground and bury it every time. But he keeps to himself, he does. And that's a fact, Longarm."

"How about two weeks ago?" the lawman asked.

"He's a loner, I said. And he has been ever since I've worked here. All the men like him, though. They just don't mess with him. They let him be."

"You're saying he's been lying to me?"

"I wouldn't say that. No, sir! Not to his face. Like I said, Longarm, he's a fast man with an axe."

"Is Gus working out here with this crew?"

Fitz shook his head. "Nope. He's on the other side of that ridge behind me."

"Maybe I'd better go have another talk with him."

"Just don't slow him down any. We need his production."

Longarm thanked the foreman, remounted, and picked his way along a steep slope beyond the clearing. Reaching the ridge, he found it alive with loggers cutting through a thick stand of juniper. Unlike the gnarled pinyon being cut downslope to be used for railroad ties and firewood, these junipers were tall and straight enough to be used for telegraph poles. As he rode past, Longarm saw the trees being barked and trimmed with almost startling rapidity in preparation for their trip downslope to the waiting skidways.

Longarm kept going, crested the ridge, then slanted down the far slope toward a small army of loggers busily cutting through a thin but valuable stand of red fir. Watching the loggers chopping at the trees—white chips flying, each axe blade sounding as steadily and surely as a pendulum—Longarm no longer questioned these loggers' gargantuan excesses at nightfall. Men who worked this hard should be allowed to play the same way.

Nearing the stand of fir, Longarm watched as one of the tall firs came crashing down among its fellows. It was so skillfully placed, he noted, that it completely missed the surrounding trees as it crashed to earth. Into the timber by this time, Longarm caught sight of Gus. The big logger was about to resume his chopping of one of the tallest of the remaining firs.

"Gus!" Longarm called out, pulling up.

Gus turned, saw him, and put down his axe. He said something to another logger stripping a fallen log nearby. This other logger took up Gus's axe and began chopping at the tree as Gus strode through the slash to Longarm. Dismounting, Longarm waited for the one-eyed logger to reach him.

"Gus," Longarm said, "I need a little more information about Ned Shortslef. You say you worked with him for a while?"

"Look, Marshal, I told you all I know. He's up north somewhere if he ain't at the Flying T."

"Gus, the foreman says you never worked with anyone. He says you're a loner—that you didn't have any such buddy as Ned Shortslef."

"He's calling me a liar."

"You look like a loner to me. I haven't seen you with anyone yet, except that time in the hotel in Silver City when you got to be spokesman for those other two bashful loggers."

"I pick my own friends. I keep to myself if I want. I told you the truth about Ned Shortslef, no matter what you or Fitz says."

The big logger was getting angry. Before Longarm could say anything to soothe the man, a shot rang out from the slope above. Longarm never found out who fired the shot, and it didn't seem to matter at that moment as a crowd of hooded horsemen swept down off the slope, encircling the stand of fir. At sight of the riders, the loggers at once dropped their axes and reached for their weapons. Longarm heard the sound of shooting coming from the ridge above and the slope beyond.

A twig from a branch over his head was snipped off by an errant bullet as a volley of shots rang out from the enclosing vigilantes. Longarm went for his gun and darted with Gus behind a tree. By this time it became apparent to Longarm that the loggers had not been completely surprised as the withering fire cut from the trees. The hooded riders pulled up somewhat indecisively. It was obvious that their appetite for bloodshed did not match their desire to intimidate the loggers.

One of the riders pulled up swiftly, turned his horse, and waved the others back. Before they could follow his lead, slugs tore into two of the riders. Longarm saw them slump forward over their pommels as other riders came alongside them to help the wounded men stay in their saddles. The firing from the trees let up a bit after that.

But the vigilante who had waved his men back away from the timber now turned his horse around and charged recklessly back toward the timber. Longarm swore softly at the rider's gallant but foolhardy gesture, then ducked as the fire from the fellow's Winchester began slashing through the branches above his head.

"Jesus!" Gus muttered. "Why's he picking on us?"

By this time the loggers in the timber had opened up once again, sending out a fierce fire at the rider. But the vigilante did not falter. He was angry. Abruptly, he ran out of ammunition. Pulling up, he began to reload his Winchester.

Longarm stepped out from his cover. "Hold it right there, mister!" he called.

The firing from the timber behind Longarm ceased, and an eerie silence fell on the scene as the gunfire on the ridge above and the slope beyond ceased also. The hooded rider looked up in surprise as Longarm strode swiftly out of the timber toward him. Then he continued in his insanely determined effort to reload his Winchester.

When Longarm had approached to within five feet or so of the vigilante, he unholstered his Colt. "This is a fool's errand, mister. What are you up to? You think those flour sacks are going to scare anyone?"

At last the vigilante looked up from his rifle and stared down at Longarm through two ragged slits in the sack. There were none for his mouth and nose. With the fellow's every inhalation the flour sack was sucked in, then blown out. It had to be as hot as a chicken's ass inside that mask, Longarm mused.

"This is a warning!" the vigilante cried, his voice muffled grotesquely by the hood. "You loggers are ruining this slope. Ruining this entire valley! If we can't stop you one way, we'll stop you another. Tell that to Slade!"

"Why, hell, man! Don't you think he knows that already? He's not logging on your homesteads. He's cutting on government territory. You can't scare him off this land. You try that and you'll be going against the law. The fact is, you ain't much better than outlaws right now!"

With a furious oath, the hooded rider swung up his reloaded Winchester and levered quickly. Longarm ducked low and crabbed sideways as he fired almost without conscious volition up at the rider. The man grabbed his left shoulder and peeled back off his horse, his Winchester discharging harmlessly into the air.

At that, the rest of the vigilantes, who had been waiting not more than a hundred yards away from the timber, immediately spurred back toward Longarm. Longarm did not think he could make it safely back to the trees. Darting forward, he grabbed the bridle of the vigilante's horse and yanked powerfully, pulling the mount down on its side. As he did this, he kicked the Winchester out of the downed vigilante's right hand, then stomped on the rifle's stock, snapping it. The man groaned and swore bitterly at Longarm. Longarm ducked low behind the horse and began to track the lead rider bearing down on him.

He fired; the shot went high. Then he no longer had time to aim. He fired rapidly, riding the recoil up with each shot. The nearest rider lost his hat. The one just behind him spun his horse when a slug whined too close. At that moment, the sudden rattle of rifle fire came from the ridge. Glancing up, Longarm saw about ten horsemen charging down the slope with their guns blazing, and two mounted vigilantes running before them. The foreman, Fitz, was leading the chase.

From the dress of the pursuing riders, Longarm knew they were Bat Lawson's men. They must have been waiting somewhere for just this kind of foolishness on the part of the ranchers. As Lawson's men swept down the slope, the rest of the vigilantes broke off their attack on Longarm and galloped away, abandoning their wounded comrade. Lawson's men, letting out whoops like cowboys on a Saturday night hurrah, galloped after the vigilantes to the delighted cheers of the loggers behind Longarm in the timber.

Fitz and one other rider pulled up. Longarm waved; Fitz waved back. Then the two riders rode over to him. The loggers had already left the cover of the timber and were forming a grim circle around Longarm and the wounded vigilante. Fitz and the other rider rode through the circle of loggers. Longarm bent down and yanked the flour sack off the vigilante's head.

He was a very young man, not yet in his twenties. His face was pale and drawn from loss of blood, but his dark eyes were alive with anger as he glanced about him. He had a lean face, deeply tanned, the jaw slightly outthrust and square. At the moment he was intent on trying to stanch the flow from his wound with his bandanna.

"What's your name, mister?" Longarm asked, holstering his Colt.

The wounded man glared up at him for a moment, but refused to reply. Then he turned his attention back to his shoulder wound.

"That's Wally Troy," Fitz said, looking down from his saddle. "Terry Troy's brother. The Troys own the Flying T. You got yourself a nice catch there, Marshal."

The rider with Fitz grinned wolfishly. He was wearing a black vest over a bright red cotton shirt. The butt of his pearl-handled Colt gleamed against the shining flap of his black leather holster. "We know just what to do with him, don't we, Fitz?"

Longarm looked up at the man. "What's your name, mister?"

"Jack Wilson."

"And just what in tarnation do you plan on doing with this man, Wilson?"

"What we do with vigilantes—string him up. That's the word from Bat. And you ain't going to stop us this time, Marshal. This man and his band of lawless vigilantes killed one of our loggers."

"Prove it."

"We don't have to."

The rest of Slade's private army was galloping back toward them now. Wilson glanced at the oncoming horsemen, then smiled back at Longarm. "Here comes all the evidence we need, Marshal."

"Wilson, if you—or any men here—take part in a lynching, I'll come after you. If I can't bring you in, there'll be other deputies, and still more after that. On this government land, I'm the law. Not Slade, or Bat Lawson, or any of you gun-happy flannelmouths."

"Guess that means you, Wilson," Fitz said, his teeth flashing in his tanned face.

"Shut up, you dirty mick!" Wilson cried.

Fitz's smile vanished in an instant and in one powerful move he brought his huge left fist around in a backhand swipe, catching Wilson on the tip of his jaw. Longarm thought he heard a bone go as Wilson went flying backward over his cantle. He landed close beside Wally Troy and sat up holding his jaw. Tears of pain and rage flowed suddenly from his eyes.

Wally Troy laughed.

Longarm pulled Troy's horse to its feet. Then he reached down to help the young man. As Wally stood up and steadied himself, he told Longarm, "We never tried to hurt anyone. We was all aimin' high, deliberate. We couldn't've hurt no loggers. He's lying."

"I was wondering how come you were all such lousy shots," Longarm drawled. "Let me give you a hand up."

With his teeth firmly clenched and his eyes closed from the pain, Wally Troy swung himself up into his saddle just as Bat's riders closed in around the circle of loggers. A rider, whom Longarm recognized as the same man who had stood in the entrance to the Paradise Valley with Bat the night before, guided his mount through the loggers toward Longarm.

"Who told you to butt in here, Longarm?" the rider demanded.

"Just who the hell wants to know?" Longarm replied testily, eyeing the man with a swift and sudden dislike.

"I'm Ruel Tyson. I'm in charge here. You ain't going to interfere in this, Longarm. I got the word from Bat. We catch any of these here vigilantes, we string 'em up."

A roar of approval came from the loggers as they pressed closer. Many of them were still carrying those ancient but formidable weapons they had grabbed when the vigilantes' attack had first begun. Longarm could not blame the loggers. They were the ones who had been the target of all that lead. It didn't much matter to them that the damn fools in those flour sacks were aiming high. And there was little chance they would believe such a thing, anyway.

"You're not stringing anyone up, Tyson," Longarm said. "Young Troy here says the vigilantes were all aiming high, just trying to scare the loggers. It was a damn fool thing to do, I admit. But scaring hell out of loggers isn't a hanging offense that I know of. So back off. I'm taking this fellow back to his spread."

"No, you ain't," Ruel said, his eyes suddenly going cold. His hand flashed down to his holster.

Longarm's Colt appeared in his hand with such speed that it seemed to have been hanging in the air between the two men all the time. In the act of drawing his own weapon, Ruel's right hand froze. His face was suddenly pale, his eyes wide and focused on the muzzle of Longarm's steady six-gun.

"Ease your gun back into its holster, Tyson," Longarm instructed him quietly. "Then tell these loggers to stand back or you'll be wearing a hole where your heart ought to be."

"Stand back, you men!" Ruel shouted, letting his Colt drop back into its holster.

Longarm heard a scuffle to his right. Glancing swiftly over, he saw a logger go down heavily. Gus, standing beside the downed man with a large chunk of wood in his hand, nodded solemnly at Longarm. The downed logger had evidently tried to save Ruel's ass. Ruel glanced in that direction, furious.

"I told you knuckleheads! Get back! Don't try nothing!"

"Gus!" Longarm called. "Get my horse! It's still back there in the timber."

Gus ran for Longarm's mount and brought it back through the ranks of grim loggers. Longarm thanked the man and swung up into his saddle, his gun still trained on Tyson. He spoke to Troy: "Start to ride, Wally. I'll catch up to you."

Slumped painfully forward over his saddle horn, Wally Troy dug steel into his mount's flanks and started up. Longarm waited until the man was beyond Lawson's riders, then told Tyson, "Now, you follow Troy. And remember, there's a Colt looking at your back!"

With a muttered curse, Ruel followed Troy, Longarm riding close behind. Once through the loggers, Longarm glanced back at Gus. "You going to be all right?" he asked.

"Never mind me, Longarm. You got enough to handle right in front of you!"

Longarm nodded and waved to him, then turned back around. Ruel glanced at him. "Keep going, Ruel. I'll tell you when you can go back to your gunslicks. Just keep riding."

Ruel did as he was told. Glancing ahead of Ruel at young Troy, he saw that the kid was doing all right. He had more guts than brains, it appeared. Longarm decided he would keep Ruel with him for a couple of miles at least before letting the man return to the logging site.

Then all he would have to worry about would be Wally Troy's friends, and after that, his reception at the Flying T.

Chapter 5

The Flying T was a good distance away. Longarm found himself riding through high, surprisingly fertile country. The floors of the valleys they crossed were covered with thick grama, the few dry stretches dotted with waist-high sagebrush. Jackrabbits leaped away through the scrub pine, and once Longarm thought he caught sight of a pronghorn antelope high-kicking his way around a clump of sagebrush.

They were crossing a narrow creek when Wally slumped suddenly forward over the pommel. Longarm had been riding just behind him. He dismounted quickly and was in time to ease the man out of his saddle and onto the ground. He took off the young man's hat and went back to the stream for some water. Wally drank it greedily. Longarm felt his forehead. It was burning up. Wally had evidently lost a lot of blood.

Easing him over to a boulder, Longarm propped him up against it and inspected the wound. It was suppurating by this time, and partly scabbed over. Ugly, raw streaks of red radiated up over the shoulder and down into the armpit. Wally Troy watched him through cold, heavy-lidded eyes, making no effort to hide his contempt for Longarm. When Longarm probed the wound with the barrel of his Colt, the young man's eyes didn't waver.

Longarm stood up and gazed down at the man for a moment, considering. Often it wasn't the bullet that killed a man; it was the infection that usually followed. And this inflammation was advancing rapidly. Longarm had seen a wound similar to this take a man in less than two days. There was nothing for it then, but to cauterize the wound as best he could.

Going to his horse, he untied his bedroll and secured his coffeepot. Filling it with water from the stream, he built a

small fire and heated the water to a boil. Then he ripped a portion of Wally's shirtsleeve off and dropped it into the boiling
water. While it boiled, Longarm took out his knife and held the
blade over the open flame until it began to glow.

Wally watched him, his eyes narrowing ever so slightly.
Longarm approached him with the glowing knife in his hand,
hunkered down beside him, and before the fellow could pull
back, plunged the blade into the wound, cutting deep and scouring the edges. The stench of burning tissue assailed Longarm's
nostrils. Only when he felt Wally's body slump sideways did he
glance up and see that the man had passed out.

It was what Longarm had hoped would happen. He took the
piece of shirt out of the boiling water and thoroughly cleaned
the wound. The blood was beginning to flow again, but it was
cleaner blood. Longarm was encouraged. He tore off another
piece of the unconscious man's shirt. Stuffing the bloody shirt
fragment into the wound to stanch the flow, he used the other
piece of shirt to bind it tightly in place.

He stood up then, and surveyed the still unconscious man for
a moment longer. Satisfied that he had done all he could, given
the circumstances and the tools he had, Longarm cleaned off the
knife's blade, emptied the water on the fire, and repacked his
bedroll. He was in the act of knotting the rawhide thong around
it when he heard a movement behind him.

Ducking low and turning in one swift motion, he was as-
tounded to see the wounded cowboy coming up behind him,
a six-gun in his raised right hand. Wally brought his weapon
down. Just in time, Longarm managed to thrust his arm up to
ward off the blow. Nevertheless, the impact of the gun barrel
on his forearm was such that for a moment Longarm thought
the fellow might have broken it. But only for a moment. Longarm grabbed the six-gun's barrel and twisted the weapon out
of Wally's hand. At the same time, he smashed the cowboy in
the midsection.

Wally Troy went down suddenly, as if someone had cut the
strings holding him upright. Longarm stuck the fellow's six-
gun into one of his saddlebags. Massaging his throbbing forearm, he turned back to the cowboy, whose head was sagging
forward, his hair falling over his face. Slowly and painfully, he
lifted his head to look at Longarm.

He spoke then in a voice so soft Longarm had to lean forward to catch his words: "You skunk! Damn your eyes to hell! I'll get you yet!"

Longarm smiled at the fellow. He liked his courage. "As soon as you're ready, I'll help you back up onto your horse."

"I'm ready," the fellow croaked weakly, and held up his right hand. Longarm pulled him to his feet.

The sun was sitting just above the mountains when Longarm followed Wally Troy into a narrow pass that led onto a vivid green flat. As he rode closer to the flat, Longarm could make out the cattle feeding on the grama. Emerging from the pass, he saw the ranch buildings, blue in the distance. They were a slightly darker smudge set against the lighter blue of the low hills beyond. The jingle of harness and the sound of shoes striking stone behind Longarm alerted him—but too late.

He swung around in his saddle and saw the semicircle of riders falling in behind him. Longarm recognized the lead rider. It was Lyle Butts. As Longarm caught the man's eye, Butts touched his hat brim and smiled coldly.

"We meet again, Marshal," he said, his stubbly, narrow face grimly serious.

Longarm glanced around at the other riders. There were six of them, all told, including Butts. Longarm had little doubt that all of them had been riding not too long before with flour sacks over their heads. But obviously others had joined this bunch, since there had been considerably more vigilantes in that gang at Wolf Creek. The ranchers were getting together then, acting in concert against a common enemy.

"Don't make a play for your six-gun, Marshal," Butts said, as he rode past Longarm to reach the side of Wally Troy.

"How you doin', Wally?" Butts asked.

The young man looked at Butts through a curtain of pain. "Hell, Butts, I'm doing just fine. All I got's a slug through my shoulder."

"You look peaked."

"I wonder why?" the young cowboy said sarcastically. "Shit, Butts, don't ask so many questions. Just get that sonofabitch riding behind me off my back."

"Sure, Wally. Sure," Butts said. He pulled up slightly and

fell in beside Longarm, then guided his mount closer. He reached out his right hand. "Let me have that weapon of yours, Marshal."

"You can take it if you want, Butts, but it'll cost you."

"Hell! I got five men backing me—each one with a hogleg pointing at you. Do as you're told, mister."

"Call me Longarm—and keep your distance, Butts. If you lay a hand on that Colt, you'll just get my balls in an uproar and all hell will break loose. They'll be sending both of us to hell on a shingle, but you'll be going in just a little bit ahead of me." He smiled. "You got a hankering to make that trip, have you?"

Butts shrugged. "I can wait. We'll be at the ranch soon enough. Just follow Wally."

"What the hell do you think I've been doing, Butts?"

The older man's narrow face darkened, but he offered no further comment and pulled his horse out and away from Longarm, then drifted back with the rest of the Flying T crew. Glancing back, Longarm saw blued steel glinting darkly in six hands. Turning around, Longarm felt a coldness creep up his spine. He felt as if he had bedded down in a nice, cool, shaded nest of rattlers—he would be all right if he didn't move too suddenly . . . maybe.

About a half hour later, with the riders still close behind him and Wally Troy keeping himself erect in the saddle just ahead of him, Longarm rode onto the Flying T spread. The low, long bunkhouse and the cookshack adjoining it were of adobe and formed two sides of a rough, sandy plaza. The opposite sides were taken up by the blacksmith shop and several wagon sheds. All of this, the working heart of the ranch, lay sprawled under giant cottonwoods. The house was separated from the work building by a high stone wall, and stood some distance away.

As Longarm rode in, a powerful stocky fellow stepped out of the small ranch office near the north end of the bunkhouse. He was wearing a black, flat-crowned hat with its brim turned down in back, a dark blue shirt, and gray pants tucked into well-cared-for boots. The man's face was handsome in a casually brutal way, with sensual lips, lidded eyes, and an habitual insolent downturn at the corners of his mouth. He looked like a man who was happy only when he was riding someone hard. When he saw the drawn guns all pointed at Longarm, he licked his lips and stepped eagerly toward the group of riders.

Longarm pulled up. Butts dismounted and hurried to help Wally off his mount. As he was doing this, the other riders pulled up in a circle around Longarm.

"What happened to Wally?" the fellow in the dark blue shirt asked Butts.

It was Wally who answered. Hurrying toward the ranch-house, he glanced back at the man who was evidently the fore-man and snapped angrily, "That lawman shot me. He's working with Slade and Lawson!"

"Hey, Russ!" a rider behind Longarm called out. "That's the marshal that messed up Teeter and Slick."

Longarm glanced back and recognized Billy, one of the four who had attempted to bushwhack him the day before. As Longarm glanced back at the foreman, the fellow took a step toward him.

"You're the one, huh? I was hoping you'd turn up. I hear your name's Long."

"That's right. Custis Long, deputy U.S. marshal out of Denver."

The foreman glanced quickly around at the grim faces of his riders, most of whom still had their six-guns trained on Longarm. He smiled back at Longarm. "Slick Hansen and Jim Teeter are two pretty sick boys, no thanks to you."

"I see. I was supposed to let them bushwhack me, is that it? A funny kind of law you've got here." The Morgan shied. Longarm reached forward and patted its neck, and settled it down. "You the foreman here?"

"That's right. Russ Blodgett's the name. You can call me Mister Blodgett."

"Russ, I reckon you better tell your men to put their guns away. There's a law against vigilantes—even damn fool vigilantes like this bunch. Wally Troy drew on me; that's attempted assault. Two of your men are already flat on their backs for attempting to murder me, and a man sitting his horse right now behind me was part of that same conspiracy. Looks to me like you've got yourself a passel of trigger-happy cowpokes who've been making a mess of things so far. You tell them to quit while they're ahead."

"And if they don't?"

"I just might have to take them back with me," Longarm answered evenly.

"All five, Marshal?"

"As many as I have to."

Blodgett laughed, and a set of crooked teeth flashed in his otherwise handsome face. "You ain't bringing anybody back with you, Marshal." The man looked quickly around. "Ain't that right, boys?"

"He's just going to have an accident," Billy drawled from behind Longarm, cocking his six-gun. The sound of the other four six-guns being cocked filled the tense silence. Again Longarm had to quiet his skittish mount. He patted the Morgan's neck gently and talked to it. Then he looked down at the foreman.

"I tell you what, Russ. Looks like I'm a dead man anyway, what with all this firepower pointed at me. The only thing a man can do in a case like this is pick one fellow and make sure he takes that jasper with him. I pick you."

"I ain't armed!" Blodgett protested.

"That doesn't make any difference, the way I look at it. Your friends have got enough artillery for both of us. I've got a Colt in a cross-draw rig under my coat. Some say I'm fast, and I guess I do practice some—for situations like this."

"Just a minute there." The foreman held up a hand and took a step back.

"Hang in there, Blodgett. I ain't started counting yet."

"It's a bluff, Russ!" a cowhand called.

"Sure! That's all it is!" another cried. "Give us the go-ahead!"

Longarm smiled at Russ. "Maybe I don't have time for counting. . . ."

"What in hell's going on out here, Russ?"

A woman had strode into view behind the foreman. She had come from the house, it appeared. Russ spun to face her. He was obviously more than a little relieved to see her. She strode angrily toward him, her fierce eyes raking the ring of horsemen.

"What in tarnation are all you men doing, pointing your guns at this one man? Put those irons away!"

She swept past Russ Blodgett and came to a halt in front of Longarm. "You're Marshal Long. Wally just told me what happened. Thank you for not killing the damned fool, Marshal. Light and stay awhile. You're welcome at the Flying T anytime. My name is Terry Troy. I own this spread."

Longarm took a deep breath, touched the brim of his hat to the woman, and smiled down at her. "Much obliged, Miss Troy."

She spun around then to face the foreman. "You heard me, Russ. Get these men back to some kind of honest work. And from now on, I don't want them playing cowboys and Indians on Flying T time. Do you understand that, Russ? They are cowpokes, not vigilantes!"

"Sure, Terry, but it was Wally's idea! he said you—"

"Never mind what that *kid* told you, Russ. I thought you had better sense than that! *That's* why I made you foreman."

With a sudden, dangerous sullenness, Russ waved the riders back away from Longarm. Looking suddenly sheepish, the riders turned their mounts toward the barn. The tension lifted immediately.

The woman turned back to Longarm and smiled. "I asked you to dismount and stay awhile, Marshal. Or do you intend to spend the night on that Morgan?"

"Not when I've got a better offer," Longarm said, swinging off the horse.

Standing before the owner of the Flying T, Longarm realized that she had appeared taller than she actually was. She wore Levi's that had shrunk to fit and looked as if they might have to be peeled off, judging from the way they clung to her full hips and lushly rounded thighs. A faded-blue man's shirt was pulled almost as tightly across her bosom, giving the shirt a shape it sure as hell never had on any man. The gaps between the two top buttons threatened to grow larger any second. High-heeled boots and a thick crown of chestnut hair were what had imparted the illusion of height. Her stance, proud and not a little arrogant, completed the picture of a woman used to giving orders and seeing them obeyed.

"What's a woman doing," she asked him mockingly, "run-

ning a ranch? Is that it, Marshal? I think that's what I am reading in your eyes. I am not usually wrong."

"And you weren't far wrong this time, either. I reckon if
you can read minds, you won't have any trouble buffaloing a
few foolish cowhands and a thousand head."

"There are more than a thousand head running the Flying T
brand, Marshal. But the cattle aren't what's giving me the trouble." She turned, called one of her hands over, and told him to
see to Longarm's horse. Then she looked back at Longarm.
"There's hot coffee at the house, Marshal, and a place to sit
that's not moving all the time."

She turned and started for the ranchhouse. Longarm left his
horse with the hand she had called over and followed after her.

The ranchhouse was massive, one story high with a fluted
tile roof. A porch extended around three sides. Deep within its
cool adobe fastness was an inner court paved with black cob-
blestones, the surfaces of which shone like glass. They crossed
the court to reach a bedroom where Terry's brother, naked
from the waist up, was being tended by a young Mexican girl.
Longarm remained behind in the doorway and watched as
Terry consulted the girl on Wally's condition. Wally's eyes
were closed, but he did not seem to be sleeping.

Terry thanked the girl and started from the room. Her
brother opened his eyes and looked at her. "Carla says that son
of a bitch did a good job when he cleaned out my wound."

"You're luckier than you deserve," Terry said, carefully
keeping her concern out of her voice. "The bullet went on
through."

Terry left the room and Longarm followed her back across
the court to a huge parlor with pine rafters. It was comfortably
furnished with leather sofas and easy chairs. A huge stone fireplace dominated the long outer wall. There were hunting tro-
phies above the long mantelpiece—the heads of a pronghorn
with an impressive pair of prongs, an elk, and a bighorn. Longarm settled into a leather chair.

This was a man's parlor, he thought, in spite of the curtains
over the bank of windows facing the porch. Terry Troy didn't
seem to go in much for frills and lace any more than she did
for petticoats.

She sat down on the corner of the sofa facing him, and

noted the way he surveyed the room. "Yes," she said, "this is still the way my father left it a couple of years ago. I saw no reason to change a thing. It is a big, comfortable room without any foolish clutter of knicknacks. It's like my father—a big man without much fuss or show."

The housekeeper—an enormous and absolutely silent Mexican woman—entered the room with a tray containing a battered coffeepot, cups, milk, and sugar. She set the tray down on a solid oak table between them, and poured the coffee. Watching her, Longarm realized that this woman was the mother of the girl in the room with Wally. The milk came out of a can and the housekeeper was quite generous with it. She handed Longarm his cup first, then served her mistress.

"Thank you, Juanita," Terry said. "Leave the pot."

The big woman padded silently out of the room. Longarm drank the coffee. Despite the generous portion of canned milk, it had the strength of a mule's kick. He savored it.

Putting down her cup, Terry smiled at Longarm. "Juanita uses aged coffee grinds, I believe. But I do like its bite."

Longarm met her smiling gaze with his own serious one.

"I am sorry about your brother, Miss Troy," he said.

"Call me Terry," she suggested with a smile.

"My friends call me Longarm."

"All right, Longarm. I understand, I think, about Wally. He's a terrible hothead, and right now—along with the rest of us—he is desperate about this logging. If my father were still alive, his action would have been a lot more drastic than Wally's was this afternoon, I am afraid. But tell me about it. Wally said he tried to shoot you."

Longarm told her everything. When he got to his account of Wally galloping back to the timber alone through the gunfire, she closed her eyes, shuddering at the picture in her mind. When Longarm was finished, she took a deep breath.

"Then you saved Wally's life. Bat Lawson's men would have hung him."

"That was their intention."

She shook her head. "Thank you, Longarm. I'm sure that when Wally comes to his senses, he'll thank you as well."

"Two other men were wounded, I noticed."

"Yes. They were Bar B hands. The Bar B is a small ranch

to the south of us. The two men will be all right, I understand."
She smiled wryly at him then. "And there are two other hurt
cowboys in our bunkhouse, one with an arrow hole in his back.
They'll be all right, too, if I can keep them quiet."

"They mistook me for a gunslinger Slade was bringing in.
What can you tell me about him?"

"Nothing much. But he's a threat to all of us. This gunslick
can call any of my hands out and cut them down easily, one at
a time. Wally would be the first to answer such a challenge. But,
Longarm, I didn't know those four men were going after you.
If I had, I would have stopped them. Butts said he tried to talk
them out of it, then went along to keep them out of trouble—if
he could."

"He wasn't very successful."

"That arrow—from the wound, I could tell it was a Digger
arrow. Were Diggers with you at the time?"

"I've been doing some thinking about that, Terry," Longarm
said, scratching the back of his neck. "In Silver City I made
Bat and his men release four Diggers they were about to hang.
I figured those four Diggers—or one of them, at least—was up
there, sort of looking out for me, when your boys opened up."

Terry frowned in thought, then nodded. "It's likely," she
said. "What's that about casting your bread on the waters—"

"Or, one good turn deserves another."

"And these Indians are like that. They never forget a
kindness—or an offense."

"That's about it, Terry," he said.

She took a deep breath and leaned back. He held his own
breath at the sight, wondering if the buttons down the front of
her shirt would hold. Her face was darkly tanned causing her
white teeth and light blue eyes to gleam like precious stones.
She wore her hair down to her shoulders, loosely curled, utterly
without concern as to how this might be regarded by others.
The lines of her face were clean, her nose uptilted slightly.
There was a faint dimple in the center of her bold chin. She was
a handsome woman—and strong. The wildness of her father
was apparent in Wally. It was in her, too, but she had her father's strength as well.

"You're staying for the night," she said. "You must allow

my hospitality to make amends for whatever indignities you suffered at the hands of my men—and the Flying T. Really, Longarm. I insist."

"That's right kind of you. But are you sure your hands will be able to understand that? They seemed pretty anxious to have me for dinner—after I'd been drawn and quartered, that is. Your foreman especially."

"This is *my* ranch, Longarm. I run it and every man on it." She smiled to take the sting out of her words. "Except, that is, for my guests."

"Even guests who shoot your hands?"

"You saved Wally's life, Longarm. That makes you more than a guest. That makes you a friend."

She stood up. As if some kind of silent command had been given, Juanita appeared, in the doorway.

"Juanita, Marshal Long will be our guest tonight," Terry informed the woman. "Show him to the main guest room, see to his gear, and draw him a bath. We'll sit down for dinner at six."

Juanita looked with large, liquid eyes at Longarm—there was just a trace of a smile in them—and waited for Longarm to follow her from the room.

As Longarm rose to his feet, Terry smiled at him. "Enjoy your bath, Longarm. Nap for a while afterward, if you wish. I'll have Juanita wake you in time for dinner. I have some business. That is, I think I should see to Wally and talk to him—and then to the rest of my hands."

Longarm nodded to her, then moved off down the long, cool hall after the massive, silent housekeeper.

Juanita spent almost a half hour lugging steaming kettles of hot water to Longarm's tub. She said nothing to him during all this time, but her eyes watched him closely, noting his long torso and its equipment with some approval. The harsh yellow soap she gave Longarm peeled the dirt off with a vengeance.

When the water was at its hottest, and filling the bedroom with clouds of steam, Juanita came back in without a kettle and fell upon Longarm, scrubbing his back with such enthusiasm that he could hear her panting in his ear from her exertions.

But it was just what he had wanted. He let her have her way with him, hoping only that she would see her way clear to leave some of his skin.

Scrubbing his chest, she dropped the soap and fished in the water for it. Her hand brushed him. She uttered a tiny cry when she discovered what her attentions had been doing to him. As she pulled her hand quickly away, Longarm reached up casually and pulled her down, kissing her on the lips. For a moment the woman tried to pull back. Then, with a deep, almost convulsive sigh, she answered his kiss, her hand plunging back down into the steaming water.

When she pulled away at last, her dark face was no longer impassive; the large eyes were warm.

Longarm smiled at her, "Thank you, Juanita. Nothing a man likes better after a long ride than a hot, steaming bath."

She nodded, reached back for the huge bath towel, and held it out for him. He stood up. She wrapped the towel around him as he stepped out of the tub, then patted him all over, leading him to the bed. As he sat down upon it, he looked at her questioningly.

She smiled very slightly, her miraculously white teeth showing for the first time. Then she shook her head, declining his invitation in such a way as to inform Longarm that she was not offended and did indeed appreciate the offer.

In a few moments the housekeeper and a tiny, much older woman—she looked part-Indian—carried the tub from the bedroom. Longarm removed his Colt from his rig and tucked it under his pillow. Lying back on the cool bedspread, bare-assed and content, he slept.

It was Carla who awakened Longarm. His nakedness did not appear to bother her. The warmth in her eyes indicated approval more than anything else. As he sat up, she presented him with fresh longjohns, stockings, Levi's, and a gleaming white broadcloth shirt that fit perfectly. His own clothing, Carla told him in excellent English, was being laundered.

As he entered the dining room a moment later, Terry, already seated, glanced up at him approvingly. "Those were my father's," she told him. "I knew you were big enough to fill them."

"Thank you," Longarm said, sitting down. "I was wondering whose they were. I'm usually a hard man to cover."

"Yes," she said. "I imagine you would be."

Sitting across the table from Longarm was the foreman, Russ Blodgett. He was startled to see Longarm enter and appeared slightly outraged at the lawman's presence at the dinner table. Longarm got the distinct impression that it had something to do with the nature of his relationship with his boss—the foreman was unwilling to share Terry with him. Longarm nodded curtly at the man.

"Wally's too worn out to join us," Terry told Longarm, "but he's resting comfortably, and Carla takes good care of him. He admitted, by the way, that most likely he would be dancing from a tree limb now if it weren't for you. I am sure, Longarm, that he will thank you himself when he's stronger."

"No need," Longarm said. "I'm a law officer. I get paid by the federal government to stop such nonsense when I can."

The meal was brought in then by Juanita and Carla, great plates piled high with thick slabs of steak, fried potatoes and steaming hot biscuits. The coffee was plentiful and even stronger than that potion Longarm had sampled earlier.

The three of them ate with quiet gusto, in a silence that grew more ominous as the meal progressed. Russ was evidently not going to dignify Longarm's presence at the table by noting it. Terry, aware of his sullenness, became increasingly irritated. Longarm could sense her growing impatience as her remarks, directed at Russ and intended to lighten the tension, seemed only to increase Russ's black, disapproving silence. In reply to her he did little more than grunt. He refused to look at Longarm.

At last, her blue eyes flashing angrily, Terry put down her knife and fork and spoke directly to the problem. "Longarm is a guest at my table, Russ. You are not being very friendly. I had hoped you would be man enough to use this opportunity to apologize for your behavior earlier this afternoon."

"Apologize!" In his amazement and fury at such a suggestion, Russ slammed his knife down upon his plate with such force that Terry visibly winced.

Her tanned features growing suddenly pale, she said quietly, "Yes, Russ. Apologize. And if that temper display cracked that plate, it'll come out of your salary."

"But—but, Terry! This man—"

"This man," she cut in, "saved Wally from a mob of rope-happy loggers. He shot Wally in self-defense. If he had killed him—God forbid—he would have been justified, since Wally turned his rifle on him. If he had left him to the loggers, he would have been justified. But he didn't do that. He took Wally from them at the point of a gun and brought him home through our own guns—"

"But, Terry, how the hell did I know all that? And what about Teeter and Slick?"

"Those two deserved what they got," she replied with some venom. "And if you didn't know all I just told you, you should have. That's the point, Russ. You had no idea; so why didn't you take this opportunity to find out from Longarm what happened? And while all this business with the flour sacks was going on, by the way, where the hell were you? If you were part of it and didn't tell me, I want to know why. If you didn't know about it, I'd like to know what the hell you've been doing masquerading as my foreman all this time."

"Why, sure, I knew what the boys was up to, but Wally wouldn't have it no other way, and I didn't want to bother you with it. You'd only worry."

"You mean I'd only stop it. If Wally had lost his life on account of this foolishness, I'd have blamed you, Russ. And I'd have wanted satisfaction!"

Russ jumped to his feet. "Now, Terry, you can't talk to me like that. Not after all we been to each other!"

"Russ," Terry said, "I pay your salary and that means I talk to you any way I want to. Right now I'm treating you like a damned fool because that's just what you've been. You can leave this table now. You've been excused. And say good night to Mr. Long before you go."

"Terry!" the man fairly wailed. "You can't *mean* that."

"Yes, I can, Russ. Now get out."

"But—but what about—" He looked with enormous embarrassment at Longarm, his handsome features suddenly turning crimson.

"You can sleep in the bunkhouse tonight, Russ," she said coldly.

"Terry! I warn you! I won't forget this!"

"Get out, Russ."

He stood there for a moment, too stubborn to be dismissed like this by a woman and too terrified to disobey.

"Git!" Longarm thundered. "You heard the woman! She means *now*, mister!"

The force of Longarm's verbal blast seemed to buffet Russ physically. He turned on his heel and lunged from the room. A moment later the outer door was heard to slam.

Terry looked down at her plate, her face pale with fury, and embarrassment. At last she glanced up at Longarm. "Forgive his manners, Longarm. And forgive me for allowing the likes of him to share my bed. It is not good for discipline, I know. But this is a lonely, barren land in some ways—and for too many things you have to make do with what you have."

"Say no more," Longarm said quietly. "I've traveled over some pretty sorry land in my time, where the pickings were just as lean."

"Some wine, then, to finish our meal?" she suggested, calm once more.

Longarm smiled. "Sounds fine."

"We'll have it served in the parlor. Nights are chilly here; I'll have the fireplace lit."

The wine warmed Longarm almost as much as the fire. As Terry talked about her father and his struggle to survive in this high desert country, the lawman developed a liking for the girl and an appreciation of her love for her dead father—as well as a strong admiration for the man himself. Everything this man had built depended on the wells that fed the ranch's water holes, and the almost miraculous cheat grasses that sprang up after even the most insignificant rain. Fortunately, as Terry explained, there was always some snow in the winter and just enough melt-off in the spring to feed the rivers and streams, which, together with the wells, gave them the water without which they would perish during the hot, almost bone-dry summers.

But now the stripped mountainsides and ridges no longer trapped the occasional rainfall. The water table throughout the valley was beginning to drop alarmingly. The wells were drying up and even the sagebrush on the valley floors was burning off. This meant that the pronghorn would soon be gone as well, leaving the land to the coyotes and the jackrabbits—and the Digger Indians.

"They can live anywhere," she said, almost in wonder.

"Well, maybe," Longarm said. "They depend on water too, don't they?"

"Yes, of course," she said, correcting herself. "And on the nuts of the pinyon. Their women go about with these enormous baskets they weave themselves, filling them with these nuts." She grimaced. "They also eat ground-up grasshoppers mixed into a kind of cake, I hear. For them, it's a delicacy."

The lawman tugged thoughtfully at a corner of his mustache. "So you're losing your water and the Indians are losing their pine groves, it looks like."

Terry nodded. Then, seeing that his glass was empty, she got up with the bottle, crossed to his armchair, and refilled his glass. As she bent close to him, intent on her task, he could feel the animal warmth of her—the sweet, clean, almost intoxicating perfume of her body. She also had bathed this afternoon, it seemed. She returned to her corner of the sofa and sat down, tucking her legs under her and smiling back at him.

He sipped the wine, knowing that she was perfectly well aware of the hell she had just raised with that brief visit.

"Tomorrow," she said, "I'll take you over our land, so you can see for yourself why Wally acted the way he did today. It was foolish, of course, and it will only bring Slade and his men down on us harder—but at least you'll be able to understand the depth of our concern. These lumber companies will be gone someday; they will have taken every tree, stripped every ridge, every hillside, leaving us with a silted-up river, gullied-out slopes, and barren valleys. It will be a dead land, Longarm."

"I wish I could tell you that telegraph poles, railroad ties, and firewood were worth all this, Terry. But I can't. The thing is, you ranchers are using government land mostly for grazing—and this government has some high and important officials who stand to line their pockets with silver and gold if they only let this company operate. The law is on their side."

"The law!" She spat out the word contemptuously.

"They *make* the laws, Terry. I never heard tell yet of a law passed *against* progress. And progress means mining the wealth out of the West, wherever you find that wealth and whatever it is—gold, silver, or lumber."

"This *land* is a kind of wealth, Longarm. Perhaps you could make a report to your superiors—someone in the federal government, anyone who might care what's happening here to this land."

Longarm sipped his wine. He knew such a course of action would do no good at all. The Western Lumber and Land Combine could not be stopped now, not legally. Their claim to cut this timber could not be withdrawn at this late date. It would be like trying to stop a boulder in midcourse down a hill. "I'll try," he said. "Raise a little hell in Denver, maybe. Speak to my chief, find out who I should contact in Washington. But I sure don't want to get your hopes up. I never saw the like of those clerks and middlemen. Seems like someone should blast away all that red tape, but if that *did* happen, the whole government would collapse." He smiled ruefully. "'Course, maybe that wouldn't be such a bad idea."

"All of us ranchers would appreciate anything you could do. I know it seems like that company is unstoppable—that they can do anything they want in order to bring out that lumber— but there's something about Slade and that henchman of his . . . I can't put my finger on it. It's just that they seem so anxious to get this lumber out *fast*. It's almost as if they were afraid of someone coming and taking it away from them. Of course, it's just a feeling. When you're desperate, you clutch at straws, I guess."

Longarm nodded. "Desmond did mention to me that he was on a tight schedule. I just figured that was normal. The faster they can cut the lumber and ship it out, the lower their expenses'll be, and the more profit for them."

"I suppose," she sighed. "That's what Tanner said, too."

Longarm looked at her levelly, and said in a quiet voice, "Tanner's dead, you know."

"Yes," Terry said. "One of my hands was in Whipsaw picking up supplies, and he heard one of Bat Lawson's men mention it. I was sorry to hear it. Tanner loved this country and had promised me that he would see what he could do."

Longarm decided then not to press any further with inquiries about the deserter. That could wait until tomorrow. He suddenly realized how tired he was. The wine and the heat from the crackling fire had lulled him. He put his glass down and stood up.

"This has been real nice, Terry—the fire, the good wine. Sorry what we talked about couldn't have been a little more pleasant. I'll be looking forward to that ride you mentioned."

She stood up also. "Yes, it's been very nice, Longarm." Her blue eyes gleamed in the firelight. "You do fill a room, you know. That's something I've missed." Juanita appeared in the doorway. "Marshal Long will be retiring now, Juanita," Terry told her. "See to his bedroom. I'll pick up in here."

Juanita nodded.

Longarm said good night and followed the housekeeper from the room.

Chapter 6

An eagle with angry blue eyes was screaming as it plunged at Longarm out of a moonlit sky. Longarm flung up his arm to ward off the raking talons. He felt himself tumbling backward off his horse. Whinnying in fright, the animal plunged away as Longarm twisted slowly in space and began to fall. . . .

He awoke to find himself sitting bolt upright in the large bed, cold sweat standing out over his naked body; he had automatically reached under his pillow for his gun and held it now in front of him, its muzzle probing the darkness of the room. There was an open window beside his bed. No moon hung in the black night sky; the sense of nightmare persisted.

He became aware of angry voices coming from down the hall. Terry Troy and her foreman were arguing heatedly. Terry seemed quite angry. The foreman's heavy voice was alternately wheedling, then demanding. The man did not sound stable. It was an ugly, dangerous confrontation. It must have been this, Longarm realized, that had awakened him.

He left his bed, slipped into a robe Juanita had left for him, and padded on bare feet down the hall. The door to Terry's bedroom was open. He stopped just outside the doorway. In front of an ample fireplace the two of them faced each other. They had already clashed physically. Terry's long nightgown had been ripped completely off and now lay in a shimmering, silken pool at her feet. A livid tracery left by Terry's fingernails extended down the side of the foreman's face. Even as Longarm stood there, the welts appeared to swell and brighten as the blood began to flow. But it was Terry who riveted Longarm's attention. She stood boldly naked before Blodgett, a quirt in one hand, her naked body gleaming from head to toe with perspiration. Hers was a powerful figure, every inch of it as darkly and thoroughly tanned as her face. A lit kerosene lamp stood on a table behind them, shedding a pale light over the scene. So intent were they on each other that they did not appear to be aware of Longarm's presence in the hallway.

"You want *him* too, don't you!" Blodgett cried, his voice thick with rage and jealousy. "You were going to go in to him! I saw you at the dinner table—the way you looked at him!"

"So I looked at him! Why not? Do you think you own me? Because I let you sleep with me, does that make me your property?"

"It should, damn it! It should!"

"Ugh! You make me sick."

"But I—but I *love* you, Terry."

"Is that your excuse, then, for stealing in here like a thief, for attacking me in my bed? You call that love? And besides, Russ, I never told you I loved you. Never! That was all your idea!"

"But why, then? You must have felt *something*!"

"Yes, damn you! Need! I felt need for a man. And that— as best you could—you satisfied, and for that I suppose I should thank you. But that's all I wanted from you. That's all I needed."

"You *used* me!" the man cried, choking now with baffled rage.

"Of course! And you used me. We used each other!"

"A whore!" Blodgett spat, aghast at her words. "That's what you are! That's *all* you are! A whoring slut!"

She stepped toward him and brought the quirt around. It whistled in the small room a split-second before it caught him about the shoulders. He yelped and reached out to grab it from her, but she was too quick for him. Again and again she brought the quirt around, driving him back relentlessly, her eyes shining pleasure, her head thrown back, her breasts upthrust, her nipples erect. Soon she was panting from the exertion as the foreman—his back to the wall now—covered his face with his arms and sank slowly to the floor while the slashing strips of plaited rawhide ripped at him, cutting his arms, his neck, his head.

Only when she was physically exhausted, her fury finally appeased, did she pull back to gaze down at the whimpering man at her feet. In a voice icy with contempt, she said, "You should always speak with respect when addressing your betters, Blodgett. I recommend it as an excellent course to follow in the future. Pack your gear and get off this ranch. Tonight. You may take two horses of your choosing from the remuda. Now get out!"

He pulled himself upright and, leaning on the wall, glared at her like some captive animal still fearful of the lash of his new master. "You . . . owe me a month's wages . . . and that bonus . . . " His voice trailed off hopelessly.

She turned and strode to the strongbox on top of her dresser. Using a key she had secreted in a small jar of what appeared to be face cream, she unlocked the box and lifted the lid. A small Smith & Wesson revolver gleamed on the black velvet cloth that covered the box's contents. She lifted out the gun, reached into one of the compartments, and pulled out a small, heavy leather pouch. Pulling its drawstrings open, she swiftly counted out several gold coins, then turned and flung them on the floor before Blodgett.

It was a regal, cruel gesture. As Russ scrambled about the floor on his hands and knees snatching up the coins, she watched him with amused, flashing eyes, her naked contempt for him filling the room. Once he had retrieved all the coins, Russ scrambled to his feet, looked about for his hat, found it on the floor by her bed, then—head down, like something wild fleeing a fire—he bolted from the room.

He was too anxious to get out to be startled at Longarm's presence in the hallway. As he disappeared down the dark passage, Longarm stepped through the doorway.

"I suppose you saw it all?" Terry asked, standing in the middle of the room, facing him, completely unconscious, it seemed, of her dark, lustrous nakedness or its possible effect on him.

"A couple of wildcats in a potato sack would have been quieter, Terry."

"I caught him in your room, Longarm, with a lantern. He was a little upset to find you in that bed, I am afraid. And back in my bedroom he was not much of a gentleman about it."

"I was able to figure that out."

"I'm tired, Longarm. Very tired. Of course, Russ was right.

I would have visited your room this evening. But perhaps you have seen too much of me already. Sleep now. We have a long ride ahead of us tomorrow."

He nodded. "Good night, Terry."

As he turned to leave, she said, "It would be best if you didn't sleep until you hear Russ ride out."

"And if I were you, I'd keep that Smith & Wesson handy," he suggested.

Longarm returned to his bed and waited. It wasn't too long before the sound of racing hoofs drummed past his window and faded rapidly as the ex-foreman fled through the gate. Longarm tucked the Colt under his pillow and closed his eyes again. The last image before sleep came was of Terry's nakedness. She stood boldly and provocatively before him, her quirt in her hand, a challenge in her blue eyes. . . .

They had been riding since the cool hours just before dawn. Now, close to midday, they rode through a steep-sided canyon and out onto a broad benchland that appeared to have been the scene of some titanic struggle between contending giants. The flat as well as the hillsides looming above it bore the familiar scars of the Western Lumber and Land Combine. Debris covered the ground everywhere. The sawed-off trunks remaining after the cutting looked like the humped, misshapen heads of defeated legions. Skid marks—slick, snaking gashes—wound down the hillsides onto the bench to a deeply rutted road that led back—Longarm had no doubt—to the lumber mill in Whipsaw. The only trees still standing were the few stunted pinyons that had been judged not worth the effort of cutting. Yet even they were not unscathed. The feverish cutting and skidding around them had left the trees with maimed branches and deep slashes in their trunks.

As Terry rode across this ruined landscape beside Longarm, she said nothing to him, content to let its appearance speak for her. Longarm was hesitant to say anything, since all that he had seen here he had seen elsewhere. He was not surprised. It was ugly. It was disturbing. But if this timber was to be cut to provide the country with the railroad ties, fuel, and telegraph poles it needed, this sad devastation had to be the result. There was simply no comfort he could offer Terry.

"You've seen all this before around Whipsaw," Terry said, glancing at Longarm. "I know that. But there's something else you probably haven't seen yet."

They rode until they reached the edge of the bench where they found themselves looking out over a semiarid valley dotted with sagebrush and grama. As Terry pulled up, she pointed without a word down the slope at a tangled mess of debris and mud lodged in a narrow stream bed. A great muddy pool was backed up behind the obstruction. On the other side of what must have been a mud slide, the stream's channel was completely dry. Gaping cracks in the ground radiated out from it to lose themselves in the dry, sage-covered valley floor.

"Look closely at that mud slide in the stream bed," Terry told him.

Longarm looked back down at the great pile of debris and thought he saw, sticking up out of the top of it, pieces of framing, a shingled portion of a roof, and the stones of a chimney. Looking still closer, he saw what remained of posts and poles that had once formed a corral sticking up out of the mass like the quills of a giant porcupine.

"Guess that slide took a house with it," Longarm said. "I see some roof shingles and parts of a corral."

"That was one of our line shacks," Terry replied. "It used to stand ten feet back from where we are now. You see what's happening to this land? A mud slide after a short rain two weeks ago and we lose a line shack and a valuable stream." She pointed to a broad slash cutting the slope behind them. "The slide came down from there, as near as I can figure, then hit this bench and rolled across it with enough force to dump the line shack. Longarm, that was a solid, two-room cabin, a corral, and a small stable. Now add to that the loss of that stream for none of us knows how long, and you'll get some picture of what we're up against."

Longarm nodded soberly.

"Can you see now why we've got to stop them? Do you understand why my cowhands go around shooting up logging camps with flour sacks over their heads?"

"Yes, Terry," Longarm replied. "I understand. I'll do what I can. I told you last night that I would, and I meant it."

She smiled suddenly, her teeth flashing in her dark face.

"Forgive me, Longarm. I know you meant it. But we are desperate, and I want you to know why."

Longarm swung around in his saddle and gazed up at the hills reaching up from the bench. "Are there any timberlands on the other side of this range, where cutting wouldn't do this kind of thing to the valley?"

"Yes, there are. That's where we thought they would be cutting. It wasn't until they began their operation that we realized they were logging this side of the range."

"Well, like I said, I'll see what I can do, as long as you realize I'm not about to promise what I can't be sure I'll be able to deliver."

"That's enough for me, Longarm."

Terry pulled her horse around, apparently satisfied, and led the way back across the bench. As they rode from it into the canyon, Longarm took one last look back at the ravaged landscape and shook his head. Once they were well inside the canyon's cool shadows, Longarm turned to Terry.

"I'm up here, Terry, to find the same man Sheriff Tanner was after—the army scout who deserted. Tanner spotted him in Whipsaw, and I think the deserter was the one who killed Tanner. I want him. I won't be able to do much for you ranchers concerning this logging until I bring that man in. Gus Dodds—one of the loggers—said this jasper left Whipsaw when Tanner spotted him, and might have ridden out to your spread looking for a job. He was a big man, and most of the descriptions I've heard say he has a heavy beard and blue eyes." He smiled at her. "Like yours, I reckon."

"I know the man," she replied. "Tanner was at the Flying T to pick up a horse thief we caught. He told us he'd spotted the deserter and was going to send a wire to Washington when he got back to Silver City. He didn't have much confidence in Washington, though. I remember his saying he'd probably end up going after the man himself. Anyway, as soon as Tanner left with the horse thief, a logger fitting that description you gave showed up looking for work. I didn't connect him with what Tanner told me until you mentioned it just now."

"Did you give him a job?"

"We didn't have anything for him. He drifted north into Digger country then. None of us has seen hide or hair of him since, but then, we haven't been looking. Like you say, though, he's a big man, all right. A bear. And he rode a horse well."

"What was he riding?"

"A grullo.

"That means he could be a long, long ways from these parts by now. Did you tell all this to Tanner?"

"He never returned to the Flying T after he left with that horse thief."

Longarm frowned at that. "So I go north, then—into Digger country, and maybe all the way to Snake River. I want him, Terry."

"I'm sure you'll get him, Longarm."

They were halfway back to the Flying T when Longarm felt the sudden chill of an impending storm. He glanced to the west. A great, dark cloud, looking like the wing of some enormous bird, was sweeping toward them from the mountains. The smell of rain was in the air. Dust devils whipped sand into his eyes and he lifted his bandanna to cover his mouth and nostrils. Lightning flickered in the bowels of the cloud. The dim muttering of thunder rolled toward them, echoing ominously in the high, rocky land through which they were riding.

Terry looked at Longarm and smiled. It was not a nervous smile. She seemed genuinely pleased—and excited—at the prospect of a storm. "We still have time before it reaches us, Longarm. I know a place where we can hole up until it's past."

"Is it near here? We don't have as much time as you might think."

"I know this country, Longarm. Besides, we were going there anyway. The view is lovely. I wanted you to see it." A sudden gust of wind made her reach up and grab the brim of her hat to keep it from flying off. "It's my favorite spot. I'm sure you'll be very impressed."

"Lead the way," Longarm told her, aware that her excitement had caught him up as well.

Terry followed a winding trail, quite steep in spots, that took them presently up onto a high bluff overlooking a vast desert valley that stretched all the way to distant peaks, dim ramparts shrouded now by the building storm. Keeping just ahead of him, she rode the full length of the bluff until she came to a boulder larger than that fancy hotel in Whipsaw, and kept on until she was in under the great rock. It seemed to be balanced precariously in the center of a large, smooth dish worn out of the cap rock.

There was a narrow trail that took them under the boulder and out the other side. Terry followed it as it wound still higher. The horses were somewhat skittish on the steep trail. At last they emerged onto a smooth rock shelf only slightly bigger than her parlor. A surprisingly large pinyon grew out of a fissure at the rear of the ledge, its gnarled, misshapen branches offering the only available shelter.

Dismounting under the tree, they tied their horses securely to it. She led Longarm to the edge of the ledge, where they stood together silently and gazed out over the desert valley, watching the approaching storm. The thunder was louder and more powerful here, and seemed to strike at the foundations of the bluff itself. The lightning lit the underside of the clouds almost continuously now, as if a series of powder kegs were being set off deep within them. Longarm could not help noticing Terry's reaction. She was watching the storm eagerly, with an excitement so intense that she seemed almost to be a part of it.

She saw the look in his eyes and laughed. "Yes, I love it," she said. "It's like we're the only ones left in the world, watching God put on one of his displays for us. To warn us, perhaps. Do you wonder, now, why this is my favorite spot?" Her eyes grew suddenly fierce. "You are the only one I have ever brought to this ledge. The only one. Do you understand that, Longarm?"

"Reckon I do. This is some spot. I can see why you'd like to keep it just for yourself."

"It's where I come to sort things out," she said. "Where I come to lie in the sun and drink in that warmth, that fabulous warmth that pours out of the sun—that pours over all of me, every bit. I can feel it drugging me, loving me, Longarm, caressing me. Do you understand what I mean?"

"You don't have to keep asking that. You speak plain enough."

"But have you ever let the sun caress you, as I have?"

Longarm shook his head. "No, I guess I ain't, Terry. I've been too busy lately to lie down in the sun."

She smiled and shook her head. "You don't understand," she said, stepping back. "You don't understand at all—but you're going to."

To his astonishment and growing wonder, she unbuckled her gunbelt, then peeled down her Levi's.

"You, too, Longarm," she said. "I want you to feel that warmth with me."

Longarm felt slightly ridiculous. There was a storm coming, even though at that moment the afternoon sun was still blazing down. Terry unbuttoned her shirt and flung it aside. She was wearing longjohns underneath her outer clothes, and promptly proceeded to unbutton them, her fingers moving swiftly all the way down the front. Kicking off her riding boots, she stepped out of the longjohns and stood before him naked.

He was having trouble with his shirt. His fingers were all thumbs, it seemed. There was a strangely tight feeling in his throat. Terry moved swiftly against him, her fingers rapidly unbuttoning his shirt. She peeled it back off his shoulders. Thunder, much nearer by this time, cracked like a giant bullwhip overhead. The ledge seemed to shudder beneath his boots. Terry paid no heed to it as she deftly unbuckled Longarm's gunbelt, then peeled his Levi's down his thighs.

"Your boots," she said softly. "Step out of them."

He complied quickly, astonished at how easily he was able to kick them off. It was the incentive, he realized, smiling to himself.

She stayed close until her help was no longer needed. Then she stepped back to survey Longarm. Like Adam and Eve before the serpent's blandishments, they faced each other's nakedness without blushing.

"Men don't often see a woman naked, do they, Longarm?" she asked. "Women are supposed to keep themselves wrapped in armor, it seems. That must be why men know so little about a woman's body. It's such a bore, Longarm, to be constantly pawed over by men who know so little about how to please a woman." She frowned angrily. "We are only supposed to be compliant receptacles into which you men pour your seed, then roll over and sleep with your mouths open."

"I reckon when you put it that way, Terry, it doesn't hardly sound very pleasureful."

A shattering crash of thunder shook the ledge soundly this time. Terry's eyes grew wide with sudden exultation. She lifted her arms up to the darkening sky and flung her head back. A bolt of lightning seared the sky over their heads and turned her figure momentarily blue. Longarm felt the hair on the back of his neck stand up a fraction of a second before another thunderclap almost flung him to the ground.

Terry was laughing wildly now as a sudden fierce wind tugged at them. The wind brought with it a damp, musty smell that reminded Longarm of a root cellar. Another bolt of lightning flashed above them. Through the deafening crash of thunder that followed, she called out to him: "Save me, Longarm! Protect me!"

"Get dressed!" he told her. "We've got to get off this damned ledge!"

"No!"

"You heard me!" he cried, reaching for his discarded clothes.

"I said no!" Terry shouted. Removing her six-gun from its holster on the ground, she cocked it and fired at Longarm—point-blank. The hammer came down on an empty chamber. She cocked it a second time. "There's only one round in this Colt," she cried as the wind wildly tugged at her hair. "It wasn't in that last chamber. Do you want me to try again?"

"Never mind!" Longarm laughed, the madness in her suddenly overtaking him as well.

"Then *cover* me, Longarm! Shield me! Keep your body between me and the storm."

The wind gusted wildly and the first faint drops of rain began to sting his naked shoulders. He stepped toward her, took the revolver from her, then dropped to one knee, pulling her down beside him. She stretched out on her back like a large cat. Longarm bent close to kiss her. She reached up, flinging an arm around his neck, and drew his mouth down hard upon her lips. Lightning played about them. A chill wind, laden with stinging drops of rain, swept over his naked body. He moved to cover her. Her tongue probed deeply into his mouth and then she fastened her teeth firmly but gently about his upper lip and began to tease it.

Another series of lightning bolts crackled in the sky above them. An almost continuous roar of shattering thunderclaps split the air. But Longarm no longer cared. There was another storm building beneath him—and within him.

Terry pulled her lips away and with surprising ease rolled him onto his side, her hand thrusting boldly, insistently, between his thighs. She found that he was ready for her, and grasped him with a strength that almost made him cry out, then buried her face in the thick hair on his chest, and began nibbling on one of his nipples. He was astonished at the effect this two-pronged attack had on him. With a deep, guttural mutter of delight, he grabbed her firm buttocks and pulled her hard against him. As lightning turned her tanned body an unearthly blue, he rolled over onto her, his knees slamming down hard on the wet rock surface.

For a moment he thought he would need something to place under her, but she thrust her thighs up with an angry urgency, and he felt the tip of his erection probing the entrance to her womb. She cried out and thrust up still higher, then wrapped both legs about his waist. He plunged deeply into her and gasped in pleasure. The rain was pounding down on them both now, and rivulets of water were pouring off his shoulders onto her. The sound of their entangled bodies slapping together filled Longarm's universe. The mindless rhythm of his thrusting caused him to lose all sense of time, while the difficulty of gaining a secure purchase with his knees kept him hovering, with a kind of maddened frustration, on the edge of his orgasm. She began turning her head rapidly from side to side, her eyes shut tight, swearing in a steady stream with a fluency that astonished him. And this was what did it for him. With a grim, wild plunge he drove into her, driving her buttocks down hard on the rock, grinding her into it. The lightning flashed, the thunder muttered and crashed over them, and the rain poured down with sudden intensity.

He felt her shudder convulsively under him. She let out a piercing scream that was more like a wail of terror. It sent shock waves of desire through him and he began to come, pulsing completely out of control. Constantly buffeted now by the wind and the rain, they clung together on the wet, slippery rock, entwined, as progressively more violent climaxes convulsed them. They grew fiercely into each other, and became one flesh, one twisting, moaning entity. . . .

Lying on his side, his head propped on his palm, he looked at her. Her long hair, soaking wet and stringy, hung over her face, partially obscuring her left eye. She smiled. The rain continued to pelt down with increasing force, and the almost continuous thunder made speech nearly impossible. She reached over and down as she moved closer. To his surprise, he found that he was ready again. She flung her hair back off her face and crawled over onto him.

"Now I'll cover you," she said into his ear, nibbling it for a moment.

She lay full length upon him, her legs closed tightly about his erection. An awesome peal of thunder deafened Longarm. She pressed her mouth hard down against his, while her tongue began probing with an insistent, delicious wantonness that caused him to twist involuntarily under her. With a sudden, delighted laugh, she leaned swiftly back, sat up, and with a violence that he was afraid would hurt her, drove herself down onto his erection. Gasping with pleasure, she began to pound on his chest—as almost continuous strokes of lightning played about them with a crackling intensity that seemed to singe the very air.

She was like some wanton female warrior, some Amazon or Valkyrie, and she rode him as if he were a beast, twisting and plunging, first forward, then sideways, gyrating around and around. She began to come repeatedly. Each time she did, she let out a cry that was like a sob. At last he found he could not keep himself from climaxing any longer. She felt his pulsating, thrusting orgasm and clung to him then, tightening her muscles about his shaft in a fierce, sobbing effort to keep him erect.

It worked. Laughing exultantly, she began to move once more—steadily, slowly this time. His shaft probed so deeply at times that its tip seemed to him to be on fire. Still thrusting gently, she leaned away suddenly, and flung her head back, drinking in the still pounding rain, allowing the thunder and the lightning to become a part of her frenzy. Longarm began to wonder if it would ever end—if, perhaps, they had stumbled into some hellish world where desire was never satisfied, where coupling became an end in itself, the only reality. . . .

He found himself coming alive again, lifting to meet her

every thrust. Suddenly he reached up to grab her thighs. He wanted her under him, to drive upon her, to plunge deeply into her as, within him, a door opened that had never opened before.

"Down!" he cried above the howling storm. "Down! I want you under me!"

"Of course!" she cried, laughing, reaching down toward him.

A surging, shattering peal of thunder rent the air. Multiple forks of lightning turned the rain-filled gloom unnaturally bright. Still riding him, Terry's nakedness gleamed in the cold, flickering light. Thunder pounded again and again—as if some maddened smith were using the ledge for his anvil. She screamed. He paid no attention as he rolled her over, his hand firmly in the small of her back, his erection still deep within her.

On top of her again, he buried his face in the wet fullness of her breast. A warm, thick wetness smeared his cheek even as the rain washed it away. But its flow persisted, its salty, metallic sweetness invading his probing lips. He pulled back with a cry. Continuous lightning flickered like a serpent's tongue about them. He caught sight of a gaping hole between her breasts. He flung himself away from her and looked down to see her blue eyes wide, unblinking in the rain, the full, ripe slash of her mouth slack now, empty of desire at last.

A movement near the tree caught his eye. He dove to the hard surface of the ledge, scrambling for his holster where he had placed it under his coat. A shot, this time not covered by the roar of thunder, rang out from the tree. Longarm felt the slug whine off the surface of the ledge just in front of him. Tiny, cutting shards of stone flew up into his face. He drew the Colt and rolled swiftly to one side. Lightning gave him another glimpse, through the sheets of rain, of the man crouched beside the two plunging horses.

Blodgett! Russ Blodgett! Longarm squeezed off a shot and saw the man stumble back. Then darkness and a sweeping, obliterating curtain of rain swept across the ledge. Longarm waited for the next lightning flash. When it came he saw no sign of Blodgett, but only the wide-eyed, plunging horses, maddened now by the storm and the shooting so close by. As Longarm started to get up, he saw one of the horses break suddenly loose. A shattering peal of thunder exploded just above his head. He heard the plunging hooves of the crazed animal as it charged blindly across the ledge toward him. When a lightning stroke revealed the animal almost on him, its eyes bulging, Longarm flung himself out of the way.

But he was unable to clear the horse. One driving hoof slammed into his chest, smashing him down on the rock ledge as the great, wet beast passed over him. Barely conscious from the force with which his head had struck the ledge, he heard the horse's sudden whinnying terror as it plunged off the ledge into the rain-filled void.

He shook his head and tried to get up. It was no use. The storm's fury made it impossible for him to concentrate. He thought of Terry, beside him on the ledge, and Blodgett, gone by this time, and groaned in frustration. He managed to roll over onto his face. The rain pounded down on him. The lightning and thunder rocked him, then lulled him. The beat of the lashing rain faded and he lost consciousness.

He awoke with the warmth of the sun on his naked body. Rolling slowly over, he opened his eyes. The sun was low on the western horizon, gleaming out of a clear, pale sky. The dark stormcloud was sweeping away over the land, smoky tendrils of rain beating the ground before it. Thunder muttered softly, Lightning still winked. But for Longarm and Terry, the storm had passed.

Slowly Longarm got to his feet, his eyes avoiding Terry's dark, sadly shrunken body. He felt his chest where the horse's hoof had struck him, and took a deep breath. There was an ache, but no stabbing pain, and he was satisfied that the horse had not stove in one of his ribs. But his head pounded. Fingering the back of it, he withstood a sharp needle of pain and felt a sticky smear of coagulating blood where his scalp had been lacerated. From the way the pain rocked behind his eyes, he realized he probably had a slight concussion.

With great care, much like a man suffering through the granddaddy of all hangovers, he dressed himself in his still-wet clothes, finding it a difficult, time-consuming task to pull on first his sodden longjohns, and over them, the skintight Levi's. Fully dressed at last, he turned to the grisly business of dressing the dead woman. The sun was setting when he stood up at last, finished. It was her horse that had bolted, leaving him the Morgan. From his bedroll tucked behind the cantle, he took out his slicker and wrapped her in it, then flung her over the pommel. The trip back down the narrow trail was an unpleasant, dangerous business that was made even more so by his unsteady vision, the gathering darkness, and the constantly shifting weight of Terry's body.

Once he reached the bluff beyond the huge boulder, he relaxed a bit, feeling grimly pleased not only to have negotiated the narrow trail safely, but also at the growing evidence that he had winged Blodgett severely. From the pink glow still remaining in the sky, he could clearly see dried puddles of blood. They grew larger with each yard or two. He was able to follow the bloody spoor all the way down to the desert floor.

Then he turned his horse back toward the Flying T. He would be back for Blodgett soon enough. He would not need a warrant, and he wanted the man to resist.

It was a good deal later when he rode into the Flying T spread. Butts, holding a lantern high, stepped out of the bunkhouse and peered up at him through the darkness.

"Hello, the bunkhouse!" Longarm called.

"It's the marshal!" Butts called to those behind him in the bunkhouse.

Dismounting, Longarm led the Morgan toward Butts. "Take my horse," he told the man.

He lifted the burden off his pommel, turned with it in his arms, and started toward the house. Behind him, he heard Butts gasp. Turning his head, Longarm spoke coldly to him. "Yes, this is Miss Troy. Russ Blodgett shot her. She's dead. Now do as I told you, Butts. Take care of that horse of mine. I'll be needing it tomorrow, early."

The housekeeper was waiting in the parlor for him when he entered. She must have seen him from one of the windows as he approached the house. Her reaction did not surprise Longarm. She simply turned her head away for a moment as he put his burden down on the sofa, then bent to fold the yellow slicker back gently. Carla entered the room with Wally and began to cry softly. Wally controlled his feelings admirably while Longarm gave him a tactfully expurgated account of

Terry's death. Only when Longarm had finished and the weeping Carla was leading him back to his room did Longarm hear—dimly—the grief that wrenched itself from the young man's heart.

The voices of angry men came to him then. He walked out onto the porch to speak to the unhappy crowd of Flying T hands. Longarm quieted them and told them what he had told Wally. None of the hands, it seemed, had any difficulty at all in believing the ex-foreman capable of such a deed.

"We'll go after him with you, Longarm," someone cried, his voice hoarse with rage.

"A rope'd be too good for him," another infuriated hand called out.

A sullen roar of agreement greeted that sentiment. Longarm held up his hand. "I'll handle it. I'm the law here. He won't get away, I promise you that. You've got a spread to run for Wally Troy. He's still hurt bad, and he'll need you. I'll handle Russ Blodgett."

With vague, futile threats and unhappy mutterings, the men filed away into the darkness, back to their quarters. Longarm went back inside. The housekeeper saw the gaunt, drained look on his face, stepped quickly closer, and kept him from collapsing to the floor. As her big arms held him, she inspected the back of his head and made a soft, sympathetic sound. In his bedroom she gently washed the wound clean, using warm water and that harsh soap he'd used in his bath, then bound a bandage around it after soothing it with a greasy, evil-smelling dressing.

He had been lying face down on the bed while she worked. Before she finished her task completely, Longarm began to drift off to sleep. Dimly, he felt her undress him and pull the sheets up gently over his long, thoroughly exhausted frame.

As Longarm rode back to the bluff the next morning, he found it difficult to shake the sense of nightmare that still clung to him. The storm and the surging, elemental passion that had grown along with it, the sight of Terry's suddenly stilled body and the crazed horse plunging through the rain toward him, all combined to fill him with an uneasy sense that none of it had really happened.

Then he saw the splayed, broken body of the horse among the rocks at the foot of the bluff. Humped, waddling buzzards were already tearing at the fly-covered carcass. He rode on past it and came finally to Blodgett's sign. The blood was barely visible now—a faint, rust-colored stain on the surfaces of a few rocks. Blodgett had taken two horses, as Terry had suggested. It soon became obvious that he was keeping the second horse with him. This would make it much easier for Longarm to track him. It would not make it easier, Longarm mused, for him to overtake Blodgett. The Morgan still had reserves of speed and endurance, but she had been ridden hard the day before. Aware of this, Longarm had nursed her along since he had left the Flying T.

Still, Russ Blodgett was wounded. Longarm hoped grimly that his slug was still lodged in the man's carcass.

Along about midday, Longarm found Blodgett's trail leading into higher, wilder country. As Longarm rode into a canyon, he realized Blodgett was no longer intent on making distance. He wanted only a place to go to ground, and, more than likely, a vantage point from which he could command the trail with his rifle. The man was probably holed up at that moment, waiting for Longarm.

Longarm forded the muddy stream that cut through the canyon, found a shaded overhang of rock face, and dismounted. Hobbling the Morgan in a lush growth of grama, he took his Winchester from its saddle scabbard and began to climb. Better than halfway up the side of the canyon, he found a man-sized cleft in the canyon wall. Straddling it, he looked through it and spotted a trail that could take him around, well behind the rim of the canyon. It was treacherous going, but when he reached a grassy bench well above the canyon floor, he found Blodgett's two horses quietly cropping the grass. Beyond them, a game trail led to what appeared to be the highest point on the canyon wall.

Longarm did not use the trail. He kept to the rocks until he found his progress barred by a steep, bald, rounded upthrust of sandstone. The incline was less than forty-five degrees; he could make it if he ran full-tilt. He removed his spurs and his boots. Levering a fresh cartridge into the Winchester's chamber, he raced up the steep rock face and burst onto a sandy

ledge. Russ Blodgett was lying facedown on the far side of
it, less than twenty feet away. He was turning swiftly to face
Longarm, but his back was still to him, his rifle barrel still
hanging out over the ledge, waiting for a target on the canyon
floor below. Before Blodgett could haul the rifle around, Longarm fired.

Nothing happened. The rifle had misfired. As Longarm levered swiftly a second time, he realized that the magazine was
jammed solidly. So eager was Blodgett, however, that as he
swung his rifle around, the barrel struck a rocky projection.
The force of it ripped the stock out of his hand. He grabbed
frantically for it, but the rifle dropped out of sight.

By then, Longarm's momentum had carried him close
enough to Blodgett to enable him to reach down and haul the
man to his feet before he could grab for his six-gun. Blodgett
cried out in pain. Longarm saw the sodden, bloody pants leg.
His round had caught the man in the thigh above the knee.
Eyes wild, panting with fear and pain, Blodgett clawed at
Longarm's coat to gain his balance.

"Please!" he cried. "For God's sake, Longarm! Take me
back for a trial! Please! I need a doctor!"

Longarm took the man's revolver from its holster and
tossed it off the ledge. Then he released Blodgett and let the
man crumple to the ground.

"A trial," Longarm said, coldly and implacably. "You'd love
that, wouldn't you? Your lips would be smacking as you told
the jury what you saw on that ledge. Hell! You'd probably get
off, the way you'd tell it!"

"No! No! I wouldn't say a word about that! You have my
promise, Longarm. My solemn oath!"

Longarm took a deep breath. The man before him was help-
less and disarmed. Longarm would have to take him in. There
would be a trial. The lawman considered what that would
mean and grew cold at the prospect. Then he shrugged and
turned away to retrieve his Winchester. He had dropped it as
soon as he had realized it was useless to him.

As he bent to pick it up, he heard Blodgett's heavy, la-
bored breathing as the man bore down on him from behind.
Dropping to one knee and picking up the rifle—barrel first—
Longarm swung it around in a complete arch as if he were

swinging a bat. The rifle's heavy stock caught Blodgett flush in the ribs and sent him reeling back.

The man stumbled, found himself on the rim of the ledge, and tried to catch himself. His good foot stepped into space. Uttering a cry of dismay, he pitched forward off the ledge. For a moment he managed to catch hold of a small pine sapling growing on the edge, but as soon as his full weight tugged on it, the sapling pulled free of the sandy soil. Blodgett tried to grab for a narrow crack in the ledge, but missed. His hands still clawing frantically, he disappeared from sight, screaming.

The scream ended too abruptly. Longarm walked to the edge and looked over. Blodgett's fall had been broken by a bristlecone pine growing out of the side of the canyon wall. He lay on his back on a narrow sandstone ledge not more than twenty feet below. The man was still conscious, though he seemed unable to move. His mouth opened, but all that came out was a hoarse, barely audible whisper. Longarm looked around until he saw a way down to the ledge. He would have given a lot at that moment for a pair of Apache moccasins. His unshod feet were painfully sore by this time. With a weary shrug, he dropped his rifle and worked his way down the steep face of the canyon wall until he was crouched beside Blodgett, peering into the man's slack face.

"I'm hurt bad," Blodgett whimpered softly. "Real bad. I hurt my back when I hit that tree! I can't move a muscle! You got to help me!"

"No, I ain't. There ain't any way I can get you off this ledge."

A shadow passed over them both. And then another shadow. Longarm glanced up. Buzzards, two of them, were circling over them, already dropping lower with each pass.

"I'm going to have to leave you here," Longarm said.

"You can't!"

"Yes, Blodgett, I can."

"Then *shoot* me, damn you! For God's sake, Longarm! Don't leave me for them buzzards!"

Longarm knew what Blodgett was thinking. The fellow couldn't move a muscle. Vultures do not smell a carcass rotting in the sun. They do not have any sixth sense concerning death. What they watch for while coasting high in the desert sky is a body lying perfectly still—unnaturally still. When they spot such a body, they drop closer. After a few passes, during which there is still no movement, they land beside the still body and waddle close.

At such a moment Blodgett would try to scream in an effort to frighten them away. For a while, perhaps, he would be able to drive the foul birds back. But only for a while. Paralyzed, there would be nothing he could do, no movement he could make to stop them as the two buzzards roosted on him. Black wings would shut out the sun and pairs of cold eyes would peer into his. Abruptly, the crooked yellow beaks and red necks crawling with lice would snap forward. They would begin to rip and tear. . . .

Longarm straightened up, then stepped off the ledge and began to climb back. Behind him, Blodgett's frantic, barely audible pleas faded. As Longarm reached the ledge, he glanced skyward. Another buzzard had joined the first two.

Chapter 7

Two days later Longarm found himself at midday taking refuge in the shadows of a narrow canyon. As he had learned from Wally before setting out, they were supposed to be coming to the end of the dry season, but this one was hanging on. That morning the air had been so dry that Longarm could barely shave. The water and soap had dried on his face even as he had reached for his straight razor. The day before, he had seen a cloud releasing rain high above the basin. Halfway between cloud and earth, the falling water had evaporated. Longarm saw curtains of blue rain dangling out of reach in the sky while the parched land beneath panted for the needed moisture. At that moment Longarm had recalled Vail's scathing description of this high desert land: *a godforsaken patch of alkali basins and black rock populated by bush Indians and a few damn fool settlers.*

Longarm pulled up. He had come at last to what he had been searching for. Water. He dismounted and took both of his canteens to the canyon wall. Water was seeping out between two horizontal formations, through a crack that looked no wider than a newspaper. Longarm had spotted it by the dark stain beneath it and by the hanging garden of orchids, monkey-flower, and maidenhair fern that fed on the steady trickle of moisture. Fortunately, even after these thirsty plants drank their fill, there was still enough water left to form a small water hole at the base of the canyon wall.

He filled his canteens while the local gnat population fought him for every drop. To keep them out of the canteens, he had to place his bandanna over the openings as he filled them. Infuriated, the miserable little bastards attacked his eyes, drawn irresistibly by the liquid shine of his eyeballs.

Longarm drank his fill, emptying one of the canteens, then filled it again. Returning to the Morgan with his hat filled with water, he gave the horse what it needed, then mounted up, the damp hat a welcome relief as he pulled it down snugly.

Once out of the canyon, he turned north again and began climbing into the same range that enclosed Whipsaw twenty miles or so south. Once into the foothills, he caught sight of a few cottonwood following the banks of a cracked, dry river bed. The shade of the trees was soothing. Longarm kept going, climbing steadily. He crossed a ridge and found himself suddenly entering a broad valley, both sides of which were clothed in juniper and pinyon. The air was heavy with the smell of pine resin, a smell Longarm had come to associate with these high, wooded hillsides.

Shots. Distant. But shots, he had no doubt. He pulled up. The Morgan blew through her nostrils and jingled her bit. Longarm patted the side of her neck softly. Then he listened intently. Nothing. A few gray desert sparrows flew from one tree to another, then seemed to wait with Longarm. A wood dove called mournfully in the distance.

The shots had come from off to his left. Longarm guided the Morgan in that direction, and after a quarter of an hour, he came to a small mountain stream. He pulled up and let the horse drink her fill, then pushed on, following the stream.

Coming around a bend, he found himself confronted by two loggers with rifles. Beyond them, Longarm saw a small campsite consisting of two large tents, three fire pits, and a rope corral with good horseflesh inside. He recognized Fitz standing in the entrance to the largest tent. Longarm pulled up and waited. Fitz called out something to the two loggers. They lowered their rifles.

Longarm rode into the campsite and dismounted. Fitz walked over. "Well, now," he said. "Fancy meetin' the likes of you up here!"

"Hello, Fitz. How are you?"

"Just fine, me bucko, just fine."

"I thought I heard shots."

"You did that."

"Game?"

The logger winked meaningfully. "You might say that, in a manner of speaking."

"Fitz, let's have it plain."

"Relax, Marshal. No need for you to worry about a thing. We handled it perfect. We kept our asses down and waited for the damned heathen to pull out. We were outnumbered, you see."

"Heathen?" Longarm echoed.

"Diggers. They don't want us here, you know. Something about the pine seeds they harvest from the valley. It's too bad, I guess, but I have a job to do. Anyway, the only casualty is one of my men. When he tried to bring up his rifle to fire on the leader, an arrow pinned the poor fellow's arm to a pine. That sort of took the heart out of my boys."

"They just cleared out? No threats? No palaver?"

"That's the way it was, Marshal."

"You'd better get back to Whipsaw—now. That was probably just a warning. The next time your men might not be so lucky."

"You call getting an Indian's arrow through your forearm lucky?"

"Have you got any idea, old son, where else that damned arrow could have gone? Like up the man's ass?"

Fitz frowned. "I see your point. "

"What are you doing up here? You're a long way from Whipsaw."

"Whipsaw is where the railroad and the sawmill are. This is where the lumber is. We'll be getting to it soon. I been scouting the area, and I figure we could put a pretty big camp right here and use the river on the other side of that pass to carry the logs into Whipsaw."

"You're going to log this entire range—use all that river?"

"That's how we're supposed to do it, Marshal." He smiled. He was an honest Irishman whom Longarm found he could not dislike.

Longarm shook his head and looked about him. This entire valley was like a miracle after his day and a half in the desert. A high, clean miracle. The pinyon and juniper stands appeared taller and more lush here. Cottonwood and aspen were mixed in with the pine. On the ridges, crowding the rimrock, he saw giant cottonwood.

He looked back at Fitz. "I still think you ought to get on back to Whipsaw, Fitz. And let me find the Indians and warn them."

"Well now, Marshal, that sounds like a fine idea. And I'm bettin' that Mr. Desmond and Mr. Lawson would be happy to know you was sticking your neck out for them."

"I just don't want to see the army in here herding the Diggers back onto their reservation," Longarm explained. "And if they keep harassing this operation, I imagine that's what'll happen. I guess I'm thinking of the Indians as much as I'm thinking of the Western Lumber and Land Combine."

"All right, then," Fitz said. "We'll move out this afternoon. I seen enough here. It's good quality timber, better than that scrub we been logging on the ridges around Whipsaw. You tell them Indians—if they *let* you—that we'll be back in less than a month and we'll stand for no deviltry."

Longarm swung up into his saddle and looked down at the foreman. "You got any idea which way the Diggers went?"

"They came out of nowhere like bloody little pixies and disappeared the same way," Fitz told him. "Maybe your coming scared them off. They're pesky, silent little savages, and that's a fact. I'm thinking of my own folk fighting the British and can't help but sympathize—but I've a job to do. You understand that, Longarm."

The lawman nodded. "I understand, Fitz. I've got a job to do as well."

Longarm pulled his mount around and prodded it toward the stream. Following the stream out of the camp, he kept with it until he had passed through a small canyon at the other end of the valley. The stream became faster and shallower, the ground rockier. Great boulders and sharp pinnacles of rock barred his way at times. He worked the horse carefully around these obstructions and kept climbing, reaching at last a long bench dotted with sagebrush and with thin stands of grama holding the sandy soil in place. Beyond the benchland rose abrupt slopes clothed with pine and juniper, but not as thickly as the valley through which he had just passed.

From what Wally had told him, he was deep in Digger country. This jasper, Shortslef, was supposed to have married an Indian. He would have no difficulty, then, in communicating and perhaps living for a while with the Diggers. If he was not with them, they would know which way he had gone after leaving them—not that they would tell him anything, he realized somewhat ruefully. And if the son of a bitch was not here with these Indians, he was more than likely well north of here in Snake River country on the Cheyenne reservation, safely hidden out with his wife's people.

Snake River country. That was high, lush land—considerably more hospitable than this basin country. Longarm found himself hoping he did not find Shortslef with the Diggers. He would not mind shaking this troubled land, and he was in no hurry to return to Denver and its smells. . . .

His thoughts were broken off by something he saw out of the corner of his eye. A small, dark figure had gone from one large sage bush to another. Dangling from its skinny, gleaming arm was a long black bow. Longarm took a deep breath, talked softly to his horse, and kept riding. He was almost to the end of the bench and could see the slope ahead of him leading into a narrow, winding valley thick with juniper.

By this time he could feel the eyes at his back. The small of his back began to crawl. Another swift movement, on his left this time, as silent as thought. They were keeping up with him on foot, making not a sound and moving only when they could be sure of cover. He kept his back straight. *Hell, might as well give them a good target,* he thought. The horse dipped down the slope. Longarm angled the horse carefully, looking neither to the right nor the left, intent on guiding his horse down the slope.

He reached a narrow trail and was soon well into the valley, with the trees crowding close upon him. A meadow spread out ahead. By this time he was sure the timber was teeming with small, nearly naked Indians, all of them keeping pace with him. Still, they had not yet loosed any arrows at him. That was a good sign.

The horse was almost to the meadow. As if that were the signal, the Indians left their cover along the trail and appeared from the deep grass just before him. He pulled up quickly as their naked bodies pressed close upon the horse, their impassive faces turned up to his, their eyes bright in their dark, wrinkled faces. There were no smiles, only the incredible silence broken occasionally by the clack of their bows. So close together were they that as they held their bows up, they knocked against their neighbor's.

One of them took the bridle and led Longarm and his horse onto the meadow. The Indians kept pace, still as silent as before. The only sounds were those of the horse's passage across the thick grama and the rustling of their bare legs brushing through it. They were—taken as a whole—the most wretched-looking creatures Longarm had ever seen. They looked even worse than those four Indians he had helped in Silver City. Many of them wore capes made of strips of rabbit skin, twisted and dried, and then tied together with strings and drawn around the neck by a cord. The capes extended to just below their hips and didn't appear to give much protection to the body, since they wore no leggings or moccasins. The men all cut their hair square in front, but for the most part it hung down in greasy streamers at the temples.

The meadow dipped, revealing a campground ahead, situated in the bend of a shallow stream. There were about ten wickiups, some conical, others domed, with a hole in the top of each for a smoke vent. They had no look of permanence about them, no sense at all that they could offer any real protection from the elements. As he rode closer, he saw that the pole frames were covered with bark and dried brush. In a few cases, mangy, matted army blankets served. Longarm had seen collapsed and abandoned sod houses that looked more habitable. The women standing in front of their wickiups, some with children clinging to their breasts, wore nothing above the waist. Their hair was filthily matted and unkempt and seemed to be growing in all directions.

Diggers. Yes, the name was apt.

When he reached the outskirts of the encampment, the Indian who had hold of Longarm's horse released the bridle and, with astonishing suddenness, trotted through the camp and plunged across the creek. Longarm watched him and was surprised to see—on a slight rise overlooking the stream on the other side, partially obscured by a stand of pinyon—what appeared to be an army tent. The Indian hurried up the slope and came to a halt in front of it.

A tall woman stepped out of the tent. The two appeared to have no difficulty conversing with each other. At last the Indian left the woman and hurried back across the stream. When he stopped in front of Longarm, he spoke in good English.

"Miss Tate say you are not to worry and she will speak to you at her tent when she has made herself ready." He peered intently at Longarm, the ghost of a smile in his black eyes. "And I say you not to worry, Marshal. Do you know my face?"

Longarm looked more closely at the Indian. The features were only vaguely familiar, but they *were* familiar.

"In Silver City," the Indian said. "You come in and sit down at the table. We have ropes on our necks and you take out your gun and free us. Yes! You remember now?"

Longarm still didn't recognize the face, but when he recalled the smoky interior of that saloon and the ring of drink-sodden faces lusting after blood, he did not wonder that the faces of those four Indians standing on the tables had failed to stay in his mind.

"Yes," Longarm said, "I remember. Where are the others?"

Immediately three Indians, grinning from ear to ear, stepped forward. Looking about him now, Longarm saw, if not outright pleasure, certainly an absence of ferocity. He was, it seemed, quite welcome.

Longarm dismounted. Admiring hands played over the Morgan's coat. A sharp command came from the Indian who had addressed Longarm, and a woman came forward and led the horse away to a pasture.

"I need the saddle and the rest of my gear," Longarm told the Indian.

The Indian nodded and said something to the squaw. She answered him without looking back, and continued to lead the Morgan away. She was heading toward the stream. Longarm relaxed, and looking up, saw the woman emerge from her tent. He started toward her. The Indians stepped aside for him and he negotiated the stream with a couple of quick strides.

Mounting the bank on the other side, he found himself as fascinated by the woman's tent and accessories as by the woman herself. Her wall tent was at least twelve feet high at the center peak, enclosing a living area the size of a good-sized living room. What looked like a rubber bathtub propped on telescoping legs peeked out from the rear of the tent, and farther back, tucked for modesty's sake behind a canvas screen, he saw what he recognized as a toilet commode. Just in front of the tent—on the front lawn, as it were—there was a scattering of folding camp chairs. Among them was a collapsible table of considerable size, upon which were piled writing materials, notebooks, and several bulky volumes.

The woman who stood regally amidst all this was at least as tall as Longarm. She was wearing a pith helmet, a tan hunting jacket—open casually to reveal a high-necked silk blouse—jodhpurs, and high English riding boots. She was blonde, her hair worn in a tight bun at the nape of her neck. Her forehead was high, her eyes hazel under clean-lined brows. Her light eyebrows had been bleached almost into invisibility. Her light chin was cleft and angular, her nose patrician, and nothing in her gaze at that moment gave Longarm any encouragement. She appeared more than ready, in fact, to do battle with him.

"You're the marshal from Whipsaw, I understand. I can't understand why Wanowi was so pleased at your arrival here. What is it you want? State your business and then be so kind as to leave!"

Longarm smiled. It did nothing to clear the air. She was adamant, her eyes cold and hostile. Longarm felt exasperation building in him and cleared his throat. Then he said, "Wanowi is a mite pleased to see me because I saved his life in Silver City. Him and three of his friends. I am not the marshal of Whipsaw. I am Deputy U.S. Marshal Custis Long and I am tracking a renegade army scout by the name of Ned Shortslef, who is not using that name, most likely, and was reported heading this way." Longarm felt his anger taking charge of his tongue. "Town marshals work for local townships and such. Deputy U.S. marshals work for the federal government and the office I work out of is in Denver. I am interested only in bringing in—"

"Enough, Marshal!" she said, smiling brilliantly. "My apologies! I am so glad you do not work for that cesspool of a town. Sit down! Relax!"

Longarm took a deep breath, and tried to hold off, but was unable not to return her smile. He followed her over to the table, held a chair for her, which astonished and delighted her, then sat down himself.

"One of the Indian women, Wahkeena, will be over soon to clear off this table and see to our supper. You will join me, I hope."

"Wouldn't think of missing it," he said, realizing suddenly that he was very hungry.

"You're amused by all this paraphernalia, I see. You think I should rough it, live as do the Indians I am studying?"

"What I think you should do is tell me who you are, since you now have the advantage of me."

"Of course. How boorish of me. My name is Barbara Spencer Tate. I am studying the Indian culture of the Great Basin before it is obliterated by lumber companies, mining interests, and rapacious settlers and cattlemen."

"You'd better get busy and move fast."

"Precisely. I have already accomplished much. These Paiute are most friendly and have already learned English with surprising speed. I only hope that somehow we can preserve this marvelous, almost purely Pleistocene culture."

Longarm scratched the back of his neck vehemently.

"You lost me some distance back, Miss Tate."

"Call me Barbara."

"And you can call me Longarm. But I still didn't get that part about Digger culture."

She took a deep breath. "Longarm, do not call these Indians 'Diggers.' It is a most crude and totally inaccurate appellation. These groups, or bunches, are members of the Uto-Aztecan family. Broadly speaking, most Great Basin Indians are either of the Shoshoni or Paiute linguistic affiliation. The Indians across that stream over there are definitely of the Paiute branch."

"I see. I'd better call them Paiutes."

"Well, that's much more accurate, certainly," she agreed.

"I guess you must read a lot, Barbara."

"Of course. Most anthropologists do."

"Then you must have read what Mark Twain wrote about these Indians."

The tall woman bristled noticeably. "Mark Twain is a humorist, not a scientist. I have only read one very crude and very vulgar and not at all informative reminiscence of his. It is called *Roughing It,* I believe. In it he calls these genuinely aboriginal people scrawny, lean, degraded, their faces and hands bearing dirt they have been accumulating for months and years. Silent, treacherous, sneaking. Oh, yes. That funny Mr. Twain. What he saw, Longarm, were Goshute Indians who had been uprooted from their culture and left to beg for food and sustenance at the various stage depots, a scene he could have duplicated in any Eastern city in this country, substituting Irish, Slavic, or Nordic affiliation for those poor Indians. Mr. Twain would be pleased to note, I am sure, that the Goshutes have embraced many of the white man's ways—they have become prostitutes and beggars."

"I guess I struck a sore spot."

"You did, I am afraid. But surely you do not feel as this Twain does. Didn't you tell me you saved Wanowi's life—and three of his friends?"

"I was just doing my job, Barbara. These Indians are wards of the federal government."

"I see. Do you want to tell me about it?"

He shrugged and told her what had happened, and when he was finished, her face was cold with fury—not at Longarm, but at what Bat Lawson's men and that crowd of loggers had been about to do to Wanowi and the others.

"Thank heavens you were there."

"Yes. But that's all behind me, Barbara. What I'm doing here, I told you before. If you could help me, I'd be much obliged."

"That deserter?"

"Yes. He's the man I'm after."

She nodded thoughtfully, "I understand. I know nothing at all about him."

"I haven't even described him to you yet. I admit you're smart, Barbara—but you ain't that smart, are you?"

She laughed. "Please forgive me. You're the first white man I've seen in months. Describe this desperado you're after."

"Well, maybe he passed through here on his way north into

Snake River country. If he did, there's a good chance one of your Paiutes might have seen him."

"They are not *mine*, Longarm," she corrected him. "But do go on. Describe this person to me."

"He's big. He was a Mountain Man once, before he joined up to scout for the army during the Indian Wars. Blue eyes. Lots of hair on the face. That's about all, I guess, except for the fact he's riding a grullo."

"That's not really much to go on, is it?" she asked, frowning.

"No, it purely isn't, at that. But I believe he killed a sheriff and I do want to bring him in."

"A sheriff?"

"Sheriff Tanner."

"Oh. That's dreadful," she said sadly. "On my last two trips to Silver City to use the telegraph, I met him. He was very nice. I am sorry to hear of his death."

"Maybe you could call over Wanowi. If he's the chief, he might be able to help me question the other Indians. Like I say, they might have caught sight of a big man like that moving north through these parts."

"Of course, Longarm."

She stood up and, with one imperious wave of her arm, brought one of the Paiute women across the stream almost on the run. Barbara told the Paiute what she wanted, and not long after, Wanowi made the trip across the stream, his small, wizened face solemn, his deference to Longarm still noticeable. Longarm realized suddenly that the Indian must be in his fifties. The smallness of their stature and the lack of tallow on their frames gave them all the appearance of little old children. It was unsettling.

Wanowi stopped before them and stood proudly, his shoulders back.

Longarm spoke first. "Wanowi, before I get down to why I'm here, I've got a question I'd like you to answer."

"Okay, Marshal."

"Call me Longarm, Wanowi. It means 'Longarm of the Law.' Okay?"

"Okay."

"On my ride to Whipsaw, did you or any of your friends follow me?"

Wanowi glanced quickly at Barbara—then grinned broadly. "Yes, Marshal."

"And was it you or one of your friends who shot that poor cowboy in the back?"

"He was going to shoot you, Marshal. When Wanowi heard the shots, he climbed to where the cattle people was and he saw what you do. Very brave! You climb the mountain like fly. But you are not like the fly. You do not have large eyes that see behind and front, too. You not see that other cattle person. I shoot him high in the back. Miss heart. He be all right with white man's medicine."

Longarm smiled. "Thank you, Wanowi. You saved my life. We are even. And you are right. That fool cowboy'll be all right, soon enough. Now how about finding out for me, if you can, whether or not a big fellow on a grullo rode through this valley a few weeks back on his way north."

Wanowi shook his head decisively. "No big man riding grullo came north this way, I think."

"Will you ask around for me?"

"Yes, Longarm. Other bands." He pointed downstream. "I will send to find out. You will stay with us?" he added hopefully.

"Yes. But not for long, Wanowi. I've got a lot of distance to travel."

"Rest here with the Paiute People. You are welcome. Wanowi and Longarm brothers."

"I'll buy that," Longarm said easily. "Do you want to shake on it?"

Delighted, Wanowi stepped forward and thrust out his small brown hand. Longarm took it and was startled at the wiry strength it revealed as the Indian wrung his hand happily. Longarm finished the handshake barely on his feet and was rubbing his knuckles thoughtfully as he watched the Indian walk back to the encampment.

He turned to Barbara. "You said something about supper not long ago."

"Indeed I did. Relax and I will consult with my lady servant." She got up and walked down the slope and across the stream, moving in long, graceful strides. Longarm saw her talking to one very old, toothless squaw, who nodded happily and hurried off with two other younger Indian women. Barbara turned back around, saw him watching, and waved.

They ate in the cool summer dusk, with the Paiute women hovering like eager children about the table. Barbara had produced some wine from a trunk in the rear of the tent. She had it cooled in the stream and then insisted on wrapping it in damp cloths while she poured the wine into long-stemmed glasses. The meal was obviously of Indian manufacture and was delicious, though Longarm did not dare to ask what it was. The main course consisted of large meat patties of some kind, greasy and quite salty—but most tasty. He recognized one of the portions: carrot root, roasted in hot stone pits. It had a delicious, sweet potato-flavored flesh.

During the meal Barbara went on at some length about what she had recorded of the Paiute culture in the almost eight months she had spent with these people. It was obvious that she was more than anxious to share with Longarm all that she had found. It poured out in unabashed abundance and Longarm did his best to listen intelligently and nod at just the right times. To his surprise, however, he soon found himself fascinated.

Though everyone, it seemed, was determined to call the Indians of the Great Basin 'Diggers,' implying that they should be regarded as little more than burrowing animals, Barbara felt that nothing could be further from the truth. To her the Paiute, Shoshone, and even the Washo had simply adapted with great skill to what she called a "desert culture." Where the white man would have perished, these Indians had found a home by a remarkable process of adaptation.

Longarm had trouble with all this. The words Barbara used with such fluency frequently made little sense to him. He insisted, therefore, on stopping her frequently and demanding an explanation. This only served to delight the woman. She said that in making her account simpler for him, she was helping herself see things much more clearly. And certainly her journals would benefit. As she continued speaking after every such interruption, Longarm found himself less and less confused.

She described the need for mobility on the part of the Paiute. The Indians had to be able to take advantage of short-lived opportunities for harvest and the hunt. Using only the bow and the net—and in some cases a throwing stick—they were able to obtain jackrabbits, cottontail rabbits, ground squirrels, tree squirrels, raccoons, wildcats, and groundhogs. Deer, she said, were taken by stalking. Frequently, when enough Indians could be brought together for the purpose, group drives and fire drives were organized to force antelope into large corrals, strong enough to hold a number of them at a time.

Because of the low availability of food, the Indians kept their bunches small, seldom more than thirty or forty people to a bunch. Wanowi was the 'captain' of this bunch, Barbara explained, but his leadership was tenuous. He had little more than advisory power. He could warn; he could suggest. But that was the extent of his control.

"Talk about a working democracy," she said, laughing. "It is pretty close to anarchy."

"Sounds like it. But if it works for them . . ." Longarm shrugged. "By the way, what else do these Indians eat?" He pushed aside his plate. "What kind of meat was that I just had? Jackrabbit?"

Her smile warned Longarm. "No," she said. "That wasn't jackrabbit."

"Raccoon?"

"Why do you think it was meat?" she asked, still smiling.

"It was salty, had a meat taste, that's why. Thunderation, woman! What was that you fed me?"

"Grasshoppers and large crickets, pounded up and mixed with animal grease, then cooked like pancakes over an open fire on a skillet I provided. I find it delicious, and I could tell you liked them as well."

"My God, woman," Longarm said hoarsely.

"You look a little green around the gills, Longarm," she teased, reaching over and filling his glass with more wine. "Drink that. You'll feel much better in a few moments. We could have served you fly larvae. Heaps of them are found on the shores of the lakes south of here, gathered up, dried, winnowed to get rid of the casings, then stored in those large willow baskets you see beside the wickiups. They are delicacies, Longarm, and Wahkeena was anxious to bring you some."

"Thank you. Now what were those small sweet balls? Or maybe I shouldn't ask."

"The women split open the cane they find in the few marshlands hereabouts, and lay the stalks in the sun until the sap has crystallized. Then they scrape it into those tasty, sugary balls you found so delicious. These Indians are very proud that you have come to visit them, Longarm. They are not holding back a thing in their efforts to make you feel at home. Nothing but the best for the marshal."

Longarm sipped the wine and glanced at her. "I see you don't mind if Wanowi and the rest of his friends go around with nothing on under those rabbit capes."

She shrugged. "And the women customarily wear nothing above their waists, while the babes at their breasts go naked. No, Longarm, I do not mind. I try to see beyond these surface indications of savagery to the heart beneath. I have come to love these people, Longarm. Can you understand that?"

"Not really. Don't get me wrong, now, Barbara. I don't mean to fault you. But it just appears to me like you look on them as happy, skillful children—something put here for you to study. Like they were some bugs under those spyglasses you people use."

"You mean microscopes, Longarm. You've heard of the work of Pasteur, have you?"

"Nope. Never heard tell of the man."

"It's not important." She frowned pensively. "But what you say—well, it has some merit, I am sure. I hope I am not in danger of looking upon these people simply as subjects for my studies. That would be—wrong, somehow—as you say."

"And if you really do care about them, you'll keep them away from those loggers. Do you mind if I smoke?"

"Not at all. I find the smell of tobacco pleasant." Longarm produced a cheroot as she continued, "The loggers are destroying their traditional pine groves, Longarm. The nut of the pinyon tree is an almost universal staple of these people. Their stores of these nuts carry them through the winter. That is what Wanowi and his people are doing in this valley now. Soon they will finish harvesting them and will move on to other pine groves. But already, vast areas have been taken from them as that infernal lumber company continues to rape this land." She blinked and started a bit as Longarm struck a match with his thumbnail.

"I know," he said, lighting the cheroot and shaking out the match. "You and the Indians and the cattlemen in the area all have a legitimate complaint. But there's nothing that can be done. This company has a perfect right to log this timber. So keep your Indian friends away from the loggers. One of them wounded a logger this afternoon, south of here. If this sort of thing continues, I'll have to alert the army—if Slade Desmond hasn't done it already. The army could make these Indians return to their reservations."

"Longarm, you wouldn't!" she said in a tremulous voice.

"I told you, I am a federal officer; this is federal land. Whoever breaks the law has to answer to me—or to someone like me. But I am not trying to run these Indians into a reservation, Barbara. I've got to find a deserter and it is turning into one hell of a job." He smiled at her. "I guess nothing is as simple as it looks to be at first."

"Then you'll be moving out tomorrow."

"That's right. North. Into Snake River country. There's a Cheyenne reservation there, and I've got a hunch that's where I'll find my ex-Mountain Man."

Mosquitoes and particularly devilish gnats were beginning to swarm about the table. The smoke from his cheroot kept them pretty well away from Longarm, and Barbara tried to ignore them, but it was getting to be a chore. Longarm stood up. "I guess you'll be wanting to get into that tent, away from these bugs."

She smiled and got up also. "Not only that, Longarm, but I have some notes to transcribe as well."

"You've got a lamp in there?"

"A camphene lamp. It does nicely."

"I'm sure."

"I'd . . . invite you in, Longarm. But that wouldn't be quite proper."

"No, it wouldn't," he said, then added, "It would be right nice of you, though."

She smiled a cool, intelligent smile, with all the passion she might have shown, all the warmth, tucked neatly behind it. An anthropologist, she was.

He touched his hat brim and started across the stream. "Thanks," he called back to her through the dusk, "for the grass-hoppers and the crickets."

Her light laugh followed him all the way to where the Indian woman had set down his gear, and its musical ringing was still hanging about him in the darkness when he rolled into his soogan and closed his eyes.

He awoke well before dawn, in a cold sweat. Something was wrong. Not outside. Not anywhere in the Indian encampment. It was wrong inside of him. He glanced up at the night sky. By the position of Orion's belt, it was near one o'clock. Dawn was a long way off, but sleep now seemed impossible.

He had been dreaming of Terry Troy. She had been implor-ing him to do something about the loggers. He had promised he would do what he could, he remembered. But something in the dream—an urgency so strong it troubled Longarm deeply—would not let him sleep. There was nothing he could do. Noth-ing. And yet he had promised her. And she was dead now. It was almost as if she had extracted from him some kind of deathbed promise.

Well, now, old son—ain't that just about what she did?

Terry's death had affected him more than he had realized. Her pleas for him to do something for her land. Her wild, ele-mental abandon. It was downright unpleasant—ugly, even—to think of all that passion, all that life, dead. Of course he wanted to keep that promise to her.

Did she make Tanner promise, as well?

The thought startled him. He almost laughed aloud. Of course she did!

Something else bothered Longarm, too. It had only just come to the surface, as if it had been hiding down inside him all this time, waiting to hit him when his doubts and questions grew too ripe to ignore.

Restless, Longarm got to his feet and walked toward the stream. Barbara Spencer Tate's tent was dark. The wickiups behind him were silent, ugly little dwellings, all but lost in the brooding darkness. There was no wind. The night seemed to be waiting for him. He stopped beside the stream and lis-tened to its passage. The clean, clear sound of the water comforted him, and brought his thoughts back to what had just started bothering him—the words of Fitz concerning Dodds.

Gus Dodds was a loner. He had no friends, Fitz had insisted. There was no trace of that big friend who had told Gus so much about himself. Sure, Gus had denied what Fitz had told Longarm. But why would Fitz lie to him? What could there possibly be in it for him? And if Gus *was* the loner Fitz described—if he had never buddied with this deserter during that fellow's stint as a logger—what did that do to Gus's credibility? How much could Longarm trust Gus to help him search out Ned Shortslef? And if Gus didn't really know this deserter, why had Sheriff Tanner gone to him first thing when he got to Whipsaw?

One more thing—the longer Longarm trailed this deserter, the more the feeling grew in him that he was chasing a phantom. Terry's description had matched Gus's, but Longarm could still not shake the feeling that something was wrong—very wrong. Ned Shortslef was not at all where Longarm was expecting him to be, or where Gus Dodds and Terry Troy had told him to look.

Longarm turned away from the stream. He was suddenly tired. *All that thinking,* he told himself ruefully. His brain was beginning to smoke. But one thing he had settled—and he felt a damned sight better for having done so. He was not going north into Snake River Country for that phantom deserter.

He was going back to Whipsaw.

He had some questions to ask Dodds. And maybe—just maybe—he might try to get some relief for those ranchers while he was in Whipsaw. He would talk to Slade Desmond, and perhaps send someone to Silver City with a telegram to send off to the chief. Someone in Washington *had* to care about what was happening to this valley. It wouldn't count for much, probably, but perhaps then the ghost of Terry Troy would let him sleep again.

Chapter 8

When Longarm rode into Whipsaw the next day a little after noon, the loggers were all off on the slopes and ridges working, so that the town had a waiting, almost deserted look about it. The whine of the saw in the mill was more or less constant, and Longarm wondered how this must affect the girls' sleep. As he rode past the Paradise Valley, he heard the tinkle of the piano and short bursts of laughter—Bat Lawson's men killing a quiet afternoon.

He rode on past the saloon, dodging an occasional wagon piled high with fresh logs for the sawmill, and left the Morgan in the livery. He did not stop in the saloon as he walked from the livery to Ruby's hotel. He was given the same room he had had before, and he left to get a shave and a bath as soon as he had stowed his gear.

When he returned to the hotel, feeling a lot lighter, with a cloud of cheap cologne following him about, Ruby was waiting for him. She was sitting in an armchair when he entered the lobby, and got up to greet him as he started across it.

"Marshal, I didn't get the chance to greet you personally the last time you were here. I am so glad you are back with us! My, don't you smell nice!"

"I much prefer it to the smell of horse manure, ma'am."

"Of course! I quite understand. Marshal, could I have a word with you? It won't take long, I promise you."

"I've got plenty of time. And you can call me Longarm."

She smiled. "Call me Ruby. Everybody does. I hate the name. Always have, but that's what my name is and that's my game, so I might as well live with it. Now, where were we?"

"You wanted a word with me," he reminded her.

"I have an office in here." With a wave of her pudgy hand,

she indicated a room behind the front desk. "Would you mind if we went in there?"

Longarm shrugged and stepped back to let the madam lead the way into her office. When he followed her inside, he found the office quite cozy. It was decorated in red. With the light coming in through the window and reflecting the various shades of red from the rug, curtains, walls, sofas, and chairs, Longarm began to wonder whether he was in some antechamber of hell, with the flames of damnation reflected on the walls—a grim portent of what was to come.

Ruby sat in a large armchair and Longarm found a spot on a sofa across from her. No sooner had she sat down than a girl entered wearing a small, neat apron over her barmaid's uniform.

"What would you like?" Ruby asked Longarm.

"Nothing," he told her. "It's too early for me."

"My, what strength of character. Or is it devotion to duty?"

"A little of both, I suppose."

Ruby ordered a bourbon and water and turned to Longarm as the girl left. "It is about Alice," Ruby said. "She is very upset."

"I'm sorry to hear that."

"About you, and what you must think of her."

"And what *must* I think of her?"

"That the only reason she went to your room in Silver City was because I made her."

"Didn't you?"

"Yes, of course I did."

"Ruby, what's this all about?" he asked, a bit impatiently. "Alice is too intelligent a whore to have taken that business so much to heart. That's not why you wanted to talk to me, now is it?"

Ruby took a deep breath and settled herself higher in her chair. Her expansive bosom seemed to grow more massive. Her eyes gleamed in appreciation of Longarm's ability to cut through her strategems. "You do go right to the heart of things, don't you, Longarm?"

"As often as I can," he agreed. "You got something to tell me?"

"Only that I had no choice but to send in one of my girls. Bat insisted on it when he found out from that little constable that you were in town. I'm sure you can understand my position here. Bat and his men run this place, and that means they run me. The company gets a third of my gross. I'm lucky they don't take half. Slade has been very good to me that way. So I do what he says. It's as simple as that. But I don't like to get on the wrong side of the law—especially federal law."

"That's good to know. Maybe I can count on your help, then."

She grew wary. "Of course—as long as you know where my loyalties lie."

"With whichever side your bread is buttered on."

She smiled. "You put it so nicely."

"All I want is some information about a logger."

"Is that *all* you want, Longarm? After all, think about where you are. I have the best girls in this county—in this state, maybe. And Alice *would* like to make up to you for that unpleasantness in Silver City. It isn't often we extend such privileges on the house."

"For now, Ruby—and no offense intended—what I want is information that only a woman in your position in Whipsaw would be able to give me. The man I am looking for is a very big, heavily bearded logger with blue eyes—a friend of Gus Dodds. And you know Gus, I'm sure."

"I know Gus. We have a lot of big loggers in this camp, Longarm. Hell's bells, most of them start at six feet and go on from there."

"I know that. But he was a good friend of Gus's. The two kept together, went places—maybe this place—together."

Ruby shook her head emphatically. "That's the funny thing about Gus. He's a loner. Keeps pretty much to himself. The girls like him at first, but after a while, they prefer others. They don't dislike him, you understand. It's just that he's kind of spooky—too quiet, if you know what I mean. And a loner. I was real surprised to see him with those other loggers in Silver City."

"So you've never seen Gus with this big fellow I mentioned."

"Never," she said flatly.

Longarm got up. "Guess I'll go up to my room, Ruby. Thanks."

Ruby pushed herself erect. She tried to do it with ease, but it was obviously a strain all the same. Her face momentarily beet-red, she managed a smile. "Why, it was a real pleasure, Longarm. Anytime I can help you, now, you just let me know."

"Just as long as I remember who your boss is."

She smiled, like a schoolteacher at a prize pupil. Longarm turned, left the office and went up to his room. He pulled off his boots and lay face up on the bedspread after rolling up some pieces of newspaper into balls and spreading them on the floor between the door and his bed.

It was still siesta time. The town was slumbering below his window. Longarm slept with the whine of the sawmill in his ears.

The knock on his door awoke Longarm instantly. In the moment it took him to sit upright, he noted the increase in the level of sound coming from the street below the hotel. The loggers were already back in Whipsaw and skid row was coming alive.

"Who is it?" he called, as the person on the other side of the door knocked again.

"Ruby!" came the urgent response.

Reaching for his hat, he went to the door and pulled it open. As Ruby entered, bringing with her an aura of tinsel and cheap perfume, he went back for his boots and sat back down on the bed to tug them on. Glancing up, he saw Ruby standing in front of the closed door. There was a look on her face that gave him pause.

"What is it, Ruby? You look like the devil's got his hooks in pretty deep."

"He has, Longarm," she said seriously.

Longarm pulled on his boots and stood up. "Okay. What is it?"

"Fitz. They got Fitz."

"You'd better explain, Ruby." He reached out to her and drew her gently onto the edge of the bed. "Who's 'they'? And what's Fitz done?"

"He sent someone to tell me to come for you," she said, looking up at him hopelessly.

"Ruby, start at the beginning. What has Fitz done?"

She looked quickly around the room as if its corners were listening. Moistening her lips, she said, "He's a union man. He's been trying to organize the loggers!"

Longarm's eyebrows rose in disbelief. "Fitz? Hell, if I ever saw a good company man, he was it."

"He cares for the workers!" she protested with sudden emphasis. "Those loggers are treated terribly, Longarm. You ought to see how Slade cheats them out of a good fifth of their daily wages. He laughs about it, he does. And that stinking freight car they have to sleep in! It's crawling with rats and lice!"

"All right, Ruby. Go on. Where're they holding Fitz now?"

"In the Paradise Valley. There's a trial going on. Slade's the judge and Bat and his men are the jury."

"And the loggers?"

"They're outside, but some of them don't care what happens to Fitz. They're yelling in to Slade to string Fitz up!"

"But not all of them, Ruby."

"No. Not all of them."

"Let's go," Longarm said, inspecting his Colt and then returning it to its holster. "We can talk on the way."

Ruby heaved herself forward off the bed and left the room just ahead of Longarm. As she padded heavily down the hall before him, a few girls and their gentlemen friends poked their heads out of rooms to see what was going on. Ruby swept past them without a word, and this obviously worried the girls more than if she had reprimanded them. Doors were slammed shut hurriedly behind Longarm as they passed.

Once they were through the lobby and out the door of the hotel, Ruby turned to Longarm, and as they hurried toward the crowd of loggers in front of the Paradise Valley, she told him what had been going on. Fitz—a man she was obviously very close to—had been holding meetings in the hills with whatever loggers were willing to form a union. Better living conditions and higher wages were the issues. The problem of wages could be settled easily enough if Slade would simply stop gouging the loggers at his company store, and maybe even throw out the crooked roulette wheels and faro dealers he had brought in.

Slade had known meetings were going on, only he hadn't known who was holding them and where they were being held. But a hired gun he had brought in the day before—Clyde Tigbee—had beat the information he wanted out of a logger, and Tigbee and Bat had gone after Fitz and brought him into the saloon for his "trial."

Longarm had heard all he needed to, and by this time they were on the fringes of the mob of loggers crowding about the saloon. Those men in Fitz's corner were raising their voices now, demanding that Slade let Fitz go. The few loggers who disagreed were being shouted down and some were being roughed up a little in the process. When those men in the back saw Ruby coming, with Longarm right beside her, they turned and shouted at those in front of them to make way.

"Hey!" a logger cried. "They got your man in there, Ruby!"

She nodded bitterly as she pushed into the crowd. Longarm had already had to swallow his surprise at Ruby's role in all this. Having seen her cozying up to Bat Lawson in Silver City, he had assumed she was Bat's woman. But then, as Ruby had reminded him earlier that day, she knew who her boss was. Fitz, from the extent of her concern at that moment, was obviously the only man in this place she really felt deeply about, a fact tacitly acknowledged by those loggers who pushed aside to let Ruby and Longarm pass.

Just as Longarm was pushing his way onto the wooden sidewalk in front of the saloon, there was a shot from inside. What sounded like Slade's voice shouted something as a warning, and the batwings burst open. Fitz stumbled out, his eyes wild, a gun in his hand. He saw Longarm and Ruby and made for them as the crowd of loggers let out a great cheer and started toward the man.

Before Longarm could reach the logger, two of Bat's men charged out after Fitz, their guns blazing. Fitz was hit high in the back once. As he twisted about in an attempt to fire at his attackers, another round appeared to catch him in the thigh, knocking him quickly to the ground. Longarm had drawn his Colt, and as the nearest of Bat's men aimed a second time at the already wounded Fitz, Longarm fired at the man. The slug caught him in his abdomen. The fellow dropped his gun and fell to his knees, his mouth opening and closing like a fish's.

The other gunman halted abruptly and dropped his gun. Slade and Bat—along with a long-nosed gent with a flamboyantly waxed mustache, a lean, cleft chin and black, unblinking eyes—pushed out through the batwings. They halted instantly at the sight of the two downed men. Longarm kept his Colt in sight and leveled it casually at Slade and the others.

"Just stand back nice and easy," Longarm suggested. "Nice and easy."

Longarm could feel the loggers behind him. Their silence at this sudden gunplay was awesome—almost frightening. It felt as if there were a great beast at Longarm's back, waiting to pounce.

"Help him to the hotel, Ruby!" a logger called out.

"Yeah," another piped up quickly. "Get Fitz away from here!"

Ruby had been bent over the sorely wounded Fitz. The man still clutched the revolver he had had in his hand when he broke from the saloon, but he no longer seemed conscious. Ruby looked up at Longarm.

"I'll need help," she said.

"Someone give her a hand!" Longarm called back over his shoulder at the crowd of loggers.

But no one stirred. Fitz was, after all, a man accused of starting a union—and there was ample evidence before all of them at that moment that such a twist in a fellow's thinking might bring him the same fate that had befallen Fitz.

"All right!" Longarm said sharply and irritably. "Which one of you fair-weather friends is going to help Ruby carry Fitz to the hotel?"

A big logger pushed through the crowd and up onto the wooden sidewalk. It was Gus Dodds. He nodded curtly to Longarm, moved past him, and bent down beside Ruby. The two spoke in quiet, urgent whispers, and then the one-eyed logger reached down and lifted Fitz in his arms. Turning, he started back through the crowd toward the hotel. Ruby moved just ahead of him, clearing a path.

The silent loggers—all of them somewhat shamed by their unwillingness to put themselves on the line for the foreman—moved back somberly, their eyes on the slack form in Gus's huge embrace. A few souls, braver than the rest, followed behind Gus and Ruby as they hurried down the street toward the hotel.

Longarm turned back to Slade. The fellow Longarm had wounded was moaning softly now, both hands clapped against his vitals. "Better get a doctor for your hired gun, Slade," the lawman suggested.

"I've already sent for the only sawbones we've got up here, thank you."

"Then I'll be warning you. Fitz will stay in the hotel under Ruby's care until he's out of danger. If any harm comes to him, I'll hold you responsible. I'm the law in Whipsaw, Slade. You'd do better remembering that."

"There isn't any law in this country that would allow foreign anarchists like Fitzpatrick to spread his doctrine," Slade said. "And no jury would convict anyone of murder for getting rid of some bomb-throwing anarchist."

"Is that what you call someone who just wants to start a union?"

Slade shook his head sadly at Longarm's stupidity. "Are you so busy riding that horse of yours up and down the backside of this country that you don't know about these anarchists? They're trying to take over our industry—our wealth! Hell, man, they don't believe in private property. They don't believe in *anything!*"

"Except maybe throwing bombs!" Bat put in. His voice was filled with outrage.

A doctor—judging from the threadbare black bag he carried—pushed up onto the boardwalk and began examining the fallen gunman's wound. He made unhappy noises and told Slade the fellow would have to be moved into the saloon, that he needed a table to work on.

Slade ordered two loggers to carry the wounded man into the saloon. As the loggers moved past Longarm to get to the fellow's side, the marshal holstered his Colt and turned to go back to the hotel.

"You haven't heard the last of this, Longarm," Slade called after him. "Protecting a bomb-throwing anarchist is no business for a federal marshal!"

Longarm kept going through the dispersing, excited group of loggers without bothering to reply to Slade's strident outrage. Of course, maybe the damned fool was right. Maybe Longarm *did* spend entirely too much time riding up and down the backside of this country. Hell, maybe Fitz *was* doing more than just trying to start a union. Perhaps Ruby had fallen for an anarchist, and maybe Longarm had just put his badge on the line for one. But he couldn't help smiling at the next errant thought that came to him.

There's nothing wrong with this company town that a good bomb wouldn't cure.

The loggers who had followed Ruby and Gus to the hotel were crowded into the lobby. Some were standing in hushed groups, while others were sitting in the soft chairs along the walls. Longarm went to the desk clerk and asked where they had taken Fitz.

"Ruby's office," the man replied, his voice hushed. "There's her private bedroom just beyond."

Longarm nodded his thanks to the man and entered Ruby's office. A door was open on the other side of it, and through its frame, he could see Fitz lying on his back, face up on an immaculate white bedspread with his boots on. Gus Dodds moved his towering frame aside as Longarm entered the bedroom. Ruby was sitting by Fitz's head while a very competent-looking young lady was swiftly undressing the now barely conscious man. Alice was in a corner, watching unhappily. Longarm realized that she had by this time become Ruby's favorite.

Fitz's dark, handsome Irish mug was pale now, like polished ivory. Sweat stood out on his forehead. He was breathing in short, ragged gasps, his mouth slightly open, the tips of his white teeth barely visible. The girl working over him was dressed in a pink shift, her red hair in an untidy pile on top of her head. She was in the act of pulling off Fitz's heavy, blood-stiffened shirt. She had to cut off the top of Fitz's longjohns.

Something clattered to the floor. Longarm caught a glimpse

of it as it rolled under a small table. He stepped over and picked it up. It was one of the slugs, battered and misshapen by its journey through Fitz's body. He showed it to the girl, ignoring Ruby, who was just sitting beside Fitz, searching his face with her eyes and occasionally dabbing at his perspiration with a perfumed handkerchief. The girl nodded and, without a word, showed Longarm the exit wound just under Fitz's right ribs. The hole was ragged and the blood was oozing out of it slowly, as if it were in no hurry to vacate Fitz's warmth.

The redhead had towels soaking in pans of hot water. She wrung out one of the towels and placed it securely against the wound, stanching the flow, and then, with deft skill, she placed a hand under his back and sat him suddenly upright. Longarm moved quickly enough to see the entry wound. It was high on Fitz's left side. A considerably smaller hole than the exit wound. Placing another compress against this wound, she then swiftly wrapped a bandage around it and the other compress, then kept working until she had him wrapped about the chest like a mummy. After this, she let him back gently on his pillow.

She pulled off Fitz's pants and finished cutting off his long-johns, tossing them onto the pile of bloody garments on the floor beside her. The thigh wound was bleeding freely, darkening the bedspread ominously. The bullet was still inside, since there was only one discolored wound. The thigh—a greenish purple—had swollen monstrously.

The girl wrapped another hot towel around this wound as well, and when she had finished, another girl joined her and together they tugged the bloody bedspread and sheets out from under Fitz until they were down to the mattress. As the second girl left with an armful of bloody sheets and clothing, the redhead looked across the bed at Ruby.

"He needs a doctor, Ruby," she said. "He's still got a bullet in him and he's lost a lot of blood."

"We haven't got a doctor. You think Slade'll let that saw-bones of his come over here? Get a blanket for Fitz! Don't leave him lying here like this, stark naked!"

Even as Ruby spoke, the second girl returned with a clean sheet and a blanket. She and the redhead quickly covered Fitz.

Longarm said to the redhead, "Clean off those scissors in good hot water and plenty of whiskey. I'll use the scissors to probe for the bullet. You can help."

The redhead looked at Ruby.

"Do as he says!" Ruby told her, her eyes never leaving Fitz's face.

"That's right," Gus said from behind Longarm. "You do as the marshal says. He knows what he's about."

The girl nodded, and snatched up the heavy scissors she had been using. As she started past Longarm, he took her arm. "Do you have longer, narrower scissors?"

"Barber scissors," Gus said.

"Yes," Longarm said to the girl. "Barber scissors. And hurry it up with that whiskey. If he comes to his senses, we'll need the whiskey to quiet him."

The redhead fled the room.

As Longarm took off his coat and gunbelt and began rolling up his sleeves, Gus stepped closer and started to roll up his sleeves as well.

"Maybe you could use some help," Gus said.

"I sure as hell could," Longarm admitted.

Then they stood silently, waiting for the redhead to return. Fitz still lay unconscious on his back, his breathing irregular. The only sound in the room was his ragged breathing. And then another sound joined it. Ruby, her face in her hands, was weeping softly.

Fitz came awake as soon as Longarm began probing for the bullet. Despite the quantities of raw whiskey they poured down his throat, he remained awake through it all. All of Gus's enormous strength was needed to keep the man on the bed. Only when the slug was in Longarm's palm, did the man rest his head back on the pillow and close his eyes. The redhead leaned over and gently took the rolled-up section of sheet from his mouth. The man had chewed almost through it, yet he had not uttered a single cry. Only the wrathful thrashing of his solid body testified to his pain.

As Longarm stepped back away from the bed, the redhead swiftly washed out the wound with soap and water—on Ruby's suggestion—and then bound the ragged hole securely to stanch, finally, the freshet of blood that poured from the man.

"He sure has lost a lot of blood," Gus said, speaking softly.

"There are some doctors who cure their patients by bleeding them, Gus," Longarm said.

"I know. There are damn fools everywhere. It ain't right. A man needs his blood—every bit of it. Look at Fitz's face, damn it."

The pallor had deepened alarmingly. Blue circles hung under his eyes, which had sunk deep into their sockets. Abruptly the man's eyes flickered open. He saw Longarm and Gus and smiled wanly. "Thanks, Longarm," he said softly. "Took you long enough, though. Where in blazes did you get a license to practice medicine?"

"Never mind that. How do you feel?"

"Empty. Light as a feather, as a matter of fact. But I'm glad that bullet is out." He began to cough, and had to turn his head away to clear his throat. Tiny flecks of blood appeared on his lips and dribbled onto the mattress. Ruby quickly reached out and wiped the blood from his mouth. He looked at her and smiled. His right hand came up and took hers and squeezed it.

She smiled stoutly back down at him. "You're going to be all right, you crazy Irishman," she said.

"Why, sure, an' there's little doubt of that! With Longarm here as me doctor and big Gus Dodds as me nurse!"

The effort required to express this optimism weakened the man alarmingly. He seemed to sink into the mattress as he let go of Ruby's hand. His eyes remained open, but he had the look of a man who is staring down a long, dark tunnel—with death waiting at the other end. Alice, who had seemed to melt into the wallpaper during all this, stepped closer to Ruby, now, and took her hand. The weary madam answered Alice's squeeze and then rested her head against Alice's breast. Alice wrapped her arm around Ruby's shoulder and held her silently. Catching Longarm's eyes, she shook her head sadly, in obvious concern for Ruby's state.

A commotion behind Longarm caused him and Gus to turn. A logger burst into Ruby's office and hurried toward the bedroom. When he saw Longarm, he halted, took a deep breath, and swallowed.

"Out with it," Longarm told him, moving toward him and out of the bedroom.

"That guy you shot—Bat's man. He's dead!"

"I'm sorry."

Gus came up beside the lawman. "I'll bet there's more to it, Longarm." He turned and addressed the logger. "Let's have the rest, Mike."

"That gunslinger Slade brought in is outside now. He's been appointed town marshal, and he told me to tell Longarm he wants him for aiding an escaped anarchist and killing what he calls 'an officer of the court.'" The logger took a deep breath. "He says if Longarm don't come out, he'll come in after him—and he'll make sure that damn anarchist don't get no better."

"That was a mouthful, Mike," Gus told him grimly. "Is that all he said?"

The fellow moistened his lips and nodded quickly. "That's all, Gus. That's what he told me to tell Longarm."

"You told me," Longarm said. "Go on back out. I won't be long."

As the logger bolted back out the door, fairly bursting with his sense of importance and the news he had ,to spread, Longarm turned to Gus and said, "You sure you want to hang in with me on this?"

"I'm already in," Gus said, his good eye glittering darkly.

"Stay here with Fitz, then, in case that jasper gets past me."

"I don't have a weapon."

"Get one," Longarm told him as he walked back into the bedroom, strapped on his cross-draw rig, and shrugged into his coat. He patted the front of his vest, felt of the derringer, then lifted his hat off the bedpost and put it on.

"Ruby," Longarm said, "I'm going outside."

"I heard," she said, her voice hushed.

"Get Gus a gun."

Alice stepped away from Ruby. Ruby reached her hand up and let Alice help her onto her feet. She took a deep breath, squared her massive shoulders, then brushed past Longarm and headed for her desk to get a weapon for Gus. As Gus followed after her, Longarm looked back at Fitz.

Fitz still had that sunken, distant look about him, as though

part of him had already gone on ahead. Longarm turned and
walked out of Ruby's office.

Longarm did not find Tigbee waiting for him outside the hotel.
Only the crowd of loggers was there, waiting not only for him
to come out, but also as a vigil for Fitz. Their faces were grim
as they stepped back to let Longarm through. Whatever loggers
there were who thought Fitz should have been hung because he
was a foreign anarchist were nowhere in evidence. This action
of Slade's had, if anything, made a union almost a certainty
now—either that or a work stoppage and the violence that usually accompanied such a course.

The logger named Mike who had told him the gunslinger
was waiting for him dashed out of the Paradise Valley saloon
and raced down the street toward Longarm. Longarm kept
walking. As the man neared him, he glanced about. The sun was
still pouring a heavy, golden light into the valley, but it wouldn't
be hanging above the ridges much longer.

The logger pulled up. Longarm kept walking and the logger
had to trot almost to keep up with him. "You said he was out
here waiting," Longarm remarked.

"He's in the saloon."

The lawman nodded. Whoever the hell this Clyde Tigbee
was—he still could not recall the name or reputation—he was
evidently a jasper who drank his courage. Good. Longarm
liked every advantage he could get when it came to using live
ammunition.

"You tell this jasper I've been doing some thinking. Tell him
I'm not so sure I want any of this to lead to violence. There's
already been too much of that." Longarm looked sharply at the
logger. "You got that, Mike?"

"I sure have, Marshal."

"Good. You go tell him that, and shake a leg, or I'll blow
your goddamned head off." He smiled at Mike when he said
this, but the logger paled and took off like a shot.

The batwing doors were still swinging slightly when Longarm pushed into the saloon after Mike. The logger was at the
end of the bar and had just finished telling the hired gun what
Longarm had said. Longarm stopped and looked around.

A crowd of Bat Lawson's men was gathered near a table, on top of which lay the covered body of the man Longarm had shot. The jasper who passed for a doctor in this pest hole was holding up the bar; a shot glass and a bottle stood at his elbow. Slade and Bat were standing with the new marshal of Whipsaw.

Longarm nodded a greeting to him. "You Clyde Tigbee, the new town marshal?"

The fellow glanced quickly at Slade and Bat, who then moved away from the bar toward Bat's men. Tigbee looked back at Longarm and nodded quickly. His uptwisted waxed mustache moved ever so slightly, his dark eyes lighting at the prospect of gunning down Longarm. The logger had evidently done another fine job of relaying a message. If Longarm didn't want any more bloodshed, if he wanted to talk, then he was yellow. And that was just Clyde Tigbee's meat. Longarm read this clearly in the man's careless contempt.

Longarm thought, *Let the son of a bitch think what he wants. Let him think I'm as yellow as a canary and just as anxious to sing.*

"Mike says you don't want no more bloodshed, Marshal." Tigbee smiled expansively. "Well, no one's going to hurt you, as long as you let us have that anarchist. He's been inciting his men to revolution, and that's against the Constitution. Hell, you're a federal officer. You should know that's treason. You let us have Fitzpatrick and you can ride out of Whipsaw, proud you done the right thing."

"Well, he's hurt bad. He can't be moved."

Longarm moved away from the batwings and started toward that end of the bar closest to him. This way he was able to keep an eye on Bat's men and Tigbee at the same time. Behind him, Longarm heard a babble of voices as loggers flocked now to gather in the street in front of the saloon. The logger called Mike burst suddenly from the group around the table and dashed out through the batwings. Longarm could hear his breathless account of what he thought was going on inside.

As he reached the bar, the barkeep—a tall, swarthy fellow with three or four black strands of slicked hair brushed straight across a shining pate—hurried warily along the bar to him.

Longarm looked down the bar at Tigbee. "Join me in a drink? I've got to think on this some, and I think better with a little warmth in my belly."

"Watch him, Tigbee!" Slade called out suddenly. "He's up to something."

Tigbee threw a quick, almost contemptuous glance at his employer, as if to say, *Let me handle this. This is my line of work.* Looking back at Longarm, the man spoke sharply to the barkeep. "Sam, give us your best whiskey and leave the bottle. Two civilized people is about to discuss an important matter."

"That's right," Longarm said quietly. "The security of the United States Constitution."

Moving down the bar toward him, Tigbee's eyes lit up. "That's it, Marshal. You put your finger right on it. I can see you're a man what understands these things."

The barkeep placed the two shotglasses down and stood the whiskey bottle next to them. Expansively, Tigbee poured for both of them, slapped the bottle down, and raised his own glass. Longarm picked up his drink. The two men tossed the liquor down. Smacking his lips, Tigbee glanced at Longarm.

"Now then," he said to Longarm. "You going back to that hotel with me to finish off that Irish son of a bitch?"

Longarm seemed to consider this for a moment, then turned casually, leaning his elbow on the bar. "I don't think I can do that. You might say he's a prisoner of the federal government."

Tigbee's dark eyes narrowed. "Maybe so. But I still got to take you in—for killing that poor man over there. He was a duly elected officer of the court."

"He came out that door shooting like a wild man. That's a hell of a way for an officer of the court to act."

"He was chasing a prisoner."

"He could have killed someone. The street was crowded with loggers."

"Loggers, shit!"

Tigbee, excited now by the argument, had taken a small step back from the bar, so intent was he on expressing his outrage that any concern need be felt for loggers. Had the gunslinger been a touch more sober, he might have been warned by the dangerous gunmetal-blue glint in Longarm's eyes, but as it happened, he was not ready when Longarm's hand reached in under his coat and drew his revolver. As the gleaming weapon appeared in Longarm's hand, Tigbee flung himself away from the bar, his right hand slapping for his six-gun. Longarm fired. He missed, and the round blew a hole in a brass cuspidor, with a loud *whang*. Tigbee's legs tangled in a chair and he went down heavily.

Longarm's first shot had gone wild because the barkeep had nudged him quickly with a logger's peavey. Longarm swung at the man with his gun barrel, smashing him across the bridge of his nose, reducing it to a pulp of flesh and blood. The barkeep was stubborn, however. Recovering, he brought back the vicious, hooked instrument a second time. Longarm fired at the man point-blank.

The round entered the barkeep's chest just beside the breastbone, veered slightly, and severed the aorta. Since the man's heart was still pounding furiously, it sent a spray of blood bursting from the bullet hole with great force, as if through the nozzle of a hose. Longarm ducked and went down on one knee to escape the sudden spray just as Tigbee got off his first shot at him. The bullet tugged at the fabric of his frock coat, shearing the flesh just above his collarbone, leaving him with the sensation that a hot branding iron had rested momentarily on his shoulder. He forgot the discomfort at once, as another shot came at him from Bat's direction. The slug bit a clean chunk of paneling out from under the bar.

Longarm snapped off a shot in Bat's direction, just to set him thinking—then another quick one at Tigbee, who was still sprawled on the floor. The round missed the new town marshal, but sent splinters from the chair he was lying near into his face. He spun away. Longarm reached up, grabbed the edge of the bar, and vaulted over it, crunching down on the upper torso of the barkeep.

His shot into the crowd around Bat had produced the desired effect—a bleat of pain and surprise, followed by a general stampede for the door. As soon as the men had cleared the room, Longarm poked his head up and saw that Slade and his crew had left Bat to handle things. The fellow was crouching down behind an overturned table. *Good*, he thought. *That makes it only two to one. Better odds than when I came in.*

Tigbee, too, had found an overturned table, Longarm noticed. But the man was still trying to dig splinters out of his eyes. Keeping well down, Longarm traveled the length of the bar and swung out from behind it, coming at Tigbee from an unprotected angle. Startled, Tigbee swung up his big Remington and fired. The round went high. The lawman heard it spiderweb the mirror behind him as he sighted deliberately on Tigbee's right eye and pulled the trigger. Longarm's slug instantly demolished Tigbee's eyeball. The eye socket appeared to expand miraculously, then deepen as a ragged triangle of bone and hair was lifted out at the exit wound. Tigbee's head snapped back so swiftly that as his body followed it, it seemed that it was his head that was pulling him over. He came to rest with his lower torso on an overturned chair, his shoulders and head out of sight on the other side.

Bat jumped up from his cover and fired quickly in Longarm's direction, then dashed for the door. Longarm aimed quickly and fired. His Colt's hammer snapped down futilely on the chamber Longarm always kept empty.

Spinning around at the door, Bat flung up his gun and covered Longarm. "Gawdamighty!" the man cried. "You're out of ammunition! Well, ain't that just terrible! Creeping Jesus! Deputy U.S. Marshal Long ain't got no more lead in his pencil!"

The man was fairly dancing with delight as he advanced on Longarm, his dark, hawklike face alight with deviltry.

"Drop it, Longarm!" he said menacingly. "Just drop that empty gun."

Longarm let it go. As the gun thudded heavily to the floor, Bat smiled. He was at peace with the world. All his prayers had been answered—and then some. This was the same man who had parted his hair with a gun barrel in front of his own men. Bat was really going to enjoy this.

Longarm smiled. "I'm an unarmed man, Bat. Don't do something you'll be sorry for."

"Hell, there ain't nothing I could do to you I'd be sorry for, lawman. This is going to be sweet."

Bat brought his six-gun back. Had the blow been allowed to land squarely, it could easily have crushed Longarm's skull. But the lawman ducked swiftly and the gun barrel whistled just overhead, taking Longarm's hat with it. Furious, Bat brought up his knee, catching Longarm just below his solar plexus. The pain that radiated out from that spot caused Longarm to gasp, then stagger back against the bar. Bat kicked him in the right side as Longarm twisted away, sending the marshal tumbling backward along the floor, his boots catching awkwardly in the brass rail.

Bat's bloodlust was thoroughly aroused by this time. He was tired of simply kicking the shit out of Longarm. Something more dramatic was what he craved now—something more final. He cocked his revolver and aimed coolly down at the figure still thrashing helplessly at his feet. Longarm had already palmed his derringer while Bat was busy indulging himself. Now he extended his right hand straight up and fired into Bat's stomach.

The muzzle of the derringer was only inches from its target. At that range the effect of the .44-caliber slug was massive. Longarm saw the man drop his revolver and clutch at his stomach; he watched him stagger back, buffeted by the awesome havoc wrought within his gut. Bat collapsed to the floor, his eyes wide; he was unconscious before he hit, and dead not long after.

Longarm got to his feet and replaced the derringer in his vest pocket. He reloaded his Colt and placed it back in his holster. Buttoning his coat, he stepped over Bat Lawson's still body and picked up his hat. Squinting painfully in the smoke-heavy air, he made his way out of the saloon. As he emerged, the loggers cheered. Longarm looked around for some sign of Slade and his men. Finding none, he acknowledged the cheers of the loggers by touching the brim of his hat to them.

"Someone had better see to those men in there," he said, stepping off the boardwalk. "But there's no hurry. They ain't going anywhere."

He pushed free of the loggers, aware that the flesh wound in his shoulder had bled a bit, causing his shoulder to stiffen noticeably. He sucked in the clear air, appreciating it as Lazarus must have when he left his tomb. The sun was now just below the mountain ridge. As Longarm moved through the gathering dusk on his way back to Ruby's hotel, he could not shake the chill of death that clung to him.

He had come here to bring in an army deserter and had ridden into a charnel house.

Chapter 9

The vigil at Fitz's bedside was a grim one that night. Alice spelled Ruby occasionally, but Ruby slept on a cot that had been brought into her office, leaving word that she was to be awakened at the slightest change in Fitz's condition. Not knowing what Slade intended, Longarm and Gus took turns sitting in the office with a shotgun in their laps. It was a short-barreled Greener that Ruby's barkeep kept handy under the bar. Throughout it all, Fitz slept fitfully. His color improved steadily, though his condition remained precarious.

That next morning an odd thing happened—in fact, it was a remarkable occurrence for a company town. Only a handful of loggers left for the ridges. The majority of them refused to report to their crew chiefs. Instead, they spent the morning milling about ominously along skid row, giving the bars and the girls no rest. Their mood was ugly, as they kept a close tab on their wounded foreman's condition.

Surprisingly, Slade and his men made no move to force the loggers to return to work. One report had it that he had ridden out early with about ten riders, heading north into the wooded slopes. By midafternoon a strong wind began picking up the dust and debris that covered the main drag and the lots between the tents and shanties, filling the air with grit and eye-gouging alkali. Clouds rolled in over the valley as thunder muttered ominously. But the rain held off.

Slade rode into town not long after, and at once the loggers realized what he had been doing. He and his ten riders were at the head of a sinister, scowling infantry of loggers—all those who had reported to work that morning. It was to be union loggers against those who disdained unions, a kind of civil war.

Watching from his window, Longarm saw Slade's loggers,

many of them armed with tall pike poles, sweep down the main
drag toward a hastily organized body of union loggers. Slade
waited until he was within twenty or so yards of the union loggers. Then he and his riders opened up on the enemy. At once,
his loggers broke into a run and closed with the union men.
The union loggers outnumbered the others clearly, but they
were disorganized and lacked the firepower Slade had just displayed. After a short, furious battle, the union loggers were in
flight, scattering throughout the tents and shacks like ants from
a ruined nest. In almost no time at all, Slade and his men had
won back his town.

Longarm turned away from his window.

As the company's manager, this was indeed Slade's town.
Whipsaw existed solely to further the fortunes of the Western
Lumber and Land Combine. Slade Desmond's job—purely and
simply—was to see to it that this purpose was fulfilled. And
that meant that nothing Slade did to further that end would ever
be seriously challenged—certainly not by those bigwigs in
Washington who owned stock in the company.

It sickened Longarm. There was no way to stop Slade.

A moment later he strode into Ruby's office. He found frightened loggers conversing with Gus, obviously telling him what
had just happened outside. At Longarm's entrance, the loggers
nodded curtly to him and darted from the office, obviously looking for a safe place to hole up until this trouble blew over. There
seemed to be no doubt that all the loggers who could would
report for work the next day and spend the following twelve
hours working off their sullen rage.

"Were any loggers wounded seriously?" Longarm asked Gus.

"Three men were hurt. They'll live. I expect Slade will be
in here next."

"Maybe. How's Fitz?"

"Better."

Longarm walked into the bedroom. It did seem a lot less
grim. Alice was sitting in a corner knitting, while Ruby busied
herself spoon-feeding Fitz, who had been propped up in a sitting position with the aid of several large pillows.

"Chicken soup!" Fitz cried as Longarm entered. "That's all

she's given me. Sure, and I'm going to turn into a chicken before long!"

"How do you feel?"

"Why, this here foreman can run faster, jump higher, squat lower, move sideways quicker, and spit farther than any son of a bitch in camp!" He smiled up at Longarm. "But if I have to say all that again, I might have a relapse."

"Be quiet," said Ruby, "or you will."

"You heard what happened?" Longarm asked.

Fitz frowned. "Yup. I been told. Slade's taken back the town. Can't say as it's any surprise. He has the firepower, sure enough. And a lot of those damn fools out there don't know what a union could do for them!"

"Look what it did for you!" Ruby said scornfully, poking a steaming spoonful of chicken broth at the man.

He opened his mouth hastily and swallowed quickly, his eyes bugging as the scalding broth boiled down his throat. "Easy, woman!" he cried. "You'll do me in faster than them bullet holes in my hide!"

Longarm shook his head, sighing. "Slade's within the law, you know. I can't see any court in this country going against a company man who's trying to save the country from the anarchists."

"No, Longarm. *Foreign* anarchists. That's what makes it so terrible, you see. After all, me bucko, there ain't a one of us here who didn't come from someplace else. And everyone's trying to hide the fact."

Longarm smiled at Fitz. He was glad the man was in such obviously better spirits. The strength of the man was astonishing. Nevertheless, he was still in great danger.

"I wish there was something I could do to stop Slade," Longarm said.

"You're the law, ain't you? Federal law. This here is federal land. You can stop him easy enough."

"In this country, for the next few days at least, the law is what Slade says it is. If he and his men break in here and kill us all, who's going to demand an investigation to find out what really happened? A union anarchist caused a riot and so many people were killed as a result. And my chief in Denver would

just have to settle for that." Longarm took out a cheroot and lit
it. "He'd raise more hell than a scalded cat, I reckon, but it
wouldn't do him any more good than a fart in a windstorm—
excuse me, Ruby."

Ruby placed her spoon down in the bowl of soup and looked
nervously over at Fitz, then turned and looked up at Longarm.
"You mean there's nothing you can do about Slade—legally,
that is?"

"I guess that's about it."

"What do you think about the way this land's being torn
up?" she asked.

"It ain't pretty." Longarm shrugged. "But it's legal."

"No, it isn't."

Fitz looked at Ruby in astonishment. Alice stopped knitting.

"What do you mean, Ruby?" Fitz demanded. "Of course it
is! How else are we going to cut these trees?"

"That's not what I mean." Ruby looked back at Longarm.
"I mean it isn't legal for him to be doing what he's doing."

"How do you know that, Ruby?" the marshal asked.

"I don't, for sure. But you let me tell you what happened a
couple of months ago. Some men came up here all the way
from Washington. They were all fat cats from the government,
here to do a check on the operations, they said."

"What department were they from, Ruby? Do you remember?"

"Department of the—" She frowned.

"Interior?" Longarm prompted her.

"Yes, that's the one! The Bureau of Land Management was
where one of them—a fine-looking lad—worked."

Longarm realized this could possibly be the survey team
that Slade had told him had not yet sent back their report to
him. So far, he saw nothing unusual in all this. But he was
willing to listen. "Go on, Ruby."

"Well, sir, they came up here to check on this town's operation, no doubt, and they were supposed to check on how the
land was being treated. That's what the young fellow told me.
But Slade didn't let them out of Whipsaw."

"How do you mean?"

She smiled. "Well, you know what attractions a house like

this provides. And they had plenty of everything—on Slade's orders. Pretty soon they drank so much and lost so freely at the gaming tables that all they wanted was comfort from our girls. I must say, the girls did a fine job. Those men never did get out of Whipsaw that week, and they were too drunk to know it when they started back to Silver City."

This was interesting, but hardly unusual. Slade was simply doing his best to keep these Washington bureaucrats in his debt by showing them a good time. "Is that all, Ruby? What's so unusual about that? The men probably had no intention of looking around. They were probably expecting just such a high old time."

"Not that young man from the Bureau of Land Management. He kept asking Slade to show him the survey map. He said he wanted to check it. And I could tell, Longarm, that he was disturbed about something. Well, sir, as soon as he mentioned that survey map, Slade went into action. All of a sudden he got my best girl and told her to stay with this fellow. Slade told her if he bothered him any more with talk about checking that survey map, he'd have her out of here on the first wagon back to Silver City." She smiled shrewdly. "This girl of mine did herself proud. She showed that young man every trick in her book and some I hadn't thought of myself—and the poor young fellow forgot all about Slade's survey map. Now, to my way of thinking, the only reason Slade would want to keep this young man from the government away from that map is because he's doing something that's illegal."

"Ruby, did you tell this to Sheriff Tanner?"

She looked at him strangely. "Why, yes, I did."

"When?"

"The last time he visited me. He was an old friend of mine, Longarm. He was on his way back to Silver City with a horse thief. Whenever he was up here on business, he stopped. He noticed how tired the girls were, so I told him what had happened earlier—like I just told you."

"What did he do when you told him?"

"Nothing much, except that he seemed interested—just like you are now," she said.

"But he didn't *do* anything?"

"No, he didn't. There wasn't much he could do anyway, was there?"

Longarm puffed pensively on his cheroot for a moment, then said, "He returned to Whipsaw a few weeks later, didn't he?"

"Yes, but he didn't stop in here to see me," Ruby replied.

"Where did he stop?"

"I think he went in to see Slade about something. But then, I was busy getting ready for my trip to Silver City to pick up Alice here and the other new girls." She looked at him shrewdly. "This is important—what I told you—isn't it?"

"That depends, Ruby. Right now I've got to do some thinking. I expect you'd better finish feeding poor Fitz his chicken broth."

Longarm left the bedroom and walked past Gus to the window. It faced out onto the main street. A few of the loggers who had sided with Slade were apparently patrolling the street. They were for the most part old-timers, Longarm noticed. A lot of them carried pike poles, their mean-looking, spiked iron sockets about even with the men's heads as they stepped along. As Longarm watched, one of Slade's men rode into town, waved to the loyalists as he swept past, dismounted in front of the general store, and hurried inside to speak with Slade.

The wind had died down and rain was beginning to fall. It was not a sudden, roaring downpour, but a steady, light fall. The rainy season, as Wally had told him, was beginning finally. Soon, Longarm realized, Whipsaw would be one vast muddy slash pile. Still, this wasn't what was occupying his thoughts at that moment.

Slade had admitted himself that those men had come to Whipsaw to extend the area Slade could log. But they had been kept from seeing where the company was already logging. Slade had not wanted that one young man from the Bureau of Land Management to check his operations against the survey map. Ruby was on to something, all right. Now Longarm remembered Terry's answer to a question of his. She had told him she had thought at first the company would be cutting timber on the other side of this range. Perhaps she had seen some of the original survey team members in that area—or had spoken to them as they rode through.

Longarm needed that survey map. It was probably in Slade's office files somewhere. If he could get hold of that—and it showed what Longarm thought it might show—he would be able to do a lot more than send a few futile telegrams. Hell, Slade would be in violation of federal law. He would have Slade by the short hair. Nothing would please Longarm more.

What about that deserter, old son? Ain't that *why you're up here?*

Longarm turned and looked at Gus Dodds. Gus saw the look on his face and got up from his chair and walked toward him.

"You see anything out there, Longarm?" the big man asked.

"Just rain and a few of Slade's loyalists marching up and down with their pike poles."

Gus nodded and peered past Longarm and out the window. "Looks like the rain's letting up some. You think Slade will try to rush us?"

"I don't know. How many loggers are holed up in here with us?"

Gus grinned at Longarm. "None. We're all Fitz's got right now—just you and me and Ruby—and the girls. They're out at the bar, enjoying their vacation."

"What's Ruby say about that?"

"Hell, she don't mind. She's finished here now, and she knows it. All she cares about is Fitz."

"And you?"

"I don't want to see no harm coming to that Alice," Gus said grimly.

Longarm nodded. "Is that why you threw in with Fitz and me?"

Gus scratched under his eyepatch with a grimy finger, and looked shrewdly at Longarm. "That's part of it, I guess. But I always liked Fitz, anyway. Best foreman I ever worked for."

"You helped me get away with that Troy kid, too. That couldn't have made you very popular with the other loggers."

"It didn't. But Fitz took my side. Like I said, Fitz and I got along."

Longarm looked closely at Gus. A curious, startling thought was taking form in his brain. "Goddamnit, Gus!" Longarm said softly. "Who the hell are you, anyway?"

"Now that's a foolish question, Longarm. You know who I am. I'm Gus Dodds."

"Are you now?"

Suddenly wary, Gus took a step back. "You feeling all right, Longarm? All this here trouble ain't made you soft upstairs, has it?"

"Maybe it has, at that, Gus. Maybe it has. But I wish you'd answer my question. I've got a strong feeling you ain't really done that yet."

"Well, maybe you'll have to wait a while before I do. Look out the window."

Longarm turned. Slade, at the head of a small crowd of loggers, was on his way down the street toward the hotel. It was showdown time, it seemed.

"Cover me from this window, Gus," Longarm said, "I'll go out and see if I can stall the son of a bitch."

Gus nodded grimly and moved closer to the window.

Slade held up his hand. The loggers behind him halted. He smiled at Longarm and walked to within a few feet of the hotel porch. The rain was sifting down gently.

"These loggers want the hotel back, Longarm. I understand you've got Fitz in there, with you and Gus Dodds standing guard. You let us back inside, nice and peaceful-like, and give these men back their girls—along with Ruby—and we won't have to do anything violent."

"No bloodshed," Longarm said.

"That's right," Slade replied easily. "No bloodshed. And you can tell Ruby I don't hold grudges. I didn't have any idea she was sweet on Fitz."

"You mean she can run the hotel—keep her girls—just like before?"

"Sure," Slade said with a smile.

"She'll be happy to hear that."

"I thought she would."

"What about Fitz?"

"Hell, you're a federal officer. Take him back with you. You can prosecute him for starting a riot, or let him go; I don't care which."

"You'll let me ride out of here with Fitz? And Gus?"

"Sure. Hell, you've done us enough damage already, Longarm. Let's say I know when I'm between a rock and a hard place. What I've got to think of now is cutting timber. It's beginning to rain now and that's going to make it a damned sight harder for me to meet my quota. Now that these loggers have learned their lesson and we've found the damned anarchist who was stirring them up, I can get back to work. That's all I want."

"Sounds reasonable, Slade."

"I'm a reasonable man," Slade replied, smiling thinly. "When I have to be."

Longarm paused, considering. Then he took a deep breath, and said, "All right, Slade. I'll take Fitz back with me. Your loggers can have their playpen back."

The man's tiny eyes narrowed shrewdly. "That's fine, Longarm. You'll be moving out, then, with Fitz, back to Silver City?"

"Guess that's the best course, Slade."

The man appeared to take a deep breath. He took off his chocolate-brown derby, swung it to rid it of the rain, and brushed a quick hand over his gleaming skull. Then he slapped his hat back on. "How soon can my men move in?"

"Fitz is still hurt too bad to move tonight—especially with all this rain. You know that pretty stage you used to bring up Ruby's girls? Have it out here tomorrow morning, first light, and we'll take Fitz to Silver City."

"Tomorrow morning?"

"That's right, Slade. Tomorrow morning. The extra night's sleep will do all of us a heap of good."

The man wanted to protest, then thought better of it. He shrugged his broad shoulders and nodded, his buckshot eyes cool, appraising. "Tomorrow morning, then. First light. And you tell Fitz I said good riddance."

"I'll do that, Slade."

Longarm turned and walked back into the hotel. Inside the lobby, he glanced through a window and saw Slade and the loggers hurrying back to the general store through the rain. He watched them go for a minute or so, trying to determine from the way they carried themselves whether Slade really had accepted Longarm's proposal—whether they really intended to let Fitz and him have a good night's sleep.

Longarm told Fitz of his agreement with Slade.

"You don't believe him, do you, Longarm?" Fitz demanded.

"Of course not. But I do know one thing. He is anxious—he has been all along—to get me out of Whipsaw."

"Why do you think he wants that, Longarm?" Gus asked quietly.

"Ruby gave me the answer to that, I think. What I told Slade out there was just a stall to give me time to get into his office."

"Why?" Fitz asked.

"I want to look at that survey map Ruby tells me that young man from Washington was so anxious to see."

"What do you expect to find?" Gus said.

Longarm looked at him. "What I think Tanner found—and why he was murdered."

Gus's eyes narrowed. "You mean Slade killed—?"

Longarm held up a cautioning hand. "Don't jump to any conclusions. Let me check this out. First of all, I figure we'd all better lay low, get some shut-eye, and arm ourselves to the teeth. If Slade makes a move against us, he'll likely do it after dark."

"You think he will?" Ruby asked, frightened. "For sure?" Alice looked up at Longarm, her face showing alarm as well.

"It all depends on how bad he wants to get me out of Whipsaw without any more trouble. Ever since Silver City that man— or one of his coyotes—has been trying to prevent me from coming here." Longarm looked over at Alice. "That's why you were sent in to search through my wallet, Alice. Slade just had to know why I was riding to Whipsaw."

Alice paled, and almost lost the knitting resting in her lap. She swallowed nervously and nodded.

"I'm going up to my room now," Longarm said. "I'm beginning to stumble around a little, so I'd better get some sleep. You too, Gus."

Gus nodded.

Longarm left the bedroom and went upstairs to his room. He kicked off his boots, took out his Colt, dropped his hat over the bedpost, and fell back onto the bed. He was asleep almost at once, the Colt in his hand.

As Longarm made his way through the foggy night, his thoughts kept returning to the hotel. He had left Fitz asleep in Ruby's bedroom and Ruby was also sleeping, on the cot in her office. Gus said he had napped earlier that evening and seemed alert enough. Still, Longarm was worried. There was a loaded Peacemaker beside Fitz in bed; Ruby, too, was armed, and Gus's Greener was loaded with number-six buckshot. Nevertheless, Slade and his men could take them easily if they wanted to badly enough.

Longarm was banking on the fact that Slade wanted him out of Whipsaw so much that he would make no move against them either tonight or when they brought Fitz out in the morning. Of course, Ruby knew enough to realize that, no matter what, she was finished here in Whipsaw.

The rear of the general store loomed out of the night. The rain had stopped, but clouds hung heavy over the valley. There was no light from the moon or the stars. The wet darkness was oppressive, but provided perfect cover for what Longarm had in mind.

He found a small back porch, mounted it cautiously, and tried the door. It was not locked. He pushed it open, stepped swiftly inside, closed the door silently behind him, and found himself in a small corridor. He moved along it and came to a door, which opened as easily as had the first. Stepping inside, he found himself in Slade's office.

He closed the door and looked around the dim room. Since the office was in the rear of the building, Longarm decided to light a lamp. He had no choice, really. He couldn't find anything in such inky darkness. Locating a lamp, he lit it, then placed it on one of three massive file cabinets. It took him almost a half hour to go through the files. His problem was that he didn't know where such a map would be filed, if in fact it was filed at all. A dead giveaway like that would probably be hidden somewhere else, but he had to check the obvious places first. He found plenty of maps, reports on the amount of lumber cut and shipped, and so forth, but no survey map.

He went to Slade's desk, then, and ransacked it in less than five minutes. Nothing. He looked about and found himself staring unhappily at a wall safe tucked in a corner. If it was inside that . . .

He walked over and examined the safe carefully. It was small. A survey map was large; Longarm had examined quite a few in his time. It would be damned inconvenient to stuff a survey map inside this safe.

He went back to the lamp and lifted it high over his head. Immediately he spotted what appeared to be a draftsman's board in a far corner. He hurried over and saw a map tacked to the board. On closer inspection, however, he found it was only a tally map, showing what slopes and ridges had been cut and how much board feet each section had yielded.

Under the drafting board there was a wooden pocket, similar to a magazine rack. Longarm reached in and removed two large maps. One he discarded immediately. It was of the Whipsaw region exclusively, and simply showed how extensive the cutting had been in this area. The other map was a different matter entirely.

Swiftly he unfolded it and spread it out over the draftsman's board. It was the official geological survey map provided the company by the Bureau of Land Management. One quick glance told Longarm what he had by now pretty well suspected. The map was designed to indicate clearly just where on this range cutting would be allowed. Longarm found the river that ran past what was now Whipsaw. But Whipsaw was not inked in anywhere along that river. Opening the map farther, he found, enclosed by an irregular red line, those tracts that were to be cut. They were well over on the other side of the range. And there was Whipsaw, inked in at least sixty miles to the west of where it now stood, in a narrow valley that opened out onto the Black Rock Desert.

The Western Land and Lumber Combine was sure as hell operating illegally, just as Ruby had guessed. Slade was cutting on government land he had not been authorized to harvest. The company had been given vast tracts, easily as rich in timber as those it was now cutting, but there was no river for transporting the logs, and no railroad. In order to get the logs to the railroad, the loggers would have to skid the logs all the way across the range and then snake them down the mountainside to the railway.

Too much time. Too much labor. Too little profit that way. So they were cutting here—illegally.

Longarm began to fold the map. This made the cheese more binding. He had all he needed now to close down this operation and put Slade and his buddies away for a little rest. At that moment he wished Terry were beside him so she could see—as he now could—an end to the destruction of this valley and the ranchers who depended on it.

The door opened and Slade stood in the doorway, a gleaming Smith & Wesson in his hand. Stepping into the office, he closed the door behind him—and smiled. In that instant, Longarm remembered Tanner's last words:

Illegal! . . . Wrong place! Settlers—right. Stop him! Stop—!

For the first time Longarm knew who Tanner had wanted him to stop. It wasn't the deserter at all. It was Slade Desmond.

"You killed Tanner, didn't you, Desmond?" he said, though he already knew the answer.

"It's not going to do you any good to know that now," Slade replied.

"When Tanner returned to Whipsaw, he demanded that you show him this survey map," Longarm continued.

Slade took a step toward Longarm. "I can see now it must have been Ruby who alerted him to the possibility when he came through with that horse thief. You've got the map there. Too bad. Alice couldn't get away in time for me to stop you."

"Alice?" In that instant, Longarm realized his mistake in trusting her.

"She is confident she can do as good a job as Ruby. I was inclined to believe her. But she's too greedy. She insisted on a larger share." He took another step toward Longarm. "Give me that map, Longarm."

At that moment the night's heavy stillness was broken by the sound of sporadic firing from the direction of the hotel.

"You son of a bitch. Your men are going after Fitz."

Slade smiled. "And Ruby. She's too smart to be a whore."

The lantern was still where Longarm had placed it, within

arm's reach on a table beside the draftsman's board. With one quick swipe of his hand, Longarm sent the lantern at Slade. Startled at the sight of the lantern coming at his head, Slade ducked away and tried to get off a shot at Longarm at the same time. But the shot went wild as Longarm flung himself at the man. He caught the small, blocky fellow in the midsection and sent him crashing to the floor under him. The lantern had struck the floor just beyond them a second before. With a tiny roar, flames erupted on the spot, and, following the kerosene, raced along the floor, sweeping in under Slade's bald head. With a terrified scream, Slade hurled Longarm's weight off him, scrambled to his feet, and dashed through what was now a low wall of flame and out the door into the night.

Choking from the acrid smoke and shielding his eyes from the flames, Longarm holstered his Colt and dashed through the flames and out into the night after Slade. It was raining steadily now. There was no sign of Slade. Longarm decided to forget about him, and raced through the slanting rain toward the hotel.

Soon he was close enough to the hotel to see a struggling mass of men just in front of it. Some were rolling in the mud, but most were still standing. A few of them were wielding peaveys, while others used the long pike poles. The sound of grunting, cursing loggers was loud enough to pierce the steady roar of the rain. Longarm saw heads snapping back and men staggering to the ground as they reeled out of the battling crowd.

And then he was pushing himself through the loggers. He narrowly escaped a couple of swinging peaveys, their iron spikes whistling close. Once inside the hotel lobby, he saw two weeping girls hovering over a bloodied and broken body that still had life in it as it tried to crawl past them toward the door.

Longarm halted and looked down. It was Tim Caulder. Half of his face and most of his shoulder were blown away. Any movement on his part now was just blind reflex. The man was as good as dead. Longarm left him and dashed into Ruby's office.

The carnage was awesome. Fitz, the Peacemaker in his

right hand, was still propped up in bed with two pillows at
his back. His fine, handsome Irish face was calm, even though
the top of his head was missing. Two men, entangled half in
and half out of the bedroom doorway, were sprawled in front
of him. Longarm recognized Jack Wilson and Ruel Tyson. Fitz
had taken them both with him.

In the office, Ruby was lying on her side on the floor, a dark
pool of blood under her. She looked like an oversized carnival
doll, all lace and petticoats and long blonde hair. Beyond her
on the floor was Gus. He was sprawled on his side, his smoking shotgun beside him on the floor, just out of reach of his
right hand. Judging from the smell of gunpowder, both barrels
must have been fired. That accounted for the man outside in
the lobby and the other sitting against the the wall opposite
Gus. The middle part of him was little more than a stain plastered against the wall behind him. His face was cold white,
frozen into a mask of sudden dismay. Longarm did not know
him by name, but had seen him many times swaggering about
the street with others of Bat's men.

Gus groaned as Longarm dropped beside him. Gently
Longarm turned him over. Gus had suffered a head wound,
ugly but superficial. The round had creased his skull just above
his left brow, tracing a deep course on its way past his temple.
His scalp was open and the bleeding was profuse, causing the
wound to look far more extensive that it really was. But the
slug had certainly knocked rather hard on the logger's head.
Longarm shook Gus gently,

Gus opened his eyes. "I'm all right, Longarm. But I think
they got Fitz."

"They got him. And Ruby."

"Jesus!" The man closed his eyes, then opened them.
"Alice! Did they get Alice?"

"She must have got out in time."

"That's right. She wasn't here when they came."

Gus closed his eyes and took a deep breath.

"Stay low," Longarm told him. "I'll get one of the girls to
clean you up. Just lie still."

"I ain't going nowhere," the big man said softly.

Longarm got the redhead and one of her chums to see to

Gus, then walked out of the hotel. The rain had let up considerably. The fighting in front of the hotel had ceased also. Not a single long pike pole was in evidence. The union loggers had won this round. But what caught Longarm's gaze and the members of the crowd standing before him was the fire now consuming the general store. A roar went up from the loggers as they saw the flames envelop the front of the structure with a dull roar and begin swiftly to climb the false front. When the loggers discovered Longarm standing on the hotel porch, they soon grew silent and faced him, waiting.

"How's Fitz?" someone called out of the darkness.

"We came as soon as we heard the shooting," another man yelled. "Them scabs kept us out!"

Longarm cleared his throat and said, "Fitz is dead."

The silence in the crowd of loggers deepened.

"And so is Ruby."

The silence broke. Cries of rage and frustration broke from many throats. Someone dashed up onto the porch, stood beside Longarm, and cried, "Burn him out! Burn out that bastard, Slade!"

"The mill! Get the mill!" an angry voice shouted.

The logger left the porch in a bound and led the loggers toward the flaming general store. As Longarm watched, a groggy Gus Dodds appeared beside him on the porch.

"I heard them," Gus said. "That sounds like a great idea."

"I'd better get my horse," Longarm said, striding off the porch, "before they set fire to the livery stable."

"I'll go with you," Gus said, falling into step beside the marshal.

The general store was now a crackling shell of leaping flames and snapping boards. Occasional muffled explosions from within, like firecrackers under a tin can, indicated that the flames were reaching what stores of ammunition the place stocked. Longarm and Gus hurried past, ducking, as the detonating rounds increased in volume and frequency. The loggers, with flaming torches in their hands, were darting through the wet night firing every structure they could find upright, not missing the tents. The small shanties and the tents went quickly. The night was soon filled with lurid islands of dancing flames.

It was surprising how quickly and easily the rain-dampened structures ignited.

Reaching the livery stable, Longarm found that the hostler had driven all the horses into the corrals and was busy quieting them down as more and more structures around him leaped into flames. Fortunately, the loggers had decided to spare the stable. Longarm saw that his Morgan was safe and gave the hostler a silver dollar to keep an especially good eye on it. The fellow's enthusiasm increased enormously.

The mill had not yet been fired. Loggers dashed past him, heading for it. A few stopped as they saw Longarm without a torch, held their flaming brands close to see who he was, then dashed off. Every one of the loggers with arson still on his mind was heading now for the mill.

Shots came from behind Longarm. He looked back and saw Slade and about six of his riders bearing down on him, with his regrouped loggers trotting right behind. The pro-union loggers were scattered and disorganized. Slade's orderly phalanx easily overmatched the isolated pockets of torch-bearing loggers. His armed riders found that the torches made excellent targets. Shots rang out in a steady fusillade. Longarm saw logger after logger stumble and fall, their torches guttering out on the rain-soaked ground.

Now the mill became a rallying point for the suddenly beleaguered loggers. Longarm and Gus also began to run toward the mill, through a rain that had begun to slant down with increased intensity. As Longarm ran, he turned occasionally and snapped off a shot at Slade. Gus, wielding Fitz's Peacemaker, fired a round or two also. Their combined effort was troublesome enough to cause Slade to pull back and regroup his riders.

In that time, Longarm and Gus reached the mill and dashed inside with loggers holding peaveys right on their heels. Soon the mill was swarming with loggers, as Slade and his own force surrounded it. The rain was now coming down with a ferocity that caused the metal roof of the mill to drum with an almost deafening clamor. Peering out of one of the windows, Longarm saw Slade on his horse, hunched under the force of the driving sheets of rain, directing his loggers to burn the mill.

"I know you're in there, Longarm!" Slade shouted above the rain's roar. "It's going to be a terrible fire!"

But his loggers were having trouble firing the mill in the rain. Flaming boards or beams that they snatched up from the burning shacks around the mill were either extinguished by the heavy rain or petered out and died before they could get the drenched mill to catch. Hurled peaveys from the besieged loggers took a steady toll of Slade's loggers as they attempted, again and again, to hurl burning brands into the mill. And then Longarm saw a few loggers rolling barrels of what he presumed to be kerosene down the street toward the mill.

Thunder crashed overhead, further deafening them. Lightning crackled. As the forks of blue fire flickered overhead, Longarm and the loggers in the mill had no difficulty seeing Slade's loggers rolling the kerosene barrels closer toward them. They began to shout obscenities at the murderous gang, which only drew the fire of Slade and his riders. Longarm nudged Gus, then led him down to the second level of the mill and in under the saw's framing. The area was almost hip-deep in sawdust that had backed up from the huge pile outside.

Here, Longarm was sure, was where those loggers with the kerosene barrels were headed. He glanced at Gus. The man nodded, understanding perfectly. A second later, a long series of rippling tongues of lightning boiled above them in the sky. In that light, Longarm saw four loggers rolling their kerosene barrels in under the mill, directly toward them.

Above the pounding of the rain and the crackling of the thunder, Longarm yelled at them to pull back. They didn't hear him. Their heads were down as they rolled the barrels still closer. Then they let go and the barrels kept rolling, bumping finally to rest against the pilings the mill was resting on. Behind them appeared one of Slade's gunmen. His revolver gleamed in the night as he aimed at the barrels.

Longarm fired at the man, the slug catching him in the chest, spinning him back into the wet night to be replaced by another of Slade's men, this one armed with a Winchester. Before either Longarm or Gus could get off a shot, the man sent a rapid-fire volley at them. As Longarm ducked low, the slugs whining off the beams, Slade's man directed his fire at the four barrels.

One barrel would have been enough. Four was too much. The explosion flung Longarm completely out from beneath the pilings and up onto the huge sawdust pile behind the mill. A stunned Gus hurtled after him. At the same time, the exploding barrels—with a fierce series of detonations—sent out ribbons of flame that caught up Slade's rifleman before he could regain his feet. The man disappeared into the maw of fire and smoke without a sound. In almost the same instant, flames began consuming the pilings on which the mill rested and started licking hungrily at the rough flooring above. Just below this, the waist-deep sawdust ignited with an explosive roar, the flames reaching out to the main pile, causing it to smolder despite the rain.

Screams and savage oaths came from within the mill. In the light of the fire, Longarm saw some loggers jumping from the mill to the ground, while others dove out of windows to land alongside Longarm and Gus on the sawdust pile. They promptly scrambled off and vanished into the darkness. It was the only course open to them now as the flames engulfed the mill. Some of the loggers remained trapped inside. Their screams infuriated and sickened Longarm.

Slade's riders appeared now out of the darkness, still on their horses, shooting up at those loggers hanging from windows or making ready to jump. One logger, perched on the steaming metal roof, hesitated before making such a jump. He was shot before he could make up his mind and plummeted to the ground. Slade's loggers began running down those loggers fleeing the mill, catching them in the back with their long pike poles.

Longarm and Gus were at the top of the sawdust pile. They kept to a prone position and were almost entirely concealed by the sawdust as they shot at carefully chosen targets. With some satisfaction, Longarm saw one rider he caught in the side tumble from his saddle to lie without moving in a flaming pool of mud. Another target, one of Slade's loggers, was busily impaling a wounded logger on the end of his pike pole. Longarm's slug caught him on the side of his head. The logger on the ground, the pole still in his side, crawled off as the first gray streak of dawn light filtered down into the drenched valley.

They had fought clear through the night and Longarm had only six rounds left in the pocket of his ruined frock coat.

Fortunately, he had two cheroots left. He handed one to Gus and proceeded to reload his Colt.

"They're wet!" Gus complained.

"I know it. Chew on it. Smoking's a disgusting habit anyway."

"You ought to quit, then."

"I'm trying. Why do you think I gave you my last cheroot? Now shut up and let me reload. Slade's men are nosing around down there."

The mill crackled in the fire. The day brightened but the rain kept up.

Chapter 10

The mill collapsed, seemingly as much from the pressure of the pounding rain as from the flames. Scalding, billowing clouds of steam rose up as the walls of still-burning logs tumbled, down onto the soaked ground. The loggers were gone from the mill area, most of the pro-union men undoubtedly forted up now in their vermin-infested railway bunkhouses, waiting for the storm to pass.

Slade had pulled his men back from the sawdust pile and now sat his horse alongside his four remaining riders, his derby pulled tightly down upon his bald skull, his bulldog chin set, as the rain slammed down onto him.

"I know you two are up there!" Slade cried suddenly, cupping his hands about his mouth. "You can't stay on that sawdust pile forever, Longarm! Not unless you aim to eat it!"

Dim, grudging laughter greeted this remark from the soaked riders beside Slade. The men had lost too many comrades this past night to be really loose. By this time it was light enough for Longarm to see Slade clearly—and for Slade and his men to see Longarm and Gus just as easily.

"Do you want to go down there and trust to the mercies of that crew?" Longarm asked Gus.

"Hell's bells, Longarm! There's only five of them. We can take 'em!"

"They're out of range of these six-guns."

"We'll trick 'em!"

"How?"

"We'll make like we're coming down peaceful. Then, when we get close enough, we can open up on them."

The plan was insane, of course. It gave them about as much of a chance as a hen at a coyote convention. Slade would not let either of them get that close while both men kept their weapons. And Longarm knew his derringer, carrying only two rounds, would not be enough. Not for five men, anyway. In addition, the flesh wound in his shoulder was beginning to ache fiercely, indicating to Longarm that he must have torn open the wound when he was sent flying ass-over-teakettle out onto this pile of wood shit.

Still, it *was* a plan. If there was little chance of its succeeding, at least it gave Gus and him something to do in the next fifteen minutes besides get rained on.

Abruptly, the rain's intensity increased. What had been a moderate, steady drizzle became almost instantly a solid, battering downpour. There was no mercy in it whatsoever. It felt like someone upstairs was emptying buckets; raindrops pounded like buckshot as they plastered Longarm's coat to his back, drummed furiously on his hat, then ran like miniature waterfalls off the brim.

And it kept up. Through the sheets of rain Longarm could no longer make out Slade and his riders. *Now!* he thought. *Now!* This cloudburst could not last forever. He tugged on Gus's sleeve.

"Let's go!" he shouted into Gus's ear. "Head for the river!"

Gus nodded and began to paddle backward through the heavy sawdust. By now the pile was so completely saturated with water that Longarm felt at times that he was in danger of drowning in the stuff. At last he pulled himself free and the two men started racing through the almost blinding rain toward the tracks and the river beyond.

By the time they reached the tracks, the downpour had run its course, and the almost solid curtain of rain began to lift. Longarm glanced back. Slade and his men were still busy quieting their mounts. In a moment, however, the man would look over and spot them. From that time on it would be an uneven race to the river—Slade and his men riding horses, Longarm and Gus on foot.

A queer vibration seemed to fill the air and then sink into the ground beneath Longarm's feet. He glanced at Gus, who was himself looking quickly and nervously about. It felt like a heavy freight barrel-assing down a steep grade—a *very* steep grade and a *very* heavy freight. Longarm looked up. Some-

thing strange was indeed happening. The mountainside beyond
Whipsaw was changing its shape—rapidly. It appeared to be
shrinking some, or perhaps settling. But, no, it wasn't just settling at all. *The whole mountainside was piling down on them!*
The trembling was no longer confined to the ground; the very
air itself was trembling, with a bone-rattling, buffeting force
that beat on Longarm like a fierce wind.

Slade and his men were bent over their horses, trying to
outride the mud slide. Some of the men began to cut toward the
river. In a panic, Slade followed. The horses had broken from
their corrals, and, like Slade and his men, were digging hard
for the river. All of this Longarm watched, fascinated, as the
entire side of the mountain—its broad slopes so recently
plucked bare of its trees and grasses—swept down in a colos-
sal tide of mud and debris. It had not yet struck the town, but
Longarm realized that when it did, it would obliterate everything. A massive, thick, pudding-like soup, it carried on its
crest a monstrous tangle of tree trunks and stumps, and a few
boulders that shone in the rain like teeth in an old man's mouth.

The hotel crumbled, then was swept along, becoming a part
of this monstrous mud slide that rushed over Whipsaw with an
ease and speed that was awesome. The still-smoldering re-
mains of the general store and the Paradise Valley went next.
Longarm turned and headed for the river at a dead run. Gus
was already well ahead of him. As Longarm reached the dark,
swollen river, he paused to look back.

Loggers were streaming from the bunkhouse toward the
river. Slade and his riders had almost reached it. The horses
were already there, plunging in. Longarm thought he could see
the hostler, well behind his horses—too far behind.

The tide of mud rolled and roared across the length of what
had been Whipsaw's main drag. It absorbed everything in its
path, advancing in a crescent shape that sent before it a forelip
almost ten feet high, making a titanic hissing sound and nosing to the right and to the left as if it were on the spoor of still
more buildings to devour—which, of course, it was. The mill's
wreckage was swallowed up and the bunkhouses were lifted
from their tracks and swept along.

Longarm turned and dove into the river. He was more than
halfway across when he felt the water under him rise suddenly

and begin to carry him with extraordinary speed to the opposite bank. Tumbling, he struck solid ground, remembering vaguely that he must keep going. Scrambling to his feet, he headed for the slope ahead of him. He might have made it if a very wet, gritty, heavy hand had not struck him down from behind.

Incredibly, the sun was out. Its warmth poured down from a cloudless sky. Longarm groaned and turned his head away from it, then pushed himself to a sitting position. He found that every muscle in his body was singing a different tune. Some springs were missing and some bolts were loosened, but nothing was broken clean through.

He was covered from head to foot with a crust of dried mud. When he turned his head, he felt the dirt inside his collar grating against the skin of his neck. In a sudden burst of concern, he reached up for his hat.

"I got it right here," Gus drawled from behind him.

Longarm turned. Gus, sitting farther up the slope, handed him his hat.

"Been sitting here with nothing to do except listen to your godawful groaning. So I figured I might as well spend my time doing something helpful, and cleaned your hat. You'll have to clean the rest of yourself in the river. Your clothes, too. All that dried mud'll scratch you to death if you try walking in them now. You don't have to worry none about going naked. There ain't a girl left over there."

Longarm placed his hat gingerly on his head and eased himself up beside Gus. From where they were sitting, they could look across the river at what was left of Whipsaw. There wasn't much—only the burnt-out shells of two shacks, and a tent at the far end of town.

Longarm looked back at Gus. "*All* of the girls, Gus?"

Gus nodded gloomily. "They all went to the hotel when the fires and the rain started. And some of them was trapped in the Paradise Valley, I guess. Don't matter where they were, they're all gone now. Snuffed out."

"I'm sorry about Alice, Gus."

"She was a fine little chippy, Longarm. She wasn't one bit like them other girls. Kind and considerate, she was. That's why Ruby liked her so much. I liked her from the start, Long-arm, the first time I seen her get off that train in Silver City."

"She was some girl, Gus, that's for sure." Longarm found he could not look into Gus's eyes as he replied "And you're right. Ruby did feel kind of partial to her." Longarm decided not to tell Gus of Slade's revelation to him concerning Alice.

"Well," Gus sighed, "there's no sense in crying over spilt milk. But I sure will miss her."

"I won't miss Whipsaw, Gus—and very few of the ranchers around here will, either."

"I guess you won't, at that. But them out-of-work loggers over there will. Some of them, anyway."

Gus was referring to a large contingent of loggers that had made it across the river and settled into a makeshift camp on this side. There were a few Digger-like shelters fashioned out of logs and slash, some fire pits, and that was about all. The river itself survived at this point only as a narrow channel, since the mud slide had almost completely blocked it. The new, narrower channel cut close to where Longarm and Gus were sitting. It looked as if a permanent and very wide mean-der in the river had been created, but the flow had not been interrupted, and for that the ranchers to the south could be grateful. The mountainside facing them from across the river looked raw—as if it were the carcass of some enormous ani-mal whose hide had been ripped off, revealing the vital organs beneath.

Longarm stood up to get a better view of it, as well as of the valley that had been so ruthlessly stamped out. Gus stood up also, and pointed to the crest of the range.

"I'll bet it all started up there," he said. "There was a ridge along that crest. It's gone now. That was the first place we cut. I remember the deep fault behind it, some nice big fir was growing in it. We cut every one, first thing. The whole ridge must have just peeled right off."

Longarm nodded. That seemed likely. He'd been up there, he remembered, and seen for himself the condition of that slope. Of course, there was no way anyone was going to be able to find out for sure. The important thing was that Slade was stopped.

"Where's Slade?" Longarm asked.

"He's long gone. While you was having your little snooze, the loggers who made it across went after Slade. He only had four riders left when he hightailed it out of this valley, heading north just ahead of the loggers. Some followed him for a while on them horses that made it across—but they've all straggled back. Slade lost them in the desert."

Longarm immediately began to undress. "What happened to that hostler?"

"He never made it."

For some reason, that bothered Longarm. He shook his head, seeing in his mind's eye the lone figure running through the rain toward the river—so far behind the horses. "Go see if you can find that Morgan of mine, will you, Gus? I won't be long here. I can ride in wet clothes; this sun'll dry me fast enough. I don't want Slade to get too far ahead of me."

"You mean *us*, Longarm. I'm going too."

"Why?"

"Didn't he kill Tanner?"

Longarm considered this for a moment. "Yes, I'm pretty sure he did, Gus."

"I'm going with you. And I don't want no argument."

Longarm smiled and began peeling off his mud-encrusted pants. "I wasn't about to argue, Gus. Pick out a horse for yourself while you're at it. And see what gear you can rustle up."

As Longarm stepped out of his pants, he glanced around and saw that Gus was already halfway to the loggers' camp.

By the time the two men reached the desert, Longarm was thoroughly baked into his clothes. He was pleased to be riding the Morgan once again. Gus had chosen a grullo. What gear they had been able to wheedle from the few remaining loggers amounted to little more than a couple of torn slickers and a total of four canteens. Gus had the Peacemaker and about ten rounds. Longarm still had only six rounds. He had cleaned his gun carefully before setting out.

Slade's tracks pointed due north across an ancient lakebed that was now only a baked alkali flat. A tumble of rocks gradually reared out of the heat haze, and it was toward this pile that Slade and his men seemed to have headed. The fierce, dry heat pounded down relentlessly. They kept their horses to a slow but steady pace. After what must have been an hour, they seemed no closer to the rocks. Longarm felt as if he were being drowned in light as the sun's rays slanted up from the table-salt whiteness of the alkali. Gus and he were moving through a brilliant emptiness without end, without hope—a kind of inspired, hellish punishment.

At last, as if some force had abruptly lifted the rocks and placed them hundreds of yards closer, they were able to see the stretch of badlands as solid reality, less than half a mile ahead of them.

"I didn't thank you," Longarm said, mildly surprised at the sound of his own voice.

"For what?" Gus didn't bother to turn his head.

"For pulling me out of that mudslide."

Gus shrugged. "I didn't want to leave you there. You looked like a beached catfish. When that slide hit the water, it was like a boot splashing into a puddle. You just got caught by a part of that puddle when it came back down. It was muddy, all right, and filled with slash, and it just about drowned you."

A canyon opened up before them. Leading the way, Longarm guided the Morgan into its blessed coolness. Once through the canyon, however, they found themselves lifting into a bleak, inhospitable graveyard of stone monoliths and spires. They passed under great, leaning gargoyles of stone.

"We better find some water," Gus said.

A shot rang out—from a revolver, judging by the sound of it. And then came another shot, the two echoes rolling frantically about them among the rocks. But no bullets whined close. Pulling up, Longarm looked at Gus.

Another shot sent its echo rolling after the others.

"Someone's in trouble," Longarm said, starting up again. "Off to our right here, I think."

Gus offered no contrary opinion, and followed Longarm into a narrow ravine. As they proceeded along the narrow trail between almost sheer cliffs, Longarm caught sight of a man propped against a boulder, his hat still on, his feet spread, a canteen resting in front of him in the sand. As they rode closer, the man raised his revolver heavenward and pulled the trigger. The man was too far gone to look up and see them approaching.

He began to tip over on his side. The gun fell from his hand and went clattering among the rocks, striking his canteen and sending it spinning away. By the time Longarm had reached the man and dismounted, the fellow was lying on his stomach. Gus dismounted, knelt quickly and pulled the man over. After one look at the swollen, greenish face, he turned to Longarm and shook his head.

"He's been drinking bad water—very bad water."

The man's eyes flickered open. He saw Gus leaning over and tried to talk to him. His eyes widened with the effort. Gus leaned close and Longarm knelt beside him.

". . . water hole. I didn't believe them . . ." the dying man gasped. ". . . didn't believe!"

"Which way is Slade headed?" Longarm asked.

"North to the pines . . . get the Diggers . . . need food . . . water . . ."

Longarm stood up and went to his horse for the only canteen he had left with water in it. He was on his way back when he saw the man's eyes close and his head dip. Gus caught his head before it tumbled heavily down among the sharp rocks, then slowly lowered the man's body carefully onto the gravelly ground.

"That's one less to worry about," Longarm said, continuing to unscrew the canteen. He lifted the canteen to his mouth.

"Better go easy with that," Gus said, "until we find a spring or a water hole in this badland somewhere. And we better be more careful than he was."

Longarm nodded, took another swallow, and handed the canteen to Gus. He took a short swig, handed it back to Longarm, and said, "Let's go. The buzzards in this part of the world will be real pleased to see a fat meal like that frying on these stones." Gus looked skyward and called softly, "Dinner is served, you bastards!"

They didn't mount up again, but led their horses on through the ravine. Once they were beyond it, Longarm cut sign once again. He found he was following a trail that now led due west. To Digger country, of course. Longarm thought of Barbara Spencer Tate and became suddenly nervous. He knew he shouldn't be. Those Diggers—no, no, *Paiutes*—would take good care of the anthropologist. But still he worried.

A water hole gleamed just before them. It was close in

under the canyon wall, an overhanging ledge offering welcome shade. Longarm was out of his saddle before Gus, kneeling beside the still pool. The water was clear, but there was a faint sulfurous stink in the air. A few wild onions grew about it, but little else. Peering closer into the cool, icy, immaculate depths, he saw no bugs, no algae scum, no worms, grubs, or spiders. Nothing alive. The smell had warned him, and the lifeless look of the water had convinced him. Gus, beside him, had seen what Longarm had. They both got to their feet.

"Looks so damn innocent and pure, don't it?" said Gus, shaking his head. "That's what fooled that poor bastard back there. The others likely warned him, but he let his eyes buffalo his good sense. He'd've been better off cutting his throat. I figure there's arsenic in that water—a good dose—along with a few other goodies."

Longarm turned back to his horse and mounted up. As Gus climbed up beside him, Longarm said, "We might as well follow those bastards as far as we can. There's water near the pine slopes. I know a spot."

Gus nodded. Longarm prodded the Morgan on. He didn't look back at the spring.

It was near sundown when they reached the barren, sage-dotted foothills of the range that still shimmered, a blue mirage, in the distance. There was not a drop of water left in their canteens, and the horses were beginning to stumble. They dismounted and led the horses through the foothills. It was a long trek, and by this time Longarm was more concerned with finding water than he was with staying on Slade's trail. He could pick that up later. The Paiutes would help. What they needed now—the horses, Gus, and himself—was water. Good old scummy, grubby, weed-infested water.

Out of nowhere, it seemed, clouds began to form over the range. They multiplied and merged, piling up like mashed potatoes, like sea foam—building upon one another like a second mountain range, greater than the one below it. The cloud forms seemed to jostle as they merged. As they walked wearily toward the building clouds, hope kindled in Longarm's breast. There was water in those clouds, plenty of it. The only question was, where would they let it down?

He heard thunder. More clouds seemed to form in the empty sky to merge with the others. The clouds began to shoot higher. Stratospheric winds began flattening their tops, giving them an anvil-like shape. Lightning glinted in their slate-gray bowels. The storm clouds began to spread rapidly now, taking over more of the sky. They were coming closer. The thunder was beginning to rock the hills around them.

Longarm stopped in his tracks. He could smell rain. Gus had pulled up also, and looked at him quizzically. They were both too dry to want to converse unless they had to.

"Dig holes," Longarm told Gus. "Line them with the slickers."

"You think we'll get it? That storm looks like it's on the other side of them mountains."

"Dig."

With a weary shrug, Gus followed Longarm's example and walked out to a flat expanse of alkali. Longarm broke the surface of the ground with his gun barrel, then scooped out the sand and gravel. Alkali dust soon covered his face and stung his eyes mercilessly. The sweat carried the alkali deep into the corners of his eyes, into his nostrils, and even into his grimly compressed mouth. But he kept digging, with his hands now, gouging out as deep a basin as he could.

When he had dug so deeply that his elbows were below the surface of the flat, he got up and untied the slicker from behind the cantle on the Morgan. He inspected it carefully, found no holes or rents in it, and then lined the hole with it. He stood back and looked over to see that Gus was about finished as well.

Then he glanced up at the sky. The storm was coming this way. Most of the sky was covered now with low, boiling clouds. Lightning stroked like gunfire through the clouds and Longarm caught himself remembering that ledge he had shared with Terry Troy not so long ago. He shook away the memory, saddened instantly by a sharp sense of loss, and felt volleys of thunder shake the air. He could smell ozone. The wind was rising. Longarm ducked his head and held onto his hat brim. When the horses began to drift back, he reached out for the Morgan's bridle and held it. Broad, dried streaks of lather covered the animal's chest and flanks.

Above them the clouds rolled in, thickening, then cracking and spitting with a roar that staggered them. Longarm clutched the horses's bridle tighter, not sure who was steadying whom. A flash of lightning—like a knife slashing open a belly—cut the clouds, and the rain came down.

Longarm took off his hat and held it out to fill for the Morgan. Then he tipped his head back and let the pounding drops clean out his eyes and face. His body absorbed the moisture hungrily, like a sponge. It took no time at all for his hat to fill. He placed it down carefully on its crown and walked over to the makeshift basins. His was full. While the rain still pounded down, he knelt by the basin and pushed his canteen under the roiling surface. The canteen was soon filled completely. He did the same with his second canteen, screwed the cap back on, then lay facedown on the soaked ground, ducked his head into the warm rainwater, and shook it.

Then he sat up, grinning over at Gus who was lying on his back, his face taking the full brunt of the downpour, his good eye closed tightly. Longarm took his canteens back to the horse and tied them to the saddle rings, then lifted the hatful of water to his horse's muzzle. She drank eagerly.

The rain began to trail off. The thunder and lightning passed over, and, soon the rain diminished to a shower, then to a sprinkling, and finally to nothing at all. The clouds rumbled in the distance. A fresh, golden light broke through. Glancing up, Longarm saw a double rainbow, one foot of it lost on the pine slopes beyond the foothills.

The pine-clad mountains no longer looked so far away. They seemed invitingly close, fresh, and clear in the squeaky-clean air. Longarm glanced over at Gus, who was in the act of bringing his two canteens back to his horse, and said, "These horses need a rest. As soon as we get into those pines, we'll camp for the night. We can pick up Slade's trail tomorrow."

"You think the son of a bitch made it?" Gus asked.

Longarm nodded. "He's too goddamned mean not to have made it, I'm thinking."

Gus nodded and turned his attention to his horse. The animal wanted some more water. Gus picked up his hat and went back to his basin of rainwater. Longarm did the same.

* * *

Longarm woke from a sound sleep and turned his head. The
bright white face of the moon was blocked entirely by the silhouette of an Indian. Longarm sat up. The Indian drove the end
of his bow into the ground and hunkered down to face Longarm. In the bright moonlight Longarm recognized the face of
Wanowi. The Paiute's bronzed, shiny countenance was troubled.

Longarm glanced across the dead campfire at Gus. The logger was sitting up warily, the Peacemaker gleaming dully in
his hand.

"It's all right, Gus," Longarm said. "This Indian's a friend.
His name is Wanowi."

"A Digger?"

"A Paiute. A member of a fast-declining Pleistocene culture."

"For Christ's sake, Longarm, speak plain."

Longarm smiled in the darkness and turned back to Wanowi.
"What's wrong, Wanowi?" He didn't really have to ask. Evidently Slade had made his presence felt in the area already.

Wanowi gestured with his left arm and another Paiute
slipped out of the pines and hurried toward them. This one
dropped beside Wanowi and spoke rapidly in his own tongue to
Wanowi, who listened intently, then turned back to Longarm.

"He say Miss Tate have trouble. Three riders in her camp.
They go in her tent. Mr. Slade—Little Man With No Hair—is
their leader. They have rifles. Shoot Indians, many."

Longarm threw back the slicker and stood up. "Where were
you through all this, Wanowi?"

Wanowi pointed south. "My people gather nuts. It is our
time—our grove. We spend week in harvest. Miss Tate stay
near stream. She speak much to paper. She study many books.
Busy."

"Okay. I understand." Longarm turned to Gus. "If Slade is
still messing up the woman's camp, maybe we can catch up to
him. I'm assuming this Indian scooted out of the place without
being seen."

"Who the hell is this Miss Tate?" Gus asked.

"It's too difficult to explain, Gus. I don't rightly know, myself. She's a different kind of woman than I've been used to.
Just get a move on. The horses are rested plenty. We should get
there by sunup if this moon holds."

"Well, this dang moon ain't going to hold, and I just wish I

could get a plain answer from you, *Mister* Longarm. I never
heard there was a girl out here living with them Indians. Why
the hell didn't anyone tell me?" He shook his head emphatically and knelt to roll up his slicker. "Never heard of such a
crazy thing. Woman's probably tetched in the head . . ."

He was still grumbling when they mounted up and started
north, the Paiutes trotting along beside them in the moon-
dappled darkness.

It was past sunup when Longarm and Gus broke onto the
meadow above the stream and started across it to the Indian encampment. A few of the wickiups had been knocked aside,
Longarm noted, but the tent was still sitting proudly on
the grassy sward across the stream. For a moment Longarm
had the absurd feeling that Wanowi—for some inexplicable
reason—had lied to him, that he had invented the entire story.

And then he saw Barbara. She was in the midst of a small
crowd of Indian women on the far side of the stream, spreading
out blankets and sheets on the grass. The Paiute women's hair
seemed more than usually wild, Longarm thought. Barbara
was directing the operation with such intensity that she did not
see Longarm and Gus at first. When she did glance up to see
them, she stood up straight, looking as cool as he had remembered, still wearing her pith helmet, the golden bun of her hair
resting on the nape of her neck, gleaming in the bright morning sunshine. She waved only once as Longarm and Gus rode
closer.

"I see what you mean," Gus said grimly. "What in hell is
that she's got on her head?"

"A sun helmet, favored by British soldiers fighting in the
tropics. Keeps the head cool enough."

"Looks like a beehive."

Longarm had reached the stream by that time. He dismounted and left his horse with the same Indian woman who
had taken her before. He told her to remove the Morgan's
saddle, then led Gus across the stream to the waiting Barbara
Spencer Tate.

"Meet Gus, Barbara," Longarm said.

"It is a pleasure, Gus," Barbara said.

"Gus, this is Barbara Spencer Tate, anthropologist."

"Howdy, Miss Tate." Gus was obviously as impressed by her jodhpurs and hunting outfit as by the steady gaze from her cool, hazel eyes.

Longarm turned back to Barbara. "Wanowi told us you had some visitors."

"Shall we make ourselves comfortable?" she asked him.

Longarm nodded, and with a quick wink at Gus, led him up the small slope to Barbara's tent. At once Longarm noticed that there were only four folding chairs where before there had been six. The table was gone as well. A small, ragged piece of canvas was lying some distance away near the pinyon grove. Without saying anything, Longarm sat down. Gus had some difficulty getting his huge frame comfortable in his chair. He seemed to be afraid it would collapse under him. Barbara ignored Gus's uneasiness and addressed Longarm.

"A small, defenseless little girl and two of the Indians left behind to guard this encampment were brutally murdered, Longarm. I shall never forget it. Never."

"How many men were there?"

"Three."

"And one of them was Slade Desmond?"

"Yes. The pig introduced himself to me. A small man, bald, wearing a ridiculous little derby."

Longarm glanced at Gus, then back at Barbara. "Wanowi said they entered your tent. I'm glad to see you're all right."

"They proposed to rape me, Longarm. Fortunately, they decided to do it one at a time. Unfortunately, Slade Desmond was outvoted by his hirelings—so he was not the first."

Longarm saw Gus's face go pale, and realized that he didn't feel so good himself. He swallowed, but his mouth had suddenly dried up.

"The first one—a pale, furtive slug—was foolish enough to be carried away by the sight of a naked woman waiting for him in a prone position. He dropped his gunbelt and hurried to me." She paused. Longarm saw her face whiten and her eyes grow bleak. "He did not see the knife I held at my side. . . ." She swallowed and went on. "Afterward, as soon as I could, I snatched up his gun and managed to shoot the next in line. But I missed Slade when the two of them rode out. . . ."

There was an awkward silence for a moment until Longarm

cleared his throat nervously and asked, "You say you wounded one of them?"

"Yes. And killed the other. I . . . was not careful how I did it, I am afraid. At the moment I'm concerned primarily with cleaning the sheets and blankets. I only wish I could completely remove the stains from the cot." Her white teeth closed upon her upper lip. She bowed her head, her forehead resting in her palm.

Longarm saw her shoulders trembling as tears began to break through what had been an iron composure. He looked sharply at Gus and got to his feet. Gus stood up also. They left her and walked toward the trees. This gave her the opportunity she wanted, and she hurried into the tent.

Well into the pines, they came upon a fresh grave. There was no marker. There didn't need to be. Longarm knew who was under that fresh earth. The first eager rapist.

"She'll be all right in a little while," Gus said softly, hopefully.

"Yes," Longarm agreed.

"You were right, Longarm. She's a different kind of woman, all right."

Chapter 11

Four Paiutes with Wanowi leading them helped Longarm and Gus track Slade and his wounded sidekick. Late that same day they came to the end of the pine forests. Ahead of them lay treacherous, gullied badlands. Gaunt, shadowed buttes and mesas poked almost straight up. The entire, savage land seemed to possess neither grass nor water. Into this inhospitable land the tracks of the two horses led.

Longarm pulled up and looked at Gus. "Ambush country. They can fort up in there for as long as they need to."

"If they got water and food."

"They can shoot food, and there's probably water. They'll work their way through in about a week and be in Utah then."

Longarm dismounted for a conference with Wanowi. The Indian seemed eager to move into the badlands after the two men.

"Wanowi, let us go on. We can track these two ourselves, now. And we can go faster with our horses."

"Wanowi go, too," the small Indian insisted grimly.

"No. This is my business, Wanowi, my job. Remember, I'm a federal marshal. I represent the government."

The Indian wavered. "We can help, Longarm."

"You already have. Please go back and see to Miss Tate. She needs your help now."

The Indian drew himself up to his full five and a half feet, stared proudly back at Longarm for a moment, then nodded solemnly. "We go back to Miss Tate. Good luck, Longarm." He turned to Gus. "Good luck, Gus."

It was the first time Wanowi had spoken to Gus, since Gus, after all, was one of those loggers who had been tearing down their pine forests. Gus was pleased and, smiling slightly, he nodded curtly in response.

As the Paiutes trotted back into the timber, Longarm remounted and led the way down a narrow ravine.

They came to a sluggish, slimy little creek and forded it easily. The tracks of Slade and the other man were still deep in the soft sand beside the creek. A swarm of deerflies attacked them. One landed in Gus's hair and attached itself to his scalp. When Longarm noticed the blood flowing down the back of Gus's neck, he alerted the man, who slapped furiously at the fly, killing it. Longarm squashed another that had taken root on his own forearm. Only when they had gone a decent distance from the creek were they free of the little bastards.

They moved still deeper into the shadowed, gloomy country. The grass was scarce, the walls sheer and striated, so tall in places that they blocked out the sky for long stretches. The tracks of the two men, however, remained clear. Longarm was sure they were gaining.

Soon they turned into a dungeonlike defile that turned and twisted like a snake under overhanging and interlocking walls so high, so close, that this time Longarm found he could catch not even a glimpse of the sky. The floor of the cleft was irregular, wet, sandy, and in places rather soupy. The defile opened up at last and led onto a wide, flat rock serving as the floor of a broad canyon. The stream that had cut this canyon was only a thin, sluggish trickle as they approached it.

Longarm dismounted, and so did Gus. They let their horses blow and get their fill of water. The two men silently filled their canteens, both of them looking idly about at the towering, forbidding walls. Slade's tracks had led out onto this canyon floor and then disappeared on the hard limestone. There were many exits from this canyon, any one of which could have been taken by the fleeing men.

But perhaps by this time Slade wasn't fleeing any more.

They mounted up, and were riding down the canyon, both men keeping their eyes on the rocks above, watching for any glint of sunlight on metal, when they heard a faint and mournful wail. It did not seem to be coming from anything human. It appeared to emanate from abysmal depths far back in the bowels of this underworld of twisted canyons and hidden passageways.

Longarm pulled up, his head cocked, trying to locate the source of this weird cry. Both he and Gus decided on a dim, shadowed cleft in the canyon wall, and spurred cautiously toward it. As they rode into the narrow wash, the cry became slightly louder and seemed to be coming out of the very rock walls themselves. A terrifying caterwauling it was, multiplied and amplified by echoes piled on echoes, overlapping and reinforcing one another. Both Longarm and Gus found themselves nervously looking over their shoulders from time to time as they continued on down the snaking arroyo.

They broke out onto a small open space and saw at once the source of the awesome clamor. Not Slade, but a man who was obviously his wounded companion was slowly sinking into a patch of quicksand, while his horse calmly cropped some grama near a small stream only thirty or so feet away.

"Help me!" the man cried. "Get me out of here! I'm sinking!"

The two riders pulled up. The stricken man was up to his waist in the stuff. It was evident that he could not get out. On the other hand, he did not appear to be sinking. His hat was gone and one side of his vest was ripped away to reveal a bloodied cotton shirt. This was the one Barbara had wounded. So where was Slade?

Gus and Longarm exchanged glances as if the same thought had occurred to both of them simultaneously. Longarm looked back at the terrified man.

"Where's Slade?"

"The bastard left me here to die! He could have helped me, but he just rode off!"

Gus lifted off his hat and scratched his head. "How the hell did you get out there, mister? You picking flowers or something?"

"My horse! It stumbled in this muck and threw me. It got out all right, but it left me, the son of a bitch!"

The man was apparently beside himself. He began struggling again, which caused him to sink just a little farther. But Longarm was wary. He had never heard of a man buried completely in quicksand in his life. Most old-timers he had talked to agreed that this was just an Eastern writer's fiction. When-ever animals and men were killed by quicksand, it was not through suffocation, but starvation or thirst. Quicksand could prevent an animal or a person from pulling free through his own frantic exertions. So Slade had left his friend trapped here to die by whichever came first—starvation or thirst.

"Shall we pull him out?" Gus asked reluctantly.

"Just hold it a minute," Longarm said. He looked around and up at the rock walls, searching for places where Slade could have settled himself while his live bait lured his pursuers into his trap. "That fellow ain't going anywhere in a hurry. Why don't we just look around?"

"Hey! You two ain't going to leave me here to die, are you?" the fellow cried in sudden panic. "You can't do that. Gus! You know me!"

Gus winced. "I *do* know the son of a bitch, Longarm," he admitted. "He was the only one of Bat's men who treated any-one decent. He wasn't exactly carrying a harp around with him, you understand."

"Pull him out if you want," Longarm said, "but I think you'd better let me look around first."

Gus paused to glance swiftly around him. "You think Slade's up there waiting somewhere?"

"What would you do if you were trying to shake two track-ers hard on your tail?"

"Go ahead. Look around. I ain't anxious to get a bullet in my back."

Ignoring the frantic wails of the trapped man, Longarm and Gus rode back into the shadows of the arroyo and dismounted out of his sight. Gus winced as the fellow's cries became even more despairing and hopeless.

"Wait here," Longarm told Gus. "Two of us climbing around up there might warn Slade off, if that's where he is. Just stay in here out of sight. Let that jasper bleat all he wants."

Gus nodded and Longarm moved back into the arroyo, looking for a way up either side. He found a rough trail, clam-bered past the loose talus, and began climbing. It took him a long time to reach the rim of the canyon wall surrounding the small pocket where Slade's man was trapped.

As Longarm searched the rimrock, he could not escape the

strident cries of the fellow so far below him. They echoed and reechoed among the rock walls and off the boulders. It was as if the screams had a life of their own. The trapped man was obviously convinced by this time that all hope was lost, that Longarm and Gus had abandoned him. This added such a keening note of terror to the man's cries that it was difficult for Longarm to push them out of his mind as he continued to pick his way over the rocks and crevasses along the canyon's rim.

Mercifully, the wild pleas for help ceased. The echoes died. Longarm straightened. *Good*, he thought. *That jasper is getting hold of himself. About time. At the rate he was bellowing, the devil himself would slam the door in his face.* As Longarm thought this, he was in the act of clambering over a particularly craggy outcropping. Suddenly he froze. He had spotted the glint of sunlight on metal on a ridge just ahead of him. Dropping lower, he started up again and moved closer to the ledge, taking his time, putting each foot down with infinite care. He had long since taken off his spurs. A large boulder blocked his path. He was moving around it cautiously when he heard Gus's voice coming from far below.

Gus! You stupid son of a bitch! I told you to let the bastard scream!

Beyond the boulder, a rifle cracked sharply. A cry of pain came from below, to mingle with the echoes of the shot. Drawing his Colt, Longarm darted around the boulder and ran openly for the ledge.

Slade was waiting. Levering swiftly, the man sent a withering fire at Longarm. The marshal flung himself to the ground, digging his elbows and knees painfully into the rocky soil. He rolled and kept rolling until he found cover. Slade's fire followed him relentlessly, the slugs whining off the rocks like hornets out of hell.

The Winchester's rapid fire ceased. Longarm looked over the boulder behind which he was crouched. Slade had disappeared. He was probably reloading. Keeping low, Longarm raced toward the ledge. Before he reached it, he heard the sound of hooves. Turning, he followed the sound, looked down, and saw Slade galloping down a narrow trail just below him. Steadying his Colt's barrel on the top of a boulder, Longarm sighted and fired.

Slade's horse pitched forward, sending him headlong over its neck. Longarm clambered down the rocky slope, jumped the remaining ten feet, and raced along the ridge toward Slade, who was crawling slowly and groggily away from the thrashing horse, his gleaming Smith & Wesson still miraculously in his hand. As Longarm approached, Slade managed to twist and get off a shot. Longarm felt the round whistle past his cheek a second before he booted the revolver out of Slade's hand.

Slade flung up both hands. "I'm unarmed!" he cried. "You've got to arrest me! You've got to take me in, Marshal!"

Longarm bolstered his Colt. "That's right," he said softly. "I do, don't I?"

"That's right! That's right! And you'll find I haven't done anything wrong! That was a mistake! A mistake! That damn foreman didn't know how to read the map!"

Longarm's dark eyes were cold as he reached his hand down to assist Slade in getting up. Slade took the offered hand and pulled himself erect. On his feet, he began to brush himself off, a swagger already creeping into his manner.

"You're acting wisely, Longarm. Very wisely. I understand that your handling of me just a moment before was . . . done in the heat of the moment. You'll find I am a man who does not hold grudges. Indeed, I can do things for you. This whole business has just been an unfortunate mistake. And I'm glad to see you're not like that fool, Tanner." The man's cold, tiny, black eyes appraised Longarm shrewdly. "After all, you don't want to be a deputy U.S. marshal for the rest of your life, do you?"

"Wasn't Tanner sensible, Slade?" Longarm asked.

"Indeed he wasn't. He kept spouting nonsense about ruining the valley. He threatened to expose me."

"So you shot him."

"I had to."

"Like you had to shoot Gus down there. In the back, most likely."

Slade caught the deadly edge in Longarm's voice. He started to take a step back. Longarm reached out, grabbed him by the shirt front, and pulled him close. He slapped Slade once, twice, then repeated the punishment. The man's eyes rolled back into his head as he slumped toward Longarm. Longarm flung him over his shoulder, then turned and clawed his way back up onto the ledge.

Looking down, Longarm saw Gus sprawled facedown close to the arroyo, a dark stain on his back. The man he had pulled from the quicksand was gone, his horse with him. Slade began to squirm. Longarm stepped to the very edge and lifted Slade over his head. Slade was immediately awake, and in that one terrible instant he knew what Longarm intended.

"No!" he cried. "No, Longarm! For the love of Jesus!"

Longarm dipped his knees slightly, then straightened and hurled his twisting, screaming burden down into the canyon. He watched coldly. The scream was cut off abruptly. Longarm turned away.

Slade's horse was still alive, thrashing feebly below him. Longarm dropped back down to the trail and took out his Colt. He moved around to the front of the animal for a clearer shot and saw the Paiute arrow imbedded in the horse's chest. Astonished, he looked quickly around him. The Indians had followed him, anyway. It was one of their arrows, not his bullet, that had stopped Slade.

Longarm glanced back at the horse. The animal was completely still now, the big eyes fogged, lusterless. He left the dead animal to the buzzards and continued along the trail Slade had been using. It led back down to the narrow arroyo. When Longarm reached the canyon, he found that Gus was still alive. Slade's bullet had chewed a nice chunk out of his back, just under the shoulder blade, exiting from the side. Gus had bled furiously, but if luck and meanness counted for anything, he would live.

Gus groaned slightly and began to curse.

Slade had struck the quicksand headfirst. All that remained visible of him was a good portion of his hind end, and it didn't appear to be sinking in any deeper. *The old-timers are right*, Longarm thought, as he pulled the barely conscious Gus to his feet and helped him to where their horses were waiting.

When Longarm and a slack, grim-faced Gus rode into the Paiute encampment close to sundown, Longarm found the Indians

gone and three burnt-out wickiups still smoldering. Barbara
was standing in the entrance to her tent, and hurried down the
slope toward them as they rode through the abandoned camp.

"Wanowi told me you were dead, Gus," Barbara said, as she
helped him down out of his saddle.

"Maybe I am," Gus grunted painfully. "I just don't want to
come right out and admit it. But give me time. I just might any
minute now."

"Don't you dare," she said.

As the big man leaned on her, she quickly inspected the
rough blood-soaked bandage Longarm had wrapped around
Gus's torso with strips torn from his shirt. She looked at Longarm with sudden concern.

"We'll take him to my tent," she said.

The moon had not yet risen, and it was dark when Barbara
stepped out of her tent, wiped the beads of perspiration from
her high forehead with the back of her hand, and walked over
to sit down in a camp chair beside Longarm. His long legs
were stretched out, and he was wishing fervently for a cheroot,
all the while cursing himself for an unregenerate tobacco fiend.

"How is he?" the lawman asked.

Barbara sighed wearily. "He's comfortable now, I think. I
washed the wound out thoroughly, despite his rather salty pro-
tests. If he can get some sleep now, he should be all right. I'll
let him have the tent to himself tonight. I can sleep outside."

"Did you say you washed out the wound?"

"Yes, with soap and water—very warm water. That's what
I was doing, heating all that water in the skillets. Of course, as
you said, you have never heard of Pasteur—or Lister, either, I
am sure—so you would not understand why I did that."

"Nope—not unless soap and water are better than whiskey
for washing out wounds. You say Wanowi was here earlier,
before we got back?"

"Yes. He returned to help his people leave here. The Paiutes
regard death as vindictive. Every effort must be made to break
the ties between the dead and their survivors. So they burned
the dwellings of those who died and have moved permanently
from this place. When Wanowi spoke to me, he was quite

pleased with himself. He said he helped you again, but did not
prevent you from using your own magic on Slade." She turned
her head toward Longarm. In the darkness, he could hot read
her expression, but her voice contained a note of cold hopeful-
ness as she asked, "Slade is dead, I presume?"

"Yes, Barbara. But the man with him escaped."

"No, Longarm. He didn't. Wanowi told me about that as
well. But I suppose, since you're a federal officer, it would be
best if I simply didn't mention it to you again."

Longarm nodded. "I'd appreciate that." He rose to his feet.
"I'm going in to talk to Gus."

"He needs his sleep, Longarm."

"I've got a few questions. I won't be long."

He could sense her looking at him sharply. "Are you still
searching for that deserter, Longarm? The one riding a grullo?"

He smiled faintly. "Yes."

She was silent for a moment before saying, "You tell Gus
I'm sorry I hurt him so when I cleaned out his wound."

"I'll do that, Barbara," Longarm assured her.

Gus was tossing fitfully on the cot. His one eye cast a fiery
glare at Longarm when he entered the tent. The lamp was sitting on a table, its flame turned low. Gus spoke first.

"That woman must have thought she lost something inside
me, Longarm, she dug in so deep."

"She's sorry she hurt you. She just told me to tell you that."

"Hell's bells, Longarm. She can hurt me all she wants. I
like that woman. I just enjoy blowing off steam once in a
while."

Longarm pulled up a canvas stool and sat beside Gus's cot.
"I've got a few questions, Gus. Shouldn't take long."

Gus looked at him and smiled through his pain. "I guess
you *must* have a few questions, at that."

Longarm chewed on the untrimmed edge of his mustache,
then shook his head and asked, "Who in blazes are you, Gus?
You sure as hell ain't Gus Dodds."

The logger seemed unaccountably amused. "Who am I,
then?"

"Ned Shortslef—with his beard shaved off and an eye lost

somewhere along the line. You really *don't* have an eye under that patch, do you?"

The big man chuckled, and lifted the eyepatch to reveal a scarred eyelid closed over a hollow, obviously empty eye socket. "You going to bring me in?"

"I have to, Gus," the tall deputy said regretfully. "I don't want to, but that's my job. That's what I've been doing up here—looking for you. I'm glad you didn't kill Tanner, but that doesn't change anything. Sorry, old son."

"You're just bound and determined to bring in Ned Shortslef. Is that it?"

"You heard what I said, Gus."

"Well, you can do it if you want, Longarm—if you don't mind digging up a grave and hauling in a corpse. You buried Ned Shortslef when you buried Martin Tanner."

Longarm pushed his hat back on his head and leaned closer. "Tanner?"

"That's right."

The lawman scratched his square, unshaven jaw. "You better explain that, Gus."

"I was in the Rosebud campaign with Ned. I scouted with him. Sat around many a fire with him and his woman and that kid of his. Hell, Ned never did kill any soldiers. All he did was drive away a foraging party from the camp, then help his wife and her clan to clear out of there before the cavalry turned up. Someone recognized Ned, though, so he had to light out and leave his people. He didn't want to bring down any more trouble on them."

Longarm shook his head. "That description, Gus. It was in the folder we got from the army. Tanner was not as big a man as Ned was described as being—as you and all the others described him. He was tough enough, I grant you that, but not a very big man."

"After the Rosebud campaign I was told to give a description of Ned to a shavetail from army intelligence. Seems they needed one, since they didn't keep very good records on scouts in them days. So I gave the lieutenant that description to throw the army off his tail. Hell, Longarm, that little fuzzy-cheeked lieutenant *expected* me to say that Ned was as big as a bear with a fine crop of hair on his face. That's what he expected an ex-Mountain Man to look like. He went away happy, and Ned changed his name to Tanner."

"Then why in hell did he telegraph Washington that he'd seen Ned Shortslef up here?"

"To bring in federal marshals like you, Longarm. To stir things up for Slade. To stop him. That girl Terry from the Flying T, and the other ranchers and the Indians, too, were in a fix. He promised he'd do what he could." Gus looked at Longarm. "And it looks like you did it for him, Longarm."

"Terry knew about all this, didn't she—along with you?"

"Why do you say that?"

"She went along with me when I described Ned to her, and said he'd been to the Flying T looking for work." Longarm stood up.

"You going to put all this in your report?"

"I think it'll be a lot simpler to bury that big Mountain Man with all the others who got caught in that slide. Besides, it's what happened to Whipsaw—and why—that's going to attract all the attention."

Gus sighed deeply and rolled over onto his back. He seemed mightily relieved. So was Longarm, as a matter of fact.

"Good night, Gus. Get some sleep."

Gus was too tired to reply.

Longarm left the tent. By now the moon had risen, and the three burnt wickiups of the Paiute encampment across the stream were skeletal in its pale glow. He found that Barbara had picked a spot some distance from the tent and put down a very luxurious, roomy sleeping bag. She was sitting beside it in a camp chair, dressed in a long white nightgown, combing out her golden hair. She had placed a camp chair beside hers and Longarm sat in it.

"How is he?" she asked.

"Better. He should be asleep soon."

"You look tired yourself."

"It's been a long day—and a grim one, Barbara."

"For both of us," she murmured softly.

Longarm nodded, took a deep breath, and leaned himself back in the chair in an effort to relax the tension that still held him. Whether he believed Gus's strange story was not important. It made sense, when just about everything else about that spectral deserter he had been tracking so fruitlessly made little sense at all. But the important thing was that he *wanted* to believe Gus.

"Longarm," Barbara said, "my father and I were very close. And one thing he told me I've never forgotten."

"What's that?"

"When something bad happens, wipe it off the slate with something nice."

"Sounds like a good idea, at that."

"Let's make something nice happen. Out here. Tonight. Under this canopy of stars."

Longarm looked at Barbara. There was a quizzical smile on his face. Then he nodded quickly. "Sounds like a fine idea."

She stood up. "I'll go in to check on Gus."

As she headed through the night toward the tent—a tall, pale, willowy apparition, her golden hair a spike of light down her back—Longarm undressed quickly, ran for the creek, and dove in. The icy waters braced him and cleared away the cobwebs and the unpleasantness of the past days.

The light in the tent was out and Barbara was waiting for him in the sleeping bag when he returned, still tingling, to her. As he settled in beside her, her fingers warmed him, playing softly over his body. He felt himself growing toward her. She moved closer and pulled him against her, the awesome warmth of her body replacing the chill in his soul, and filling it with wonder—and desire.

The canopy of stars Barbara had mentioned rolled well across the heavens that night before either of them thought to look up again.

GIANT-SIZED ADVENTURE FROM
AVENGING ANGEL LONGARM.

BY TABOR EVANS

penguin.com/actionwesterns

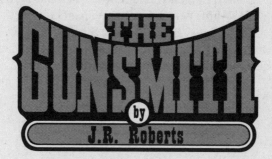